MOONLIGHT DESIRE

Christina heard Jason's light step in the darkness. Somehow, she'd known all along that he would seek her out.

She felt her heart beat crazily as he stood across from her and slowly reached out his hand. She met his gaze, and did not flinch from the desire, and the purpose, she read in their depths.

He pulled her toward him and lowered his feverish lips to hers. She yielded to him; her slender arms slipping about his neck to draw him closer as her body molded itself to his hard, masculine length.

Crushing her in his strong arms, he let his lips trail a path of fire across her slender throat as he carried her to a bed of forest moss. The sparkling pool, the stars that gleamed like flickering candles, and the shaft of moonlight which lit his way, all served as a perfect backdrop.

Christina felt so wicked, so alluring, as she felt the coolness of the ground moss against her bare skin, and the magic of his fingers as they played expertly across her body.

There were no yesterdays, or even tomorrows. For Christina, there was only this moment . . .

Rebel Pleasure
Mary Martin

ZEBRA BOOKS
KENSINGTON PUBLISHING CORP.

ZEBRA BOOKS

are published by

Kensington Publishing Corp.
475 Park Avenue South
New York, NY 10016

First printing: October 1985

Printed in the United States of America

To my husband, Tom
This one is for you, blue eyes

Beginnings

Prelude

Natchez, Mississippi
1861

"Christina! Christina!" The voices drifted farther into the distance as the little dappled pony, his rider perched sidesaddle, galloped full speed past the main house and out onto the road that led from the Duprea mansion. The young girl laughed rebelliously, her smoky-green eyes sparkling with mischief.

"Whoa, boy. Slow down a bit, Domino," she commanded as she pulled back gently on his reins. The pony shook his shaggy head as she patted him lovingly. "Do not run too far Domino. Poor old Sam will have a hard time finding us then. We wouldn't want to ruin the game for Sam now, would we?" She smiled in amusement as she visualized the old groom plodding out after her on his mule.

Christina Duprea, thirteen-year-old daughter of one of the richest cotton barons in Natchez, allowed her pony to wander from the river road and graze contentedly on the thick, green grass that skirted the banks of the winding Mississippi. Sliding down from the confining sidesaddle, she gave a small gasp as her reed-slim body made contact with the hard ground; she would have to find a place to hide. Sam would be expecting it, be looking forward to it. Holding her pink ruffled bonnet securely in place, she scampered toward the towering willow that was one of her favorite hiding places. Bubbling with mischievous glee, she surveyed the gently swaying limbs, head craned back, green eyes shining in anticipation.

"You are like a lovely weeping lady," she whispered, as she nimbly climbed the jutting branches. Christina thought and spoke in a series of quotations memorized from her demanding tutor's lessons, plus her own, very vivid imagination. "You conceal your mournful face with long silken tresses that flow gracefully about you, hiding your deep sorrow from prying eyes. But I will not reveal your secret. You and I are old friends, beautiful lady. Now spread your wispy mane and embrace me with your slender arms. I do not want to make it too easy for Sam to find me."

When she had reached the highest, most obscure branch of the tree, she planted her small feet firmly in the fork, and gazed out over the flowing, turbulent water. Taking a deep breath, she stared as though mesmerized by the river's power.

"Today as yesterday you continue on your constant course. Never do you waver from your goal until you have reached the Gulf!" she yelled into the blowing wind. "Oh, to be that free! It would be grand, simply grand!"

So engrossed was Christina in her dreams of independence, that she did not hear the approaching horse and rider as they cantered over to investigate the riderless pony.

"Where in the blue-blazes has that sprite gone off to now?" exclaimed twenty-year-old Jason O'Roark, his sapphire eyes beginning to darken with growing concern.

In the five years that the Duprea and O'Roark families had known each other through their mutual interest in steamboat lines, young Jason had appointed himself guardian of the wild, gypsylike Christina Duprea. As often as possible, he would travel from his birthplace, St. Louis, to visit with Christina and her brother, twenty-year-old Curtis Duprea. Both families got on splendidly; and if, to the casual observer, it appeared as though the dashing Jason treated Christina a bit harshly, their families knew otherwise. The spirited beauty had already managed to snare his heart, though neither Jason nor Christina seemed aware of their growing fondness for each other. The Dupreas and the O'Roarks were delighted at the prospect of uniting their prestigious families with a bethrothal between Jason and Christina.

Jason halted his prancing stallion and swung his long legs down from the saddle. "Come on, Christina," he urged. "The game is over. Everyone is waiting dinner until you return." He stood impatiently below her hiding place, long arms crossed in front of his chest. "Five minutes, Christina, that's all, and then the search begins." Jason closed his eyes and began to count slowly.

His imperious figure, so broad shouldered and stern, filled the young girl with a sudden feeling of inflexible determination.

You're not going to spoil my fun today, Jason, she vowed to herself as she glanced down at the handsome youth beneath the willow. Her tongue clucked rapidly against the roof of her mouth as her thoughts raced furiously. The crunch of leather upon gravel signified that Jason had stopped counting and was now searching for her.

11

"You're trying my temper!" he warned, peering into the tall river grass that grew in abundance along the sloping bank. "I'm not old Sam, you know! If I get my hands on you, scamp, I shall put an end to these unescorted romps once and for all." He walked toward several massive oaks, parted their gray-green manes, and said smugly, "Aha! Now I've found you!" When his words were met with silence and his pretense exposed, he grew even more impatient and, sighing in defeat, resigned the victory. "All right, I give up, Christina. You win. Now come on out! I'm starving and wish to indulge in a bit of Dulcie's fried chicken before it's all gone!"

Christina clapped her hands together with glee. She'd won! He was giving up already and she, Christina, was the victor! As agile as a cat, she quickly scooted down the wide tree trunk. Hitting the ground in an unladylike heap, she moaned in distress as the hem of her dress gave a resounding rip. She imagined her mammy scolding her disapprovingly, and perversely blamed Jason for her own impetuous behavior. She glanced at his now retreating back and threatened him under her breath. "I'm going to tell Mammy it was all your fault, you pain in the neck, you! If you'd just mind your own business where my fun is concerned, we'd all be a lot better off."

She picked herself up from the moss-covered ground and made haste toward her waiting pony. With grim determination she pulled herself into the cumbersome sidesaddle and then urged Domino forward at breakneck speed. "Be swift, Domino. We cannot let Jason catch us now." Her satin bonnet was torn free from her unruly curls.

Laughing to herself, her tawny-gold hair blowing wildly in the wind, Christina once again allowed her uninhibited spirit to capture the freedom of the moment. But it was all too shortlived. To her amazement, she heard the sound of hoofbeats rapidly approaching from behind, until at last the pursuer rode up beside her and returned her laugh directly into her startled face.

"I knew I'd smoke you out, vixen!" Jason shouted over the thundering hooves of the galloping horses. "One thing you must learn about me, Miss Duprea, is that I never give up—never! It was just a form of bait to lure the unsuspecting little wildcat from its hiding place." He indicated by a jerk of his head that he wanted her to pull back on her mount's reins.

But it was as though a small demon sat on Christina's shoulder urging her to ignore the brash, overbearing, young man who refused to accept any of her unending pranks.

Christina stuck her small tongue out directly in Jason's overly confident face.

Surprise stripped the mask of self-righteousness from Jason's lean good looks, followed by amusement. Then something else took fire in his brilliant blue eyes. As he stared without blinking for one breathless moment into Christina's wide-eyed, rebellious face, he found himself thinking just how beautiful and challenging this untamed minx had become. He searched the exquisite, gold-flecked orbs that stared back boldly from beneath dark, feathery lashes and found the answer hidden in their velvety depths.

Without even realizing the message she conveyed to him by that brazen, unreserved look, Christina's breath caught in her throat as a sudden gust of wind swept Jason's low-crowned hat from his leonine head. Ebony waves, as blue-black as a raven's wing, spilled forward

13

over one dark, arched brow. His expressive eyes shimmered like quicksilver. She almost felt sorry she'd challenged him now. What was it about this young man that always seemed to bring out the very worst behavior in her? Any why did she think she despised him one minute, and then the next, when he looked at her so intently, imagine that she read more than friendship in his regard? Of late, these strange feelings invaded her senses at the mere sound of his voice. Even his image— his brash, handsome face—managed to intrude into her dreams at night.

She shivered under his appraising gaze. Before she could utter one feeble protest, Jason reached out and swept the defiant Southern belle from her pony into his arms. Stunned, Christina allowed him to enfold her into his embrace, marvelling all the while at the iron-firm muscles that rippled beneath the flawless cut of his tailored coat. The deep blue of the material matched the flash of fire now dancing in his eyes.

She is really no longer a child, Jason thought, *but still so very young and innocent.* He held her tightly against his beating heart, and wondered what the future held in store for him and this child-woman who drove him to such total distraction every time she was near.

"It is time for us to go back now, Christina," he said, his voice revealing none of the confusing emotions that he felt within. "And you and I both know that these games between us must now come to an end." He sighed a bit regretfully. "Do you understand what I am telling you?"

Unknowingly, his warm breath had caressed the delicate shell of Christina's ear, sending delicious frightening quivers of pleasure racing along her spine.

14

Christina replied softly, *"Oui, monsieur,* I understand."

"I want you to promise me, Christina, that you will not gallivant unchaperoned about the countryside again. It is not proper for a young woman of your position to do so. Will you promise?"

Christina shrugged indifferently. *"Oui,* I will think about it, *monsieur."*

"It is not a request that bears much thought," Jason swallowed. His resolve began to slip and thoughts of retribution began to take shape. "I am ordering you to stop this wild, irresponsible behavior!"

"Don't shout in my ear, you insufferable dolt!" She flounced her golden curls indignantly.

Jason stopped his horse and swung them both from the saddle to stand upon the dusty road. Barely suppressed fury gave a threatening quality to the tone of his voice.

"You know, someone needs to take a switch to that petite derrière of yours, my sweet. You are quite impossible or, more accurately, spoiled rotten!"

She didn't so much as bat an eyelash as she purred her reply. "You wouldn't dare. I would have to inform my brother, and then he would be forced to call you out."

Jason threw back his dark head and burst into peals of laughter. She stood her ground, glaring daggers at him, wishing at that moment that she were a man so that she could call him out herself.

Her brother Curt's sudden appearance added a boost of confidence to her rapidly flagging spirit.

"What is so funny, might I ask?" Curt Duprea inquired as he swung a leg over his saddle and slid to the ground beside his sister and best friend. He too began to laugh as he caught the look of unveiled fury on

15

Christina's face. "Don't answer that, Jase. I can see right now she will run you through if you intimidate her any further."

Jason wiped at the moistness in his eyes and shook his head unbelievingly at Christina. "You never cease to amaze me with your boldness." He turned his attention to his friend Curt. "Be careful of this one. She is going to have you so busy fighting duels to protect her honor that you will not have time to do much of anything else."

Curt slapped Jason across his back, grinning broadly. "It is not I who has to be the wary one, *mon ami*. No, . . . not I."

Jason's face suddenly became blank of all expression.

Christina began to sputter with rage. Not knowing how or upon whom she wished to vent it, she contemplated both men with her most withering glare. "Pig-headed jackanapes," she muttered, "both of you."

Jason's full, chiseled mouth narrowed into a grim line. "What was that I heard coming from those innocent, pure lips? A vulgar expression no less, and directed at your brother and myself." He gazed down at her trying his best to hide his amusement. For a moment, a fleeting second, he almost thought she was going to apologize. She was suddenly so quiet, so angelic looking as she stood demurely, staring at the motion of her shuffling feet. Then his eyes followed the direction of hers, and he saw at once the reason for her acquiescent manner. Her dawdling kid slippers were deliberately stirring up the dust around his feet until his shiny, black boots were covered in a thick coat of brown grit.

"My God!" Jason exclaimed in exasperation, "What in the deuce are you going to think of next?"

Curt jumped between the two adversaries and feigned

16

a proper duelling stance.

"Okay, ladies and gentlemen, choose your weapons," he teased. "Whoever draws first blood shall emerge the victor."

In deference to Curt's presence, Jason resisted the urge to paddle Christina's backside until she screamed for mercy. Instead he vented his anger with cutting words.

"There is no contest here, my friend. A mere slip of a girl will never get the better of Jason O'Roark—never." Without giving Curt or his volatile sister time to reply, Jason grabbed Christina and hoisted her over his shoulder like a sack of potatoes. He strode purposefully to his waiting horse, tossed her across the saddle head-first, and swung up behind her.

"See you back at the house, Curt," he stated nonchalantly. "Bring Domino, will you?"

Curt stared dumbstruck as Jason urged his horse with its additional passenger into a leisurely trot toward the Duprea mansion.

Christina's feet dangled helplessly in midair. She could feel the breeze as it whipped her hem about her ankles, exposing her pantalets to any who happened to be passing by. Her head was whirling with bitter, angry thoughts as she stared down at Jason's boot tops. This was the worst form of degradation he could possibly inflict upon her, and she vowed silently to find a way to repay him if it took the rest of her life to do so. One slim hand wiped at a tear that had trickled down her flushed face; a streak of dirt instantly smudged one cheek, left there by a hand dusty from her adventuring.

"One of these days I'm going to repay you for all of your meanness, Jason O'Roark, and then we'll see who gets thrown over a horse like a dirty, old sack of laundry!"

Jason appeared unconcerned by her childish threats as he rode in stony silence down the oak-lined drive that led to the impressive three-story home of the Duprea family, Oak Meadow.

Standing in the shade of an enormous, flowering mimosa, Matthew Duprea awaited the return of his beloved daughter.

He was at last ready to admit that Christina was indeed a spoiled and willful child. Something needed to be done immediately to change her tomboyish behavior. And her manners left much to be desired as well. Perhaps his wife, Elizabeth, was correct. Maybe it was time to send their unruly daughter abroad to finishing school.

Pulling his gold watch from his brocade waistcoat, he checked the time. Then sighing with dismay, he called to the large black woman who stood in fretful silence on the veranda.

"Mammy, I'm going to walk down the drive a short way and see if I can catch sight of the children."

Mammy's turbaned head shook back and forth woefully. Christina had really done it good this time. Mr. Duprea was none too happy, and she feared Christina was in a heap of trouble.

"Don't be too hard on her, Massa. She just a bit of a thing, an' she don't mean no real harm."

"No, Mammy," Matthew called back. "Don't worry about your precious lamb. I'm not about to start whipping her now. It is too late for that, I fear."

Matthew hurried down the road through the canopy of

18

trees and caught himself wishing that things could have turned out differently. If only . . . That was something he seemed to wish for more and more of late. If only Elizabeth had been a proper mother to their daughter, a good deal of this misery might have been avoided. He shook his dark head sadly as old memories skirted across his mind. Beautiful, passionate Elizabeth . . . at least, in the beginning. The perfect wife and—before Christina's birth—the perfect mother to their young son Curtis. All that changed the day that their tiny daughter had been born. Elizabeth had almost died giving birth to Christina. Her recovery was slow, and the doctor discreetly told Matthew that she would risk death if she had any more children. They were both saddened by the news, but Matthew did not expect the form of retaliation that followed. Elizabeth moved her belongings into an adjoining bedroom and locked Matthew and their children out. From that moment on, she tolerated Matthew and ignored her son and daughter.

Matthew quickened his pace, as though he wished to outrun the hurtful, awakened memories, and almost collided head-on with Jason, who rode hellbent-for-leather toward the beckoning mansion. Jason deposited Christina none too gently onto the hard, red dirt at her father's feet.

Scowling fiercely at Jason, Christina smoothed her skirts back down over her knees. Her golden curls were in total disarray, and smudges of dust clung to the tip of her nose.

Matthew Duprea stared at her in astonishment. This was the last straw! Christina looked like a street urchin, with leaves and twigs clinging to her hair, and her torn hem dragging raggedly along the ground.

"Young lady!" Matthew shouted. "I demand to know the meaning of this outrageous behavior, at once!"

Christina appeared properly remorseful now that she was confronted by her angry papa. But Jason knew her only too well, and was not fooled for one minute by her ladylike charade.

"I'm sorry, Papa," she offered apologetically, "I did not mean to worry you so. I promise not to do anything like that again . . . I really do." She then turned her attention back to the opposition. "Thank you for offering me a ride home, Jason. I hope I didn't put you through too much trouble." She curtsied politely and, bowing her tawny head, hid a telltale smirk from his knowing stare. When she lifted her gaze to meet his, their eyes locked in silent battle. Smoky-green clashed with icy blue. Her rosebud mouth lifted at the corners in a sly, secretive smile.

Jason didn't know what to feel. Beneath that hoydenish charade, lay a most refreshing young woman. He was intrigued with her beauty, no doubt. But it was not her beauty alone that held him captive. Something about her wild irrepressible spirit drew him to her, like steel to magnet. As if she knew what he was thinking, Christina chose that moment to favor them with a dazzling smile.

"May I please be excused, Papa?" she asked sweetly.

"Yes, daughter. Run along up to the house. Mammy is most anxious about you."

When she'd taken her leave, Matthew turned to Jason. "I am disturbed by Christina's unruly behavior. She is becoming more of a hellion and a scamp with each passing day. I do apologize to you, my boy. I really do."

Jason grinned, and tried to console Christina's distraught father. "Don't give it another thought, sir. All is forgotten."

Matthew followed the path of his retreating offspring as she skipped along. "I know Christina can charm the eyes right out of a snake . . . probably has, for that matter." He shuddered at the thought. "It is a complicated business, this raising of a daughter. I am grateful for all your help, son."

"Yes, sir," Jason replied.

"I've made a decision today, my boy. Decided to send Christina to finishing school in Paris, immediately."

Jason's eyes turned toward the distant mansion, where the enchanting, melodious sound of Christina's laughter filled the air. "I suppose that will be for the best," he replied huskily.

"Yes, it will, I'm sure of it," Matthew said, feeling a bit more secure with his decision now that he'd voiced it out loud.

Curt Duprea's shouting interrupted any further conversation between the two men, as he reined his weary, lathered horse beside Jason's mount and began to excitedly relay what he'd been told.

"You are never going to believe what I've just heard from Conrad Templeton. I can hardly comprehend it all myself." He placed his palm over his rapidly beating heart as if to still the pounding in his chest.

"Curt, are you all right?" Matthew inquired, his voice heavy with concern.

Swallowing convulsively, Curt nodded. "We are at war with the North . . . Fort Sumter was fired on by the Confederate forces of South Carolina, and the North has vowed to preserve the Union . . . no matter what the cost."

"Dear lord," Matthew said grimly. "May God bless the Confederacy."

Jason felt something akin to deep sorrow wash over him. His eyes never left those of Curt Duprea. He felt compelled to hold this moment for as long as he possibly could. For he knew, as he put to memory the picture of Curt as he now looked sitting before him, that their time—and their friendship—was drawing to a close. Jason smiled sadly at his sandy-haired friend and Curt returned the gesture. It would be a memory that Jason O'Roark would treasure in the long, bitter years that were to follow.

Chapter One

Coming home . . . could it finally be? After seven long years, twenty-year-old Christina Duprea repeatedly asked herself that question, as the stately riverboat churned down stream toward Natchez . . . to her home.

She had grown into a beautiful young woman, and presented a vision of loveliness. She stood at the guardrail appalled at what she saw: the aftermath of the brutal Civil War. It had been three years since Lee's surrender at the village of Appomattox Courthouse, but still the evidence of destruction remained. Her slim hands twisted the gloves she held as she fought to remain calm and not run along the deck screaming curses at every Yankee she saw. And they were everywhere; the brazen conqueror come to view the defeat of a proud adversary. Angrily, she brushed at a tear that had escaped before she could prevent it, and fiercely reminded herself that Dupreas did not show weakness of any kind. Especially before Yankees. Sighing, she closed her eyes for a moment of quiet reflection.

"Is anything the matter, Miss Duprea?" inquired

Sarah Pennswick, Christina's hired travelling companion.

"No, I'm fine," she assured the plump, matronly woman as she opened her eyes and gave her companion a reassuring smile. Christina was most grateful for Sarah's company and would never forget the woman's kindness throughout the long, tedious journey from Paris to the States. But at that moment, Christina wanted to be completely alone. It was difficult and rather overwhelming to realize that when she reached Oak Meadow, neither her brother Curt nor her mother would be there waiting for her as she'd so often dreamed. They were both dead—victims, each in their own way, of the brutality that had been the Civil War. Her mother had succumbed to yellow fever, and Curt was listed as missing in an explosion of a Confederate troop boat. Everyone on board had been lost in the fiery burst of the ship's boilers, which spewed death and destruction hundreds of feet in every direction. She shivered even now thinking of his remains lying on the cold river bottom, forever lost to those who loved him. Bitterness threatened to consume her and she gripped the edge of the guardrail until her knuckles turned white.

"I believe we should be going in now," Sarah said with an understanding pat on Christina's arm. "Perhaps a nap would refresh us for our dinner tonight at the captain's table."

"Perhaps," Christina replied, taking a deep breath, "but I don't think I can stand the confinement of our cabin just yet. You go on ahead, I'll follow in a bit."

"Well," Sarah Pennswick hesitated, pursing her lips, "I suppose it wouldn't hurt, just this once." Clutching at her straw plait bonnet which the river wind threatened to

24

whip from her head, she turned to leave with a final plea. "Don't tarry long, dear. It appears a storm may be brewing." She scurried away.

Christina's gaze followed her companion's bulky figure as she disappeared inside. As her eyes swept the length of the deck they came to rest upon a sole male figure leaning casually against the rail not far from her. Before she realized that she was staring at him, he removed his flat, low-crowned hat and swept it forward in a deep, exaggerated gesture.

Mon Dieu! Christina breathed as she stared into his handsome face and piercing blue eyes. *I think the man's a gambler.* Taking a quick survey of his attire—the dove-gray trousers and coat that fit his broad-shouldered frame impeccably, the snow-white cravat and silk shirt, the large diamond ring on his finger—she was even more certain of it. But still, she found something unusual, undeniably different about this man. Their eyes never left each other's face.

"What is it about him?" she mused under her breath, as she surveyed his rugged good looks, the close-cropped beard that concealed the lower portion of his face.

True, he was very handsome, and appeared quite friendly. She watched as the wind caressed the wavy black hair causing it to fall forward over one dark brow. Impatiently, he brushed it from his face as the full, sensuous mouth continued to smile invitingly at her. His even white teeth flashed wickedly in his sun-browned face as he returned her brazen look.

Odd prickles, like invisible fingers caressing the length of her spine, caused her to turn away from his demanding stare, his searching blue eyes. She was trembling uncontrollably, and it suddenly dawned on her why.

Jason O'Roark . . . he favors him so, she thought unbelieving, *but surely he couldn't be. My father wrote that Jason had disappeared since the war. No one has any idea what happened to him.* She shook her head at her foolishness. *No, you're just wishing Christina. Jason, a gambler? Hardly!* Veiling confused emotions with thick, curly lashes, she turned her attention to the passing landscape. She could feel her cheeks flush under his scrutiny as she tried to calm her rapidly beating heart. "I wish he'd just go away," she murmured.

But the man did not move one inch. For he was experiencing an emotion he could not readily identify. He regarded the enchanting creature who had so brazenly invited his attention and found her absolutely breathtaking to behold. At first he'd thought her bold, perhaps a bit loose with her affections. Upon closer observation he altered that hasty first impression, and became totally mesmerized by everything that he saw.

"Who in God's name is that lovely, tempting morsel?" he asked himself breathlessly. "Surely she has an escort." But looking about he could see no one. "Wonderful," he snorted confidently.

He took a step forward, intending to approach the lady and introduce himself. But upon taking a closer look at the beauty's face—the way the setting sun transformed the petal-smooth complexion into shimmering satin, and the fiery rays shone on her tawny-gold curls, he stopped dead in his tracks. He choked on the trite words he was intending to impress her with and quickly resumed his post at the guardrail.

I know what you're thinking, Jase, ole boy, he admonished himself, *but you're quite crazy if you think that could be her.*

Cautiously, he observed her out of the corner of his eye. The hair color was indeed the same, the eyes as green and fathomless. She was slim, and her willowy figure was becomingly dressed in a seagreen gown that clung everywhere it should, exposing creamy flesh in just the right place. The haughty features of her face in profile allowed him to notice the defiant thrust of her petite chin and the proud, erect way in which she carried herself.

"Oh, God . . ." he moaned, "don't do this to me now, not when I have a game with Marcus Trudeau—the sole purpose for my return here."

Someone tapped him on the shoulder from behind. Startled that he'd let his guard down for even a moment, Jason pivoted in an aggressive stance, hands ready to protect himself.

"Whoa, man, it's just me," the intruder exclaimed in a pretended effort to defend his life.

Jason relaxed upon recognizing the thin man as a gentleman with whom he frequently played poker. A hint of a smile brightened his face. "What's up, partner? Is it time?"

"Just about, Jase. Trudeau has been asking for Jason Woods. That is you, . . . correct?"

"So they tell me," Jason said lightly.

"Well then, you're on."

"And ready," Jason replied with a satisfied grin. All thoughts of the lovely young woman at the guardrail disappeared. It was time for the battle, and Jason was at his best when it came to keeping his emotions shuttered, closed to everything that could possibly come between himself and his goal. The Secret Service for the Union had listed him as one of their best, and their most ruthless. "Wish me luck," Jason asked as he extended his

27

hand to the smaller man.

"You know that Jase, . . . always." The man accepted Jason's hand in a firm grip, and then watched silently as the tall, dark gambler strode by the golden-haired beauty and into the gambling saloon without so much as a backward glance.

Dinner at the table of Capt. John McGurk was a pleasant affair, and Christina berated herself for her obstinacy that at first had included the captain and his lovely dinner companion, both Yankees.

There were four people at the elegantly set table and scarcely a pause in the conversation. Still, Christina could not take her eyes off the empty chair before the precisely placed china setting. Who was invited and did not attend? She shrugged indifferently and turned her attention to Captain McGurk's interesting tale of the mysterious, revolutionary rebel they talked so much about around here.

"Not one soul has any idea who this man is, or for that matter has ever seen him without a mask. They call him the Silver Wolf because of his silver-gray locks, and story has it he wears a mask to hide some sort of disfigurement he received during the war. A Confederate rebel, that one, but dedicated to his cause of equality for all men."

"Is the man dangerous, Captain?" inquired Sarah Pennswick with a shudder.

"That depends, ma'am, on just whose side you're on. He is a great danger to the folks who prey on the less fortunate, the innocent victims in this political upheaval called Reconstruction." John stroked his chin thoughtfully. "Seems . . . let me just recall this now . . . yes, it

28

was just last week that the Silver Wolf and his band of followers interrupted a raid by those parasites, the nightriders. Scattered them good, he did!"

Christina observed the fleeting spark of admiration that touched the rugged captain's eyes when he described the mysterious rebel.

"It is indeed a fascinating tale, Captain," Christina said, "but I must say I hope I never encounter this individual. I'm sure I would faint dead away."

"I agree, Miss Duprea." Martinique Summerfield, Captain McGurk's dinner companion stared pointedly at the captain. "These poor ladies are going to think the entire South has become nothing but a haven for relentless carpetbaggers and vindictive scalawags who sell out their own people."

"That's not far from the truth, Martinique," the captain stated quietly, his gaze flickering briefly to Christina. "I hope I haven't spoiled your homecoming, Miss Duprea. But what I told you is fact, and I'm sure you're aware of the dissension in the South right now."

Christina's voice was a bit strained when she answered. "Yes . . . I've heard this and much more, Captain. Don't worry, you've not spoiled my homecoming. I'm afraid that was accomplished several years ago."

There was a flicker of compassion on everyone's face at this beautiful Southern woman's impassioned statement. The moment was eased by the steward as he refilled everyone's wine glass.

"I'm sorry to have to leave such lovely dinner guests, ladies," said the captain rising. "But it's time I looked in on the pilot. He's liable to think I've deserted him" He smiled down at Martinique, who returned his smile. Then he inclined his copper-streaked head at the women as he prepared to depart, but paused for an instant longer. "Oh, and ladies, please don't tarry on the promenade deck tonight. There's a regular April thunderstorm brewing topside." He gave a final wave as he left the dining salon.

The raven-haired Martinique turned to Christina. "I was very pleased that you could join us tonight, Miss Duprea," she said. "And you also, Miss Pennswick."

"Thank you," Sarah replied smiling warmly.

"Yes, thank you very much," Christina added politely. "I found the company most refreshing and the dinner absolutely delicious."

"I'm told shrimp Creole is a specialty on board," said Martinique. Glancing at Christina's half-eaten dinner, she said sympathetically; "It's hard coming back after so many years away."

"More than you can imagine," Christina returned softly.

"Oh, I think that I can, dear," Martinique replied. "There isn't one of us who hasn't been touched in some way by that God-awful war."

"I don't mean to give the wrong impression." Christina said, "I don't blame every Northerner I see, or at least I try my best not to do so. But it is hard to return to one's homeland and find only strangers. And to know that these people are responsible for the destruction!"

"Yes, I know," Martinique replied with a sigh.

Christina found, much to her surprise, that she liked this pretty woman who was so sincere in her sympathy for the plight of the South. And yet, this was the woman whom the captain had introduced as a visitor from Boston—a woman very much a Yankee.

"Will you be staying long in Natchez, Miss Summerfield?" Christina inquired.

Martinique sipped thoughtfully from her crystal wineglass before replying, as though to compose her thoughts. "I can't really say at this point, Miss Duprea. Let's just say it depends on a great many things."

Christina stood and smoothed the wrinkles from the rich silk apricot gown that she had chosen to wear for tonight's dinner. "If you do decide to stay in Natchez for a while and find time on your hands, please do not hesitate to call on me." She offered her hand to the woman and smiled warmly.

"Thank you, that's very kind of you," Martinique returned gently. "And I hope everything works out just fine for you dear."

Martinique sat alone for some time after Christina Duprea and her companion had departed, her thoughts troubling. "Why *am* I here?" she whispered to herself. "There's something John's not telling me.... He's acting so peculiar at times." She took a deep breath and settled back in the plush chair. "Well, I suppose the enigmatic Mr. Woods and I will find out all about it later tonight." She chuckled. "I'm glad he could not make it tonight for dinner. He would have found Miss Duprea most charming I'm afraid, and the last thing the poor girl needs is to become enamored with that rogue!" She wondered then just how he was faring in the long-awaited poker game with Marcus Trudeau.

Knowing Jase, she was sure he was faring very well indeed.

The unusual clamor that drifted out through the opened doors of the gambling saloon became louder, almost frantic.

Captain McGurk flexed his broad, muscular shoulders and did up the silver buttons of his dark blue uniform and left the pilothouse. He was anxious to discover what the fuss was about in the saloon, although he had his suspicions.

"Be back in a little while, J.W.," he called to the steamboat's pilot. "Got to see for myself what in the hell's goin' on down there."

The pilot laughed to himself while he watched Big John, as the gentle giant of a man was known to his friends, hustle down the stairs to the deck below. J.W. glanced overhead at the eight-day clock, and felt assured of reaching Natchez by early the next day. He waved at the rousters who were lighting the many lanterns along the deck of the *River Queen*. A storm seemed to be brewing, which was not unusual in these parts, considering it was early spring. He hoped it wouldn't cause the river to rise too much, for it might necessitate stopping for the night in Vicksburg and falling behind schedule. A rising river would set driftwood afloat, making it virtually impossible to navigate safely after nightfall. He swung the wheel expertly through his hands and hoped for the best.

Captain McGurk was not the only individual wondering what was taking place in the boisterous saloon.

Christina Duprea, who had chosen to disregard the captain's warning, strolled along the deck enjoying the wind and the wildness of the threatening storm. She knew that Miss Pennswick was upset with her for doing so, but life was so terrible short and they just couldn't cower behind closed doors merely because they were born female. Intrigued by the raucous noise flowing from

32

the open doors of the saloon, Christina chose to be even more daring. She decided to see for herself just what a gambling establishment looked like. Gently-reared ladies were not supposed to wonder about such things, but Christina was more independent than that. She hurried across the deck, pausing to catch her breath just outside the entrance to the vast room.

The night was warm and sultry; the shuttered saloon doors thrown wide to catch the breeze drifting in off of the river. She paused at the threshold. This was close enough. She had a perfect view of the exciting casino without actually entering the saloon. She started to shiver, her legs trembling so shakily that she put a hand out to the doorjamb to steady herself.

Bright, baize-topped tables occupied every available space in the richly appointed room. Long velvet draperies outlined the windows, and thick carpet covered the floors. Overhead, crystal chandeliers glittered in magnificent splendor, sending streamers of mellow gold filtering through the air, softening the intense faces of the gamblers seated beneath them. Two men sat at a table before Christina. They were playing one on one. And if the size of the pot in the center of the table was any indication, it appeared to be a high-stakes game.

Christina did not know how long she stood there, just watching. Suddenly the fervor of the crowd gathered about the gamblers appeared to change. Men began pressing closer as one of the gamblers pushed the last of his funds into the center of the table. Two merry revelers weaved past the awe-struck girl, accidently bumping into her and sweeping her along with them into the gambling saloon. The lure of the forbidden quickly overrode her fear and she found herself eagerly elbowing her way through a horde of slack-jawed men to reach a front-row position.

The captain, too, edged his way to the front of the circle of fascinated bystanders. Turning to the man at his left, he said. "Who's winning, sir?"

"The younger fella," the man replied, never once removing his gaze from the two gamblers who had been entertaining them so adeptly throughout the evening. He snorted derisively. "That young man can play poker. Trudeau's a damned fool for continuing."

John McGurk ran one great hand along his side whiskers. "You don't say. Now that is surprising news." McGurk knew that Marcus Trudeau, the *River Queen*'s owner, was a cheat, a cardsharp, and most of all, a rotten scoundrel. He almost laughed out loud he was so pleased. The son of a bitch deserves this, he gloated. He observed both gamblers' faces as they intently studied the cards in their hands.

Marcus was disturbed, was sweating it; John could tell by the twitch of his eyelid that belied his otherwise, calm demeanor.

With the stack of notes in front of the young gambler, Marcus must be just about desperate. No wonder he was beginning to come apart at the seams.

The captain had to smile at the look of satisfaction on the tall, dark conqueror's face. He was ruthless and unconcerned, as though he knew he had his opponent by the throat and was just waiting for the most opportune time to go for the jugular.

The steely eyes, which assessed Marcus with a cool air of disdain, suddenly glanced up and locked silently with John's. Not a flicker of emotion passed between them, but John McGurk had read their intent and gave a prayer of thanks that it was not he who was up against this man.

The cocky, young gambler raised one slashing brow and drawled. "It's up to you, Trudeau. Can you cover my bet, or not?" His long, agile fingers swept the huge pile of winnings forward, depositing his entire sum in the center of the baize-topped table. "This is it . . . all of my winnings against whatever you've got to equal that amount."

Uncontrollably, a shudder ran through Trudeau's body, and a sheen of sweat glistened across his swarthy brow. A distant murmur of surprise circulated among the resplendently dressed bystanders as the riverboat's owner signed the note that could mean the end of his empire. It was for ownership of the *River Queen* and his shipping trade. With a feigned air of self-confidence, he tossed the note onto the stack of paper money that the young gambler had bet.

"I'm covered, Woods. I'm calling you," Marcus said as he smiled wolfishly and flung down his hand. "A full house, kings over." As if from somewhere outside of his body, he watched as his challenger's cards hit the bright cloth table . . . four aces! Then his beady eyes looked up and met those of his master, the man who had just ruined him.

He cursed violently as the brash devil's mouth lifted at the corners into a grin. The man was flaunting his victory in Trudeau's face. A feeling of sick revulsion gripped Marcus and his insides seemed to turn to jelly as the realization of what he'd lost fully dawned on him. His leathery face became livid with rage.

"You think you're smart, don't you, Yankee? Think ole Marcus don't know how you managed to pull that off."

Jason O'Roark, who for the sake of anonymity had

assumed the last name Woods, answered with a deliberate sneer of his upper lip. "I'm sure you do, Trudeau. You've always been a master at it, haven't you?"

Marcus sat up straight in his chair as though the gambler had physically assaulted him. "Just what are you insinuating, sir?" he snarled, his hand slowly sliding below the table.

"Let us just say I am familiar with your type of skill at cards. But no doubt, you are one of the best I've ever seen," Jason retorted, as he too allowed his hand to reach downward and rest securely upon the pearl-handled knife within his boot. "But then, you've had many years of practice, haven't you, Marcus?"

Marcus knew the cold, steely-eyed bastard was goading him for some reason. But damned if he could think of why. He'd taken everything of value Marcus had, totally wiped up the floor with him. And for what reason? He stared purposefully at the lean, hard face; his blood pounded so loudly in his ears he felt certain everyone could hear it. Damn it! He would force the man to tell him if need be—he had to have an answer.

"Why, Woods?" he asked grimly. "Why in the hell did you do this to me?"

Jason took his good time in answering. He wished to savor the moment a bit longer; it had been a long time in coming. Like the predator who has trapped his prey, Jason continued to toy with the broken man. "Let's just say I took back everything you cheated and swindled out of innocent folks . . . everything."

Trudeau sprang to his feet in outrage. "Sir, I demand satisfaction for the slur you have cast upon my name!"

Jason laughed harshly. "How could I possibly debase

something that is already scum? But if it will give me the added pleasure of running you through, then I heartily accept your challenge."

Even Christina, who was still glued to her spot, had to gasp at the young gambler's brazen affront. "Name your weapons, Marcus. Choose how you'd like to die."

Trudeau's eyes, showed fear when they looked into Jason's.

The young gambler appeared cool and unconcerned. He glanced downward, flicked at a speck of dust on the cambric ruffle of his shirt. "Be quick about it old man," he sneered. "I don't have all night."

Marcus realized his challenge had been hasty, but that unlicked cub had left him little choice. The insult had been publicly cast. He'd had to retaliate. But now he knew what a fool he'd been. Woods had acted out the scenario with skilled perfection. He'd trapped Marcus, had him right where he wanted him.

The cardsharp knew he lacked skill with weapons. Fear welled up in his chest, overwhelming him, and only one thought hammered in his head. He had to get the drop on Woods first or he was a dead man! Quickly, he raised his pant leg above his calf and grabbed a derringer from a strapped-down holster and took aim.

But in less than a heartbeat, Jason had pulled the knife from his boot and hurled it forcefully at Trudeau's extended arm.

Trudeau howled in agony as the blade was embedded into his beefy shoulder. The spectators stared in stunned disbelief as the unfired derringer flew from his fingers to land with a soft thud at Christina's feet. The cardsharp swayed uncertainly for a moment before pitching over onto the carpet. Shocked gasps at Trudeau's lack of

37

gentlemanly honor could be heard throughout the room.

Jason rose to his feet and stared dispassionately down at the groaning form of Trudeau. "I would have preferred to face you on a field of honor, Trudeau. But you left me no choice." He began to gather his winnings from the table. "There will be another time, cardsharp, you can count on that."

Marcus raised a weak hand and pointed a finger at Jason. "I have . . . to know . . . ," he whispered hoarsely. "why you played me so ruthlessly."

Jason hunkered down beside the man. He bent his dark head toward Trudeau so that he was the only one to hear his reply. "Four years ago, my family owned this very riverboat. My father's last name was O'Roark. You destroyed everything, including my father, with your cheater's game. He committed suicide because of his shame. I am the only one who could have avenged his death. And I swore to his memory that I would."

Long, well-muscled legs spread in an arrogant stance as he pulled a cheroot from within his tailored coat. After lighting it, he turned his back on the wounded Trudeau, tugged at each ruffled-tip shirtsleeve, and dismissed the broken man as just another piece of the puzzle put back in the proper place. He could feel no sorrow for tonight— only a deep sense of satisfaction.

Jason's eyes met those of the boat's captain. McGurk tipped his hat to Jason in a show of respect, and something more. He grinned as the gambler returned his welcome, then sauntered away.

"Thomas!" Big John called to the riverboat's bartender. "Come lend a hand here, will you?"

Between the captain and the bartender they managed

to remove the wounded Trudeau from the saloon and see that he was provided medical attention. He would be put off in Vicksburg when they docked for more fuel. Big John McGurk couldn't help smiling at the thought.

Christina's face was flushed with excitement as she fled the pandemonium of the gambling saloon and collapsed into the nearest deck chair.

I don't know if I feel sick, or fascinated, she said to herself. She closed her eyes to think and calm her jangled nerves.

He was absolutely cold-blooded the way he tore that man to pieces. Surely that cannot be the Jason I once knew. I am mistaken. And I heard his last name was Woods. She shook her head to clear her thoughts. Burying her face between her fingers she tried to dismiss the image of Jason Woods's savagery.

The brooding gambler had left the gaming room and now strode briskly over to the guardrail. The thunderstorm would break any minute by the sound of the low-rolling clouds and the lightning that flashed in brilliant arcs of fire across the pitch-black sky. His blue eyes assessed all of this with a sleepy, lazy look as he inhaled the fragrant tobacco of his cigar.

It was obvious to Christina, who sat watching him from the shadows, that the man deliberately portrayed an illusion of indifference. As if he had worked hard to project such an image. She found herself wanting to shatter that confident, arrogant air. Impulsively, she called out to him.

"Congratulations, *Monsieur* Woods! I understand you have emerged the victor in tonight's game!"

Jason whirled about, eyes peering into the mist-enshrouded night for the person behind the lilting voice. It was impossible to distinguish who had addressed him. But whoever she was, she was a brazen little chit. He would gladly settle for a soft, warm body to curl up with for the night.

"I give up!" he chuckled, "come out from the shadows so that I might see who it is that has congratulated me."

"I do not think that would be too wise," Christina replied suppressing a giggle. She was finding this game most exciting. Being young and quite inexperienced in the ways of men, she did not see the seriousness of such folly.

"And why is that?" Jason inquired, his dark brows forming a bemused line over his sapphire eyes. Where the deuce was the vixen?

"Because this way I have the upper hand, *monsieur*, . . . and that suits me."

A half smile tugged at one corner of the gambler's mouth. "And I think it is because you are afraid, little one."

Christina's spine stiffened. "I am no such thing, you conceited peacock!" she flung back at him.

His laughter rumbled deep from his chest and danced pleasantly upon her ears. "I have not been called such names in a long, long time." He caught his breath as memories of a beautiful girl flooded his mind. Swallowing convulsively, he turned back to lean over the rail.

Silence prevailed, and Christina leaned forward. What had she done or said that had caused his mood to change so swiftly? She bit her bottom lip, unsure of what to do next. Perhaps nothing. After all, she was playing with fire. She decided to stay hidden in the deck chair until she could slip away without the gambler noticing.

40

Jason heaved a sigh as he gazed out over the river. He removed the half-smoked cheroot from his mouth and tossed it wearily into the swirling water. Suddenly he was tired, very tired. Even the thought of the saucy filly behind the unknown voice sharing the night with him could not pick up his flagging spirits.

He had travelled hundreds of miles, yet it seemed he had come full circle. Tomorrow he would once again be in the one city in the world he wanted most to forget. Natchez. Just the name running across his thoughts made him feel depressed.

As if the heavens interpreted his mood, they suddenly unleashed a slashing downpour. Torrents of rain and wind buffeted anyone foolish enough to still be lounging around on deck.

Holding her skirts well above her trim ankles, Christina fairly flew across the deck toward shelter. She gave a small cry as her satin bonnet was whipped from her golden hair and blown from her reach. Before she could decide whether she wanted to give chase or not, the gambler made a gallant dash for the wind-tossed bonnet.

In one swift, sure movement he had captured the bonnet with agile fingers.

She watched him approach her, her breath fairly catching in her throat as she sensed the savage strength of the man. As he handed the bonnet to her a flash of lightning lit up the night sky, and Christina found herself staring in wide-eyed wonder at the dancing, mocking lights in the cocky young gambler's eyes.

"So, it is you," Jason surmised with astonishment, "the girl I saw earlier. Do you make a habit of prowling the deck picking up stray men?" he taunted.

Christina wanted desperately to make some clever retort—snap his head off his shoulders! But for once in

41

her life her tongue remained firmly glued to the roof of her mouth.

Just then the captain's voice called out to Jason and the man's attention was turned elsewhere.

It gave Christina the time she needed to view him closely. And what she saw behind the cynical mask, the dark, neatly trimmed beard, made her senses reel!

Jason! It had to be Jason! There were no two men so similar. But why the fictitious name, the ruthless card playing? And how had he become such a cold, callous gambler?

Christina wanted desperately to reach out and touch him but she forced herself to remain still and do nothing. Something about this man told her he would not welcome recognition. She stood like a foolish, half-drowned kitten watching him. When he tipped his hat to her and turned toward the captain and Martinique Summerfield, she could not help the stab of longing that pierced her heart. Mouth agape, she watched her Jason stroll out of her life. Then he turned and looked back at her for a moment.

Christina hurried toward her stateroom. Her companion would be pacing the floor with worry by now. As she walked briskly through the dimly-lit corridor she thought once again of the man that she'd just left. He was so changed, so wild; wild as the storm that had caused their chance meeting. She felt as though her blood flowed faster and hotter through her veins after the mere sight of his face.

Sleep was a long time coming that night, and when at last she drifted off, her slumber was disturbed by haunting dreams. Dreams of another time, another place, and the laughing, blue-eyed youth who had been the center of her young life.

Chapter Two

One piece at a time, the broken, supressed memories made their way to the surface of Jason O'Roark's mind. Regardless of how hard he tried, they refused to be put back. He knew it was because of John's telegram, and the fact that he was once again in the one part of the country that he'd sworn to avoid.

He had accepted the shattered youthful dreams, the loss of his father, and the family fortune, in addition to the disillusionment of the Civil War. He had accepted all of these things; but it had left him a cold, hard man and he was not yet thirty years old. As he returned John McGurk's enthusiastic handshake and listened to his warm words of welcome, a sudden rush of feeling washed over Jason. Perhaps he was getting soft; after all, Marcus Trudeau was still alive, wasn't he?

"You're looking great, both of you," Jason said. "Looks as though you've at last realized your dream of travelling the river, John."

"That I did my friend." John replied, as he regarded his wartime protégé closely. He glanced down at

Martinique Summerfield. "You always did say ole Jase here was a friend you could depend on, didn't you, Marti?"

The female member of the Secret Service replied, "He's always been there when I needed him. Whenever I was caught in a bad situation and there seemed no way out . . . Jase was there."

Jason smiled appreciatively. "It was my pleasure, ma'am," he said. "After all, we couldn't allow our prettiest agent to fall into enemy hands. Then I would have been stuck looking at Big John's ugly face for the duration of the war, and that would be above and beyond the call of duty."

Big John's deep chuckle reverberated throughout the stateroom. "And to think I was almost beginning to feel that I missed you, Jason," he taunted mockingly.

"Well, I certainly missed both of you," Martinique intervened, "and I can't tell you how delighted I was to get your wire, John, suggesting this little get-together."

"That goes for me too," Jason replied sincerely, his tone now serious. His eyes drifted once again to Martinique's. "I was very sorry to learn of your mother's death, Marti. I know how devoted you were to her and what a comfort it must have been for her to have you by her side when she needed you most."

"Thank you, Jase," she replied softly. "I'm glad I made the decision to go home after the war. Her illness left her an invalid and I was the only one left to care for her."

"One has to do what one thinks is right," John sighed, "and even though it was terribly hard on both of us, it's over now. And perhaps this lady of mine will at last consent to become my wife."

Martinique felt his warm, appreciative gaze and looked

up at him. "It seems as though it were meant to be, after all, doesn't it, John?"

He squeezed her hand, grinning from ear to ear. "There's no doubt in my mind, pretty lady."

"Well, we shall see if you feel the same after the completion of this trip," she replied in a teasing voice. "You'll probably be ready to throw me overboard by then."

"Never," he chuckled. "I intend for you to be a permanent fixture around here from now on."

"And just what am I to do while you fellows are busy running the show?" She gave him a questioning look. "I'm not like most females, John. I must be an active participant in your life. It's only fair to warn you now."

"And that's exactly how I want it too, Marti," he assured her. "I believe I know you well enough to realize you're not going to be happy sitting in my cabin darning my socks. I know you're accustomed to being your own woman, and I hope you'll stay that way. I want you to interact in the business and help in every way." He glanced over at Jason. "If it's all right with the new owner, that is."

Jason shrugged his broad shoulders. "Sounds just fine to me. I'll be needing all the help I can get." He walked over to a marbletopped sideboard and picked up a crystal decanter of bourbon. "I want to propose a toast to our new venture," he said, as he filled three glasses, picked them up and carried them to his friends. When each person held a glass, he raised his. "To the future, and to the *Lucky Lady*."

"The *Lucky Lady?*" John questioned.

"That's what I've decided to rename my new enterprise," Jason hastened to explain. "It seems befitting, considering everything that has taken place today."

The three friends touched glasses, happy to be together, and happy to be getting on with their lives.

"And to my long-awaited victory over Trudeau," Jason added, "thanks, John, for wiring me that he was here."

"It was my pleasure," John answered sincerely. Suddenly he cast his friends a sheepish look. He decided there was no better time than the present to break the other half of his news to them. "Ah, . . . Jase, Marti." He cleared his throat nervously.

"What is it, John?" Martinique inquired, as she searched his face for the cause of his sudden discomfort.

"There is something more I'd best tell you."

Jason became at once wary. "What's that, John?"

"Last month," John began, "not long after I sent you each a wire to meet me in Memphis, I was contacted by our former commanding officer."

"The colonel—whatever for?" Martinique questioned, her face registering her surprise.

John heaved a sigh, rose from his seat, and crossed the room to refill his glass. "Our services have been requested, that's why." He sipped at the amber-colored bourbon and then calmly asked if anyone would care for a refill.

"Yeah, me," Jason drawled, "I have a strong feeling I'm going to need it." Both men were silent as John refreshed his friend's drink. He turned toward Martinique, his eyes questioning.

"None for me, thank you," Martinique replied softly, her voice somewhat strained. She glanced at John. "Are you actually serious John?"

"Yes, I am."

"I don't believe this," Martinique moaned.

"Believe it, Marti," John hastened to add, "he was most precise in explaining the government's position on this matter."

Jason shook his head, remembering the pain of the war, the days and nights when he couldn't remember who he actually was or what alias he was using. "I don't like anything about this. But I'm sure that the colonel was most convincing." He sailed his hat across the room to land on a nearby buffet. "And I suppose I may as well get comfortable. I have a feeling I'm in for one of your long-winded, patriotic speeches, Big John." He leaned back to rest one hip upon John's desk as he regarded his companion from under hooded eyes.

John did not back down from Jason's penetrating stare, which he had been subject to many times in the past; the frostiness of those chilling, blue shards could not sway him from his task.

"I believe you'll both understand if you'll just allow me a few more minutes of your time."

"By all means," Jason responded dryly. "You have my undivided attention."

The big man returned to sit beside Martinique. "And you, Marti?" he inquired softly, "will you listen?"

"Yes, . . . although I don't know why," she replied, sounding dismayed.

John took a deep breath. "Well, here goes. . . . I know both of you are aware of the Reconstruction in the South and the serious problems the government is facing with the corruption and violence of the Northern politicians—some of whom have arrived with their only possessions contained in a carpetbag slung across their

47

arm—and the Southern aristocrats who once ruled everything and everyone around them by their own code."

"I've heard," Jason replied. "I'm not immune to the hardships of the Southern people, and I certainly sympathize with what they've had to endure since the war. But I have no idea how the government feels they can use my services in this matter."

"I agree with Jase," Martinique added.

John held up his hand. "I know you both are sick of sleeping on the hard ground, and sticking your neck out just to get it shot at," he said, "but this time it will all be different. The colonel assured me."

"I hope they're not the same assurances he gave us the last time we went on assignment for him." Jason stated harshly.

"The war had a way of interfering with everyone's best-laid plans, Jase," Big John replied, his eyes resting upon his friend. "Times are better, and particularly for you." He swept his arm before him to include their surroundings. "This is all yours now. We won't have to sleep on horse blankets and eat rotten grub on this venture. We just don't have to any more."

Jason viewed his eager friend with skeptical eyes. "What's the assignment? Get to that."

Big John displayed a boyish grin, indicating he was confident they would not let him down. "The South has been divided into five military districts under Reconstruction. The colonel has been assigned this district. Congress cannot persuade Mississippi to accept the Fourteenth Amendment. She must be convinced that it is for the good of her people that she comply with the Constitution. The government is of the firm belief that if we clean up the corruption among local politicians, and the violent, secret organizations that oppose them, the next time the Union submits the amendment to the people of Mississippi for ratification, it will not be rejected."

"Sounds like just another political power play to me," Jason quipped sarcastically. "And Mississippi, you say . . . just where in Mississippi, Big John?" he inquired.

"Natchez," Jason replied.

Jason sat up ramrod straight. "Natchez! Of all the goddamned places!"

"What's wrong with Natchez?" John asked, somewhat perplexed. "We had some nice times in that city during its occupation."

Martinique laid her hand upon John's arm. "I think I can explain. Jason swore after the war that he would never return to Natchez. He wanted to put everything behind him, begin fresh."

"It's different this time, Jase," John explained. "If you don't wish to run into any old acquaintances, just keep low and continue to wear that beard. And if you use Woods as your last name, I can't imagine there being a problem."

Jason laughed shortly before replying. "What the hell! I can't say as though it isn't for a worthy cause. And I do feel we owe them something after what we did to their culture and their lives."

"Great!" Big John shouted, and looking at Martinique said. "How about you, pretty lady. Can we count on you?"

Martinique gazed deeply into his eyes and saw the love and commitment there. How could she continue life

49

without him now that they'd just found each other again? "Yes . . . you can count on me, you big lug!" she responded, her face brightening.

"I knew neither of you would let your country down," John cried exuberantly. "Everything is all set. In the morning we land in Natchez and meet the courier at Rose's place. He will inform us whether or not he managed to inveigle an invitation to a man named Simon Baker's political ball. He is definitely under government suspicion. A shady sort, from what I've heard."

"Simon Baker," Jason mused, "I remember the name from somewhere." He shook his head at his inability to place the man.

Big John clapped his large hands together in a gesture of conclusion. "That's that, then." John snapped his fingers. "Oh, I almost forgot. The colonel said that if you're going to use Rose's establishment as we did during the war, that you are to keep a low profile this time and not go acting like a wild houligan." John fairly choked on his laughter and moisture formed in his hazel eyes from the effort of suppressing it. "Your last adventure there apparently cost the government plenty. The colonel wants you to remember that the war is over. Damages can no longer be blamed on cannon fire. Is that clear?"

The agents all regarded each other wryly.

"Cannon fire? Is that what he actually told them?" Jason inquired incredulously.

"So he says," John answered with a chuckle. "But do promise, old boy, to keep your entertainment low-key . . . all right?"

Jason's brow arched upward. "What?" he quipped exaggeratedly. "Business and no pleasure? Your age is beginning to catch up with you, my friend."

John scowled darkly at his friend. "I'm thirty years old and far from having my foot planted firmly in the grave."

Martinique swatted him playfully as Jason strolled across the room to retrieve his hat. "See you in the morning then, John. I'll be waiting with a glass of warm milk for you, old timer." His laughter was rich and deep as he disappeared into the shadows of the Mississippi night, but his thoughts did not match the light-heartedness of that sounds. They were concentrated single-mindedly on just one thing, one person: the ravishing creature who earlier had compelled his very thoughts to intermingle with her own.

"Is it you?" he whispered to the bewitching little face that floated about in his thoughts and would not be put to rest. "And if it is so, whatever am I to do about you," he groaned. "Go away, you green-eyed temptress. . . . Damned if I'm going to fall under your spell again."

But even as the words were being spoken, he knew exactly what he was going to do, and what a fool he was for allowing his emotions to rule his heart once more. "I want you, my love," he murmured as he stepped over the threshold to his stateroom. "But I do not intend to pay that price ever again for anyone . . . not even for you."

Chapter Three

Christina Duprea gazed upon her beloved Oak Meadow and beamed with pleasure as she stepped from the carriage. The house was in dire need of paint and repairs, and the once immaculate gardens were now thick with overgrown weeds. But to Christina's eyes it was still the most beautiful sight that she had ever seen. The imposing structure was graced by tall, Corinthian columns that extended about the entire house. The gleaming windows, adorned by green and ocher shutters, allowed cool southern breezes to drift into the high-ceilinged rooms. It was a reminder of the plantation way of life, a life that Christina was determined to resurrect.

As she hurried forward, two people rushed out of the house onto the veranda. Her pace quickened until she found herself running toward them with outstretched arms.

"I'm home . . . I'm home," she repeated as she threw herself into her father's comforting embrace.

"Yes, you are, and welcome, darling Christina," Matthew said emotionally, his dark eyes, once so vibrant and alive, looking at his daughter with only a hint of their old spark.

"Oh, Papa, it is like a dream! Home at last," Christina cried brokenly.

"I know daughter, I know," he whispered, hugging her fiercely to his chest.

Christina rested her head upon his shoulder, wondering at his lack of height. Once she'd thought him so tall and invincible; he now appeared almost shriveled and frail. The past seven years had left their mark on her papa. He was a broken, defeated man. Anxiously, she glanced over at her childhood mammy and reached a shaking hand toward the familiar, loved figure. Gray hair now peeked from beneath the colorful kerchief, but her stout body had remained as proud and straight as ever. The doting woman shook her head sadly at Christina's questioning look. The girl read the message that Mammy conveyed by that look, and knew with a sudden icy grip of fear that her papa had all but given up on life.

"I'm home now, Papa. We shall never be parted again, I promise you." Christina stroked the crisp, white hair of her sobbing father, and gently took him by the arm and led him inside the house. A house, Christina thought painfully, as she stepped into the still impressive entrance, that had once been filled with life and children's laughter. Now the rooms rang with anguished cries of the past, and the future lay shrouded.

The afternoon meal passed pleasantly for father and daughter. If Christina noticed the way in which her papa picked listlessly at his food, she did her best to hold her tongue. Mammy had Dulcie prepare everything that Christina had loved as a small child: fried chicken;

hominy; light, fluffy biscuits dripping with honey gathered from the plantation's own bee colony; and an assortment of pies and rich, gooey desserts. After their hearty meal, Christina and Matthew went for a walk about the gardens. Spring seemed to have arrived just to welcome Christina home. The surrounding grounds were aflame with flowers of every color.

"Are you getting tired, Papa?" Christina asked, as she led him over to one of the marble benches that graced the weed-infested garden. She held his hand as she sat beside him.

"I have been tired for so long, little one, that I don't know how to feel any other way." He sighed defeatedly. "Christina. I tried . . . heaven knows I've tried so hard. But there are times when I just can't remember what I've said from one day to the next." He cleared his throat, and rubbed his fingers across his temples. "No use in trying to keep it from you any longer, daughter. Your step-cousin Simon is managing our affairs now . . . everything."

There was no way for Christina to conceal her shock. She was appalled. "No!" she cried in distress. "Papa, how could you allow this?"

"Oh, it didn't happen overnight," Matthew explained, "but Simon bided his time. When the carpetbaggers and Federals swarmed over the South to pick its bones clean, well, Simon was only too happy to welcome them. The ravens and vultures have swooped down to pick the nests of the eagles, and we've had no choice but to stand back and watch them plunder and destroy everything they touch."

"Surely there is some way we can stop them!" Christina blurted out.

"How?" Matthew replied in a broken voice. "Some of our own are finding it easier to give in to these vermin than to stand up to them. There are so many! And Simon is one of the worst. Since his stepfather's fatal fall at Falcon Hurst, and then Simon's mother's passing—well, Simon has been like a man possessed. He's drunk on power and wealth."

Christina drew a deep breath. "What you're trying to tell me is that Simon has his clutches on our business, our investments."

"Yes," was the mournful reply.

"Dear God, . . . that means I am dependent on the lecher for the very food that is on our table."

"I'm sorry, daughter," Matthew said in an anguished voice. "I had no idea what he intended to do when I appointed him manager of our funds and investments. And then there were the taxes that came due. You don't realize, Christina, the Reconstructionists have inflated taxes beyond any of our means. They're determined to bring us to our knees." Matthew turned tormented eyes upon his offspring. "I didn't know who to turn to. Simon said he knew some people who would help see to it that Yankees didn't get their hands on our lands."

"I'm sure he did," Christina replied with a bitter laugh as she wrapped her lace shawl tighter about her shaking form and tried to still the fury that now gripped her.

Matthew clasped his trembling hands in his lap, his head bowed forward. He had made a mess of things. It was hell to grow old, but even more so in these times when the vultures were perched out there . . . waiting.

Christina whirled around to face her father. "Papa, tell me, what of my deed to Oak Meadow that was in trust? And the one on our riverboat that I loved so much, the *Christina?*"

"They are still yours, daughter. He could not manage to get his hands on anything that was held in trust. And he didn't bother with the shares of railroad stock that we have, so that is still ours too, worthless as it is."

"Nevertheless," Christina replied determinedly. "It is ours! And with that small mistake on Simon's part, we can begin anew. Do not worry, Papa, it was through no fault of yours that this happened," she assured him lovingly. "We shall overcome these times. We *will* overcome these times!" she repeated firmly, a plan already beginning to form in her mind.

Matthew rose shakily to his feet and took his fiery, ever confident daughter by the arm. The odds against us are more formidable than you imagine."

"Since when has a Duprea been afraid of a few odds?" She threw back at him. "I will put fire back in your step once again . . . just you wait and see."

Matthew Duprea felt proud at that moment—a feeling he hadn't experienced in many years. How unlike her mother she was. Thank the lord his wife hadn't lived to see this day. She would never have been able to live without her refined, Southern culture. She had been appalled by Matthew's refusal to shackle his slaves to him by ownership. No, he'd said even then, a man works harder when he knows he is doing it to put food on his own table. And he had been right. His slaves were free to come and go as they chose. And many still remained with him today, even if there wasn't any money to pay their wages. Oak Meadow was home to all of them.

Matthew's pace quickened to keep up with his daughter's. The little girl who had caused him so many sleepless nights because of her wild, untamable spirit

57

was home at last. Matthew smiled as he observed the stubborn thrust of Christina's chin and the excited bounce of the tawny curls as she strode briskly toward the main house. She would give Simon something to lie awake nights thinking about. Matthew grinned broadly. *Simon*, he thought, *you are about to meet the one person who will not be intimidated by your power. And may the good lord have mercy on your black heart when she's done with you.*

Despite being weary from her journey, Christina could not seem to keep her eyes closed. They kept popping open, staring at the lacy canopy that crowned the fourposter bed. Unconsciously, her slim fingers began tapping persistently against the cool sheets. The house was quiet, as was usual in late afternoon.

"There isn't anyway I can rest," she finally admitted as she sprang from the bed and crossed over to the rosewood armoire. Reaching inside, she hastily withdrew a cream silk shirt and dark blue riding skirt. She smiled as she observed the neat contents of the armoire. Mammy had wasted precious little time in transferring Christina's clothes from her trunks to their proper place. It gave her a warm, secure feeling to have her clothes in her own room. As she changed she gazed about the bedroom. It was the same as the day she'd left, painted a soft yellow with frothy white curtains at the windows. Christina was amazed at how familiar it all seemed. While she was away she had remembered every detail. She walked over to a picture that had been placed slightly askew on one wall. A sad smile appeared on her face as she gently lifted the watercolor painting and stared at the indentation in the wall. Hesitantly, she reached out to trace the jagged edges that were so painful to remember. Her brother Curt had put that mark there. He had been giving her a demonstration of his skill with the rapier, and misjudged his distance when he'd lunged forward. The tip of the blade had torn away a portion of the plaster. Christina had put the picture there to hide it from Mammy. She returned the picture to its place and hurried from the room and down the stairs. She didn't hesitate for one moment, but flew along over the path that would lead her to the stables.

The spirited mare felt the expertise of her rider as they raced over the rolling countryside. Christina's mood brightened as she lost herself in her surroundings. It was a beautiful day, and the birds sang gaily as she urged her mount along the river road. The sky, lightly tuffed with white, wispy clouds, had the vibrant color of fresh morning-glories. A cool breeze whipped off of the great river, over the towering oaks, and slid invisible fingers through the girl's thick, golden hair, wooing it from the tight bun until it lay in a wild mass of gilded sunshine. Her smoky-green eyes misted as the familiar black fields, pierced by endless rows of cotton, met her wandering gaze. She leaned over the mare's neck urging the horse forward past her willow, past the turn that led to the sparkling pool in the forest, onward until at last she caught sight of her destination looming starkly in the distance—the lovely guest house that her father had built for the O'Roark family to stay in when they visited. There was a charm about the little cottage named Gardenia Place because of the many scented gardenia bushes that surrounded it. So intent was Christina in viewing the estate, that she didn't notice the group of rooting hogs along the curving road. Too late, the horse and rider were upon the squealing animals. The frightened horse swerved. As if suspended in time Christina felt her body float over the lowered head of her mount, fly freely through the air and land in a crumpled heap admidst the startled, bristly beasts. A searing pain coursed through her body as she landed. Later, she was to remember an angry curse that had exploded the air as a pair of strong arms reached around her. Then nothing. . . .

Her head spun dizzily as she opened her pain-filled eyes, and looked up into the most vivid blue eyes she'd ever seen. Fringed by thick, spiky lashes, they looked down into hers with serious regard.

"Are you okay?" he asked.

"I do—don't know," she stammered, attempting to sit up.

"No, no," he hastened, pushing her firmly back. "I do not think it would be wise to try and move too quickly. You've been unconscious for a long time."

Wide green eyes started back at him in disbelief. "Oh, dear, I had no idea." Dazed, she looked around but the rapidly setting sun had taken the brightness of the day with it, and she found it impossible to distinguish her surroundings. "Where am I?" she inquired, touching a shaking hand to her bruised forehead.

"You're in a deserted cottage," he replied, rising from his chair beside her. "I would imagine that there are some candles around here somewhere," he said as he

60

rummaged about the dim room.

Even in her disoriented condition she could not take her eyes from his rugged face. He was tall, lean and firmly muscled as he strode across the room to search a nearby buffet.

"Ah . . . I've found some," he exclaimed, withdrawing a candle from an open drawer. He struck a match and held it to the candle.

Her curiosity piqued, Christina propped herself up on one elbow to better discern his face in the flickering candlelight and was startled to realize that she was lying on a sofa in Gardenia Place. His harshly handsome features were thrown in to sharpy relief, and she gasped her shock.

"Sweet *Jesu!*"

The room became extremely still as they warily studied each other.

"I'm afraid this cottage was the only comfortable place to bring you. I hope you understand." He walked over to set the candle on a nearby table and thereby removed the revealing light. Turning toward her, he continued. "I happened to be passing by as you were approaching, but I'm afraid you didn't hear me call out to you. I'm sorry I couldn't manage to prevent your accident."

He is acting so cool, she thought, as though their meeting was purely coincidental. *But I know better, you scoundrel.* "So am I," she replied, trying her best not to remember his primitive, unleashed fury as he'd faced the cardsharp in the gambling saloon—recalling instead how he'd looked in those precious years before the war. "Are you staying near here?" she asked innocently.

"No," he replied noncommittally, "just passing through on business." He looked coolly back at her. "I

61

have my carriage outside. Whenever you feel up to it, I'll have the driver take you back to wherever it is you came from."

"Oh, that won't be necessary," she replied quickly. "I'm sure in a few minutes I'll feel just fine and can return on my own."

His eyes seemed to burn into her from across the room. He walked slowly toward her. Without thinking, she drew back.

He grinned crookedly at her. "And I think it is necessary, so no more need be said."

Her chest felt suddenly constricted as she stared at this man who wrapped himself within a cloak of secrecy.

"What is a young, pretty lady doing out riding all by herself, with no one to look out for her?" he asked, his tone becoming soft, almost coaxing.

Christina found her voice at last and managed to stammer. "I—I just felt a need for some fresh air, to be alone with my thoughts."

"Ah, yes," he commented agreeably. "I know how it is." He reached inside his coat and withdrew a cigar. "Do you mind?" he inquired politely.

"No. By all means, please go ahead."

The gambler appeared completely at ease with his surroundings as he resumed his seat. He lit his cigar and inhaled deeply.

Christina watched as the tip of the cheroot glowed bright orange in the barely lit room. After a moment the long fingers withdrew it from between his lips.

"Are you cold?" he asked solicitously.

"It is getting a bit chilly," she said as she watched him stand and remove his suit coat. Leaning over her, he draped it across her upper body.

"There, how's that?"

She stared into his face in bold assessment. *So tall, so very handsome*, she thought. For a moment time seemed to stand still.

Jason was overcome by her loveliness, and the initial reaction in his loins did little to alleviate the situation. He wanted this haunting beauty, had to have her. Why? The very moment he had seen her riding in the wind had confirmed his earlier suspicions. What in the deuce was he going to do about her—and the damnable mission? He looked upon the thick mane of flaxen silk, the glittering jade eyes, like those of the sea siren calling the doomed man into her beckoning arms. So green, so fathomless; if a man wasn't careful he could easily drown in their depths. Jason mentally shook himself, forced his thoughts away from his desires, and willed his voice to sound normal when he spoke.

"Perhaps I should be getting you home now."

"Yes, perhaps," Christina managed to whisper; then she gasped slightly as he stood over her, his gaze resting on her moist, inviting lips. He laughed softly.

"I must say I am tempted to keep you here forever," he drawled in a teasing voice.

Christina blushed becomingly. Even in the shadows that danced against the candlelight, she saw his lips cease smiling, become serious. "Your family must be getting worried about you. Come," he said, as he leaned over and effortlessly scooped her into his arms. "Let's see about getting you returned home safe and sound."

Instinctively, her hands reached up to wrap themselves about his neck, accidently brushing the blue-black hair that curled over the back of his collar. And when he straightened with Christina enfolded in his embrace, she felt the muscles in his corded chest ripple beneath her. His long legs, encased in tight-fitting breeches that were tucked into high-top boots, moved with the grace of a sleek animal as he carried her toward the front door. He stopped by the lit candle, and lowered her a bit so that she could blow it out. That done, they left the little house and stepped out into the cool evening air. The driver watched them approach and swung down from his seat on the carriage to open the door. Her rescuer placed her inside the carriage; after making sure her horse was tethered to the back, he hopped in lithely to sit beside Christina.

"Do you think you are feeling up to the journey?" he inquired politely.

"Oh, yes. I only live a short distance down the road."

He grew strangely silent, and she wished with all of her might that there was a full moon instead of the scant sliver of light that barely lit up the interior of the carriage. She still could not see him as well as she would have wanted.

"Which way?" he asked a bit gruffly.

"Down the river road," she instructed, "until you come to a sharp bend, then turn into the roadway there. It is the entrance to my home." She regarded his face, hoping to see some sign that would tell her he remembered.

He tossed the remains of his cheroot out of the open window, and allowed his gaze to follow after it. Damn! he thought as he called the directions up to the driver. There was no point in denying it now. It was indeed her.

"Is anything the matter, *monsieur?*" she asked, unable to hide the slight tremble in her voice.

"Not at all," he replied thickly. His face, when it turned to meet hers, was quite blank of any emotion. His eyes took on a wary, guarded look, that lazy, assessing stare that revealed nothing about his true feelings. She was so lovely sitting there next to him, and so untouchable. He felt as though someone had just taken their fist and rammed it into his stomach.

Her eyes looked away from his. "I thought you might be upset with me for detaining you. I apologize if I've ruined your plans for the evening."

"How could anyone be upset with such a charming diversion?" he grinned at her.

"You are very kind, *monsieur* . . ." she waited expectantly for him to announce his last name.

"Woods," he offered without hesitation.

Why does he persist in playing this charade with me, she wondered?

"Ah, . . . Monsieur Woods. Well, at any rate, I wish to thank you for all that you've done. Might I detain you a moment longer so that you could meet my papa?" she inquired of him.

"I don't think that would be too wise," he replied dryly, his nostrils flaring slightly as the lavender scent of her sweet perfume seemed to envelope him in its intoxicating embrace.

"And why is that?" she chuckled, as she envisioned how he must be squirming.

"Because," he offered with a touch of sarcasm, "I happen to know how these planters are when it comes to their darling daughters. When their precious has been gone unescorted for half the day, and to places unknown, only to return on the arm of a man—well, let's just say that your reputation would suffer."

Her delightful laughter filled the carriage. "As you wish, *monsieur*," she returned with a toss of her head. "I have taken enough of your time at any rate." She cast him a sideways glance. "And I'm sure there are many more hands of cards yet to play this evening . . . *oui?*"

"And how would you know of such things?" he asked; even in the shadowy interior of the carriage she could see the look of surprise on his face.

"I know many things ladies are not supposed to know," she returned with a saucy smile. "But if you would really like to know the answer, it is because I was witness to your card game with that wicked man, Marcus Trudeau."

"You were what?" he cried incredulously.

"You don't remember because you did not have eyes for me then," she replied. "But you do remember saving my bonnet from blowing into the river during the rainstorm, do you not? I had just left the gambling saloon."

"Of course," he whispered thoughtfully, "the drowned little kitten."

At that moment she felt like kicking him in the shin. Drowned little kitten, indeed! "I suppose you're accustomed to a somewhat larger species," she chided. "Perhaps a tigress. At any rate, I do think you play cards remarkably well, although I wasn't very impressed by the rest of your act."

Jason grinned. "Ah, . . . little cat," he whispered. "You have a most refreshing way about you. And I can see right now how you could most assuredly be a pain in a man's backside."

Christina shifted uncomfortable, very much aware that his muscular thigh brushed against hers with each bump of the rumbling carriage. She could not prevent the flow of warmth in her veins, nor the limpness in her

66

limbs at his nearness. Just as she was about to reply, the carriage turned into the drive, and Jason moved away from her to call out to the driver.

"Stop down the road, before you get to the house," he ordered.

She stared at him, wondering just what he had on his mind—and how she would react if he were to kiss her. His male scent seemed to surround her—quite pleasant, heady. She breathed in the virile mixture of fine brandy, cigars, and leather. Shockingly, she realized that she didn't want to lose him again. She wanted desperately to be held in his arms, to feel his lips upon hers, in the way that she had dreamed so many times—for seven long years.

"Why are we stopping?" she asked, her eyes wide, softly shining.

"I do not think it wise for your family to see you arrive with a complete stranger," he explained wryly to her questioning look.

"Ever the gallant . . . *Oui, Monsieur* Woods?"

With you a role I am quite used to portraying, he felt like saying. But he did not. Instead, he removed his broad hat and inclined his dark head toward her. "Always, beautiful lady." He opened the door of the carriage and stepped down. "Your servant, madam," he said as he bent forward from the waist, his thick, dark hair shining lustrously in the moonlight.

His large hands encircled her slim waist and lifted her forward to place her on the ground before him. The feel of those lean, agile fingers gripping her waist so possessively caused a strange, exhilarating feeling to course madly through her.

Jason looked down at this golden vision, looked down

into those jade cat eyes that had haunted his dreams for so many years.

"Is there something wrong, *monsieur?*" she inquired of his scrutinizing appraisal.

"Quite the contrary," he replied as he continued to regard her with that sleepily, assessing stare.

She blushed furiously. There was no mistaking the intent of his words, nor the desire she saw within his eyes as they boldly raked her from head to toe, approving of the lithe, willow-slim frame, and the high, firm bosom that strained against the material of her blouse.

She has grown taller, he thought, *but even so, standing here so close to me she just barely reaches my shoulders.* He liked that. Good things were known to come in small packages. Jason thought she appeared like a tawny-gold cat as she stood blinking those wide green eyes at him so boldly, curiously. Very slowly he lowered his mouth to capture her pink, moist lips. The shock of their sweetness almost jolted him off his feet. He was surprised, and knew that if the kiss deepened he would surely lose himself in her soft, delightfully innocent femininity. With a muffled groan, he pulled her closer until she lay pressed against his hard, masculine length, their hearts beating rapidly in unison.

Christina knew that she should stop him, but as she felt his tongue probe gently at her trembling mouth, then more forcefully, as he demanded entrance, she parted her lips. A low moan escaped her as expertly he explored the soft inner recesses of her mouth, awakening feelings that thrilled, yet frightened her. She had been kissed a few times before by inept schoolboys. But never had she experienced anything that could equal this delicious new feeling that made her want to forget who they were, and that they now belonged to different worlds. Throwing all caution to the wind, she allowed her arms to steal upward and entwine themselves around his neck, her fingers weaving their way into his thick mane of black hair. She sighed as his stroking fingers caressed the high, delicate cheekbones of her face, then moved lower to grip her slim shoulders almost roughly.

Their embrace, the intimate contact of their bodies, was almost too much for Jason to bear and not possess her completely. And he knew that this was not either the time nor the place. Reluctantly, and with a ragged sigh, he pulled his mouth from hers and gazed deeply into her passion-drugged eyes.

"I am just a man, sweet thing. And if I continue to hold your tempting body in my arms much longer I will lose what little control I have left . . . and then we both know what will happen." His blue eyes glittered recklessly, as though he were daring her.

Christina did not move from within the circle of his arms, nor did she remove hers from about his neck. He could feel every luscious curve and valley of her body pressed against him. His breathing, as well as the obvious response of his male body, told her of his desire for her. She knew that he had truly meant his warning to her. And she knew she must end this rapturous torture before it was too late.

"I do not want this to end, Jase," she murmured unashamedly. She touched his bearded jaw with a finger. "Will I ever see you again?"

"I don't know the answer to that right this minute," he replied softly. "You know the life I lead, what my profession is." He gazed at her coolly, and inclined his dark head toward the house. "What do you think your family would have to say about this? I doubt very much if they would approve."

She appeared a bit taken aback by his harsh words. "Whatever they would think, *Monsieur* Woods, is certainly no concern of yours. My family—and my life—are my own."

He shook his head with disbelief. "Jesus, but you're a cool one. Here I thought I had a sweet, innocent virgin to worry about, and she turns into a spitting, little vixen."

Christina glared back at him. "Is it so awful for a woman to know her own mind, and speak it?"

"No," he replied, "but the lady in question should be very careful as to who she voices her wishes to. He could be a wolf in sheep's clothing."

She bit her lip to keep back the angry words she wanted to hurl at him, and instead replied candidly. "Perhaps I find you a bit intriguing, different from the eager, fresh-faced boys I've met abroad. There is something wild and untamable about you that appeals to me." She shrugged helplessly. "It is a terrible fault of mine. . . . I know it. But I have never been one to go along with society's wishes."

He grinned wickedly, thinking how well he knew the truth of that statement. "Nor I," he said as she returned his amused smile.

She searched his face one last time before she reluctantly turned in the direction of the house. "You will not forget me," she said brazenly. "And somehow I think that you do not want to." She started in the direction of the mansion, but was stopped. Jason grabbed her hand before she got out of range and swiftly pulled her back into his embrace.

Christina thought for one breathless moment that he

70

intended to kiss her again, but instead he pressed her smooth hand to his lips, and kissed it.

"I am your talisman, love. The protector of your dreams. Whenever you need me I will return to you . . . no matter where I may be at the time." Then he released her, and stood watching as she led her horse toward the brightly lit mansion . . . and out of his life once again.

As Christina strolled casually toward the house, her thoughts remained on the strange events of the day. They had been destined from the very beginning to become lovers. She felt no shame whatsoever at the thrill that raced through her upon the realization. Yankee or no, she loved him, had always loved him. And she would have him . . . by God, she would.

Her worried father was waiting for her when she entered the house. He was relieved to hear that she was all right, and after explaining that she'd just lost track of time, Christina retired to her room for the night.

With the morning came a new set of problems for the headstrong young woman. She stormily paced the floor, pausing to gaze out of her bedroom window at the surrounding countryside.

"I just don't know, Mammy," she ranted, hands placed firmly on her narrow hips. "That overblown toad, Simon, may think he has won—and perhaps he has, for now. But this is only round one. The best is yet to come!"

Mammy's ebony face brightened at the fire in her lamb's voice. "Dat's my girl! Ah done told George Washington, dat new man your pappy hired to work the south field, jist you wait, when Miz Christina gits home

71

she settle things wid dat no account white trash."

Christina tried to smile with conviction at Mammy. "I have to—for all of our sakes. Poor Papa just didn't realize how evil a person his stepnephew is." She shuddered. "Taking advantage of poor Papa's illness like that. Why, Papa didn't even realize what he was doing when he signed over to Simon the right to manage our interests. He is living in the past so much it is beginning to frighten me."

"I know, darlin'. It is awful, but der was nothin' we could do 'bout it. Your pappy jist give up on dis here place after your brother and de missus die."

Christina's green eyes narrowed in anger. "I should have known that son of a she-dog would try and pull something underhanded like this." She at last gave way to her emotions, and issued a string of expletives that nearly caused Mammy's curls to stand on end. "I'm going to send George Washington into town with a note for Mr. Worthington at the bank. I want an immediate audit of everything that we have left." She chewed thoughtfully on her forefinger. "Tell him to freeze all of our accounts immediately. Then we'll see just how much cousin Simon is able to steal from us."

Just then Mammy reached inside her apron with a gasp and withdrew a note. "Ah almost forgot dis wid everything dat went on last night." She frowned disapprovingly in the girl's direction. Christina still hadn't told her the full story, she was certain of it!

Christina walked over and accepted the pale green envelope. "What is it, I wonder?" she said.

"Open it, chile, dat's de only way you goin' to find out!" Recognizing Simon's wax seal, Christina felt her heart lurch. The note was brief, but not direct.

72

My dear cousin,

Your presence as my hostess is requested on Saturday, the tenth of April, for my annual masquerade ball. Come dressed to compliment my Chinese warlord attire. I look forward, dear Christina, to our reunion.

Your devoted servant,
Simon

Christina ripped the invitation into tiny shreds and threw the pieces into the fireplace.

"The nerve of that man!" she ranted. "I suppose if I should refuse we'd be lucky to have any food on the table. Come properly attired to compliment his costume indeed!"

Mammy's face became a picture of concern. "You be careful, chile. Dat man's up to no good wid yo, I jist feels it."

"Mammy, I suspect that you are absolutely right," Christina replied glumly.

"What you goin' to do now?"

Christina stared moodily into the glowing fire that Tyrone had built earlier to ward off the early April chill. Her almond-shaped cat eyes reflected the flames of the firelight.

"Why, begin my costume, of course."

Mammy was quick to react, "Oh, now darlin', I done saw dat look you tryin' to hide from your ole Mammy." She drew her sturdy frame up to its full height. "You's not goin' to do anythin' you shouldn't, is you?"

There was no answer. For already an image of the costume she intended to wear danced in the corners of Christina's mind. A secret smile stole across her lips as she pictured her cousin's face as she paraded before his friends.

The house that Simon Baker called Falcon Hurst was situated on the highest, lofty bluff overlooking a panoramic view of the Mississippi. He had purchased it dirt cheap after the war when the original owners could not pay the back taxes. It helped to have connections in government. And this, Simon did indeed have as was evident by the guest list that his house servant Lucinda now held in her hand as she went over it one last time with him. She was a very pretty octaroon, and had been in Simon's employ since the house had changed ownership. Her sloelike eyes regarded him with fear as she waited for his final approval.

The crafty Simon paid careful attention to each and every name before him. "Yes," he said at last, "everything appears to be in order. No one has been left out." He turned cold eyes upon the young woman's soft features and smiled when he observed the slight stiffening of her slim body. "Come closer, dear," he said, "come closer and let me thank you properly for a job well done."

"Yes, suh," she replied weakly, feeling sick as she drew near him. She saw the all-too-familiar gleam in her employer's eyes and knew that those stubby fingers would soon be creeping up and down her flesh. She willed her mind to go blank.

Simon paid little heed to the lush, young body that now lay over his lap enduring his funbling caresses. His mind was preoccupied with another's face, another's slim form—that of his stepcousin, Christina Duprea. How her

74

sweet body must have bloomed since last he had seen her.

"That's it, sweet," he cooed as Lucinda began to unbutton his shirt and massage him from his chest downward. "Yes, . . . oh, yes," he blubbered, "just like that, Christina. Just like that."

Lucinda was not surprised in the least when he whispered another's name. But she did feel pity for the poor young woman whom Simon sought with such relentless fury. Silent tears flowed down her light brown cheeks as she fixed her eyes upon the heavy, dark furniture in the study.

"Something the matter, Lucinda?" Simon's steely voice was as frigid as the Mississippi river which flowed below his huge mansion.

"No, suh," she whispered, "nothing is the matter, nothing at all."

"I didn't think so," Simon taunted, favoring her with a slick smile as he lowered his lips to her heaving bosom. As his tongue flicked over her quivering flesh, he sighed with contentment when he thought that soon, his long wait would be over. Christina Duprea would be his.

Chapter Four

To Jason it seemed that he had just emerged from a dream. Almost in a trance, he stepped down from the carriage, handed the driver a generous tip, and strode briskly toward the impressive front door of Rose's. But he knew it had not been an illusion; she had been there, he had seen her, held her achingly in his arms, and tasted her soft-honeyed mouth. His senses were filled with her; he was blinded by her haunting beauty, lost within the rapture of her satiny skin, and driven by the need to possess her. Never had he felt such a desire to be bound to someone.

Knocking once on the leaded glass of the door, he waited patiently to be allowed entrance. It gave him the time he needed to clear his thoughts of Christina. When a huge impeccably attired black swung the door open, Jason was composed.

"Good evening, Samson," Jason said stepping into what Rose liked to call the "greeting room."

"Good evening, Mr. Woods, sir," Samson replied, accepting the gambler's hat. "Your party is already here, sir. Captain McGurk has been most anxious about you. He's in the front parlor." Jason was very familiar with the accommodations at Rose's. He had spent many pleasant evenings during the war playing cards in Rose's back room. Here they catered to an exclusive clientele—there were no seedy cowpokes or river rousters here. But there was a brand of pleasure that could be found nowhere else in Natchez. Beautiful women, luxurious accommodations, and any fantasy that a man or a woman could think of was available at Rose's—for a price. It was a house of pleasure; even New Orleans could boast none finer.

Big John McGurk jumped to his feet when Jason entered the crowded parlor. "Where the hell have you been? You were supposed to be here hours ago."

"Detained," Jason replied, striding over to pour himself a healthy shot of whiskey from the intricately carved decanter. Downing the fiery contents in one gulp, he poured another and turned to his friend. "Have you been here very long?"

John scowled. "Long enough that I began to get worried about you. Damn it! You didn't say you were going to go on a tour of the countryside!"

"I didn't know I was going on a tour of the countryside."

McGurk shooed away a buxom brunette dressed sparingly in a red, gauzy wrapper who had been parading back and forth before him trying to catch his eye. John's gaze met Jason's.

"The courier had the information we needed. I sent him along with one of Rose's girls to relax a bit." McGurk grinned slyly. "Guess who just happened to sashay in: none other than Simon Baker himself. He's in the back room playing poker."

78

Jason threw him a satisfied, predatory look. Like the cat who has caught the canary and is now looking forward to the kill.

The two men exchanged meaningless small talk as they ambled into the smoky back room of the brothel. Their eyes narrowed in the dimness of the room, searching the hazy interior for Rose's familiar figure. She noticed them first and could not help the exclamation of pleasure that burst forth at the sight of them. She hurried forward.

"Big John! Jason! My, but it's nice to see you two rascals again." Her generous mouth widened as she smiled warmly. "You two haven't been back to see the new bathhouse that I had built." She winked conspiratorily. "What's the matter fellas . . . find greener pastures for your romping?"

Jason's blue eyes danced merrily. "Now, Rose, you know us better than that."

Big John surveyed the occupants of the gaming room and gave a low whistle at the air of wealth prevalent at the tables. "How is it the South is in a state of financial ruin, yet everyone still manages to find money to gamble?"

Rose stood between the two men, her petite frame practically engulfed by their size. She patted the cluster of auburn curls that were arranged artfully on her head, and turned snapping brown eyes on McGurk. "Some rascals are turning a nice profit by lining their pockets with the misery of others. As long as it's the color of gold, it don't matter to them how they get it." Her sharp eyes were focused directly on Simon Baker.

Both men allowed their gaze to casually roam the room before directing it toward Baker's table. A chilling pair of

79

steel-gray eyes appraised the two strangers as new blood for the game.

Jason withdrew his wallet from inside his coat and made a production out of checking the contents. He could feel the hair on the back of his neck rise as Simon's eyes fastened upon him.

Jason indicated for the captain to lead the way. "After you, Big John," he murmured, his blue eyes full of mockery. "Another adventure awaits us."

It was an unusually warm night. The moon, though little more than a crescent shape in the star-laden sky, promised an enchanted evening for all those who ventured forth. An air of magic swirled about in the velvet shadows that enveloped the Mississippi delta. Christina stood before her cheval mirror and knew it would be a spellbinding evening. She gazed at the reflection of her costumed figure and smiled becomingly.

"What manner of specter are you, oh, mysterious maiden?" the vision demanded, as the flashing emerald eyes sparkled merrily above the scalloped fan that concealed the lower portion of her face. "Who shall come to claim your hand, to pledge his heart, to steal your love this night?" Quite suddenly, her eyes ceased to shine so brightly, and the fan was lowered dispassionately to her side. "To the winner of tonight's round, cousin Simon," she proclaimed with determination in every word. "But I think even you shall be thrown off guard by my appearance tonight." A bubble of amused laughter drifted from Christina's bedroom and caught Mammy's attention as she passed by the door.

The old woman rapped firmly on Christina's door and

called her to unlock it at once. "Darlin', you open dis door dis minute! You up to no good again, ah jist knows it!"

Christina paused from arranging her cloak about her shoulders to open the door.

"What you tryin' to hide away for? Ah knows what you is up to." She leaned back on her heels, and the whites of her eyes widened like two round saucers in her ebony face as she glared at Christina's costume. "Your ole Mammy gonna have a fit of apoplexy tryin' to keep up wid you now, chile. You jist remember dis body might look like it got action in it, but des bones is a sight older dan de was seven years ago."

Christina laughed as she hugged Mammy around her wide shoulders. "I am a grown woman now, Mammy," she said gently. "It isn't necessary for you to worry over me."

Mammy sniffled and patted Christina on her back. "Ah knows dat, ah gots eyes!" she snapped indignantly. She pulled back from Christina's arms. "What you up to . . . you tell Mammy?"

Christina answered truthfully and without hesitation. "I believe it is time for the Duprea family to challenge Mr. Simon Baker to a duel that has been a long time in coming."

Mammy gasped. "No! No, darlin'! Don't you go doin' somethin' foolish! Dat evil man kill you faster dan you say, General Lee!"

"Oh, Mammy, dear. I do not intend to literally challenge Simon to a duel, but it will be a calling out, of that you can be sure." Christina hastened from the room before anything further could be said.

Involuntarily, she shivered as Simon's cruel face took

shape in her mind, smiling malevolently. She tried to still her terrifying thoughts as the coachman helped her into the carriage. After all, it was a magical night, and her prince charming awaited her.

An invitation to the ball had been received by every corrupt, influential politician in Natchez, Mississippi. Simon had been anticipating this evening for weeks. He had been dressed in his Chinese warlord costume for hours. It suited him perfectly. One by one the gaily costumed guests began to arrive, and Simon made it a point to personally greet each and every one of them. He didn't want to take a chance on possibly snubbing the wrong person.

As he stood in the entrance hall, his eyes kept straying to the front door of the mansion. He could hardly wait! Unconsciously, his fingers wandered to the mustache that he had attached to his upper lip. Soon she would be walking through that front door and he would have her within his grasp.

The young woman who had just offered him her hand, winced as Simon, lost in his musings of Christina, crushed the dainty limb in his grip.

A guest stood on the grounds of Simon's estate, watching with growing interest the entourage of eager arrivals. His piercing, amber-gold eyes peered from behind the slitted mask as he remained in the shadows of the surrounding shrubbery. He was sleek and lithely muscled; as he lounged against a nearby oak tree, his silver-streaked gray hair glowed almost luminous in the shaft of moonlight that shone between the parted limbs of the oak. It was not yet time to make his entrance.

"Patience, Silver," he ordered himself, "the night is still young."

And so the notorious highwayman known throughout the Mississippi delta as the Silver Wolf remained enshrouded by the cover of darkness, watching his sworn enemy. He was alone, having left his band of faithful followers on the outskirts of the city hidden deep in the swamps.

"Wait for me here," he had told his men. "I shall have a better chance of gaining entrance to the ball if I can slip in by myself. Even though Baker's protégés will be in costume, I will take note of each name mentioned; have no doubt."

As he stood observing the last of the guests arrive, the Silver Wolf found his attention drawn to a most astounding vision. His eyes warmed as he studied the daring gown that had been fashioned into a geisha costume. It was indeed a shocking but highly sensual piece of handiwork. An intricate design of golden butterflies and nightingales had been stitched on the front panel of the dress. Deep slits pierced either side of the shimmering black silk. Her long, golden hair was gathered into a single braid, and swung freely across her slim hips. As she ventured toward the double doors of the mansion, Silver found himself wishing that he could see the face behind the gold satin mask. Never had a woman's presence demanded his attention in such a way. This was no simpering maiden, but a daring beauty of strong-willed, singleminded, determination. It was evident by the sure step, the straight carriage, and the proud thrust of her delicately shaped chin.

The crisp, chisled line of his jaw tightened beneath the

mask that concealed his profile; eyes followed her steps until she disappeared into the brightly lit mansion.

Streams of ethereal moonlight reflected on his dark clad figure and caught the flash of fire that burned deep within his gaze.

The soiree was going along nicely by the time Christina stepped over the threshold and toward the huge double parlors, whose doors had been thrown wide to form one, immense room.

As expected, the dress caused an instant sensation among the guests as she walked into the vast ballroom. Fixing a bright, confident smile upon her lips, she swept forward across the floor until she reached her stepcousin's side. Taking him completely by surprise, she executed a formal Chinese greeting, bowing from the waist forward. Every eye in the room was upon the beautiful, daring young woman who flaunted her rapturous charms before them as though she owned the world.

"Good evening, Simon," Christina purred, lifting her blazing eyes to meet those of the man she'd sworn to destroy.

"Yes, it is," Simon replied with a cold smile, his narrowed gaze fastening upon her scandalizing attire. "And your presence makes it even better. However, I must say that costume you're wearing leaves little to the imagination. I'm afraid it may offend some of the less-worldly citizens here."

Christina smiled brazenly. "I happen to think this costume most appropriate in respect to the status of your guests. After all, I understand that these people are in the shearing business. If the sheep is to be shorn, then why not make it easier on everyone? Have it done with so that all may be witness to it. Not on the sly, behind the good citizens' backs."

Gasps of shock circulated about the costumed guests that surrounded Simon. Simon's reptilianlike eyes blinked back at Christina. At that moment, she thought he would draw the curving sword strapped to his side and run her through. But then Simon never did anything in front of witnesses. That was not his style.

"Touché, my dear," he muttered icily, as he grabbed her elbow and whisked her away to a secluded alcove off of the parlor. After he had seated her and stood towering over her, he said, "You haven't lost that sharp little tongue of yours, have you?"

"No, I have not," she replied as she glared at him, "and you haven't lost your ability to poison everything that you touch."

He feigned a shocked expression.

"And to think that all the time I missed you, my pet, you were honing that viperish tongue to use against me." He appeared contrite.

She stared at him sullenly. "I know what you've tried to do to my family. I intend to put a stop to your clever manipulation of our monies, your perfidy in regards to our business holdings."

He appeared amused. "What a clever imagination you have, my dear. Where did you get such an insane notion? From that senile father of yours, no doubt." His hot gaze roamed at will over the creamy fullness of her bosom that peeked invitingly over the top of the flesh-toned shift beneath the transparent gown. His eyes glittered with lust as he moved closer. "No one will believe you. A mere slip of a girl involving herself in business affairs. . . . Come now, pet, . . . who will pay attention to your ravings?"

"I have proof, Simon. Or at least I shall shortly," she snapped.

His eyes regarded her with a sadistic light that bared his sick soul to her, she remembered that same look from earlier years, when Simon had captured grasshoppers just to pull off their legs and watch them flop helplessly.

"I have many influential people that back my every move, Christina. They will see to it that your unjust accusations are not backed by any substance." He drew her to her feet to stand before him. "But let us not talk of such nonsense tonight. I did not invite you here to match words with you. Quite the contrary." He brought his face close to hers. "Why don't you think about putting that pretty little head to better use. Leave the management of such things to me. I do not approve of my future bride becoming involved in financial matters."

Christina managed to sputter in outrage, "I would sooner marry a low-down blue-belly than the likes of you!"

Simon chose to ignore her words as he pulled her behind him to the dance floor, his arms encircling her. His fingers played along the sheer fabric that covered her shoulders as his beady eyes glittered hotly into hers. "I do not mind your wearing this gown privately for me, sweet, but never again before my business associates. I don't want them to see what is only for my eyes." Pulling her indecently close to his over-sized body, he whispered in her ear as he led her clumsily around the floor, "I wish to announce our engagement, my dear—tonight."

"You may announce it if you wish," she retorted, her eyes holding his. "But it will not make it so. I will laugh in your face if you do. As for my costume," she continued heatedly, "I wear what I want to wear. Look around you . . . some seem to appreciate my efforts."

"That 'appreciation,' as you put it, is nothing more than pure lust, Christina. Every man in this room is undressing you with his eyes, feeling his body pressed close to yours, as mine is." Simon moved his huge body closer, until Christina felt certain she would be sick if he continued. Simon observed her cheeks flush hotly as he molded himself against her. "This is where you belong, Christina, have always belonged."

Christina pulled back from him. "I would sooner be in the arms of the devil, sir," she retorted, twisting away. She felt a slight tearing of the delicate cloth as she pulled free of him and walked briskly toward the terrace. The darkness beyond beckoned, and she gave a sigh of relief when she realized that she had managed to elude him for now. She was alone and could take a few badly needed deep breaths. The man had to be insane. Her shaking fingers found the small tear in the flowing sleeve, close to her throbbing wrist. He was a beast! She must take care not to underestimate him. At the slightest opportunity he would tear her apart. *Mon Dieu*, she thought miserably, *what have I gotten myself into? How can I manage to best him on my own?*

Seemingly without reason, Christina suddenly felt the hairs on the back of her neck prickle, and send shivers racing along her spine. She was facing the inky blackness of the estate grounds, and had the distinct feeling that someone, or something, was watching her, gauging her next move before she'd even made it. A manly shape seemed to take form in the wavering moonlight that beamed across the grounds—his golden eyes like fire in the night, his hair glowing ghostly white in the darkness. She didn't understand why she wasn't afraid when he began to walk toward her; she held her ground, waiting for him. But just when she thought he would join her, he changed direction and walked toward another entrance. He disappeared inside the crowded ballroom.

A deep voice broke through her silent musings and shattered the spell. "Good evening, my little cat."

Jason Woods had been watching her all evening, and now made his presence known. Christina whirled about and was more than startled to see the handsome gambler walking toward her, his eyes mocking as he smiled lazily at her.

"Wha—what are you doing here, if I might be so bold as to ask?" she stammered, "and how did you manage to gain entrance with no costume?" She observed the finely tailored suit, the wide-brimmed hat, the snowy cravat with the diamond stick pin.

"I'm visiting friends here," he replied, his smile widening. "And I am in costume. What every well-dressed gambler should wear. And you?"

"Unfortunately, I was invited by my stepcousin, Simon Baker."

"I see," he said, remembering now why the man's name had sounded so familiar to him.

"I don't think you could possibly," she said dejectedly.

Jason immediately noticed the tears that hovered threateningly in her eyes, and the silkiness of her costume as it swirled about her ankles in the evening breeze. He slowly covered the distance between them and drew her gently into his arms, laying her head upon the broad expanse of his chest. Her lavender-scented hair filled his nostrils as she clung to him.

"What am I going to do about you," he whispered huskily. "You seem to fill my every waking moment, little rebel," he murmured against her hair. "And now you are filling my arms."

She nestled deeper into the safety of his embrace, revelling in the strength she felt in his rock-hard arms, and the clean, mildly scented cologne that touched her senses. "Have I conjured you up from some unknown depths to destroy my every strength," she stated breathlessly, "or are you truly as you say, my talisman, the protector of my dreams?"

Jason savored the feel of her body pressed to his, it was as though she'd been formed with his body in mind. "I am no demon, love," his lips brushed her sweet-smelling hair. "But I think that this attraction between us will cause trouble."

"Then let it," she replied unhesitantly.

Jason's fingers took her dainty chin and tilted it up so that her lips lay within inches of his. "I do not think you can even begin to know what you are saying."

Her green eyes flashed angrily. "I know my own mind and feelings, *monsieur*."

He smiled a crooked grin that could melt any woman's heart. "Ah, . . . little cat. You are a spitfire, and I'm quite certain you shall lead me to an early grave. . . . But God help me, I would go willingly if I could spend but one night with you." He lowered his mouth to capture her, but before he could feast his lips upon their softness, a giggly pair of masked lovers stole onto the terrace to exchange a few moments in the concealing darkness. Jason cursed and disengaged Christina's arms from around his neck. He tilted her face up to gaze into his. Christina there is much between us that needs to be explained. I know that . . . and I'm quite sure by now that you do also." His deep voice became intense. "But not now, not just yet. Bear with me but a short while and then I will tell you everything. . . . I swear it."

"You are asking me to deny what my eyes and my heart

are telling me." She shivered from the intensity of her emotions. "Why? Why must I Jason O'Ro—"

His hand pressed firmly against her mouth to still the name she so desperately wanted to call him. "Because I have asked it of you. Damn it, Christina, for once in your life you must do exactly what I say without fail."

Her pert, little nose wrinkled itself in agitation above his hand. He knew she was hopping mad, but still he felt he could trust her to not reveal his true name. He prayed he was right.

Removing his hand from her mouth, Jason replaced it with a kiss upon her stiff lips. Then he turned her in the direction of the ballroom. He watched her until she was safely inside, and gritted his teeth when he noticed Baker approach her. With his fists clenched at his sides, he too reentered the room and quickly became lost within the crowd.

Jason was forced to spend the remainder of the evening silently observing Christina as she played a brave game of wits with the ruthless Simon Baker. Big John never strayed far from Jason's side. It was a sixth sense with the two of them.

Big John surveyed the charge of emotion that seemed to eminate from the very beautiful girl, whose daring costume left little to the imagination, and his partner, who acted as though he were coolly unaffected by it all. A hint of a smile graced John's lips as he attempted to goad his friend.

"You sure manage to find them in all shapes and sizes, don't you, Jase?"

Jason's blue eyes swept over him as he answered with a trace of a grin upon his lips. "They're lovely, tempting

90

creatures, my friend. Lovely, tempting, and very dangerous."

Martinique stepped between them and looked up at Jason. "How about a dance? Let's see just how proficient you are in that social grace."

Jason escorted her to the center of the highly polished floor where Simon was dancing with Christina. Martinique felt the slight stiffening of Jason's muscles as they drew near the oddly matched couple.

"Lovely, isn't she?" Martinique's words broke through his grim thoughts.

"Yes, she is," he replied as he looked down at his partner, "but then, so are you."

"Ever the flatterer," Martinique countered smiling.

"I wouldn't ever tell a lady something I didn't mean," he said with a wide smile. "Especially my best gal." His eyes returned to Simon and Christina.

"But it's not your best gal, as you say, that you wish to hold in your arms at this moment, is it?" Martinique stated with a knowing glint in her amethyst eyes.

"You're imagining things, Marti," Jason replied.

"Am I?" she insisted.

"I can see that wild Irishman of yours giving me killer looks," Jason said, smoothly changing the subject. "It won't be long before he steals you right out of my arms."

To Christina, the evening seemed to drag on forever. Simon must have taken her warning under serious consideration. There was no announcement of an engagement. Still, he kept her beside him for the remainder of the evening and talked of nothing else but the day she would become his. He was most attentive and catered to her every need. She felt as though she would surely smother if she did not escape him soon.

Jason was given to much the same thoughts as he stood silently raging, obvserving Simon fawning over Christina. It took every ounce of his will power to keep from pulling Christina from Simon's embrace and punching the man in his leering face. Only the threat of exposing himself as an agent kept him from doing so.

Finally, after what seemed an interminable amount of time, the last dance of the evening was announced.

Jason didn't see Christina after the soiree ended and the guests began to depart. But he knew he would seek her out one last time. He had to ease this hunger for her, which threatened to consume his every thought, his every breath. But would that really be enough for them, he mused as the carriage rumbled along the deserted roads toward the levee. Would he be able to leave her without guilt, after once having loved her? The thoughts persisted.

He returned to the riverboat, bid his companions good night, and then headed for the seclusion of the saloon. Damn it! he would drink the vixen from his thoughts, even if he had to consume the entire contents of the bar to accomplish the task.

His handsome features marred by a fierce scowl, Jason strode into the saloon and walked purposefully to the bar. "Thomas!" he called to the young bartender. "Pour me a healthy one." Gripping the glass, he watched as the bourbon was generously served. *Damn*, he thought, *it promised to be another long, sleepless night.* He sighed as the shot hit his stomach and spread slowly throughout his system. "Another please, Thomas. And while you're at it, why don't you just leave the entire bottle."

Complying, the bartender nodded and set the bottle down on the bar. "Very good, Mr. Woods. It's all yours.

Determinedly, Jason poured another, and another, until at last his mind grew numb of all thought and reason and he stumbled wearily toward his cabin.

The Silver Wolf rode toward the designated spot in the bayou where he had left his trusted comrades. It had been a long night for him also but, unlike Jason, he looked forward to reaching his home—and his woman. She would be eagerly awaiting him, his Rhea. She hadn't wanted him to come tonight, and they had parted after exchanging harsh words. His fingers absentmindedly reached up to touch the mask that covered his face. Removing it, he put it in his pocket. Then, taking out an eye patch and halting his mount long enough to allow him to tie it in place over his weak eye, he continued his ride. The vision in one eye was not very strong, and after leaving it uncovered any length of time, it began to blur considerably.

"Perhaps you are right, Rhea," he mused verbally, as he urged his horse forward, "perhaps this is too big a fight for one man to take on alone." He rubbed his throbbing leg, where a mass of scar tissue still pained him, even after three years. "How much longer?" he murmured, "how much more pain?" He thought then of his friends; it gave him the will to go on, the means to keep fighting.

The Silver Wolf had been born out of a desperate need to help a confused, proud people redeem their self-respect. It was bloodsuckers like Simon Baker whom he sought to uncover and destroy. Tonight had been a small victory for Silver. He had moved freely among the many guests in attendance, chatting about their political views, listening for any hint as to where their loyalties lay.

Baker padded the pockets of the newly freedmen to gain necessary votes for his corrupt friends for the North. Simon was known —at least to the people of Natchez—as a scalawag, a traitor to his culture. His Southern neighbors were not aware that he was known by yet another guise, but the Silver Wolf was. Simon was the leader of a secret band of nightriders that sought to eliminate anyone who attempted to exercise their new rights under the Constitution. Simon carefully played both sides, taking great care not to expose himself and his double dealings.

The Silver Wolf had a personal vendetta against Simon Baker and his band of murderers, and swore he would not rest until he'd destroyed them all—the entire filthy clan. The highwayman sought only unity, for all people. And if it took every last ounce of his strength and his life to ensure this, he would give it unhesitantly. As always, whenever he pushed his thoughts to search his soul, a searing pain began to eat away at his brain. Slowly, agonizingly, the silent fingers reached out to squelch his power to think; immediately, Silver pulled up on his snorting mount to slide shakily to the ground. His entire body fought against him, and soon he was trembling uncontrollably. He fell upon his knees and raised his scarred image toward the heavens, issuing an anguished plea.

"Why? Why has this happened to me? At least allow me to remember some of my past life!" he cried despairingly. "Am I the one chosen to lead his people, as you once were? Answer me, damn it!" But as usual, there was no reply. There was nothing. Nothing but the low, keen groan of the sighing wind as it blew through the damp, misty bayou and embraced the tortured man.

Silken

Seduction

Chapter Five

Christina's independent, strong-willed spirit was un-
daunted. The memory of last night's battle of wills
between herself and her stepcousin was already beginning to lose some of its clarity as she strolled over her
land in the bright afternoon sunshine. She had a single
objective in mind for today. She had come to a decision—
a major one—and she hoped it was the beginning of a new
breath of life for Oak Meadow. Quickening her pace, she
lifted her dress as she walked briskly toward the cabin of
their black hired hand, George Washington. With a
definite plan in mind, and a driving need to defend what
she held most dear, the young woman mustered up her
courage and rapped lightly on the worn door. She chewed
pensively on her bottom lip when at first she received no
reply to her knock. She knocked again.

"Mr. Washington! It is Christina Duprea. I must speak
with you!"

The door opened slowly—just a crack—and a timid,
little black face peered out at her, eyes blinking at the
unaccustomed brightness.

"Is your father here?" she asked.

The small child nodded and then darted past Christina to point in the direction of the distant garden. "He over der, workin' de garden." The youngster, having decided that the pretty lady was harmless enough, raced past Christina to show her the way. Before woman and child had covered the few hundred yards to the family's meager vegetable garden, Christina knew everything there was to know about the moppet, whose name was Lucy.

George Washington—a name he had chosen upon receiving his freedom papers from his former owner—looked up from his backbreaking work and grinned at Lucy, who had been known to make friends with the forest animals without suffering dire consequences. He grinned at Christina. "She talk your ear off if'in you let her, missy."

"She's a fine girl," Christina complimented, offering her hand in a show of friendship. "I am Christina Duprea, sir. And I take it that you are the man my father hired, George Washington."

George drew himself up to his full height of five feet four inches and accepted Christina's hand in his. "Mighty nice to meet you, ma'am. Heard your pappy tellin' some of de other field hands bout you comin' home. He a good man, your pappy."

Christina thanked him and decided to get straight to the point. "George, I am here to offer you a business proposition—one that may very well benefit both of our families."

George appeared perplexed. "Don't know, missy. Your pappy already done promise me if I keeps workin' the south field dat he pay me soon as we pay off all dat tax money he owes your cousin."

Christina gave her head a negative shake. "That's just it, there is not going to be any money to pay you . . . for a very long time."

Afraid she was confusing the issue rather than clarifying it, she continued. "Listen to what I've got to say. If you like it, then please pass my offer on to everyone who is working for us."

"All right," he replied, his curiosity fully aroused. "But let's git outa dis sun and sit a spell under dat shade tree yonder."

By the time the sun had set, leaving nothing more than a pink hue in the evening sky, Christina had put all of her carefully laid plans into motion. Even Morris Worthington at the bank could not deny that Simon had been careless with their money. She had paid him a brief visit after conferring with George Washington.

"Have you frozen my accounts, Mr. Worthington, as I requested?" Christina had confronted the nervous banker with a stern face, ready to become forceful if she thought it necessary. But Morris Worthington was a spineless whimp, and he knew that she could cause him trouble if he didn't watch his step. *Simon would know how to handle this overbearing female and put her in her rightful place. Imagine, a female discussing business! Unthinkable!* But he voiced none of these things out loud, at least not to Christina.

"I have the matter well in hand, Miss Duprea," he coughed nervously. "Yes. . . . Well in hand."

"And I do not know why you ever allowed it to get out of hand in the first place, sir," she scolded.

99

Worthington's Adam's apple bobbed convulsively as he hastened to cover his ineptness. "I did what I thought best, Miss Duprea." He wiped his moist brow. "After all, your own father gave Mr. Baker the power to manage his accounts as he saw fit."

Christina viewed him with obvious contempt as she sat across from his impressive desk staring at his frightened face. "And to think that, at one time, my family considered you one of our friends."

"I still am," Worthington choked.

"Hardly, sir," Christina snapped. "You knew Papa was not well!"

Sensing the hostile feelings directed his way, Morris was forced to remember how Matthew Duprea had helped him hide from his wife the fact that he had a mulatto mistress and five illegitimate offspring. Was it possible that the girl knew, and was attempting to blackmail him? Worthington jumped to his feet. "What is it you want of me?" He did not miss the deadly purpose in her eyes.

Christina smiled innocently. "Why, nothing that should present too much of a hardship, I'm sure." She quickly produced a paper with the terms of her wishes. Wasting no further time, she handed it to the sweating banker.

There was a moment of absolute silence while he read the contents. His jaw went slack as he went over her requests. "Young woman, you have got to be mad to attempt something of this size—and to expect this bank to back you!"

Without so much as batting an eyelash, Christina let him know he'd best not deny her what she sought. By the time Christina left, her every wish had been granted and more. Worthington gave her a note to use as collateral to refurbish the *Christina*, and accepted a mortgage on the boat in good trust.

She left the bank highly satisfied, and assured of the fact that sometimes it paid to eavesdrop on private conversations. After all, it was her father's kindness that she had traded on.

Christina was proud of herself. Her best-laid plans were now at work. And the deed had been done without help from anyone. An exhilarating feeling rushed over her as she directed her coachman to take her back to Oak Meadow.

Stepping from the carriage, Christina was eager for a nice long soak before dinner. But as she prepared to enter the house, she was stopped by a breathless Mammy who greeted her at the front door.

"Honey lamb, you jist gots to see the pretty animal dat's down at the stable for you." She hurried the astonished young woman back down the front steps and toward the rear of the main house. "It arrive jist after you left dis afternoon," she said. "Go on, you git down der!" She shooed Christina forward, flapping her hands impatiently.

Christina quickened her pace until the stable loomed a short distance ahead. She called out to Tyrone, who had just pulled the carriage into its space under the overhang.

"Mammy says someone left a surprise for me earlier! Hurry and join me—let's see what it could be."

The faithful Tyrone smiled broadly at his mistress's enthusiasm. He hadn't seen her so excited since she was but a bit of a thing and used to ride her old pony across

101

the plantation like a spirited gypsy. He hurried to join her, and together they entered the stable.

Christina heard the soft nicker as she approached the stable, but she wasn't prepared for the magnificence of the animal as she peered inquisitively inside the stall at the golden palomino.

"Would you jist look at dat!" Tyrone squealed.

Christina's eyes shone like a small child's on Christmas morning. "Who in the world would want to give me such a gift?" she said in wonder.

"Ah don't rightly know," Tyrone chortled, "but whoever he be, you can bet your bottom dollar he think right highly of you."

The distant sounds from the bayou beckoned her. Standing alone on the upper gallery just off of her room, Christina thought over the events of the day. She felt good—very good! Everyone had retired hours ago, but she was much too full of excitement to sleep. She pushed up the heavy fall of gold-streaked hair from her neck and held it atop her head. It was an extremely warm night for so early in the spring; it promised to be a hot summer. She stood staring out into the darkness, puzzling over her gift. Mammy had no idea who had sent her the horse, and no one else did either. The man who had delivered him just said it was from someone who knew she appreciated fine horseflesh. *Whoever could that be,* she thought. Her stepcousin Simon would not part with any money to woo her, and if she suspected that the animal was from him she would have returned it without delay. No, Simon hadn't sent it; he wouldn't know the difference between a thoroughbred and a jackass. Still perplexed, she padded silently back to bed.

The minutes turned into hours and still she tossed restlessly, unable to sleep. Finally, she rose from the feather mattress and pushed aside the mosquito netting that surrounded her. Christina crept on tiptoe to the armoire, not wishing to disturb anyone. She chose a simple lawn dress and hastily put it on, replacing the nightgown she'd just discarded on the floor. Without a second thought, she slipped quietly from her room and down the wide stairway.

The night air felt soothing to her after the stuffiness of the house, and she paused a moment to run her bare toes through the dew-laden grass, savoring the coolness. She felt so wanton and uninhibited running barefoot through the wet grass and wearing only a thin, white dress to cover her nakedness. Like a wild thing, she embraced the mist-enshrouded night as she flew over the grounds heavy with the scent of night-blooming jasmine. Nocturnal creatures of the swamp called out to her as she passed the bayou that bordered one side of her land. She headed for the stable.

The palomino whinnied his welcome as she entered the blackness of the stable and approached his stall. Taking a rope halter from a peg above his head, Christina soothed the spirited animal by talking reassuringly as she prepared him to ride. She climbed up on the boards of the stall and pulled herself carefully onto his back. He was over eighteen hands high and could have easily thrown her from his back, but he seemed to know that she meant him no harm and that they were going to share something special. Together, horse and rider anticipated the excursion of their midnight adventure as Christina leaned low over his silky mane and urged him forward.

"Go, boy! Quickly!"

He reared slightly off the ground, giant hooves pawing the air, and then they were but a brief whisp of white and gold as they raced headlong into the Mississippi night.

Her excursion could only end in one place, and she urged her mount in that direction. She hadn't had the opportunity to go there since her return, and she found herself eargerly awaiting the first glimpse of her private oasis. Christina now ventured deep into the cool, green forest. She gasped with pleasure when the crystal-blue pool came into view. Pulling up, she sat motionless, admiring the moonbeams as they danced upon the smooth surface of the water. Giant, live oaks, gnarled and nearly a century old, blended with cypress and creeping myrtle to form a thick, lush canopy overhead. A sliver of moon shone through the spreading branches, illuminating Christina's way as she slid from the horse's back and approached the pool. She stood silently peering down into the clear surface, peace finally settled within her. An owl hooted above, his blinking eyes fixed upon the Gypsy-like creature who had hiked her skirts up well above her knees and now waded at the water's edge, completely alone—or so she thought.

Jason had also chosen to pay a visit to the quiet, little refuge. He had been here many times in his youth with Christina and her brother Curt; he had returned because of the memories that her reappearance had stirred. Now, as he stood silently watching her from the edge of the thick forest, he could not help but marvel at her uninhibited beauty. Her tawny-streaked hair lay thick and tangled about her shoulders, the silvery light turning it to liquid gold. How he longed to crush his fingers in those sweet-scented tresses and bury his face in its luxurious texture. A low groan escaped his lips as the blood began to flow hotly through his veins; the very sight of her was enough to turn his fiercely beating heart into putty in her hands. A sharp stab of longing began in his lean, flat belly and spread like wildfire to throb achingly in his loins, Unconsciously, Christina furthered that desire by tucking the front and back hem of her dress in the sash at her waist. Long, shapely legs, as sensual and finely formed as any he'd ever seen, captured his appreciative attention. Then she raised her arms gracefully above her head, as though she were worshipping the moon or beckoning to her lover. The thin, white dress left little to his imagination, and he allowed his eyes to feast upon the lines of her firm, high bosom, slim hips, and those sleek legs revealed through the transparency of the dress. His gaze wandered the length of her and came to rest upon her face, and in the single shaft of moonlight that spilled upon its petal-smooth softness, he read the unspoken message that was revealed there. The half-closed eyes, the parted lips expressed a longing; it was a rapturous, seductive look that he could not misinterpret. Jason could only pray that it was because of her burning desire for him that he heard her sigh with longing. Tonight, by God, she would be his! Nothing would stop them now—nothing!

She heard his light step as he approached her from the darkness, and she knew that she had nothing to fear. This was what she'd been waiting for, why she'd chosen to come directly to this spot. Some how, she'd known all along that he would seek her out. But the actual reason for his coming here she had yet to fathom, or perhaps she chose not to. She only knew that he was here, coming toward her, a shadow in the moonlight that came to possess her soul.

Christina felt her heart beat crazily as he stood across from her and slowly reached out his hand. She met his eyes and did not flinch from the desire, and purpose, she read in their depths.

Her slim fingers shyly bridged the breadth of space that lay between them and curled around his larger, stronger grasp that met hers halfway. The touch of their fingertips was an intoxicating flame that burned them both with its intensity. There were no words spoken, there was no need. The message was written clearly on both their faces, for each of them to see. All barriers that lay between them were down. There were no yesterdays, or even tomorrows; there was only this moment, and two lovers who would not be denied.

Christina's breath caught in her throat as his penetrating look ran the length of her slim form, drinking in every detail as though he had thirsted for her desperately, and now could have his fill.

He stood quietly before her, and it took all of her will power not to throw herself headlong into his arms. She urgently needed the reassurance that she found only in his embrace, in his strength. Surely this attraction that lay between them was based on more than mere lust for each other's bodies. She looked up into his face, saw the blue-black hair that lay rakishly over one brow, the sapphire eyes that held hers mesmerized, and shivered at the desire that overwhelmed her. The creamy white shirt that he wore lay open at his chest, revealing a fine dusting of dark hair. Christina could almost feel the roughness of it as she thought of how it might feel crushed against her bare breasts. At the erotic vision, her nipples grew taut and hot against her thin dress. *I am simply shameless where he is concerned*, she thought!

Very gently, he drew her toward him, and she felt her flesh quiver with longing as she read the silent purpose in his assessing stare.

Here is a woman made for loving, Jason thought. *A goddess that is unequalled in her beauty, or the intensity of her passion.* He wanted her so! But after he once possessed her body, and held her next to his beating heart, would he then be free of her spell? He did not have an immediate answer, nor did he wish to. But deep in his innermost thoughts, he realized that with this enchanting creature once would never be enough. He would seek her out again and again, until her body, as well as her soul, belonged exclusively to him.

With an impatient growl of deep-seated need, Jason lowered his feverish mouth to hers. His heart sang when he felt her eager response.

Christina's pulse raced madly as his tongue slipped into her mouth and caressed the softness he found within. She yielded to him, her slender arms slipping about his neck to draw him closer as her body molded itself to fit his hard, masculine length. She felt him respond to her boldness.

Crushing her in his strong arms, he let his lips trail a path of fire across her slender throat as he carried her to a bed of forest moss. The sparkling pool, the stars that gleamed like flickering candles, and the shaft of moonlight which lit his way all served as a perfect backdrop for the two lovers.

His restraint was gone the moment he laid her upon the carpet of soft moss and stretched out beside her.

107

Gently, his hands slipped beneath her to unbutton the only barrier that lay between them. She arched her back to further his cause. His agile fingers made short work of the tiny buttons, and he silenced her tiny gasp of fear with soothing words of love. He lowered his lips to once again revel in the taste of the sweet, heady passion that he found there. Very slowly, he slid the dress from her shoulders, down over her trembling arms toward her slim thighs, until at last her provocative body lay naked beside him. He stroked the satiny flesh unhesitantly with a killingly sure touch.

Christina felt so wicked, so alluring, as she felt the coolness of the ground moss against her bare skin, and the magic of his fingers as they played expertly across her body.

His mouth left hers to taste of each breast, and unhesitantly, she encouraged him as she murmured how good he made her feel. Her lush breasts were explored by his lips and tongue as they nibbled a scorching path across her tawny skin to fasten possessively around one nipple.

She clutched at him desperately, her fingers curling in his wavy hair, encouraging him to continue, as she moved her breasts seductively against his mouth. He continued his gentle seduction, caressing the satiny globes until the hot waves of desire, that had started as a gentle, lapping ripple, washed over her and inside of her, causing a cry of need from her lips.

"Now," she panted unashamed, "make love to me—show me everything there is to know."

Pulling his lips from her breasts, Jason murmured huskily. "I will teach you all there is, little cat, everything. When you leave me tonight you will be a woman, and I will surely be like a man possessed by your beauty, and the memory of how you feel lying in my arms." He buried his lips against the lavender-scented hollow of her throat.

Christina sighed with bliss and gave herself up to his hands and lips which tenderly moved over every inch of her, caressing everything they had discovered. Her body was all that he'd known it would be, and more. It was exquisitely formed; all sleek and satiny and warm. He feasted his eyes on every part of her, and his lips upon the silkiness that she offered him. But when his tantalizing fingers travelled lazily down her taut belly to the golden curls between her long legs, she stiffened and held them tightly closed against his fingers.

Jason understood her shyness, knew that she had never known a man's caress before. He sought to assure her of his purpose. "Don't, sweet," he whispered in her ear. "Open your legs for me, love."

At his soothing words, and the message she read in his firm tone, Christina timidly unlocked her legs to allow him free access to what he desired.

Gently he stroked her; the light motion of his fingers on the bud of her womanhood was the sweetest agony she had ever experienced in her life. She began to move her hips against his hand, unable to remain still beneath his touch. She moved her head from side to side, moaning softly at this unexpected attack on her senses.

"It's all right, sweetheart," he urged her. "Let go . . . come to me . . . let me show you. . . ."

She strained upward against his persistant motion, until her hips moved faster and faster against the rhythmic stroking of his fingers. Christina had no idea what she so desperately sought by her frantic motions, or what he was doing to her—only that she wanted more, so much more.

"Oh, God," she breathed raggedly, "what are you doing to me? I'm afraid, I'm afraid," she sobbed.

Tenderly he touched his lips to hers and reassured her, calmed her breathless sobs. "Just relax my beautiful, little cat . . . let me love you. Trust me to know what's right for both of us." He rained ardent kisses along her neck and whispered what she longed to hear.

She lay panting beneath him as he continued to woo her with words meant just for her. It was something he'd never done before in his life. "I'll be gentle, love. God, I want you more than any woman I've ever met," he admitted truthfully. "You're like the siren that calls the doomed sailor upon the reefs, bewitching him with your beauty until he can think of nothing but your face, hear only your voice, and desire only . . . this." He ran his lean fingers up and down her silky flanks to gently slip inside her, and at last probed the satiny warmth that he yearned to possess. She denied him nothing now, and like the perfectly formed bud of a rare and beautiful flower, he very gently unfolded each petal, preparing the way for his entry and the sweetness he knew lay within. Leaving her for just long enough to remove his clothing, Jason was amazed and highly pleased, when her fingers reached up to help him. When he was naked, he lowered his body to cover hers. Boldly she ran her hands along the thick muscles of his back, and then lower to shyly brush across his lean buttocks. Mouth sought mouth, as hands, eager to explore, sought every valley, every curve, every pleasure spot.

His lips adored every inch of her body, and this time, when he sensuously tongued the taut flatness of her belly, nibbling softly at the hollows on either side of her hips, she let him. He was drunk on the clean, sweet smell of her velvety skin, and lost within the realm of his desire. He lowered his mouth to the heart of her and began to swirl his moist tongue upon the trembling mound, glorying in the heady nectar that met his flared nostrils, fanning his passion to searing heights.

Christina gripped his thick-muscled shoulders, afraid if she let go that this heavenly, all-consuming sensation would vanish from her grasp. She began to feel as though she would explode and her legs trembled as each wave washed over her, pushing her toward such unbearable ecstasy that she felt she would lose all reason. He held fast to either side of her hips, his fingers biting into the soft flesh of her buttocks as she rocked and moaned against his lips. She cried out to him as the first spasms of pleasure began to pour through her limbs and veins until she felt such heat in her loins that she felt she might swoon from it. When at last she lay still, her breathing more normal, Jason lifted his head and whispered huskily.

"Don't think that's all there is, sweetheart. There's still more . . . much more." Exerting no pressure, he lay over her.

His eyes stared at her with a driving intensity. A faint whimper escaped her as she felt his hard, throbbing manhood probe demandingly between her thighs, seeking what she now knew she'd been saving just for him. As she closed her eyes, she felt him take his knee and part her thighs, and then lower his hips to fuse against hers. A small shudder escaped her as he eased partly inside her tightness, and she whimpered. Immediately, she received assurances from him.

"You're all right love," he soothed. "I'll go slowly." His mouth closed over hers as she felt his swollen staff thrust forward to claim her virginity in one swift stroke. She cried out in pain and felt sure that she had been betrayed. His voice continued to soothe as his hands and lips moved tenderly over her body.

"Trust me, sweet. Now I shall show you how good it can be." Gritting his teeth to delay his rapidly mounting passion, Jason began to slowly move inside her, all the while murmuring words of love in her ear. She would never know how much the effort cost him as his body screamed for release. She was so warm, so untouched, that his emotions threatened to explode. But determinedly, he refused its cry, and waited until he felt her begin to respond. He knew that the fire was building in her when she locked her ankles across his back without hesitation. Arching and twisting, the pain forgotten, she matched him thrust for thrust. She ground her lips against his, emitting soft, mewing sounds in her throat that were driving him wild. Running her untrained hands over his corded back, she felt the muscles respond and quiver beneath her touch. Bravely, she lowered her fingers to his buttocks, clasping him to her, holding him as though she would never let him go. Together they sought the heavens and the stars, and were not to be disappointed. Christina clung tightly to him as the flames of desire began licking at her loins, spreading throughout her body until they burst forth in a shower of white-hot intensity that sent her spiralling into the throes of ecstasy.

Jason, sensing that she received what she'd been seeking, lost himself in her velvety grip, and followed the same lover's path.

Afterward, when their world had righted itself, they lay entwined in each other's arms for a long time. Jason was the first to move as he reached out to brush the thick, damp hair that lay wild and unruly about her face. His hands gently caressed her, and his lips rained feathery kisses upon her flushed cheeks. She gloried in their closeness, their oneness, and in his tender concern. Reluctantly, Jason rose to his feet, and reached out both hands to help her up. She was surprised when her legs almost gave way beneath her. His arm grabbed her.

"I don't think I—I can stand just yet," she said shyly.

Lacing his fingers in hers, he urged her body against his. "Rest a minute. There's no hurry."

Christina liked the warm contact of their bodies. It felt so natural, so perfect. And when he kissed the top of her head, she smiled to herself. They stood silently for awhile, and then he said, "Let's have a moonlight swim."

She stiffened immediately. "Oh, I don't know," she replied. "I really should be getting back home. . . ."

But Jason refused to release her, and in the end she did exactly as he suggested. The water was cool and refreshing and they swam and frolicked until they were both exhausted. Jason swept her up in his arms and carried her, both of them laughing like two children, back to their lovers' nest. His body held hers close and his hands warmed her chilled flesh as the two of them lay completely lost in the wonder of what they had shared.

"You have surely bewitched me, rebel," he concluded as he lay propped on one elbow, head resting upon his hand. His fingers began tracing intricate patterns along her skin. "And I want to make love to you again." A deep groan rumbled in his chest as Christina reached out to caress him, shyly at first, then boldly. Urgently, he

113

pulled her over him and positioned her hips across his. Both of them sighed with bliss when their bodies joined as one and their souls soared together on the wings of love.

Daylight crept across their secret place and roused Christina from her dreamless slumber. Nestled against Jason's warm body, she had felt safe, at peace, and loved. As she gazed upon his sleeping form, she couldn't help but marvel at the love that now swelled within her breast. She knew she had always loved him. But this overpowering new emotion that clutched her with such aching intensity was nothing like her feelings for him before this night, this moment. She could not allow this love for him to muddle her reasoning, to sway her from the goal she had set for herself. Sobering, she slipped silently from him, disengaging his arm from around her bare waist and sliding from his reach. She had been a fool to allow her heart to rule her head. Not once had he spoken of love, of marriage. He cared in his own way, she truly believed that. But this night of passion, this ecstasy that they shared, had been nothing more than the silken seduction of her senses.

Chapter Six

Unfolding her long legs, Christina stood and stared down at Jason's sleeping form. Confusion was mirrored in her eyes as she silently observed the first rays of dawn come stealing through the treetops to play upon his dark, rugged face.

His black wavy locks lay in disarray about his wide forehead, concealing his eyes but still affording her a view of his finely shaped nose, firm jawline, and mouth, the full curve of his lips appearing relaxed, innocent. But Christina knew this to be deceiving. She knew only too well how those lips could be drawn harsh and tight in anger one minute and then soft and coaxing the next. He was a man of many faces, of many moods; at the moment, she felt as though she would never really know any of them.

Suddenly overwhelmed by emotions that threatened to tear down the last of her defenses and send her rushing back into the blissful security of his arms, she spun around. Snatching up her crumpled gown from where he had hastily discarded it hours before, she slipped it over her head. A small gasp of surprise escaped her at the touch of his fingers entwining forcefully around her wrist.

"Christina?" he questioned, his voice soft, belying the intensity of his grip on her arm.

"Yes," she replied noncommittally, struggling to pull her thin dress over her nakedness and wiggle free of his grasp all at the same time.

He would not release her. "Were you going to leave without so much as telling me goodbye?" The words were cynically spoken and she knew that if she turned her eyes to meet his she would see anger shimmering like blue fire in their depths.

"I must go before the household rises." She stared over his bare shoulder, avoiding the sight of his muscular torso.

"Not so fast, love," he commanded huskily. Dropping her wrist he pulled on his breeches and then ran his fingers through his tousled hair. "Just wait for one moment . . . please."

She used the time it took him to dress to straighten her attire; all the while her eyes observed the gradual dawning of the new day. The household would be up and about soon; she must leave if she was going to avoid an encounter with the household staff, and with Mammy.

Startled, she realized that he had finished dressing and now stood beside her. Gently, he turned her toward him and drew her into his arms.

"You were wonderful," he whispered as his lips sought hers and his fingers played along the satiny valley between her breasts.

Reluctantly, she drew her lips from his and dropped her eyes to hide the nervousness they revealed. Her pulse was racing and she longed desperately to stay with him, to capture once again the closeness, the ecstasy that they'd shared so beautifully throughout the night.

"Please, Jason . . . you must allow me to leave. Do you want me to be shamed before the household?"

"I would never want that," he assured her. But still his hands and lips could not seem to release her and continued to caress her, his warm breath against her cool skin causing goose flesh to follow in its path.

"Jason," she pleaded in a short gasp, "you must stop . . . at once." He brought his face up to meet hers, his eyes devouring her. "I am bewitched by you, completely captivated. But I will allow you to leave me under one condition."

"Which is . . . ?" she inquired softly.

"Promise me first," he demanded, his eyes narrowing, his fingers grasping the golden flesh of her upper arms.

"Promise? Promise you what?" she asked somewhat apprehensively, a bit frightened by the intensity of his request and the possessive grip of his fingers.

"That this is just the beginning for us—not the end."

Her green eyes were unwavering as they met his and held them. "Do you really want that?"

"Yes," came the simple, honest reply. He laid her head upon his chest, feeling her heart beating rapidly against his. At that moment, he wished with his entire being that the rest of the world, and the damnable mission, would just fade away. Christina's petulant sigh broke through the moment. "What is it?" he questioned.

"This is going to complicate many things," she stated, her eyes searching deeply into his, missing nothing. "You know that, don't you? Everyone will begin to put the pieces together, Jase."

"Yes," he half-snarled, as he entangled his fingers into her flowing hair and brought her mouth within inches of his. "I expect they will." His lips touched hers in light, searing kisses. "But right now all I can think of is you, and how perfect you feel in my arms." His lips were demanding and hungry against hers.

"I care for you very much, Jase," she whispered, her eyes half-closed as she breathed the words into his mouth. "And I believe the feeling is mutual."

"Beyond any doubt," he replied.

"But . . ." she returned.

"But what?" he demanded, setting her apart from him and waiting expectantly for her answer.

"But I think that we should get a few things straight between us first." She held her head proudly. "I will not be your whore."

He cupped her face within his big hands. "Trust me to do what's best for both of us. I would never want you for that sweetheart, but the rest must wait . . . for awhile, anyway."

She swallowed over the lump in her throat. "There are many questions to be answered. I have given myself to you, Jase . . . completely. Don't you think I am entitled to have some of my doubts laid to rest about you?"

"Yes, of course," he replied thickly. "And you shall."

"When?" she persisted.

He dropped his hands to his sides. "When I say so, that's when," he replied a bit more gruffly than he intended. His head-strong lady-love had not changed at all. "You must respect my wishes on this, Christina. The telling will come later."

Tears glistened as she lashed back at him defiantly. "Don't wait too long, Jason Woods, or whatever it is I'm supposed to call you now. I am no longer a mere child that you can toss across your saddle whenever I do something that displeases you. I am a woman, Jase, and one who is used to directing her life as she pleases."

118

"And one who is still issuing childish threats," he replied cuttingly. Damn if she still didn't have a way about her that could drive a man to gnashing his teeth, he thought.

Hurt was evident upon her face. His manner softened and he reached his hand forward to caress her cheek, but she was having none of it.

Spinning around on her heel, she strode briskly to her horse, dismissing him completely. "Be off with you, you seducer of innocent women!"

"Will you just listen a minute, you little hothead!" he pleaded. He hurried his pace to catch up with her. Stalking up behind her, he grabbed her about the waist and held her thrashing body tightly against him.

"Let me go, you honey-tongued, one-way, no-good scoundrel!" she ranted as she stood rigid as a board and unyielding in her temper.

"I know what you're thinking," he said against her ear, "and it's simply not true." She kicked his shin with one foot. "Ow! You are as fiesty as a cat that's about to be shoved in a rain barrel, you know that?" He wrapped one firm-muscled leg about hers to prevent further damage to his limbs. "Now just quiet down, Christina. Don't fight me so, sweet."

"I will fight you until my dying day, Jason. No man will ever make a fool out of me!"

For a long while he held her, talking soothingly into her ear, caressing her stiff, angry limbs gently. At last she quieted. With one sure, swift movement Jason lifted her long legs and tossed her up onto her stallion's back. She glared down at him but her lips stayed tightly clamped.

"We didn't ask for any of this, Christina," he told her. "But now it's happened. Fate intervened to bring us together and I've made love to you as I have no other. I

119

care very much about you," he admitted, regarding her with that compelling, hard stare of his that released butterflies in her stomach once again.

She looked deeply into his vivid blue eyes.

"I want to believe you, Jase. But I also remember those others."

"What others?"

"The ones in the hayloft—at Oak Meadow," she blurted out, her cheeks flaming at her own admission. "I know you thought no one else knew about the Dalton twins. But I followed you one day and . . ."

"You were witness to the Dalton twins?" he fairly choked.

She nodded mutely.

"Sweet Jesus, Christina! I'm surprised I had to teach you anything!"

"I had my eyes covered half of the time," she said quickly. "Well, almost half."

His fingers stroked his suddenly throbbing temples as he shook his head from side to side. "This is not the same thing. That was . . ." he struggled to find the correct words. "That was lusty adventure, a young boy's way of sowing his wild oats." His hands returned to his sides and he breathed deeply. "What you and I shared together was something very beautiful. Filled with deep meaning and emotion."

"I thought so," she professed softly.

"And I would do anything for you," he whispered.

"Very well," she replied slyly. "Then prove it."

"In any way that you see fit, madam," he replied, then caught the triumphant uplifting of her sweet lips. *The crafty, conniving little wench! I should have known!* he swore to himself.

"I accept your generous offer, *monsieur*. There is one small thing you could do for me," Christina said, a wicked gleam in her eyes.

"And just what would that be?"

"Something that will suit you perfectly."

His blue eyes narrowed.

"Deal faro on my riverboat," she said lightly.

"For a woman?" he snorted. "Why, they'll run us out of town."

She sat up tall and proud. "Hardly, *monsieur!* But if you are intimidated by having me as your boss and by what people might say, then I will not hold you to your offer." She dismissed him with a haughty toss of her tawny locks.

His blue eyes danced merrily. "All right, I agree. And just to clarify matters, I could not give a damn what your upstanding citizens think, madam. But there is one stipulation." He grinned crookedly at her. "That you always remember who takes the dominating role of our, ah, other activities."

"I'm sure you will not allow me to forget!" she laughed throatily. It was the soft, silky kind of sound that could stop a man dead in his tracks.

"Be off with you, then," he ordered gruffly. "Before I change my mind and keep you here with me forever." He swatted the palomino on the rump. "Ride with care, my beauty."

She waved in his direction as her fiery mount trotted along the path that would lead her toward Oak Meadow. Just as her horse crested the hilltop overlooking the leafy glade, she called back to him. "Thank you for Wildfire!" she said patting her mount.

"You're most welcome, my little cat," he whispered. He watched her ride like the wind, trying desperately to outrace the rising sun.

*   *   *

"It about time you wake up, darlin'." Mammy stood, hands on her broad hips, clucking her tongue. "Your pappy say let you sleep, so's ah did. Now it's bout time for the noonday meal, so's you best git up and git goin'."

Christina withdrew her head from beneath the eiderdown comforter and peered up at the old woman. "It can't be that late," she mumbled, still half-asleep and content.

"Yeah, it is," Mammy persisted, as she threw open the windows and flooded the room with sunshine.

Christina blinked, and propped herself on one elbow to mull over what she thought in her sleepdrugged state had only been a dream. For a few moments she stayed safe within that realm that separates fantasy from reality. But all at once her mind remembered vividly everything, and every word that had been shared between them. She hardly noticed when Mammy had left the room. Throwing back the covers, Christina slipped from the bed and padded softly to stand before the cheval mirror.

"Was that actually me? Were Jason and I really together . . . like that?" she inquired of the bewildered face that stared back at her in the glass. Hastily, she shed her nightgown and stared at the soft curves of her body. Thoughts and images drifted back to her as she remembered each place his hands and lips had touched, and brought to life. Strangely, she found that she was not embarrassed to think of herself in that way, with him.

"It was beautiful," she whispered, "and I love him so." Shyly she touched each breast and wondered, as she remembered how his hands had felt there, if he found her body pleasing to the eye.

She smiled to herself, recalling his heated passion and his words praising her loveliness. Swinging around in circles, she cried joyfully. "You are mine, Jason

O'Roark, only mine. And I shall hear you say you love me . . . Believe me, I shall!"

The rattle of her bedroom doorknob prompted her to swiftly slip into her pink silk robe.

"Bout time you're up an' about," Mammy sniffed as she carried in a tray laden with dishes. "Brung you some vittles. You's gettin' a mite puny from all dat fancy-dancy stuff de feed you over der in dat Paree place." She wrinkled her nose distastefully. "Nothin' to dat food but names a body can't understand, let alone say."

Christina smiled. "Paris, Mammy. And I am not puny." She strode over to the armoire and began drawing out one dress after the other. "I'm just fine," she replied, "and I'm afraid I don't have time to eat."

"Why dat?" Mammy plunked down her offering and appraised the flushed, excited face before her. "We not had time around here to even say how ja do before you's flittin' about all over."

"I must take care of some business in town. I'll be home before dark," Christina explained as she chose a very fetching India muslin dress with a full, embroidered flounce in soft blue and matching jacket. "I'll return in time for dinner with Papa." She glanced over at Mammy. "When you go back downstairs, would you be so kind as to have one of the boys fetch me some hot water for my bath?"

"Ah s'pose dat's a polite way of sayin' you's heard enough from dis ole woman." Mammy ambled in the direction of the door. "Ah knows when ah's bein' told to skedaddle. Ah be expectin' you for dinner." She peeked her head back around the doorjamb. "No excuses, neither!"

*　　　*　　　*

123

The pleasant ride through the Mississippi countryside allowed Christina a few minutes to prepare a mental list of everything that needed tending upon her arrival in Natchez. The ride also gave her a chance to admire the quiet beauty of her homeland. For as far as one could see lay white and yellow dwarf dandelions, black-eyed Susans, cinnamon ferns, and tiny pink and white Cherokee roses that gleamed like jewels in the sunny fields and in the shade of the heavy forest. Being surrounded with such beauty should have filled any young woman with a feeling of tranquility. But her mind continued to review the many details that needed tending before they could start home again.

She had informed Tyrone earlier that he was to drop her at Madame Tulane's dress shop on Main Street and should then proceed directly to King's Tavern.

"Yes, ma'am," Tyrone had answered in a bewildered voice. "But what is ah s'pose to do when ah gits der?"

"Post this for me," Christina had said as she handed him a large placard, upon which was written in bold letters Able-Bodied Persons Needed for Hard Work and Fair Wages.

"And Tyrone, tell anyone that should happen to inquire that we will be interviewing at three o'clock sharp down on the levee."

Tyrone had averted his eyes from her face as he'd assisted her into the carriage. She knew he was confused and did not understand why she asked this of him. But it could not be helped, and soon it would all become quite clear. In hard times one called upon every resource, even if it meant hiring a Yankee card dealer—and a mysterious one, at that.

The memory of Jason's astonished face when she had

revealed what she wanted him to do brought forth a bemused chuckle from her.

This has got to be the answer, she told herself hopefully. *I know there is money to be made in gambling; after all, didn't I see with my own eyes the sums of money that exchanged hands during just one such game?* Her green eyes flashed. *I would just about promise my soul to the devil himself if it meant pushing Simon's nose in the dirt.*

As the carriage approached the edge of the city, Christina caught sight of the imposing mansion, Dunleith, sitting like a regal queen in a jewel setting of brilliantly colored Japonicas and delicate-hued azaleas. As a child she had visited there many times, and with her friend Anna had listened for the sad, mournful strains of the ghost, Miss Percy, who reputedly still wept each night for her lost French lover. Smiling to herself, Christina remembered the night she and Anna had sat on the stairway watching the elegant soiree that Anna's parents were hosting, and observed two fashionably attired ladies carve their names in a window pane with their diamond rings. A whim of the very rich? Or perhaps, as she thought of it now, a bit of themselves forever captured in time.

Up ahead in the distance loomed the steeple of St. Mary's church, and the city itself. Her venture was about to begin.

As instructed, Tyrone delivered Christina to Madame Tulane's small but fashionable dress shop that sat in the heart of the city on Main Street. Christina stood alone on the banquette and watched as he continued toward his destination. Her eyes scanned her surroundings with just a hint of sadness.

Natchez had remained an imposing, dignified city, but

there was an idleness about it now that had not been evident before the war. Back then, it had been the cotton empire, a city of magnificient wealth.

But the golden years of prosperity, which had allowed her fellow Natchazians to build their temples on her alluvial bluffs, had ended.

"Unbelievable sums were made here and invested back in the land. But no more," Christina hissed angrily as she lifted her skirts with a swish and opened the door to Madame's shop.

Madame Tulane, a small woman whose sharp, dark eyes missed nothing, came forward to greet her customer.

"Good day to you, *madmoiselle*," she said in a cordial, refined voice. "How can I help you?" Her gaze travelled the length of Christina and rested upon the girl's face.

"Good morning, madame," Christina replied with a charming smile. "You don't remember who I am, do you?"

Madame took a closer, more critical look at the lovely young woman before her. Her eyes lit up with recognition. "Can it be?" she exclaimed with a clap of her hands. "Tell me it is!"

"*Oui*, I am Elizabeth's daughter, Christina."

"I should have known," the dressmaker said with a delighted laugh. "I have yet to meet another with eyes the same sparkling green, and with just a hint of mischief always lurking in their depths."

"Yes, well, a great deal about me has changed since those days, I'm afraid," Christina replied softly.

"I have heard, little one, and I am deeply sorry for the misfortune that has fallen upon your family." Her eyes were sad as she took Christina's hand in hers and patted it comfortingly. "But, come now, tell Madame what it is that you are looking for." She drew Christina along with her toward the heart of the room, which was a kaleidoscope of materials in every texture and color. "What is it? H'm . . . a gown for a welcome home party?" She picked up a deep rose silk. "This would be perfect on you."

Christina shook her head. "That is beautiful, Madame, but not quite what I need just yet," she explained. "I need some advice—" She clenched her hands nervously—"On apparel for my new business that will open soon."

"Marvelous!" the woman enthused. "A shop! Or is it an eating establishment? Heaven knows we need something exciting in this city. It has declined so since the war."

"Yes—well—it will have a place to dine," Christina stammered, "but what I need are gowns to compliment the interior of a gambling room . . . on a riverboat." *There!* she thought, *I've said it!*

"And these gowns are for you . . . personally?" Madame questioned curiously, her face blank of any expression.

"Yes," Christina replied proudly, "they are."

Madame did not tarry a moment longer, nor did she lecture Christina about the dim views society took upon women of such positions. "I believe I have the perfect thing, dear," she said as she rang the brass bell at her fingertips and summoned her helpers from the back room. She turned back to Christina after conferring with her girls. "We will have you fixed up like a queen, *mademoiselle.* A most deserving one, I might add."

Christina gave the dressmaker a look of astonishment. "Then you do not think my idea foolish and shocking, Madame?"

"Daring, uncommon, *oui*, even shocking." Madame finished with a wag of her finger. "It is survival, my dear, plain and simple. Rich and poor alike are doing what they can just to live. And I know, believe me, what it is like to try and keep one's head above water." She led the girl over to sit upon a brocade settee beside the enormous stone fireplace. There she told Christina much of her own young life when her beloved husband had passed on and she'd opened this dress shop, praying that it would prosper. She encouraged Christina to follow her instincts and not give up just because someone may view it as foolish.

Sometime later, Christina happily stood before a mirror in the fitting room surveying a sample of a gown that Madame suggested she have made up.

"It is nice," she said. Just as she turned once again to glimpse her image in the floor-length mirror, she caught a sight of a fashionably dressed man reflected back at her in the glass.

"*Sacré bleu!*" she gasped, as she noted the dark brown, superbly cut jacket and the light, fawn-colored trousers that hugged his slim hips and enhanced his muscular legs. "What ever are you doing here?" she exclaimed.

"Looking for you," Jason drawled, his eyes registering their approval of her appearance. "And I must say, I do like very much what I've found . . . yes, indeed."

"Really, *monsieur!*" she gasped, as she glanced at Madame, who smiled knowingly. "A gentleman does not belong in a lady's dressing room!" She continued to glare at him through the mirror.

"I'm happy to hear myself thought of as a gentleman," he said as he leaned a shoulder against the frame of the door. "I was beginning to have my doubts about what you thought of me."

She blushed furiously. "Do you think this will befit my new role, *monsieur?*" she asked him, attempting to divert the conversation.

"There hasn't been a gown made that is worthy of such beauty," he breathed softly. "But, with further help from me, perhaps we can improve it." He strolled casually toward her.

"I don't need your help," she said firmly. "How did you happen to find me, anyway?"

"I was at King's Tavern when Tyrone put up your advertisement. He said you were here."

She viewed his image with renewed interest. "Did anyone take notice?" she inquired hopefully.

Jason shrugged. "A few, I suppose." He fingered the taffeta material, surveying the cloth critically. "That's one of the reasons I'm here. Figure you're going to need some assistance with a good many things from here on out."

She jerked the hem from his grasp. "Oh, . . . you do, do you?"

"Yes," he insisted, "I do."

"Well, I have all the help I need here. Now kindly leave!"

Christina gritted her teeth as Jason once again rubbed the gown between his long fingers.

"This one will do nicely," he said to the dressmaker. "And I would like to order several more."

Madame fairly glowed as she nodded for her girls to bring her pad and pen. She assured Jason that she would personally supervise each gown so that every stitch was sewn precisely right.

And when, despite Christina's protests, he actually spent several hours choosing styles, materials, and accessories to accompany each one, Madame could have danced with delight. *Mon Dieu! Such a man, and a rich one at that!* His substantial down payment had her beaming with approval. Yes, this was a man after her own heart.

Christina could only sit dumbfounded as Jason summed up her new wardrobe. There was to be a rich moiré, embroidered in gold from the bodice through the entire skirt, taken up and fastened on either side with gold trimming; the amber underskirt, trimmed in Brussels lace, would peek out from under the slightly elevated hem of the dress. Mauve colored satin, ice-blue silk, velvet cloaks for chilly, damp evenings along the Mississippi . . . and, of course, a crimson taffeta, lined in creamy satin and boasting a flowing train that could be fastened when not needed by tiny rosebuds at her shoulders.

"No," Christina had attempted to protest, "I do not need fans inlaid with jewels. Absolutely not!"

Jason had brushed her outburst aside and increased his order.

"Slippers, Madame," he'd instructed, "and this." He had picked up a piece of gossamer-thin material. "Night clothes and underthings. I want them all made from this." He handed Madame the wispy silk.

Christina blushed furiously and threatened to hang him under her breath. Madame only smiled secretively. After satisfying himself that all would be done as he'd ordered, Jason secured the arm of a furious Christina and walked toward the front door.

Madame had hastened to add, "Your taste is excellent, *monsieur*. Your lady shall be the talk of the town in my lovely gowns."

Jason had favored Madame with a lazy grin as he'd propelled the steaming beauty through the open door. "I fear, dear woman, that you are quite correct."

Chapter Seven

Christina insisted from the beginning that everything connected with the *Rebelle Christina* should be first-class. With Jason's guidance and Christina's observant eye for even the smallest detail, the old riverboat soon glowed elegantly under a new coat of crisp, white paint. Her appointments, while not as luxurious as some, bespoke of good taste and comfort. Great care had been taken to painstakingly repair her intricate gingerbread trim and polish all of her brass fittings until they gleamed like molten gold in the bright Mississippi sun.

In the weeks that followed, it appeared that Christina would soon begin to realize her dream of becoming self-sufficient. The riverboat was booked solidly on each excursion from Natchez to New Orleans. She carried minimal freight on the short journey; the boat had been revitalized strictly for pleasure trips.

Jason and Christina sat in companionable silence in the dining salon, enjoying an after-dinner drink and watching the last rays of daylight disappear like sifted sand through the cottonwoods that lined the shoreline.

He studied her with admiration, knowing that this beautiful, spirited woman was the main reason for the droves of passengers, who now lined the deck to catch a glimpse of her as she passed by on his arm.

"I'm very proud of you, you know," he said softly as his eyes feasted upon the creamy-gold shoulders revealed so becomingly above the décolletage of the crimson gown. "I knew that I was completely charmed by you, sweetheart, but I must say if you continue to pull at my heartstrings in this fashion I will undoubtably become your willing slave."

Her eyes left the scenic countryside and met his, which sparkled mischievously as they regarded her. "I would like to believe those words, you handsome rogue," she teased as she mentally noted how especially grand he looked this evening. Every bit as impressive as the splendor that surrounded him, Jason was dressed in a black jacket with satin lapels, brocade vest, and a crisp, white-ruffled shirt. A thin black cigar was clamped firmly between his teeth and she watched mesmerized as a small puff of blue smoke spiralled lazily upward to settle about his dark, curly locks. "I suppose we should be departing for the saloon before it gets too late," she said.

"It can wait a few more minutes," he replied, a speculative glint in his eyes. His fingers reached out to touch the cameo locket that lay about her throat on a gold chain. "Is that new?"

He noticed her hesitate before she answered him, but he was not prepared for the shock of her reply. "No, it is not. It was a gift from my brother, Curt . . . one of his last." He watched dazed as her fingers wrapped tightly around the necklace. Her eyes held deep sorrow.

He watched in silence as she opened the locket and

revealed a picture of his friend, Curt, the way Jason remembered him from his youth. "You never told me how it happened."

"It was an explosion on a Confederate riverboat just outside of Vicksburg." A tear trickled down her cheek. Jason reached out to brush it aside. "His body was never found, Jase," she sobbed. "He's lying on the bottom of the river somewhere. We've lost him . . . forever."

Jason took the locket in his hand and snapped it closed. The sound was as final as her words. "I'm so sorry," he whispered as he laid her head upon his shoulder, "so damn sorry."

"With my mother gone too, all I really have left of my family is Papa, and, of course, Mammy." She sighed heavily. "But others have borne worse."

"You'll always have me," he murmured against her hair. "You do know that, don't you?"

Her slim finger traced an invisible pattern around the rim of the hand-painted dinner plate before her. "But not all of you, Jase," she replied, her voice sounding somewhat bitter.

"All that I can give you right now," he returned huskily.

"And does that include after we dock in Natchez?" He did not answer immediately, and she cursed him for it. "Damn you, Jase! Why must I go through hell to love you?"

"There is nothing easy about love," he said drily.

Her throat tightened as she observed the shuttered expression fall into place over his dark features. *Don't do this to us,* she silently screamed. *Don't put me outside of your life when it suits you and then expect me to fall into your bed when you but crook your little finger.*

"Perhaps I can manage it later," he replied quietly. "We'll just have to see. Now I need to drop by and attend to some business on board the *Lady*." He hated appearing so coolly indifferent, but it was imperative that she not find out about the mission.

Jason had been cleverly working his way into Baker's elusive circle of friends for weeks. He had joined in their poker games, spent evenings in their homes, and appeared to share their same greed: money and power were everything. Baker's business contacts in New Orleans and Natchez wished to avoid paying the enforced tax on alcohol. Simon Baker was only too happy to accommodate them. He turned a healthy profit from rum smuggling; presumable, Jason did likewise. Tonight Jason had to check that the last shipment of rum smuggled from Cuba had arrived safely in Natchez. He hoped all went smoothly; for if so, other runs would follow, and more evidence would be confiscated. Jason was secretly sending a number of barrels up North to the O'Roark warehouse, to hold as evidence against Baker.

"Will you greet Martinique for me?" Christina asked, her words bringing Jason's thoughts around. Christina knew John and Marti from the *Lucky Lady*, where John served as captain. She knew nothing of their activities for the Union.

"Of course," he replied, fixing his gaze upon her perfect features and taking note of the sadness that still lingered there. "Why don't you meet John, Marti and myself after you wrap things up around here and you can tell her yourself."

"I'd like that. I'd like that very much," she replied warmly.

Still, he felt she was deeply troubled by something

more. "Come on, Christina, tell me what's bothering you," he coaxed.

"I can't go on playing this charade of yours much longer," she interrupted. "I hate it! I hate everything about it!" The determined look in her eyes was a sign he'd learned to associate with impending trouble.

"And do you think that I like it?" he posed tightly.

"Sometimes I think that you do."

"I'm going to repeat this one last time, Christina," he warned, the authority in his voice silencing any further protest by her. "My business in Natchez will be completed soon. Until it is, you will keep that pert nose of yours out of my business and quit badgering me about it."

"I don't think I can do that," she answered honestly.

"You will . . . and you must," he emphasized. He took hold of her wrist and drew her close to him. "It is time for our evening appearance, madam. Our poker-playing customers are most likely chomping at the bit, eagerly anticipating your arrival." He bent his head to hers and nibbled a dainty ear lobe. "Not that I can say I blame them. In that enticing number you're wearing tonight sweet, you look positively good enough to—"

"Jase!" she choked.

"Where is your mind, darling?" he said with a chuckle. "I was merely implying that you looked enticing enough to distract even the most ardent of poker players."

He grinned lopsided at the becoming blush that stained her cheeks. "Let us depart, innocent."

"To our continued success," she proposed as she lifted her wine glass.

"And to our poor customers, who upon your arrival in

135

the gambling saloon will have eyes only for your beauty, while I will be doing my best to relieve them of their money." He winked. "Although, with your presence in the room, even I shall find it difficult to concentrate on the game."

"You'd better," she threatened softly. "I need you."

His fingers played along the scalloped neckline of her gown that clung to each ripe curve he longed to explore. "If you need me, then why the cold shoulder of late whenever I attempt to woo you to my side of the bed?"

She was a bit startled by his directness, although she told herself she should be accustomed to it by now. Taking a deep breath, she replied. "I believe you and I are seeking two entirely different things from this relationship, Jason. I hear the words *want* and *desire*, but not once has the word *love* crossed your lips." She did not stop when his face became dark as a thundercloud. "A woman needs more than honey-tongued words. She needs to hear she's loved. Especially after she's given herself to a man freely and without asking very much in return.

There was silence between them as the steward came to clear the table and to hand Jason a fresh, miniature, red rose that he wore in his jacket lapel each evening at the gambling tables.

"Good luck, sir, madam," the steward offered before departing.

"Thank you," Christina acknowledged as Jason nodded his reply.

Jason took her hand in his, his face once more relaxed. "You are right to some extent. A woman does need to know that she is not being played false. But it's my opinion that if a man and a woman care about one another, then the woman should sense what is in his heart, and not worry about things such as words, which are easily spoken and not necessarily meant." He placed his plam against her breast and felt the pounding of her heart against his hand. He touched his lips gently to hers. "Your heart tells me much, Christina," he said, lifting his mouth from hers and placing her palm upon his own chest. "Mine is beating much the same as yours." He forced her to look up into his eyes. "Do you feel it?"

"I want to believe you," she whispered.

"If you don't know what I feel by what was shared between us the other night," he replied between clenched teeth, "then you really don't know me, and you never did." He suddenly laid his hand on the back of her neck and kissed her passionately upon her half-opened mouth. He broke the kiss first. "Come, my beautiful lady. It is time to go to work and I need you by my side; you're my good-luck piece, sweetheart. I wouldn't want to ever lose you." He stood, pulling her to her feet beside him.

Damn him! Damn him! Christina mentally swore her frustration; this man drove her to complete distraction and jumbled her emotions until she was not certain whether she would ever think straight again. And the audacity of him to ply her with kisses and caresses until she forgot she was upset with him and yearned for the heated passion that they had shared the other night. Physical desire ate away at her days and slipped into her dreams at night. She could barely think of anything else. And she knew that he knew.

"Lead the way, my Yankee gambler," she said coolly, her small steps gliding behind his light tread as he directed them to the loud, gay laughter of the gambling saloon.

When they walked across the brightly lit threshold, side by side. And together they felt the powerful magnetism that they possessed as a couple. They had the ability to turn every head in a room merely by entering it. She felt a moment of intense pride as he took her hand and kissed it.

"For luck," he whispered huskily before turning away.

"For luck," she replied. She watched him saunter confidently to his place at the faro table. "And for love."

Lunch with John and Martinique lifted Christina's spirits considerably. There existed such genuine warmth between Jason and his friends that anyone else in their midst was affected by it also.

Conversation flowed easily as they dined on baked white fish and an excellent bottle of white wine. It was a relaxing time.

"This is a charming place, isn't it?" Christina remarked to Martinique as they left the two men to their brandy and cigars and retired to the brick patio that overlooked the winding river.

"Yes, it is," Martinique agreed. "I understand that during the war this was a Confederate hospital. The owners have made quite a few changes since then."

Taking note of the quiet, luxurious surroundings, Christina replied, "And much for the better. It is simply marvelous to be here after the hustle of travelling the river the past few weeks."

The two women took seats on a stone bench that provided a perfect view of the countryside that lay rich in green foliage, the air delightfully scented by sweet-smelling clover.

"What kind of reaction are you getting to this new venture of yours?" Martinique inquired in a voice that revealed her concern.

"I am sure people think me quite mad. But it is the only way I can make enough money to keep us all together at Oak Meadow, so I have no regrets."

"I'm glad to hear that," Martinique returned sincerely. "I know people sometimes take a dim view of such things."

"Sometimes it doesn't matter what others think of you does it, Marti," Christina stated as more of an opinion than a question.

"Not if in your heart you know what you're doing is right."

"I do," Christina answered immediately, but then her voice faltered, "however, I don't believe Jason shares the same feelings. He doesn't understand that a woman needs to be told that she's loved, as well as shown." She sighed despairingly. "Oh, Marti, I don't know this man that he's become . . . not at all."

"It has not been easy for him," the other woman remarked. "Sometimes things happen in a person's life that cannot be so easily set aside." She turned a compassionate gaze upon Christina. "Christina," she said hesitantly, "there is something about Jason's past life that I don't think you are aware of. And I have never talked about it with anyone before, not even Jase."

Christina looked pleadingly at her friend. "Oh, please tell me." She laid her hand upon Martinique's. "I promise to keep it to myself."

"Yes, well, you must," Martinique warned her gently. "For he will not want you to talk of it with him. He never has discussed her with any of us."

"Her?" Christina whispered, her eyes round and apprehensive.

139

"Yes. Her name is Teressa St. Clair. She is the reason Jason does not believe in committing himself to promises of love and lasting relationships. He was hurt badly by giving all of himself to love once before."

"I had no idea he had been in love before." Christina could not hide the jealous reflection in her voice. "So, there is someone else for him. Someone he loves . . ."

"Loved," Martinique hastened to add, "that is the word I wish for you to keep in mind. He loves you now; he loved her. She's his past."

"If he does love me, he certainly is doing his best to keep silent about it!" Christina replied in a biting voice. "He's as stubborn as an old mule!"

"Yes," Martinique nodded, "I'll have to agree with you. I'm afraid one of his worst traits is his hard head."

Christina could not help but smile at her friend's intuitive remark. "You are his best friend, Marti. No one can doubt that you certainly know him well." She turned searching eyes upon the woman once more. "But please, go on with your story."

"It is not going to be easy for you to hear."

"Nothing about this relationship with Jason is easy," Christina retorted. "Why should this be any different?"

Martinique sighed. "She was a singer he met in New Orleans, in the Vieux Carré, at a place called Diamond Sal's."

"I've heard of the place," Christina sighed. "Three stories of elegance; the finest gaming room in all of the Vieux Carré."

Yes, it is at that," Martinique agreed. "And it is the perfect setting for a young woman of Teressa's aspiring nature. Dark hair, snapping dark eyes, and French bloodlines through and through."

140

"A singer . . ." Christina whispered, "it is hard to believe."

"Teressa St. Clair is not just any singer, dear," Martinique replied, admiration for the woman's talents in her tone of voice. "She is one of the finest I've ever heard, and I hear tell that she is a smashing success in Europe."

"Oh, my word!" Christina cried. "Teressa . . . of course! The one they call the Golden Girl in Europe. I saw her once in Paris. She is certainly lovely and very talented."

Martinique continued. "Jason was in New Orleans after the occupation. He was assigned to duty there. He was young, far from home, and very lonely. It was in New Orleans that they met and fell in love." Martinique kept her eyes upon Christina's face so that she could comfort the girl if need be. "Her career finally came between them. Jason was left out in the cold when she departed to tour the country. She promised to write, and he promised to join her as frequently as possible. But it was wartime. The travelling and the long separations finally drove an irreparable wedge between them."

"Has he seen her since then?"

Martinique shook her head. "No."

"Thank you for telling me, even though it is painful to hear. At least it helps me to understand him a bit more."

"I only revealed this to you because I believe you are the woman to show him that love can be deep and lasting—to be shared without fear of heartache."

Christina searched her friend's face. "You believe that, don't you?"

"Don't give up, Christina," Martinique encouraged her. "You are the woman for him . . . I know it."

141

"If I could just get one promise from him," Christina said wistfully.

"I know that deep in his heart Jason loves you," Martinique persisted. "Even if he does act like a jackass at times. It is in his eyes each time he looks at you."

"Yes," Christina replied with renewed confidence, "I must learn to be patient." She grinned. "Not one of my best virtues.

"Mine either," Martinique laughed.

"I am going to do my best to win that rogue over, Marti. But if you are wrong about his feelings for me, and he is only toying with my affections, I swear I'll personally carve that honey-tongue right out of his head! I assure you that I shall be the last woman to hear his sugar-coated phrases!"

Martinique burst forth in laughter, her amusement bringing forth a giggle of laughter from Christina also. Neither woman was aware of the light-footed Jason as he walked up behind them.

"May I ask what is so funny?"

"I'm afraid, my friend," Martinique chuckled to Jason's bland expression, "that you have met your match. I don't think you should do her wrong, for she will make a terrible adversary."

Hands resting on his lean hips, Jason answered mockingly. "I hope I never have cause to find out either, my dear Martinique. I've grown rather accustomed to this voluble tongue of mine." He grinned crookedly. "It would be rather a shame to deprive me of it, now wouldn't it, ladies?"

Both women viewed him speculatively. Martinique doubted whether he had overheard much of their conversation; it was not Jason's style to eavesdrop. But his bemused smirk proved he had caught the end of Christina's statement, and Martinique could only stare as Jason took possession of Christina's arm and propelled her toward their waiting carriage.

In fact, the conversation between the two women was not the reason for Jason's abrupt departure with Christina in tow. When their carriage finally halted before the *Rebelle Christina,* Jason made no attempt to escort Christina to their stateroom. She threw him a questioning look, with what she hoped appeared a reassuring smile.

Jason had received some disturbing news from Big John, and it was weighing heavily upon him. Simon Baker's henchmen were beginning to ask questions: questions about Christina, and her role in Jason's life. The answers they received were innocent enough. Christina Duprea had hired Jason to deal faro on her riverboat. That was the extent of their relationship. But would they probe further? Jason would have to watch his every move with the golden beauty. And that was getting increasingly harder to do. He sighed. Tonight, more rum than ever was coming into the country via New Orleans. It was the *Lady*'s responsibility to meet that shipment— and without attracting the attention of the Coast Guard. It was important that Jason be there to assist Big John. If they were to fall, it would be together.

"Aren't you coming onboard with me?" Christina asked. The hour was growing late and he was to deal faro this evening.

"Not tonight." He gave her arm a gentle squeeze. "Something urgent has come up. I've got to beg off for this evening, sugar."

"Oh, Jase!" she wailed, "however will I turn a profit if you aren't there?"

"Look," he offered, "why don't you try your hand at dealing? Take my place, you'll be great at it."

"Perhaps I could do that . . ." she said speculatively. "I've played faro countless times with you and won." She favored him with a brilliant smile. "This should be easy."

"Just don't allow those smooth-talking devils to pull any fast ones on you," Jason warned, his face set in hard lines. "I wouldn't want to have to call anyone out for taking advantage of my woman."

His woman, she mused dreamily. When he referred to her so intimately, it felt like she had a stomach full of butterflies all flying in opposite directions. "Will I see you later?" she asked.

"I'm not certain . . . perhaps."

"Well," she snapped, seeing the mask of indifference on his face. "Don't go out of your way, Yankee, by any means."

He laughed, a rich, deep rumble in his chest. "For you, princess, it is with pleasure."

She spun about and stormed up the gangplank, her ruffled petticoats rustling about her trim ankles. She called back over her shoulder: "I am not certain I shall like it if you leave me to sleep alone tonight. But then on the other hand . . ."—she paused effectively—"I just may find that I like it very much . . . very much, indeed."

His dark brows snapped together as he watched her proud, straight carriage ascending the gangplank.

"The war's over, rebel. Remember?" he called after her.

She smiled with forced sweetness. "That one, anyway," she called back.

The *Lucky Lady* lay jut beyond the city limits of Natchez in a remote bayou. The crew had been instructed to pick up her illegal contraband outside of international waters and proceed with all due haste to this designated area.

The riverboat carried no passengers or cargo—legal cargo, that is. But it did carry countless stacked barrels of illegal liquor, stowed in its hold beneath heavy canvas.

"Jesus, but I do hope the colonel is right on this one," remarked Big John McGurk. "I'd hate to think of the explaining we'd have to do if we were caught by the Coast Guard with these barrels of liquor on board."

"I don't like it either," Jason said, "but if there's one thing I learned working with the colonel during the war, it's that he's very thorough when he lays down a plan. Nothing is left to chance."

"You're right, of course," McGurk said as they walked over the riverboat's creaking deck. "I suppose these godforsaken surroundings are getting to me." He snorted, pointing to a gnarled cypress that stood partially submerged in the brackish water. "Look over there. See what I mean?"

Jason laughed as a huge snake slowly slithered into the water. "He rather reminds me of someone I know."

"No one I care to know, I can tell you that," Big John shot back.

"But you've already made his acquaintance," Jason grinned. "Christina's stepcousin."

"Baker?" John found himself laughing. "You're right, you know. Especially around the eyes."

"Did you find out the name of the party we are to deal with from now on?" Simon Baker gave the agent of the Freedmen's Bureau a chilling stare that left him with the feeling of being under a magnifying glass.

"John McGurk and Jason Woods. Two Yankees seeking to make a buck from Reconstruction, just like the rest of us," the agent sneered. "They are money-hungry bastards. They made the run to New Orleans and are now back in Natchez awaiting further instructions. It was a clean run and they made it in record time."

"The same two men I met some time ago when they first came to Natchez," Simon mused. "One, the Woods fellow, is a hell of a card player. Met them over a game of stud at Rose's. After I found out what they had on their minds, I invited them here to my annual ball." He smiled slyly. "Men like them are so easy to control." He glanced over at the bureau agent. "All it takes is money. Doesn't it, my friend?"

"Still, we should be cautious until we learn more about them," the man advised.

"That's your department; mine is running my empire and making certain all goes smoothly."

"Very well, Mr. Baker. I shall see what I can find out for you—if anything."

"There is always something, you idiot!" Simon snapped.

"Yes, sir," the sweating man replied.

146

"Find out what it is and report back to me," Simon ordered. "These two men have maneuvered themselves into my empire, and I want a full report on them on my desk by the end of the week."

"I'll do my best, sir." The man scurried from the study and out of the garish mansion to collapse against the closed door and wipe his forehead. Damn the Bakers of this world for their power and influence while men such as himself had to grovel at their feet and do all of their dirty work. Being born to a rather well-to-do class of Northern politicians did not mean a damned thing in these times. The Simon Bakers, the scalawags, were the ones with the political power. While everyone else struggled in vain to get a foothold in the southern states, Simon Baker ruled the town and everyone associated with it. Even the Freedmen's Bureau, and organization founded to help the freed slaves adjust to their new lives, found Baker a powerful foe. Either you did his bidding or risked injury—or death. Clutching his briefcase under his arm, the intimidated bureau agent hurried to his carriage. Fear was a most powerful persuader; he knew he would have to come up with something—anything—on the two men who had just joined their ranks. If not, he would be signing his own death warrant.

Christina was sparkling tonight, a rare gem that Jason O'Roark could only watch from afar. The deep blue silk gown, with a narrow skirt and over-drape brocaded with silver throughout, glistening luminously like so many stars each time she moved. A magnum of champagne, empty now, sat neglected on a serving cart between them. The last of the *Rebelle Christina*'s passengers had departed

147

on the Natchez landing at the foot of Silver Street, after a very leisurely trip up from New Orleans. Even the saloon was reasonably quiet. Jason sat transfixed by Christina's slim finger that daintily travelled over each careful entry in the ledger book.

Without looking up she remarked gaily, "We are doing well for ourselves. I am pleased."

"Was there ever any doubt?" he queried softly as he leaned back in his chair, his long legs stretched before him.

"Of course not," she replied. "But we've only been in business for a little over a month. And look at the profits we have been realizing." She unfolded her legs from the chair she was reclining in and moved across the space that separated them to push the ledger book under his nose. "See?"

They were sitting in her office that overlooked the gambling saloon. This evening's fast and hard card game had left Jason drained. But even so, he took the time to go over each figure in the book.

"Very good," he praised, his eyes registering a gleam of admiration as they met hers. "You have a head for figures and an astute, keen judgment in business matters. You are to be congratulated on what you've managed to accomplish."

"And we both know the reason behind this success, don't we?" she said with a knowing smile.

"Do I take it you may be referring to our respective talents?"

"Thirty thousand for one night's work," she said smugly. "Not bad for a Yankee and a stubborn rebel, is it?"

"Not bad at all, sweet. And at this rate, you can retire

before you're even twenty-one."

"What?" she feigned mock surprise at his words. "Just when I've managed to start all the tongues up and down the river wagging and those Yankee dollars flowing right into my cashbox?" she chuckled throatily. "Why, I'd be a darn fool to even consider it."

A frown creased Jason's forehead as he scowled darkly in her direction. "Damn it, woman! Don't let all of this glitter go to your head. It is shallow and deceiving, and can be very dangerous.

"And very profitable," she retaliated with smooth assurance.

"But it will hardly keep you warm nights," he remarked sarcastically.

"I thought we were discussing my business," she responded in a tight voice. She could not help but notice the dark look of desire that now smoldered intensely in his eyes. Turning away from that heated gaze, she stood and walked across the room to stand behind her desk, feeling safer now that she had something solid between them.

"There are other things to consider besides business, Christina," he said silkily, slowly rising to his feet and advancing toward her.

She was suddenly frightened by the hardness of his eyes, which bore into her with relentless determination. He was unsmiling, and the purpose she read in those unwavering blue depths turned her knees to watery objects that felt disoriented from her body. She sagged against the desk for support.

"Jason," she breathed huskily. "You told me at one time not to push things, remember?"

"Yes, I remember," he returned with a twist of his

mouth. The distance between them slowly closed as he walked toward her. She shivered as he came to a halt on the opposite side of the desk, facing her.

"Jase, I'm asking the same of you," she pleaded in desperation; a final plea for him not to touch her, not to kiss her, or her carefully constructed wall of indifference would come tumbling down around her feet.

"And I refuse," he replied, his voice firm and increasingly demanding. "I want you, all of you, not just when you have a few moments to pat the hired help upon the head." He held her gaze. "Is there someone else taking my place in your bed?"

For a moment she was bereft of speech. "How dare you!" she spat out finally. "Do you think me like all your other whores? That I am nothing but a warm body to lie next to at night?"

His hands clamped hurtfully on her upper arms.

"Don't talk like that. It sickens me!"

"And your other life sickens me!" she shouted in his face. "You want me beside you all of the time. Yet, you are the one that is never there for me—you are forever on some mysterious journey. Then you return and I don't even know you, you are so distant and cold."

The expression on his face was unreadable. "I've told you, it's business—not pleasure—that takes me away from you."

"Then why are you so close-mouthed and secretive when you return?"

"You want a pledge from me, all the sweet words and phrases that mean so much to women. A vow to love, honor, and obey. One thing you will have to learn about me is that you can't twist me around your finger. I will never sacrifice myself for love again." As soon as he'd uttered the words he regretted them. He watched the light die in her eyes, all of the spark and anger that had drawn him to her, gone—replaced by a haunted expression he would never forgive himself for putting there.

"So it is only desire between us," she breathed, her eyes bright with unshed tears.

"Damn it! I need you, I want you with me always," he responded fiercely. He extended his arms across the desk which separated them and pulled her unyielding form over its surface.

Without Christina knowing exactly how it happened, she found herself sprawled unwillingly across his lap as he reclined one hip upon the desk. His eyes burned into hers with such intensity that she felt frightened.

She attempted to slip from his grasp but was stopped by the imprisonment of his arms that were like two steel bands around her. He drew her against his chest. "I don't ever want to hurt you, sweetheart, and I won't," he whispered as his lips nibbled her neck and his hands caressed the length of her arms.

"Not physically," she moaned, "but you will."

His dark visage and the deep timbre of his voice made her shiver with suppressed desire. "You're all I'll ever need, all I'll ever want, little cat. There is no one but you in my life . . . no one." His words and his emboldened caresses, which now teased one, taut, throbbing nipple beneath the material of her dress, brought forth tiny gasping sounds of pleasure from her throat. But still she fought his advances and refused to admit her need of him, and the burning ache inside her that was demanding to be sated.

"I do not want this," she panted, "no . . ." She felt her

resistance weakening with each touch of his fingers upon her skin, and so did he.

"Your lips tell me no, Christina, but your traitorous body is not listening." His strong, lean fingers pulled her roughly, almost hurtingly against him, until before she could reply, her bosom had been bared from her gown and laid against his muscular chest. She was only dimly aware of him yanking forcefully upon the long, tight sleeves, which encased her arms by tiny pearl buttons that ran their length, and the sound of buttons as they fell this way and that upon the hardwood floor.

Desire was now a painful, throbbing knot in her belly and she eagerly tore at his clothing, as he did hers, to sigh with bliss when they were both naked. He slipped her legs over his arms, moving to the plush desk chair and settling her in it. He towered over her boldly, demandingly, positioning her slender limbs so that he might have better advantage for his now obvious purpose. Her eyes showed alarm briefly as his sensuous lips began exploring every inch of her.

"You want me," he whispered huskily, bestowing light kisses upon her quivering stomach, "just as much a I want you."

"Sometimes I think I hate you," she moaned. "But not tonight, not at this moment." Her fingers wound themselves into his thick hair as she urged his mouth upward to press hungrily to hers. She closed her eyes, wishing to lose herself completely in this world of desire that he alone seemed to control. When it came to the physical side of their relationship, he had the advantage. And when his lips, moist and hot, continued to roam every inch of her, from her sweet-scented hair to the tip of her slender toes, she felt herself once more transported into his world . . . where only he existed.

His hands were gentle as they stroked her full breasts, thumb lightly circling each sensitive nipple until they rose rigid and hard to his touch. She writhed and gripped his shoulders, hungry for the feel of him, the taste of him. She moaned softly, pressing her parted lips to the thick mat of curls upon his chest. A hoarse gasp escaped him.

Emboldened by his groan of pleasure, she slid her hands from his wide shoulders down his broad chest, along the tightening muscles of his abdomen to weave through coarse hair, at last finding what she was seeking. Like warm velvet, she thought, as she wrapped her fingers about his throbbing member, teasing, stroking, working him into a frenzy of desire.

He attempted to control her sliding grip with the rhythm of his hips, but Christina had the initiative now, and she only increased the motion of her wrist, enjoying her brief power over this man. Jason gasped for breath and stilled her hand with his.

"I want to bury myself within you, little cat, and feel you thrash beneath me."

"Then do," she purred beneath him, "now . . ." Consumed by insatiable desire, she wrapped her long legs about him and drew his lean hips into hers.

They came together in a blazing fire of passion. A primitive cry escaped her as he entered her, consumed her, and brought her to the edge with his powerful thrusts. She gyrated her hips to match his feverish rhythm, uttering one small gasp as she felt herself whirling, falling, the world around them dissolving away until there was only the two of them and the white hot galaxy of ecstasy where only lovers were permitted to go.

Later, after she had retired to her stateroom alone, and Jason had left on another of his "business trips" with John McGurk, she lay wide-eyed upon her bed and promised herself that tonight had been the absolute last straw. She could not go on this way any longer!

"Tomorrow morning I will go home to Oak Meadow for a visit," she whispered into the darkness. "I must get some sort of perspective on my life, some sense of direction. And to do that I have to get away from him for awhile, for he overshadows everything around me here." She continued to lay there staring up into the darkness. She knew she was not separate from him any longer; he had weaved himself so completely about her that even her thoughts were becoming confused with his and her body controlled by his killingly soft touch. She closed her eyes to slumber and unconsciously wrapped her arms around his pillow, drawing it snugly against her breasts.

Even her rebellious thoughts could not stop the invasion of her senses by the lingering scent of him that crept into her dreams and evoked visions of their earlier love-making.

In her dreams she was a willing slave to the desires of her healthy young body—and to the man she could only know as Jason Woods, her welcome master.

Chapter Eight

The odor of lemon and beeswax drifted through the open door of Oak Meadow mansion and mingled in the afternoon breeze with the musty smell of dust that Christina determinedly pounded from a carpet. She had the hooked rugs from the bedroom slung over a line in the shade between two broad, sweeping oaks.

Mammy stood off to one side under a towering willow, a pitcher of lemonade in one hand, while the other wagged a chunky finger in the girl's direction. "Don't know why you doin' dis yourself for!" she ranted, her coffee-brown eyes taking note of each carefully aimed swing of Christina's arm as the rug beater connected with a dull thud upon the intended target. "Dere's folks round here fo dis kind of work. Not right for lady like you to be doin' dis!"

The mistress of Oak Meadow did not glance up from her gruelling battering of the carpet. Instead she replied firmly, "And they are just as busy with other chores. Look how much we've all managed to accomplish since I arrived yesterday, Mammy."

"S'pose you might be right dere," Mammy reluctantly agreed after careful deliberation. She ambled over to a wicker table to place the lemonade alongside a plate of sugar cookies that had been her first offering and squeezed her rounded figure into a lawn chair. "Least you kin do after ah goes to all dis trouble jist for you is to have some of dis refreshment. Ah didn't squeeze all dem lemons jist fo de exercise, missy. Now you sit down awhile fo you drops!"

Wiping her brow with the corner of her white-starched apron that protected the simple cambric gown, Christina walked over to join Mammy for a moment. She sat down in an adjoining chair.

"It's beginning to look as it once did, isn't it, Mammy?" she said, viewing the pleasant changes around them.

"Dat it is, chile." Mammy smiled.

The workers that leased land from Christina had been more than happy to volunteer their services in shifts to help their mistress. She was well liked and respected among them, and there was nothing they wouldn't do for her in return for the homes and land that she'd offered them. They hurried to and fro, some painting the exterior of the house, others replacing and whitewashing worn fencing, and still others replanting the gardens and trimming the hedges that surrounded the estate. And the interior was being just as lovingly restored. The household staff and Christina had been up since early norming, cleaning and polishing, washing windows until they sparkled, and waxing floors that once again shone with a rich, burnished glow.

Matthew Duprea sat in his rocker on the veranda viewing the activity around him with vague, listless interest. Once in a while he would bob his head from its resting place upon his chest, and gaze with a flicker of his old pride at his surroundings. But just as quickly the spark of recognition would be extinguished and he would slip without a struggle back into his other world where there existed the gentler, less-demanding pace of life that Matthew preferred. His white head dropped like a stone upon his thin chest, prompting Christina to jump apprehensively to her feet.

"Mammy!" she cried in alarm. "Is Papa all right?" Placing her empty glass on the wicker table, she started toward him.

Mammy was on her feet in one agile motion that surprised even Christina. "Ah take care of de massa," she ordered the girl, "you stay puts where you is at." She strode briskly toward the wide veranda, her arms swinging purposefully at her sides. "Bin takin' care of dat man fo nigh onto forty years, and ah s'pect ah be doin' it fo another forty."

She directed her heavy body up the stairs and to his side. She placed one large hand upon Matthew's frail chest. Nodding her head assuredly at Christina, she grinned. "Ah told ya. Dis ole man goin' to outlive all of us." Her spirits restored, Mammy headed back inside the house.

With a sigh of relief, Christina rested her own head for a second on the back of the lawn chair. Before she realized, her eyes drifted shut.

A child's voice calling to her from a distance woke her. "Miz Christina! Miz Christina!"

Waking with a start, Christina thought for a moment that she was back in another age, a time when she had been but a youngster herself and had romped so freely about the plantation. She shook her weary head to clear her thoughts. It was then that she spied little Lucy Washington skipping over the rolling lawns, a yapping coon dog at her heels. She waved for the child to come join her.

"What brings you all this way?" Christina inquired as Lucy, breathless from her jaunt, collapsed in a heap upon the cool, green grass.

"I came to ask you to have dinner at our house dis evening," she said with a bright smile. "My mama done said ah was to make sure dat you comes, too." She reached eagerly for the tall glass and two sugar cookies that Christina extended to her.

"That is very nice of your mother, dear. And I'd love to."

"Mama will be proud to have you," Lucy beamed as she promptly devoured the cookies with a sigh of ecstasy and then licked the sugar from her upper lip. After exchanging a few more minutes of idle chatter, Lucy thanked Christina for the treat and reluctantly rose to her feet. "S'pect ah best go tell Mama dat we's goin' to have our company. She bin lookin' fo a reason to use dat new tablecloth you gave her from dat New Orleans place."

"I'm so glad that it pleased her," Christina replied.

"Yes, ma'am, it surely did."

Christina walked along beside the child, chatting about the girl's family and what a splendid job her father, George, was doing in overseeing the plantation. When they reached the end of the vast lawn, Christina leaned against the winding fence that surrounded it, and watched Lucy until the child disappeared along the wooded path that would lead her back home. It was a hot, sultry afternoon, but Christina knew that the closely growing trees within the dark, damp forest would shield Lucy from the elements. It was not one of her favorite places on the plantation. But it was the only efficient way of reaching the bottom land where the tenant farmers made their homes. Turning away, the young woman strolled leisurely up the sloping incline and back to her task.

At first, upon reaching the main yard, she did not notice the buggy with two strange men in it that sat before the house.

Then the sound of harsh, angry voices—voices with the distinct nasal twang of Yankees—reached her from across the lawn.

Matthew Duprea stood clutching one of the great, round pillars that supported the house, his face a mottled shade of red, his breath rasping in his throat. That was all the warning Christina needed to lift her skirts and withdraw the petite pistol that Jason had insisted she carry at all times. Silently she crept up behind the men. As one argued heatedly with her father, and the other kept his eyes on the mansion's main door, Christina surprised them both.

"And what may I ask brings the likes of you to our home, suhs?" she demanded in a thick Southern drawl. In one glance she had taken in the dandified clothes and derby hats, that bespoke their occupation, and their intent. They were carpetbaggers through and through. And they were not here to pay a social visit.

One of the men stood up and leaned one arm in a cocky manner against the buggy frame. His eyes did an insolent sweep of her figure before coming to rest upon her pale, wide-eyed face.

159

"Well, well, Zeke," he chuckled, his swarthy face breaking into a cynical grin. "Looky what we got here." At that moment he noticed the pistol pointed at his midsection and his bravado suddenly disappeared. "Little Miss Hot Shot thinks she's scarin' us with that little pop gun," he said with an unconvincing laugh.

"You'd best quit your stammering, suh, and talk fast, for we Southerners do not take kindly to Yankees on Oak Meadow property." Though her heart was pounding wildly, she held the pistol steady.

"Now, girly, we was just funning with the ole geezer . . . honest."

"We got us permission, ma'am," squeaked the other man in the red, blue, and gold buggy.

"Permission from whom?" Christina demanded.

The slick Yankee who had remained standing shot back with an icy smile. "From one of your own relatives. Your stepcousin gave us permission to come out here."

"He had no right to do that!" Christina said softly. She advanced with deadly purpose toward the two wary men.

"Now, lady, don't go gettin' all riled up!" He glanced apprehensively at the gun. "That little popgun can still do a hell of a lot of damage to a man's innards."

Christina swung her gun hand back and forth from one man to the other. "I suggest you get your Yankee butts off my property before I forget that I am a lady and shoot both of you."

The man who was seated in the buggy did not move a hair as the lively young woman brandished the gun in front of his face. Never before could he remember himself being so frightened by the purpose that he read in anyone's eyes. This green-eyed hellion meant to shoot them if they so much as took a wrong step. He could see it in her eyes. A warm, constant trickle spread over the seat of his trousers and ran slowly down the inside of his pants leg. Mortified, he closed his squinty, bespectacled eyes and prayed that no one else had noticed. His partner's loud burst of laughter told him his worst fears had been realized.

"Now, look what you've made old Zeke go and do, missy. Ole Zeke, he ain't used to spirited gals like you, but I likes 'em. I likes 'em a lot. I reckon you and I might come to an understanding," he grinned smoothly, exposing yellow, tobacco-stained teeth.

"The only understanding that we could possibly come to is which one of you would like a bullet in his hide first!" Their eyes clashed.

"Your cousin Simon ain't going to like the way you treated us. Bet soon as you and him are married you'll be changing your tune about Yankees on this here property!"

"Get out!" Christina screamed. "I'd sooner burn this place to the ground than marry the likes of Simon Baker!" She moved forward and jammed the gun in his ribs. "I said get out."

At that moment Mammy hurried through the front door swinging her broom threateningly.

"What goin' on out here?" she demanded. Bustling down off of the veranda, she swooped over the slack-jawed men who were staring at her, and focused her attention to the Yankee who stood by the buggy.

"Y'all gits away from my lamb! Gits, ah say!" She swung a vicious blow to his midsection that sent the air whooshing from his lungs, rendering him helpless as a baby as he sprawled upon the ground.

Grasping at his stomach and coughing jerkily in an

attempt to refill his lungs with air, he never had time to recover from Mammy's first assault when she issued yet another.

"Ah teach da likes of you to mess wid us decent folk, dat ah will!" Her hand snaked down to grasp the seat of his britches and the other closed mightily around his scrawny neck. With a powerful heave-ho she sent him flying through the air to land with a thud right at his startled constituent's feet. "We not partial to Yankees on dis here property, so's ah s'pect y'all better leave real quick like!" She swished the broom at the gawdy buggy as if to prompt it along.

The astonished carpetbagger driving the buggy needed no further urging; he spun the team of horses around, almost upsetting his wounded friend in the process, and lashed out at the horses with a whip.

The buggy careened crazily down the road with Mammy standing like a sentinal in the center of the drive. She was going to make certain that they did not return again.

"Y'all remember," she called after them, "next time dis ole woman say git, ah means jist dat—git!" she huffed, "An don't you ever forgit it neither!"

All through dinner at the Washington home, Christina's thoughts wandered to the awful confrontation with the two carpetbaggers. The meal was excellent, but it was with relief that she rose from the table with George to go for a stroll about the bottom land, which lay thick and abundantly planted with cotton, as it had for several generations. This was her family's legacy, this land, these fields that stretched for miles upon miles. And tonight,

162

Christina was deeply troubled by how open and vulnerable it all appeared in the soft haze of twilight that slowly settled a curtain about the land. Some strong, inner instinct called out to her, pleading with her to guard this heritage closely, with her life if need be.

"Somethin' bin on your mind all evenin'," George's voice interrupted her dark thoughts. "Come on now, missy, you can tell me bout it." They stood on the edge of the fields. The tenant farmers' freshly whitewashed cottages, with lights glowing warmly from the windows and smoke curling fragrantly from the chimneys, lent a peaceful atmosphere to their surroundings.

"I suppose it's just that scene today with those awful Yankees," she replied, the tenseness evident in her voice.

"Ah s'pect dat would pry on your mind some," George agreed. "But ah thinks dey got de message, don't you?" He chuckled. "Dey won't be back none too soon."

"I'm glad you can see some humor in the situation," Christina returned, finding herself smiling right along with him.

George kicked at a clump of black earth with his booted toe. "Ah believes dat you have to see de humor in lots of things, s'pecially when things is a might down and out. Sure would liked to have seen dat ole woman raisin' a ruckus wid dem boys."

"Yes, well, it was a sight, I have to admit," Christina grinned.

"Dat's my girl!" he replied as he directed them along a winding, shell-covered path that skirted the edge of forest, past the carefully tended vegetable gardens of her workers. "Let's take a walk to see dat cotton gin. We gots it all fixed up again."

163

Christina nodded in agreement. "I always did like watching that machine during ginning time. When I was a child, my brother Curt would bring me down here to spend the day and watch as the planters from other plantations would arrive with their own cotton. The machine was the only one around, and Papa was generous with its use."

"Ah bet dat was a sight to see," George said. "Watchin' dat machine separate de fluff from de seeds by pullin' it through de narrow teeth of dat wonder machine."

"It went on like that for days until the last five-foot bale was loaded on flatboats for the journey down river to New Orleans. Then the real fun began. We'd have parties and barbecues, and everyone would celebrate until they were ready to drop from exhaustion."

"Maybe we will have dem times again soon," George said wistfully.

"Maybe," Christina replied solemnly.

They approached the darkened building that housed the machine. Christina waited outside for George to light a lantern inside. She was gazing off into the darkening horizon when something drew her attention to one area of the dense forest that lay in the distance. It appeared as just a brief flicker of something silver-white against the eery backdrop of the mist-covered limbs of the giant oaks. Startled, she stood transfixed by the scene as the seemingly fluid object moved through the forest. It travelled over the ground with apparent ease, as though perhaps it never really touched the ground at all but glided above it.

"George!" she cried out. "Come here, quick!"

George picked up a nearby hoe and hastened to her

side. "What is it missy? More Yankees?" His sharp eyes followed the direction of hers.

"Don't you see it? That faint silver-white glow over there in the woods. It is unnerving the way it floats so ghost-like among the trees and the mist."

"All de workers say dey bin seein' dat of late. It never comes any closer, jist stays out dere in de woods."

Christina watched closely as the strange, glowing light seemed to evaporate into the gray shadows. "I'm certain it is nothing unnatural," she sought to reassure him. "Just a trick of the moonlight among the trees, that's all."

"Ah don't know bout dat," George said skeptically. "Some folks are sayin' dat it is a ghost of some dead soldier hauntin' dem woods."

"Oh, George, that's just scary talk and you know it. There are no such things as ghosts and spirits. And don't go letting them spread these tales or we'll never get any more workers here again."

"Yes, ma'am," George replied, his head filled with stories that two workers had already told him: a body that seemed to be disconnected altogether from the head, and a dark cloak that swirled about the enormous horse that it sat upon. George followed along behind Christina as she began their trek back to the cabin. He turned one last time as they crested the hill and looked back in the direction of the forest. It was still there glowing softly, flowing freely through the trees. George shivered as though chilled and turned his eyes away. Whatever it was George hoped it stayed in those woods; they wouldn't have a worker left on the place if it didn't.

* * *

165

"I just don't understand any of this," Christina wondered out loud, giving the reins she was holding a firm snap of her wrist to encourage the leisurely-paced team to quicken their pace. "Ghosts . . . spirits. Fiddlesticks!" she continued over the crunching sound of the buggy wheels as it rolled along in the direction of her home. "Now, of all times, for some unexplained apparition to suddenly pop up. Every worker on this place will be leaving unless I can get to the bottom of this, and I've just about enough cash to make the next tax payment."

As the prancing team of horses moved through the dense forest, a hushed silence seemed to settle in about her. She drew the folds of her lace shawl tighter about her shoulders.

Just keep your wits about you Christina, she reminded herself. *There is nothing here that can harm you. All of those stories are nothing more than scary talk.* She smacked the horses with the whip. "Giddy-up, there! Take us home quickly!"

There was no immediate warning, not even a hint of impending disaster. But danger and evil lurked in the forest that the young woman was passing through. Horrible catastrophe was preparing to strike. None of the people chatting inside of their cabins before their cheery fires had an inkling of what was about to take place in the rich, bottom land that nurtured their cotton. Even the old plantation bell that tolled when such occurrences took place, lay silent. For it came unannounced out of the twilight darkness, slipping through the shadows: one

166

hundred riders, their faces covered by masks painted with images of hideous demons. They converged upon the cotton crop, like hungry boll weevils intent upon one thing: destruction of the tender fluff that had been so carefully cultivated.

"Trample it all!" came the gruff order from their leader. "Every last goddamned twig is to be destroyed! And burn what is left!" He jabbed his heels viciously into the heaving sides of his snorting mount and rode forward to toss a flaming torch into the unending rows before him. He watched with malicious satisfaction as it ignited the cotton and spread rapidly, destroying everything in its path.

It was the sharp burning in her eyes and the acrid smell of smoke that first alerted Christina. Swinging the team around and back in the direction of the fields, she struck each animal an encouraging blow once again. They raced madly through the undergrowth toward the orange-red glow spreading wider in the distance. Her stomach churned in revulsion as she quickly ascertained what was burning.

"Oh, no, it cannot be, . . ." she uttered in a stunned voice. "Not the cotton fields. . . . Not the cotton fields!" Hysteria rose like bile in the girl's throat as the full impact of her statement began to sink in. She would be ruined!

His sharp, predatory eyes, like those of the devil's viewed the hellish scene before him with a jeering smile.

"It is done!" he yelled over the roar of the fire. "Be off

with you, Night Riders of the Superior Empire! You have served your leader well."

The hooded leader motioned toward the approaching girl in the buggy. Needing no further urging, the hideous figures obeyed.

Like a pack of demented demons, they tore across the land before Christina's horrified eyes, almost upsetting her buggy as they thundered around and past her, intent on preventing her from sounding an alarm. Thundering rapidly closer, the leader maneuvered effectively alongside her buggy. She watched with dawning awareness as he stood up in the stirrups, swung his bulky frame forward, and landed with a heavy thud in the seat next to her, grabbing the reins.

"Get away! Get away!" she sobbed as she fought to loosen his hold on the reins. The buggy careened wildly amidst the trees; branches and sticker bushes tore at her face and arms. She was hardly aware of the pain she was struggling so desperately to keep from fainting. She stared deliberately at the hooded figure who had torn the reins from her grasp and was now driving the team of terrified horses deep into the darkness of the forest.

"What are you going to do to me?" she demanded. "I insist you tell me!"

The voice was muffled and deliberately garbled when he answered. "Teach you that a woman's place is beneath a man. And I intend to show you just what I mean firsthand."

For a moment Christina experienced fear so overwhelming that she doubted she would be able to lift a finger to stop him. Finding her voice at last, she hissed, "You are like a vicious killer that shreds everythings it comes near to pieces, just to revel in the sweetness of the kill." She managed to raise the buggy whip unnoticed for a fraction of a second. It was just enough time to give her a brief advantage. She swung her arm, bringing the whip down forcefully across his back. Emitting a scream of pain, the man clamped his hand around hers.

"God save me!" she screamed as he threw her to the floor of the buggy and ripped the whip from between her fingers. He was strong as a bull and Christina doubted she could do anything to prevent it if he intended to ravish her. But perhaps . . . she reached for the pistol that normally lay strapped securely beneath her petticoats. "*Mon Dieu*," she whispered in dismay as her fingers met nothing but billowing cloth. She remembered all too clearly now the scene between Mammy and herself after the confrontation with the carpetbaggers.

"No lady dat ah heard of goes bout wid a gun strapped to her leg!" Mammy had lectured her in a most authoritative tone. "Now y'all give dat thing to me fore somebody gits hurt."

Christina had reluctantly obeyed, telling herself that she would retrieve it from the old woman's room later.

Silently she prayed for herself and hoped that her workers had been alerted to the rapidly spreading fire by this time, and were attempting to bring it under control. Her heart lurched in fear as she felt her abductor direct the buggy off the narrow roadway and into the thickest, darkest part of the land. There were just the two of them thundering toward an empty creek bed that lay hidden with heavy shrubs. As she strained her eyes upon the evil figure that loomed threateningly over her, Christina vowed that he would have to kill her before she would allow him to do what she knew that he was intent upon.

The buggy came to an abrupt halt that knocked her

head against the floor and caused flashes of light to explode beneath her eyelids. She groaned in pain as she slipped toward unconsciousness. It was then that the fiend struck.

"Come here, you little bitch!" he growled beneath the hooded mask. "Let me show you how it is to have a real man between your legs."

Don't faint, Christina, she willed herself as she became aware of being pulled from the floor to lie across his lap on the buggy seat. Cunningly she feigned a swoon, seeking to buy herself a bit of time and an element of surprise. He continued pawing at her.

"How does that feel?" he purred. Realizing at last that he was receiving no response he shook her roughly, his hurtful fingers roaming at will where only caring, loving ones had touched her. "Wake up! Speak to me!"

His anger began to increase as she lay silent in his arms and endured his cruel fingers tearing at her bodice. She fairly gagged as moist, wet lips nipped along the curve of one alabaster white breast. His slobbering, brutal assault upon her quivering flesh seemed to excite him to a fever pitch. She forced herself to remain still until the time was just right. His lips were upon her own now, the hood lifted a bit so that he had better access to what he so desperately sought. Brutally his tongue ravished her soft mouth, and just when she felt the need to vomit, she willed herself to strike.

Reaching deliberately under his mask she raked her long nails down one side of his face and gloried in the sound of his anguished scream of pain. Her knee lay between his, and before he had time to recover she brought her knee up savagely, inflicting a blow to his engorged privates. His ardor cooled instantly as he crumpled belly up beside her, looking every bit like a great, beached whale.

"Ah . . . you filthy little whore!" He wailed as she pushed him with all of her might, sending him toppling over the side of the carriage to land with a bone-crunching sound in the rocky creek bed.

"That will teach you, you low-down, yellow skunk!" she screeched as she recovered her mobility and picked up the reins where they lay on the floor. "Hah! Get going, horses!" she screamed to the team. But the narrow wheels had settled into the moist earth between the gravel; no matter how hard the horses pulled, it would not budge. "Sweet *Jesu*," she moaned in panic, glancing over to where her assailant still lay moaning. Knowing she had not other choice, she leaped clear of his body and landed agilely a few feet away from him. The sharp gravel dug through the delicate kid slippers and bit into the soles of her feet as she darted off into the thick growth of trees. She didn't know how long she had been running when her ears picked up the distinct sound of another's footsteps directly behind her.

"Oh God, no," she groaned, almost to the point of losing her mind to the fear that overwhelmed her. "This time he'll kill me." She ran faster, but still she could hear the footsteps gaining on her. She ran like a person attempting to out run the hounds of hell. Just when she caught sight of a clearing that would lead her out of the forest, a shadowy image stepped out of the trees and stood before her, completely blocking her escape.

Chapter Nine

"Do not fear, chérie." The unexpected, humanlike quality of his voice brought forth a sob of relief from Christina.

Breathless, swaying dazed upon her bruised feet, she impeached the figure with frightened, doelike eyes and an anguished plea. "Oh, please, help me! He is trying to kill me!"

The darkly-clad shape moved slowly out of the shadows and strode toward her. It was then that the terrified girl began to have doubts as to who, or what, she was addressing. She peered into the darkness where his face should be. Her eyes were surely playing tricks on her. For his features were not there—he had none! All that remained was a pair of pale topaz eyes that gleamed back at her. She held out her hands as if to stave him off.

"*Monsieur,*" she whimpered. "If you are some kind of monster like that I just escaped from, then tell me now of your intentions. I am too weary to fight any longer," she moaned, placing her face in the palms of her hands. "Kill me . . . do what you will. Just do not play with me further." Uncontrollable sobs racked her body as the shock of her earlier encounter at last caught up with her.

"You are wrong, *mademoiselle*," the refined and masculine voice replied at once. By the closeness of that voice she assumed he must be standing right before her now.

Her hands dropped from her face and she willed herself to look directly into his eyes to gauge the truthfulness of his words. There was a black void where his face should be, and she felt her knees give way beneath her as she slowly sank toward the ground.

"Whoa, little one," he stated as his strong, solid arms secured her; he held her against him as though she was his alone to protect.

Her wobbly head lay upon his shoulder; drawing in deep, life-giving breaths, the young woman noted that his form was solid, not the mere nothingness as she'd expected. Pushing away from him she gasped, "What are you? Who are you? Are you man or phantom?"

His deep chuckle gave her a moment's pause. "I didn't realize," he said. "I suppose it is not unlikely that you would think me some kind of ghostly spirit that haunts these woods." He grasped her hand in his before Christina had a moment to pull away from him. "Do not draw away, *chérie*," he said in a determined voice. "Here, feel." He ran her fingertips along his seemingly featureless face. At her cry of astonishment, he reaffirmed her discovery. "It is a mask. Nothing more than that."

Her trembling hand roamed freely over the black material that covered what she now eagerly touched. "It is . . . it is," she replied in a relieved tone. "Tell me, who are you and why are you following me?" She stared

174

transfixed as he unbound a dark scarf that had been secured about his head. Upon seeing the thick mane of silver-gray hair revealed, she remembered the fleeting silver vision that had seemed to glow in the moonlight in the forest earlier that evening. "It was you," she whispered.

"I am here in answer to a need . . . a need for justice."

"And you hide your face and wear those garments to conceal your identity, do you not?" she queried, intrigued.

"No, it is not to conceal," he sought to explain. "I do not believe my identity is the issue here. But my cause most definitely is."

"Surely you have a name?" she persisted. She swore she heard him chuckle at her straightforwardness. There was a pause before he answered.

"You have spirit, you have beauty, and you have an insatiable curiosity, do you not, *chérie?*" he quipped wryly.

She brought up her chin in a defiant gesture. "And brains, *monsieur,* to go along with it all,"

"That is most evident."

"And I know what you are trying to do," she shot back unhesitantly.

"And what is that, *chérie?*"

"You seek to draw the conversation away from yourself to me."

"A much more interesting topic, I assure you."

"I disagree."

He was doing his best to bite back his laughter as he observed the beautiful young woman intently. "I would love to stand here forever and argue that point. However, might we postpone this discussion for another time and place? Suffice to say that I am known as the Silver Wolf. Now I strongly suggest we make ourselves scarce before someone discovers where you are."

Awareness took hold of her, and it was as though she'd just been doused with any icy bucket of water. "My cotton!" she wailed, "They've destroyed it!" She began to run, completely forgetting the stranger that followed behind. "Everything I've worked so hard to obtain. Damn them!"

"Mademoiselle Duprea, please do not run out into the clearing!" he called out to her. He cursed his stupidity for not holding on to her, and quickened his long strides until he had her within arm's length. Just as he reached out to grab her flowing hair, Christina stopped dead in her tracks.

"This cannot be happening," she whispered in a shocked voice. She had come to the edge of the trees and stood horror-stricken by the sight she had stumbled upon. It was like a scene from one of her worst nightmares.

"I tried to stop you," he said softly, reaching her side and watching closely the play of emotions revealed on her face.

"I cannot be awake," she breathed. "Surely this is nothing more than a bad dream I will not even remember in the morning." She stared dumbstruck by the fierce battle that was taking place on the edge of the cotton field between the masked devils and the Silver Wolf's followers. It was an awful sight to behold.

The smell of burning cotton and the yellow-orange tongues of fire that licked persistently at the tender, half-grown crop made the diabolical scene even that much more deplorable to witness. The pounding of horses'

176

hooves as they trampled everything around them intermingled with their frightened screams as the smell of blood and death assaulted their nostrils. Through the dense smoke and the hordes of men in hand-to-hand combat, Christina's eyes could only see one thing. The field was virtually destroyed. She heard him speak to her and turned her head in his direction.

"We did our best to stop them," he attempted to explain, "but I'm afraid we weren't able to save very much. But you have other fields, do you not?"

"Yes, I—I do," she stammered.

"I believe we at least prevented them from getting to those."

"Why would you want to do this for me?" she asked incredulously.

He answered without a moment's hesitation. "It is my purpose in life—the only one I have at present—to fight these parasites who have been sucking the very life out of our beloved South."

Christina's expression was totally sober. "The night-riders?"

"Yes, men who have recruited our young people by telling them they will be fighting the Reconstructionists who threaten to destroy the South's honor." He snorted disgustedly. "They end up losing all of these ideals along the way when they find out they're also murdering many of their own neighbors."

"So you are a Southerner?" she inquired.

"I am," he returned with pride, "until I have no breath left in my body."

"As it is for me," she agreed.

He took hold of her hand and tugged gently. "Come, I think it best that you let my men take care of things here.

It is not the first time we have clashed with these fiends, nor will it be the last." He began to lead her back into the protective covering of the trees. She immediately cried out in fear.

"What if he is still in there . . . waiting for me?"

"He is not," her rescuer assured her. "He knows that I am here and that's a confrontation he'll avoid at any cost. Even if the price is you."

It was strange, how completely safe she felt in this mysterious rebel's presence. How had he known her name? And how strange that he should be called Silver Wolf, though with his lithe, dark form and silver-streaked mane, she supposed it was appropriate enough.

When they returned to the creek bed for her carriage, the fiend was gone and the Silver Wolf retrieved the vehicle from the mud. Christina thanked him, knowing her life had been saved by this brave man. He mounted his black steed and escorted her back to the road that led to her home.

"This is where I leave you, *chérie*," he'd told her gently. "I will watch until you are safely inside."

"Thank you," she'd said.

"*Au revoir*," he replied, "till we meet again."

And somehow, as she'd started away from him toward the main house, she knew that his parting words were sincerely spoken.

The next morning Jason was furious to find that Christina was not on the riverboat. Christina had enlisted Martinique as the riverboat's hostess in her absence, leaving not so much as a note explaining her whereabouts.

178

"Where in the hell did she say she was going, Marti?" he demanded.

"I'm not certain she wishes you to know," Martinique responded honestly.

"I have to know!" he said. "Baker's men didn't show up last night for the usual run to New Orleans. Big John and I went alone. Baker is up to something, ... and I don't like it."

Martinique gasped. "Could he be involved with the nightriders?"

"It's quite possible. And if he is the leader of those vigilantes then Christina is in even more jeopardy. That bastard will do anything to possess her and her lands. She went home, didn't she?"

"Yes," Martinique said.

"I only hope I'm not too late." He turned and strode out of the room.

Christina sat before the ornate fountain in the center of the stone patio and watched as fat, contented goldfish swam lazily in the cool water. She had explained as much as possible the events of last night to her father, Mammy, and the concerned workers. This morning she had come to a conclusion.

"I want guards posted around the plantation," she had instructed George Washington. "No one is to get in or out unless they darn well have a reason to be here." The overseer had nodded in agreement and departed, leaving his mistress to mull over the nightmare of last night once more.

Dressed in a black velvet skirt and a silk blouse of pale gold, she looked every bit the grand lady of Oak Meadow plantation. She had been served her breakfast of croissants and iced coffee earlier but, finding that she had very little appetite, it still lay uneaten on the black iron patio table.

As was his custom, Jason appeared before her as though he had simply materialized out of thin air. She just happened to glance up, perhaps sensing his presence as she always did, and there Jason stood, looking as though he hadn't slept a wink, glaring at her.

She jumped, startled. "How did you get in here? I just posted men around here to keep out trespassers."

He grinned sarcastically. "You have always accused me, madam," he drawled, "of being half-Indian in my 'skulking around,' as you so aptly refer to it. Or have you forgotten, as you've forgotten your duties running the riverboat." His words were crisp and direct, and she sensed the fury beneath his icy veneer.

"I have forgotten nothing, Jase, and I certainly don't remember appointing you as my guardian either."

"Well, you sure as hell need one!" he retorted. "That was a pretty stupid thing to do." He flung himself down in a chair beside her and proceeded to help himself to her uneaten breakfast. "You'll excuse me," he said nastily, "for forgetting my manners. But I'm hot, tired, and damn hungry." He bit into the flaky pastry.

She arched one brow as she quipped dryly, "Aren't you afraid, Mr. Woods, that someone will come along and recognize you? You did spend considerable time here in the past." She brushed at some crumbs that had fallen on the tablecloth. "Or is that little charade over with?"

He banged the china cup he held forcefully against the saucer and she thought for certain that he'd broken it. "That is still none of your concern. But if you must have a reason for my coming here like this then I will give it to you, plain and simple." He leaned his dark head toward hers; his hand snaked out so quickly to rest on the nape of her neck that she jumped noticeably in her chair. In a deceptively soft voice he reminded her, "I am your talisman, Christina, the protector of your dreams. Whatever you desire, I will but sense it and come to you." In one swift motion he threaded his lean fingers in her tousled curls, pulled her lips to his, and kissed her savagely until she became weak and willing. Willing then to do anything that he asked. Just his wonderful, familiar male scent was enough to send her whirling through time, back to the night that he'd first made her his. Pulling his mouth reluctantly from hers, he whispered in a voice thick with desire. "And it will always be this way between us, little cat. You are mine . . . belong only to me."

"You are certainly sure of yourself, aren't you?" she couldn't help but reply; she was angry at herself and him, because for once she had to admit that he was right.

His face loomed over hers and she tried to resist the pull of the bright blue eyes that gazed so heatedly into hers.

"You wanted me to come and get you, and so I have."

"You are insufferable."

"I agree," he mocked with a grin, "I am. But I do know you very well, . . . don't I?"

"I'm glad that one of us is certain of the other," she said with a bitter laugh.

"You can no more stay away from me, Christina, than I can you."

"Let's get one thing straight here," she replied crisply. "You are the one that came looking for me. I was fine all by myself."

He was watching her closely, and she realized as soon as she'd uttered those words how hollow they sounded.

"I don't believe you're doing as well as you'd like me to think."

"Nonsense," she insisted. "I haven't thought of you one time since I came back home."

He raised one dark brow in a speculative gesture. "You expect me to believe that?"

She watched him in stony silence. Her heart began to pound against her rib cage as she watched him lazily stretch his arms above his head and then stand to rub his bearded jaw. The rasping sound of the bristles against his fingers was the only sound to be heard—that and the methodical rhythm of two hearts that beat as one.

Dropping his hands to his sides, he unknowingly drew Christina's attention to the gun in a tied-down holster on his hip, the clothes he now wore were so out of character for the man she'd once known. He had on a rust-colored shirt under a buckskin vest, dark pants, and brown leather boots that reached practically to his knees. But it was the sheathed Bowie knife attached to his gun belt that held her gaze. The carved, pearl handle was all that lay visible.

"This is what I will never get accustomed to," she suddenly blurted. She threw her hands up in despair. "A stranger sits before me."

His overall appearance continued to command her attention. So it was with a cry of surprise that Christina felt him grab her possessively around the waist with one hand, while the other clamped tightly under her firm backside.

"I've just about had enough of this for one day," he

said in a most threatening manner. "We're going somewhere where it will be just the two of us. Maybe then you will listen, or realize, what I'm trying to tell you." With one mighty tug he swept her up into his arms and over one broad shoulder as he began to stride determinedly toward the French doors that led to the dining room.

She attempted to kick him but acquired a resounding smack upon her rump for doing so.

"Ouch!" she yelped in total surprise. "How dare you beat a defenseless woman!"

She received only an amused snort as his reply as he strode uncaring, and bold as brass, through the open French doors with her still hoisted over his shoulder.

"You despicable *canaille!*"

"Don't use any of your fancy French name-calling on me, Miss Duprea," he ordered sharply. "If you have a mind to swear at me then do so in good old American cuss words. . . . Got it?"

Her face flaming and her temper seething, Christina muttered between clenched teeth, "No man has ever treated me in such a fashion as you! I despise you for the ill-mannered brute that you are."

"Spare me, please," he drawled sarcastically, making his way across the elegant room and almost colliding with one of the servants. She jumped aside, her eyes bulging from their sockets at the sight of her mistress lying bottom up over the shoulder of the scowling Yankee.

"What goin' on here?" she demanded, her words sharply spoken.

At a bone-chilling glare from Jason, she quickly turned around and headed back in the direction of the kitchen. Mammy would surely want to know that yet another

Yankee had his greedy paws upon her lamb.

"What is dis world a comin' to," the servant mumbled as she quickened her pace. "Yankees all over de house, and all over de mistress to boot!" She shook her turbaned head in absolute disbelief.

No one stopped Jason as he made his way through the mansion, out the front door beneath the prismed glass of the fanlight, and down the wide stairway with Christina hanging to him for dear life with one hand and frantically grasping with the other at any inanimate object that could possibly deter his departure.

Where is everyone when you need them, she thought dejectedly as she observed the solitude around her. A fleeting movement behind the honeysuckle-entwined trellis caught her attention. A small, cherubic face, thumb firmly planted in his mouth, peeked back at her with curious, solemn eyes.

"Mikey!" she called to the little boy sitting cross-legged and content in the cool dirt. "Go find your papa immediately! Tell him that some low-down Yankee skunk has kidnapped Miss—" Jason's palm clamping firmly about her mouth silenced the last of her words effectively.

Jason favored the boy with a winning smile and a consorting wink. "Don't listen to her, Mikey. We were playing a game and Miss Christina lost. And now she has to pay her dues." He grinned one last time at the boy as he swung himself and his prize up into the saddle of his waiting mount. "And you know how much girls hate to lose to boys, don't you son?"

Mikey nodded with a gleeful giggle and sat firmly

rooted to his spot.

Christina could only gape incredulously as they rode away from the house and toward the river road. Was there no end to the people who fell for this blackguard's charm and glib tongue? *I swear by all that's holy he's going to find himself without it one of these days yet!* she promised herself as she felt his arms tighten beneath her full breasts as the horse broke into a leisurely trot.

With helpless fury she watched the scenery for some indication as to where he was taking her. When he passed the turnoff to their private pool and did not alter from his course she knew then, beyond any doubt, where he was headed.

"I don't wish to go there with you," she said, gritting her teeth.

"You really don't have very much to say about it, now do you?" he replied uncaringly.

Quiet now, she could only stare at the cottage looming ahead in the distance. The intoxicating scent of flowering gardenias brought forth overwhelming memories: pleasant, comforting visions upon her mind's eye that conflicted with the jumbled, confusing emotions shared between them now.

Sensing her feelings, he whispered, "It's the only way, little cat. We need to be alone together desperately."

"Like hell," she replied tersely, although in truth she was tired too of all of this fighting.

"We can't go on like this, loving one minute, and then fighting like worst enemies the next. Why is there no common ground for us to meet upon? Why?" Jason whispered huskily.

"Has there ever been?" she replied softly, wishing that they could come to terms with one another, and simply

185

and openly express themselves and their love. She hoped for all of these things as he slid to the ground with her body cradled snugly to his chest, his arms holding her close.

With ease, he carried her toward the cottage, nudged open the door with his booted foot, and stepped into the dimly lit hallway. She began to realize that perhaps his thoughts were not so very far from her own, and felt her heart soar. He closed the door, shutting out prying eyes, anger, and misunderstanding, and all of the things that had brought them to this moment, to this confrontation.

The first hour at Gardenia Place had been spent in bitter squabbling with one another. And then, after all of the hurtful, angry words had been spoken, stubborn silence. But later, as they'd stood staring across the room at each other, he suddenly grinned crookedly, and they found themselves laughing good-naturedly. He swept her up in his arms and carried her to the cozy bedroom, where he laid her tenderly upon the feather mattress.

"There is no one but us, sweet thing," he murmured against her perfumed hair, "and we have the rest of the day to become reacquainted once again."

"Someone may come looking for me." she said. "What then?"

His lips moved over the satiny smoothness of her throat, to nip gently the place where her graceful throat joined her shoulder. "Then we shall tell them to go away, that you are mine . . . forever." He wooed her with his moist lips, and when his tongue traced tantalizing circles to her ear lobe, she purred her defeat.

With agonizing slowness his lips travelled the smoothness of her cheek, brushed her closed eyelids, and moved along her nose to fasten almost savagely upon her full, pouting mouth. He began removing her clothing piece by piece, caressing her satiny skin with knowing fingers. Bending his head to her aroused nipples, he tongued them teasingly, achingly, then nipped each bud to rigid peaks. His fingers found their way to her long, lustrous hair, lacing their way in the silky strands, encompassing her small skull to press her close, their breaths mingling as one.

"I want you, Jase, I want you so," she gasped, almost pleadingly. Her fingers hurriedly removed his clothes.

The warmth of his mouth surrendered to hers, their tongues entwining lazily, then savagely, as desires flamed out of control.

He tore at the rest of her clothing, tossing it aside; then, pressing himself between her legs, he took her with fierce abandon. While he had always been a considerate lover, making certain each time that she reached her peak of pleasure before surrendering to his own, today he appeared to give more of himself than ever before.

And later, when they lay sleepily contented and she cradled his dark head upon her breasts, she wondered if it was because he was beginning to admit to himself that he belonged to her. No longer just his body, or his passion, but his very being.

Sometime later, after they awoke from a nap, she murmured against his cheek. "You were right to come here." She stroked his curly locks that appeared to wrap themselves about her slim fingers of their own accord.

"H'm," he replied somewhat sleepily, moving his head deeper into the soft cleavage between her breasts. "We've both got pleasant memories to recall of this cottage."

"Yes, of your family and mine, and of Curt." It hurt so

to say his name, and she couldn't help the soft sob that escaped her.

A wave of tender concern washed over Jason as he rose up on one elbow to look down at her. "Are you all right?"

She nodded, her eyes squeezed shut so that he could not see the tears glistening in them.

Studying her through lazy-lidded eyes he knew there was no denying it now. Goddamn, how he'd fought it. *I'm caught*, he screamed to himself, *I love her. I love this infuriating woman with my entire being and I don't know what in the hell to do about it!* He sighed; she opened her eyes to peer up at him. *She knows*, he thought. *She knows I love her.* The emotions that he'd battled since he'd first laid eyes upon her again came tumbling down around his bruised and battered ego. The admission was like a soothing balm upon his wounded heart.

Her fingers reached out to caress his face, trace a path along his sensuous lips. "I know what you're feeling, Jase, it's the same with me."

He longed desperately to reveal his feelings, to share this all-consuming, wondrous emotion with her. To tell her that just the touch of her flesh to his had the power to heal all of the hurt and pain that had remained since he had lost Teressa. But before he could tell her, his mission had to be completed.

Christina's fingers traced feather-light patterns along his broad back. "I love you, Jase, with all my heart." She felt his body tremble at her declaration. He turned so that his soft gaze met hers. The words hung between them and echoed back in her face. She sucked in her breath when he did not speak, her hand dropping limply upon the bed.

His fingers reached out to grasp hers and squeezed reassuringly. His expression was somber. "Nothing about my journey to Natchez has worked out like I had planned. My life since the war has not been one of much purpose, I'm afraid. I'm not proud of the fact that I've seen my mother only a handful of times since my father died a few years ago." He stroked her smooth cheek. "I was resigned to my wandering ways . . . until now, until you." He leaned over toward her, a tender smile touching his lips just before they pressed to hers. He raised his head a bit to look deeply into her eyes. "Somehow, I've found that my values have changed and my life means more to me now. I think we can contribute my sudden change of attitude to a certain beguiling young woman who has stolen my heart."

"Are you trying to say that you love me?" *There, she had said the words for him,* she thought.

"I think I am," he replied somewhat in wonder himself. "Although I'm not doing a very good job of it, am I?" He grinned crookedly.

She wrapped her arms about him and hugged him to her. "Oh, . . . you're doing just fine, I think. Just fine indeed."

His hand gently smoothed the tangled, damp hair away from her face. "We are two of a kind, little cat. Two hearts that beat as one, two souls that are united. Each time I hold you, make love to you is like the very first time." He kissed her half-closed eyes, her petite nose, and the soft lips that she offered him. "You drive me crazy with desire for you whenever you're near," he choked. "What I'm trying to say is that I want you with me, in my life, until the end of time."

"And that is exactly where I want to be," she

whispered, rising up on her knees and raining feathery kisses along his chest, working slowly down his flat belly. "Forever . . ."

"Oh, God," he groaned, eyes closed to the magic of her lips upon every part of him. "When you do that . . ." he grinned, "and that . . . I am totally lost to you." He gripped the thick tangle of curls in his fingertips and gave himself up to pleasure. Slowly she eased his big body back onto the bed and took him once again to the heavens, to soar mindlessly, helplessly, and completely upon the wings of love.

Later, he reminded her that there was a vow between them now as lovers. "A promise," he whispered huskily, "that I do not take lightly."

She knew that he was remembering another vow, and the tragic way that love had ended. But she was not Teressa. "Nothing can separate us now, Jase, and no one can come between us."

"Christina?" he inquired, as they rode back in the direction of the main house. "There was some trouble in this area last night, and you had guards around your place when I arrived. Did any trouble reach Oak Meadow?" He felt her grow tense.

"Wha—what kind of trouble, exactly?" she inquired innocently.

"Prowlers—the kind that like to rough up pretty girls and burn everything that gets in their way."

She shivered, remembering.

Jason nuzzled his chin on the top of her head. Then he stopped the horse in the middle of the road and turned her head to force her to look at him.

She swallowed still trembling. "It was like some horrible nightmare that I have tried to make myself believe did not happen." Her voice faltered.

"It's all right, sweetheart. I'm here now, no one is going to harm you."

Haltingly at first, tearfully in the end she told him what had happened. And when she came to the last of the story she was weeping bitter tears that tore at his heart. He handed her a handkerchief. "Here, wipe your eyes. It's all over now, I promise you."

"How are you going to prevent them from coming back again?" she asked raggedly.

"Let's just say I have ways." His tone was deadly and menacing. He urged the horse forward once again.

"How's that?"

"Don't worry your pretty little head over it."

"Oh, no!" she bristled. "You're not shutting me out on this, Jason!"

His arms rightened about her. "Keep still, Christina, and do what I tell you for once in your life!"

Her angry silence was worse than her sharp tongue. Fortunately it lasted only as long as it took him to reach the road that led to the main house. As he lifted her from the saddle she cried out.

"I am not leaving here until I know what you have in mind. I refuse, do you hear me! And you can't force me!"

He slid out of the saddle. "This time I'm just going to make a suggestion. One that will make me very happy if you will accept it."

She glared back at him.

"It's as simple as that," he smiled blandly.

"You'd match words with the devil, Jase. I know when I'm being sweet-talked," she retorted smugly.

His hand reached forward to grasp her hair and draw her to him. "Do you?" he breathed in her ear as he laid her head upon his chest. "Do you, indeed?"

"I do," she whispered breathlessly.

"I'm just going to suggest a solution."

"All right," she at last agreed, "but I'm only going to listen."

He wrapped his arms tightly about her, half to feel her close to him, and half to prevent her from escaping. "I want you to pack some things and be ready to go with me by tomorrow." She began to wiggle in his embrace. "I mean it, Christina. I don't want you staying here. It's too dangerous for you."

"What about my father?" she cried.

"I'm going to have the army post a few men around your house to keep an eye out. But not you—you're mine to look out for. I'm going back to town while you pack and talk to some friends of mine about you staying with them."

"I don't want to be shut away somewhere!" she protested. "I have too much to look after for that!"

He gripped her chin in his fingers. "Martinique, John, and I can run things just fine. And it won't be for long. It's all going to explode wide open soon anyway."

Awareness swept over her. "That's what you're here for . . . to put an end to the nightriders." Her wide eyes blinked unbelievably. "You're an undercover agent. . . . You're gathering information." She pulled back, stunned.

"Now, sweetheart, don't be so melodramatic," he replied smoothly.

"Am I, Jase? Am I really?" She stepped back further, putting distance between them. "I'm so confused."

"Don't be," he smiled persuasively. "Just believe in me, in our love."

At the word love, her retreating footsteps halted. "Don't play me false. I'm going to believe in you and trust you, although for all I know you'll be taking me to some horrid, out-of-the-way place that will be full of other individuals with uncertain pasts and last names."

"You've read too many penny novels, love," he chuckled. But in a way she was most astute in her prediction. Christina would be sharing her temporary residence with quite a few flamboyant inhabitants. Dancing Janey, Alma Amour, and Fast-fingered Patsy all lived at Rose's.

Jason felt certain she would be safe under Rose's protection. Simon Baker would not dream of harming her under Rose's roof, for she wielded as much political power as he did. And Baker was well aware of it.

"I'll be back in the morning, bright and early to get you. I'll meet you at the cottage."

"I'll be ready," she replied.

"Don't let me down, love," he said as he remounted his horse. "A promise is a promise."

"Yes," she responded with tenderness, "I know."

193

Chapter Ten

"Rhea!" the silver-haired highwayman shouted to the small, dark figure that had just stalked unhappily away from him. "Will you listen for one moment to what I'm trying to tell you?"

"No!" she snapped. "I have heard enough already of this golden one. I do not wish to discuss her anymore!" She disappeared inside the house.

The man stared after her. Perhaps there was some truth to her accusations after all. Was he obsessed with the tawny-gold beauty whose life he had saved? He gazed out over the sprawling land that stretched for miles in every direction. It was his land, paid for with good old Yankee money: greenbacks that had been begged, borrowed, and stolen. He felt no guilt whatsoever for his deeds. But he did feel uneasy—yes, even a bit guilty—for these feelings that occupied his thoughts both night and day since he'd first laid eyes upon her.

Why did he feel compelled to ride the meadows and forests that surrounded her land? Was she indeed in his blood? His mistress of three years, Rhea Francesco, thought so. It was evident by the heated exchange of words between them.

"I know now, Silver," Rhea had accused in a caustic clip, "why you roam each night across the lands of Oak Meadow plantation. It is because of that *gringa* who lives there! She occupies your thoughts each day and creeps into your dreams at night." Rhea's coal-black eyes blazed with fury and unhidden jealousy as she'd continued. "And the dreams have returned, haven't they? You're not sleeping well, you hardly eat, and the nightmare is back. Leave her to her own. They will take care of her."

"You're acting like a jealous shrew," he'd retaliated. Angry because he knew what she had accused him of was true, he felt the need to suddenly lash out for all of the pain and misery he had endured for so long. "Leave me, woman! I grow weary of your unendless prattle!"

Dark eyes filled with tears assessed the man sitting before her. "You do not wish to face the truth, *querido*. You are obsessed with her, . . . perhaps even in love with her," she'd finished somewhat chokingly. When she did not receive a response to her statement she had left him sitting under the willow and turned away. The fiery Spanish beauty tossed her flowing black hair over her shoulders as she walked straight-backed and proud, toward the home that they shared.

She had heard the confusion and desperation in his voice. He did need her, whether he realized it or not. But still she had not turned back. There was something she urgently needed to check out. She had to reach her room, the secret, hidden pouch. The answer to her terrifying suspicions was in there.

Silver Wolf sighed heavily as he rested his head back upon the tree trunk. He tried to dismiss Christina Duprea from his thoughts by surveying the land that stretched before him. Generally it never failed to revive his flagging spirits, this place he so aptly called Willow Wind. It was here the legend began. Three years ago on a blustery day, his life had taken on a purpose. Rhea had been by his side in the beginning and he knew he owed her much. Without her and the people who lived and fought and died for this cause they all believed in, there would have been no Silver Wolf, no life for him at all.

"Yes, Rhea," he acknowledged, "I do owe you, I owe you my very life as it is now, I would say. But damn it! What of her? This golden beauty who has appeared in my life also without my wishing it. Who is she? Why do I feel the need to hold her close, to protect her, to love her?" He tossed a stone he'd been toying with into the small brook that cut a path across his property. It skimmed briefly upon the clear, gurgling surface and then disappeared into the green depths of the water. "Like my very thoughts," he growled in frustration. "Here one moment and then swallowed up by muddled memories the next. All that remains for me is my cause, and my vow to restore my beloved Mississippi to dignified government once again. At no matter the cost to myself." He closed his amber-gold eyes in an attempt to shut out the pain. The face that was turned toward the warm sun bore no concealing mask; the body was not covered by a dark cloak. The man sat as he was, just a man filled with the same agonizing self-doubts as most, but with one undeniable difference that set him apart: a slashing curve of a scar that ran along the side of his face from temple to chin and marred his otherwise aristocratic features. His fingers absentmindedly traced the path of the scar and once again he tried to recall the events that surrounded that day; that particular day which remained as dark and elusive as the legendary reputation that surrounded him.

True to his word, Jason arrived back at Gardenia Place early the next day. He'd investigated their suspicions about Simon Baker and alerted the colonel by ciphered message of Baker's connection with the nightriders. He also told him that Simon used many men within the government in his quest for white supremacy. He either bought them, or threatened them with their lives, but he always managed to have them on his side. Christina Duprea was being taken under Jason's personal care for this very same reason and the colonel would see that her plantation, Oak Meadow, was put under military security.

Now, as Jason stood in the river road, his eyes scanning the distance for a sign of Christina, he began to wonder about the wisdom of taking her to live in an area that was the "sin town" of Natchez. Rose's house was an exception, being situated on the far end of the levee at the top of Silver Street; but the nightly brawls of the river men could still be seen and heard from the gallery surrounding her place. It was the boatmen's pastime, this gouging of eyes and biting off of ears, and was said to keep them strong and virile. The meanest, brawniest man on each boat fought to maintain his distinguishing title "cock of the walk" and even wore a red turkey feather in his hat to boast further of the earned name. Natchez Under the Hill lay under the affluent bluffs of the city and had rightly earned its reputation as the devil's den.

* * *

Rose's glittering game room was alive with activity when Jason and Christina entered. The swift whirring of the roulette wheels, the clink of silver coins, and the high falsetto laugh of Rose's girls fell upon Christina's ears as they entered the room.

"Right this way, Mr. Woods, suh," the doorman said, showing them into Rose's private office. "And will you be stayin' long, suh?"

"At least a couple of weeks," Jason replied, casting Christina a for-once-in-your-life-keep-your-mouth-shut look.

The young woman glared back at him, a simmering, heated stare that told him she would remain silent but that revenge would be forthcoming.

Rose observed both young people as they stood before her, one appearing apprehensive and sullen, the other a bit uncertain and nervous.

"What can I do for you, Jase, my boy?" Rose inquired as she left her comfortable chair to greet the couple. "And just who have you brought to meet me?" Her alert eyes did an imperceivable survey of Christina and she knew immediately that Jason would not have brought this young woman of obvious good breeding to her establishment for a casual visit.

"This is Christina Duprea," he introduced his companion, "of the Duprea family, and I desperately need a place for her safekeeping."

Rose nodded her head in Christina's direction. "I know who she is, Jason." She scrutinized Jase, who held his hat in fidgeting fingers. "And you are certain that this is where you will find it?"

"Yes, I am," Jason returned without hesitation.

"And you know where you are going to be staying?"

she questioned Christina straightforwardly.

"Yes." Christina met the woman's hard stare without flinching.

"Very well," Rose agreed. "Consider yourselves most welcome guests."

"Thank you," Christina replied with a smile.

"I'm glad to help out," she replied. "You can have the rooms over the casino. It's secluded, and the only entry is by the outside stairway on the side of the building. I'll post Tiny before your door when you're away, Jase. For added safety." Rose looked up when one of her giant bodyguards, summoned by a pull of her bellcord, entered the room. "Tiny will take you to your quarters, Miss Duprea. Jason, you wait up a spell and fill me in a bit more as to what is going on." Her stern face brooked no refusal and Jason obediently remained behind.

"You tell that worthless son of a bitch that if he has thoughts of winning the next election in this town then he'd better get some men together and put a stop to this highwayman!" Simon Baker sat behind the massive desk in his study, fists pounding the wooden top. He paused in his tirade just long enough to light a pipe and inhale deeply. His fingers found their way to an angry, red scratch that was fresh upon his face. He seethed in silent fury while he remembered why it was there, and who gave it to him. "I hear the Silver Wolf was on my stepcousin's land last night—burned one entire field of cotton to a crisp! You get your ass back to your office and rouse that drunken bum of a sheriff and go after this highwayman." His eyes narrowed. "Do I make myself clear?"

"How do you know for sure it was them fellas?" the bumbling deputy made the mistake of asking. "Did somebody see 'em?"

Simon snarled. "Are you doubting my word?"

"No sir, never, sir," the man hurried to reply.

Simon glared at him. "I didn't think so. Now get out of here and don't come back until you have him in hand!"

The cowering deputy bobbed his head up and down. "Right away, sir!"

As soon as the deputy departed, Simon rose from his chair and pulled a lever on the wall that was hidden behind a loose panel of wood. A secret door slid open and a dark complected man stepped forward. He was a swaggering, confident henchman who bore the same deep-rooted prejudices as his fellow nightriders. They talked of Southern ideals and fighting for the restored dignity of the aristocratic South, yet they felt no qualms about wheeling and dealing with the Yankees for monetary gain. Most would sell their souls for a profit. Simon Baker, and the man he extended his hand toward, were two such individuals.

"Did you have a good trip from Cuba?" he inquired.

The man accepted his handshake. "As good as can be expected, I suppose. I'm not exactly accustomed to travelling second-class." He sat in the chair Simon indicated.

"It won't be something you'll have to do much longer. Things are beginning to look good." Simon poured two brandies, handing one to the man. "You did a good job in Cuba. The rum is arriving at regular intervals."

The man smiled satisfactorily. "Ah, . . . good. And you found someone trustworthy to smuggle it from international waters and through New Orleans?"

"Yes, so my contacts have assured me."

"Who is the rumrunner?"

Simon resumed his seat behind his desk. "A fellow from the North, Jason Woods." At the mention of the Yankee, his companion's face turned a mottled shade of red.

He slammed the brandy snifter down upon the desk top. "Woods! For God's sake, he's a bigger con artist than you and I put together, Baker!"

"Woods knows his business," Simon replied, stung by the man's rudeness.

"That isn't even his name! It's O'Roark, and he is as clever a pirate as I've ever seen."

"How do you know this?"

"He and I have a fortune we keep passing back and forth. At the present time, O'Roark holds it all in the palm of his hand."

"And you believe this fellow is attempting to do the same with me?"

"I know he'll wipe you out without so much as blinking an eye if given the opportunity."

Simon rubbed his heavy jowls in pensive concentration. "I need him . . . at least for awhile longer. He knows every inch of the rivers and bayous. But perhaps I do have a way to control him, use him, and then discard him, thereby leaving more profit for us."

"How is that? I would be interested in reclaiming back what he took from me."

"A young lady here in Natchez appears to have captured his fancy. She has captured mine as well." Simon smiled coldly. "I think I am about to get two birds with one stone.

The man nodded. "Now you're thinking . . . Together,

we'll have it all. The money, O'Roark, . . . and the woman."

"The woman is mine, . . . only mine," Simon interjected, "and don't forget it."

"All of the aces are in your hand, Simon?"

"Yes, just where I like them. The only problem, is the Yankee has the girl over on Silver Street at Rose's. The place is like a fortress, and it's impossible for anyone to get near her." He stroked the folds of his double chin. "So, if the bee won't come to the honey?" He snapped his fingers. "Bring her news that the banker, Worthington, wishes to speak with her regarding her ledgers and the little bee will fly straight to him . . . and right into the fruit jar." He sat back, feeling triumphant.

"Shall I tell the boys to take care of anyone that gets in the way of the honey bee's flight?"

"Discreetly . . . it all has to go unnoticed. Leave no witnesses," Simon stressed. "Nary a one. But the girl is not to be killed. I want her brought to me along with the ledgers. Both are to remain intact."

"And then we go after the bastard who gave me this!" The other man indicated the arm that hung useless at his side. "He will be mine."

"I'm sure as hell glad we're on the same side, Trudeau," Simon told him. "I wouldn't want you for my enemy. Of that I'm certain."

Marcus Trudeau grasped his lifeless arm to keep it at his side as he disappeared behind the hidden panel once more.

While Christina's accommodations at Rose's were most adequate, the young woman still felt as though she

203

were confined to a jail cell. At least a dozen times a day she found herself pacing back and forth in the cozy room. It was cheery, furnished with comfortable, bright furniture: a pine cupboard, a cypress dry sink, and a Mississippi hunt board. A large, wood-burning fireplace flanked one entire wall. Both the main room and the small bedroom opened onto an upper gallery which overlooked the bawdy goings-on of Silver Street and the slowly meandering Mississippi River. Only after the sun set was she permitted to venture outside onto the gallery for a breath of cool air that came in off of the river.

"Rules! Stipulations!" she fumed to herself. "That's all he ever seems to impose upon me. And I'm expected to follow his orders without so much as one complaint." She peered out of the wide windows that overlooked the steep incline of the street that led up onto the bluff. She was not aware of the door opening until his voice called out to her. She spun around to meet his mocking, smiling face.

"See anyone in particular out there that captures your fancy?"

Chiding herself for being caught with her head craning out of the window in search of him, Christina felt her face redden to a crimson flush. "And what if I did?" she said tartly.

"I was only teasing you, darling," he said.

She flounced away from the windows to gather up a tray containing a teapot and several cups.

"Did you have the ladies up for tea?" he asked.

"They're the only company I've got," she replied testily.

"I realize that," he acknowledged. "But the next time they leave latch the door. It was unlocked when I came in. Anyone could have walked in on you."

She laughed shrilly. "I'd be ecstatic to have someone to talk to besides Dancing Janey and Alma Amour."

Jason dropped into a chair and cast her a sympathetic smile. "Come here, little cat," he said gently. "I think I may have just the solution for this cabin fever which is making you so jittery."

Christina stood watching him from out of the corner of her eyes. "What would that be?" She sat in a chair beside him and watched him closely.

"Perhaps a night under the stars, with just the two of us, will do much to improve both of our dispositions," he surprised her by answering.

Excited at the prospect of some change, Christina found herself nodding enthusiastically. She rose to her feet and strode toward the bedroom. "Just give me a few minutes to change and I'll be ready."

Jason silently observed her retreating figure and mused upon his inner thoughts. He wasn't certain of the wisdom of their venture, but Christina did need a break in her monotonous life style. Being under constant surveillance was enough to get anybody down, especially an independent young woman like Christina. He also wished to discuss her reasons for sending Tiny to speak with Worthington about picking up the results of the audit she had been awaiting. Jason had seen Worthington one too many times with Simon Baker. Just the thought of Baker knowing that Christina was nearby gave Jason plenty of reasons to worry. Damn the woman! Why couldn't she have kept a low profile like he had told her to! He smiled wryly to himself. Christina keep a low profile . . . not as long as she had any breath left in her body.

* * *

It was a wonderful evening—one that Christina would not soon forget. The night was hot and sultry, most typical for a summer evening in mid-August. Jason had hired a horse and gig for their clandestine adventure, and they'd had a late night picnic under the full moon on the bluffs overlooking the river.

Sitting with her golden hair pinned high upon her head and becomingly gowned in a lavender creation, Jason thought that he'd never seen a woman so beautiful. He reclined with his head in her lap and continued to drink in the sight of her.

"Oh, I'm so full I don't think I can eat another bite," she moaned in mock distress.

"Nor I," Jason agreed. "It was delicious."

"I must say, if Rose caters to all of her guests the way she does to us it must be easy to tell which citizens frequent her establishment."

"And how is that so?" Jason queried.

"They would have smiles on their faces and roundness to their bellies." She proceeded to pour champagne into their empty glasses, and delighted in his deep laughter.

Jason smiled up into her face, pleased that she appeared to be enjoying herself. Compulsively, he reached up to draw her lips down to his. "I haven't seen you this light-hearted before. It's a side of you I like." He kissed her ardently.

"Maybe it's the company?" she whispered.

"I would like to believe that."

"Then do," she smiled.

He took her hand in his. "Would you care to stroll along the bluffs?"

"Yes, I would love it," she replied.

He pulled her to her feet. "A stroll beneath the moon

with my favorite girl," he teased as they started forward. "What more could a man ask for."

Walking hand in hand along the tree-lined bluff, with only the soft sounds of the crickets and the persistent hooting of owls to disturb the night, Jason and Christina felt as though they were the only two people in the world. They stopped to look down upon the river below and noted the lights from the riverboats that lined the shore which twinkled up at them like so many fireflies upon the vast, dark water.

"Before the war, the port of Natchez was so busy with river traffic that you would have been blinded by the lights below," Christina exclaimed quietly. "But it's just not the same now . . . it's changed so."

"All things must change, Christina," Jason replied. "Change is necessary to promote new growth."

Christina stared at him with a sudden feeling of resentment beginning to well up inside her. "And is this what you and your government are intending to do here, Jase? Change everything and promote new growth from the devastation of our lives."

"Must we always talk in terms of my government, and your government? They're one and the same now."

"Yes," she responded peevishly. "I've heard. But I refuse to accept it."

"Whether you accept it or not, we are one country, one government, and together we certainly could better things. So why don't you try and help me and the Southern people by getting rid of your prejudice, and persuade others to do likewise."

"Accept your Union, you mean," she said, glaring at him.

"It's inevitable anyway."

"I will never do that!"

"You'll have to change your mind sooner or later."

"Just because your flag flies over our city does not mean that her people have turned their backs on everything they once believed!"

"It isn't a matter of that anymore, damn it! The war's over!" He found himself suddenly as angry as she. "There is no more Confederacy!"

"I'll always hold on to my culture and my beliefs," Christina said, her green eyes flashing.

"Is that why you ordered the results of the audit to be finished and ready for Tiny to pick up on Friday and delivered to you?" He knew he had taken her by surprise when she fell silent for a few moments.

"How did you find out about that? Did Tiny tell you? Or did you spy on me?" she taunted. "It is a talent you're good at, isn't it, Jase?"

"I only wish you trusted me more than you do," he said icily. "This personal vendetta of yours to ruin your stepcousin, Baker, is leading you straight into his arms."

"I'm not afraid of Simon Baker," she declared.

His dark brows drew together as he viewed her stubborn refusal to accept anything he said as fact. She was as difficult as an old mule. Always had to learn everything the hard way. Never took an easy path if there was a rockier, harder path to follow.

"Come on!" He took her arm once again, but this time he led her back toward the gig. "It appears as though our delightful evening together is over, and it has been most enlightening," he mocked.

"Yes, it certainly has," she responded coolly, as he assisted her into the vehicle.

She stared stonily forward without saying a word the

entire trip back to town.

Jason cursed his love of fair-haired women, especially ones with sharp claws and even sharper tongues.

In the days that were to follow, Christina felt a coolness in their relationship that had not been there before.

Jason believed one thing, she another. It was North against South all over again, even in the bedroom. Both of them knew they could not continue this way much longer, but each was too stubborn to make the first move.

So Jason was not overly surprised when one morning, following a night of tussling together, Christina stated firmly that she was going back home. She'd had enough, and security be damned!

"Very well, if you find being under the same roof with me so repulsive, then go. Only the men I've posted around your plantation stay. Yankees or no."

She observed his cold, hard expression and felt a stab of pain in her heart. Why had they come to this? What had happened? If he would only insist that she stay and never leave him, she would. Oh, God, she would!

Jason turned his face from hers and went over to look out of the opened gallery doors. He felt like a part of him was dying inside. Why didn't she come to him and put her arms around him like only she could do and tell him she was sorry, that she hadn't meant any of the things that she'd said? There was complete, heartbreaking silence for several minutes. Finally, he sighed. "I'll have Tiny take you home today."

"Good," she replied without hesitation, "the sooner the better." For a moment she thought she saw him flinch at her cold declaration. Then he moved back in the direction of the door that led to the stairway. "I'll drop by Oak Meadow later in the week."

She heard the sound of the door closing softly and she could not help the bitter, hot tears that began to stream from her eyes and down her face. "You cold-hearted bastard," she whispered. "I hate you . . . I hate you." She was listening, hoping, for the sound of his footsteps returning to tell her that he'd changed his mind. But there was only the distinct sound of retreating footsteps as he walked out of her life.

Christina tried to focus her attention on the ride to her plantation. The wooded, gently sloping country that had first surrounded them when they'd driven out of town had given way to the familiar scenery that lay all around her. She was in an almost lethargic mood as she observed the bright afternoon sun slanting across Tiny's broad back as he sat perched in the driver's seat. Upon her lap lay the findings from the bank audit. All things considered, she should feel triumphant. Instead she felt so miserable that she hadn't even taken the time to examine the records in her possession.

Tiny had told her that he was to remain at Oak Meadow as her constant companion. "Mr. Woods, ma'am," he hurried to explain, "told me he'd skin me alive if'n I didn't." The huge man smiled warmly. "But it's my pleasure, ma'am."

She had thanked him sincerely, inwardly glad that the man was with her and secretly pleased that at least Jason was still concerned for her physical welfare.

Something prompted Christina to turn her head. Her

eyes widened as she saw the sun gleam brightly on the hideous masked faces of the nightriders. A shot split the tranquil atmosphere in two, and Christina watched in disbelief as Tiny's massive bulk fell forward and beneath the hooves of the terrified horses. The buggy jolted sickenly as it careened over him. Christina clutched at the sides of the buggy to keep from experiencing the same fate as her bodyguard. She heard herself scream only once when the buggy wheel hit a deep rut in the road, the wheel bouncing in, then out, and then tearing loose all together from the frame to fly into a nearby field. The frail buggy separated from the team of charging horses and scooted briefly, almost hopefully, along on three wheels before it began to flip, end over end, and landed upside down in the center of the road.

Christina's body was thrown clear of the buggy, a fact that not only saved her life but changed the course of it as well. All of the papers from the bank were scattered by the wind.

Simon Baker's men had managed to prevent her from examining the ledgers with the altered figures, but they'd failed in their attempt to kidnap her. They could only watch from afar in seething anger as gentle, caring hands reached out to gather her up before they could get to her. In her unconscious state she did not know that she had been rescued once again by the silver-haired highwayman so obsessed with her haunting beauty.

"Simon's going to be madder than hell!" one of the nightriders yelled as he ducked his head to dodge a bullet that whizzed by him.

"Yeah, well, that's just too damn bad," his companion

called out. "I ain't sticking around here and get my ass blown off just because he's got a hankering for some Southern tail." He sawed at his mount's reins. "Let's get out of here!" A cloud of dust marked the band's passing as they disappeared into the forest.

The amber eyes that desperately sought some sign of life in Christina's were filled with relief when a soft moan escaped her lips. He cradled her against him, his lips caressing her bruised cheek.

"Do not fear, little one. I am here . . . I will watch out for you." He carried her toward his waiting horse. "You belong in my care now, for he has failed to protect you."

The Snarling Wolf

Chapter Eleven

Night had descended when Christina finally stirred from the depths of unconsciousness. For one brief moment she could not remember anything at all. But then with startling clarity it flooded back, and with a cry of fear she struggled vainly to free herself from the strong arms that held her so tight she found it difficult to breathe. She touched the tenderness in her ribs and knew that the cloth that was bound snugly around them was the main reason for her difficulty in breathing. It felt as though every bone she possessed had been broken. She was bruised and battered everywhere but she knew that she was fortunate to be alive. She was on a horse, in someone's arms, and they were moving steadily through the blackest, most threatening country that she'd ever had the misfortune to see. This man had killed Tiny and kidnapped her, and now she was completely at his mercy. The night was so black she could not see his face, but when he spoke she knew immediately in whose hands lay her fate.

"I shall take care of you from now on," the

highwayman stated. And Christina, not knowing that she owed him her life, fought him as though her very existence depended on her resistance. What was he planning to do with her, and where was he taking her? Whatever his intentions, she vowed he would never take her without a fight!

"You filthy no-good son of a stray dog! You gutless *canaille!*"

Her captor gave no sign that her hurled obscenities even penetrated his indifferent facade. She began to whimper softly, her hands covering her dirty, tear-streaked face.

Still he did not show any sign that her tears moved him in any way. His arms remained a steel band from which there was no escape.

A slow misty rain began to fall as night veiled the landscape in gray whisps of swirling fog.

Night creatures along the Natchez Trace called out to them as they galloped over the marshy bayou, on and on until finally, becoming weary from her constant struggle, she fell into a fitful sleep. Pulling her close, he wrapped a blanket about her shoulders to ward off the bone-chilling dampness.

Sometime around midnight they reached the very core of the swamp; they were so deep in the forbidding marsh that even in the light of day not one ray of sun seeped through the enclosed shroud.

When they reached the area that would be their campsite, Silver slid from the saddle with Christina's slumbering form pressed to his chest. He held her protectively for a moment, and then kissed her lightly upon the mouth. He carried her to a warm spot near the fire that had been built and laid her gently upon a blanket.

Christina would have been surprised if she would have awakened and saw the almost tender way in which he brushed her cheek with the tip of his lean fingers. As a curious afterthought, he unclenched her tight fist and stared down into her palm, puzzled as to what could be of such great importance to guard so fiercely. His amber eyes showed a flicker of surprise as a cameo locket attached to a velvet ribbon spilled out onto the blanket. With something akin to caution, he touched the necklace. His expression seemed puzzled, thoughtful. He shook his head slowly, wondering what it was about this particular girl that stirred feelings within him not experienced before.

"I know you think me heartless and cruel right now," he whispered. "But when you awaken and are less frightened, I will explain it all to you . . . then you will understand why I had to do this thing." He rose to his feet, peered intently at the locket in his hand, and shook his head slowly from side to side. Then, hunkering down beside Christina, he laid it back in her hand. He rose and stared down at her one last time; then, without so much as a backward glance, he tread lightly to the campfire where his men were waiting expectantly. He took a seat upon the ground in their midst, the man they all called the Silver Wolf, and attempted to explain to them as best he could why he had brought the beautiful girl along as his captive.

Christina's fear soon turned to anger when they

arrived at his home. "I demand to know why you have done this thing!" Furious green eyes, so hostile and cold, regarded the figure lounging against the black marble mantle of the fireplace.

"For the hundredth time, *chérie,* it was for your own well-being," the highwayman replied patiently.

"So you say."

"I do not lie."

"No, only kidnap people!" she retorted waspishly.

He clucked his tongue upon the roof of his mouth. "My, my, such ungratefulness I am faced with. Perhaps I should have just left you to the mercy of your cousin's men?"

"You are one and the same it appears."

"I hope you do not mean that," he replied in a tight voice.

"Just tell me where I am, for God's sake!" she cried heatedly.

He appeared to ignore her as he strode over to pour a glass of bourbon from a crystal decanter. Taking a long drink, he sighed and said, "You are at my home in the Natchez Trace. I have brought you here to protect you." He poured a glass of sherry for Christina and walked over to join her on the settee. She accepted his offering, feeling she was going to need it. Sipping from the glass she watched him over the rim. He appeared calm.

"What gives you the right to keep me here?" she inquired. "And how long am I to remain?" She set her glass down forcefully on a marble side table. He still wore the mask that obscured his face from her. Curiously, she wondered whether it was to protect his identity, or was it to obscure something about him that he alone could not face. He was observing her coolly. "*Monsieur,* I demand

218

an answer to at least one of my questions."

"I don't think I can answer you with what you want to hear just yet."

"You said that my stepcousin is responsible for my accident and poor Tiny's murder. Yet when I awakened, I found myself in your arms, and now I am in your home. It all is a bit hard to swallow, *monsieur*."

"It is the truth," he returned.

"And I am here strictly as your guest?"

"If that is how you wish it," he replied softly.

"Am I a guest of your bedroom . . . or house?" she said sarcastically.

He did not flinch at her tartness. "House," he replied dryly.

"Then we understand each other on one count, *monsieur*." She stared into his piercing amber eyes.

"I believe we do, *chérie*. On that, at least."

She bowed her head, suddenly weary and depressed. "Oh, lord, what a mess my life is. Will anything ever be as it once was?"

"I wish I could make it so for you," he said.

She raised her eyes to gaze into his and found that she almost believed him. But still, she did not trust him.

"You need time," he said gently. "Do not force your thoughts and emotions. Believe me, if anyone should know this it is I. Just allow me to take care of you, be my guest here for awhile. I think that you will find in a short time you will have no desire to leave."

"I have a plantation to run," she reminded him. "What of that?"

"I believe that your Yankee friend is taking care of that for you, is he not?"

Christina made a gasping sound of shock. "How did you

know of this?"

"I have my ways."

"There is a side of you that can be very dangerous," she whispered, somewhat in awe of him. "And yet you assure me that you're not."

He held up one finger in her direction. "I said *you* have nothing to fear from me. I did not make any promises concerning the others."

He stood and indicated that Christina should follow the servant who now waited in the arched doorway. "Jenny will show you to your room. Have a good rest."

Christina could only follow wearily behind the girl, her mind numb from all that she'd been through. As she ascended the stairs her eyes were unknowingly drawn to a magnificent mural on one wall of the stairway. It depicted a scene from a fox hunt. The hounds were baying at the heels of a terrified fox as it ran desperately over the countryside, fleeing, searching, looking anxiously for any means of escape.

Christina stared at the dancing flames of the firelight as she sat wrapped in a fluffy white robe, dreaming quietly and sipping a glass of white wine. The warm bath had soothed her jangled nerves, as had the maid's firm brushing of her freshly-washed hair. The maid's voice droned on in her ear as she felt herself slip into slumber, grateful that at last she could manage to forget the madness that surrounded her.

She was not certain how long she had been asleep in her chair. Vaguely she was aware of her body being lifted in strong arms, and the sensation of security before she rested her wobbly head against a firm shoulder. She was laid ever so gently on sweet-smelling sheets, sinking back into slumber as soon as her head hit the soft pillow.

"Pleasant dreams, my lovely captive. . . . Pleasant dreams."

The dominating figure stood beside the fourposter bed and gazed entranced at the beautiful girl. His golden eyes flared in the dim room. Again, he bent forward and captured the cameo locket between long fingers. Gently, so as not to disturb Christina's sleep, he opened it. But just before he was able to look upon the contents Rhea crept into the room in search of him.

"I woke and could not find you, darling. I became worried." She frowned visibly at the scene confronting her. "Why is it I find you here beside her bed? Did I not please you? Am I not still your only lover?"

He turned on her instantly, dropping the locket softly on Christina's chest. "Be quiet, Rhea! Do you want to wake her with your endless questioning of me!" He spun around to face her. "Go back to bed, in your own room. I will be needing you no longer."

Even in the darkness Silver saw her wince, a look of pain in her snapping dark eyes, before she turned on her heel and left in a quiet huff.

He only stayed for a moment longer—to pull the mosquito netting around the bed, he assured himself. His glittering eyes rested upon the silken curve of her shoulder, then upon the cameo locket that lay beckoning between her breasts. Fighting his emotions, Silver struggled within himself to keep his hands at his sides. How he longed to open that locket, to see if it was the Yankee that she carried next to her heart. But instead, he strode quietly to the door and took his leave as swiftly as he'd arrived.

Christina slept on throughout the remainder of the night. She dreamt of being pursued by a sleek silver wolf

221

with amber eyes. But just before the stalking wolf brought down his prey, another animal appeared: a huge, powerful panther with eyes as blue as the sky. He stood growling fiercely at the silver wolf, his body rushing forward to tower over Christina protectively. *How strange that I am not afraid of the snarling black beast,* she thought. She reached out her hand to caress it, and immediately the image faded. Still she slept on securely, feeling almost safe for the first time since she had been taken captive. Her blue-eyed talisman would protect her from the snarling wolf.

It was Rose herself who first broke the news to a stunned Jason.

"No trace of her was found," she finished in a hushed voice. "She appears to have vanished into thin air. Tiny's was the only body near the wreckage, poor man. He died instantly."

"How could this have happened?" Jason wondered brokenly.

"They figure it was the work of the nightriders," Rose told him. "Who else would do such a thing?"

Jason smashed his fist into the panelled wall of Rose's study, his grief overwhelming. "I should never have allowed her out of my sight. It was my damned stubborn pride . . . and now she's gone." He pressed his anguished face against the cool wood's exterior. "I'll find her, I swear I will. And when I get my hands on the bastards that did this they will know no mercy."

Christina prayed nightly for Jason to come for her. She

222

had only been at Willow Wind for a week and already it seemed like months. A persistent tapping upon the bedroom door disturbed her thoughts and drew forth a sharp response from her. "Come in! You don't have to beat the door down."

Rhea Francesco stepped across the threshold, prompting Christina to rise from the trundle bed that she'd been resting on and acknowledge the woman. "What is it, Rhea?" she inquired warily.

Ignoring Christina's question, Rhea's eyes followed the girl's movements instead. "You do not have to nap on the trundle bed unless, of course, the big bed does not meet your comforts . . . or your tastes," she finished with a cool smile.

Christina felt anger rising within her. Couldn't the Spanish witch say anything that wasn't meant to be an insult! Well, two can play at that game, she thought. "The big bed is most comfortable, however, where I come from it is considered poor manners to muss the feather mattress after the servants have smoothed it." She returned Rhea's forced smile. "Of course, good manners are something you wouldn't know about. . . .

Rhea's face grew as dark as a thundercloud; she tossed a colorful array of gowns that had been draped across her arms onto the bed. "Here, fancy lady, I was told to bring these to you."

Christina eyed her warily. "For me?"

Rhea's voice was thick with resentment. "It was not by choice. I could care less whether you have anything to wear or not. But Silver insisted that I bring you these."

"How sweet," Christina purred, "that you should allow me to wear something from your very own wardrobe."

Rhea's eyes did a critical survey of Christina's slim figure. "Anyone can see that you are taller and noticeably larger than I. So take care when squeezing into my gowns—I do not want them stretched completely out of shape."

Rhea stormed from the room and slammed the door behind her.

Christina had never known anyone who hated her so intensely, and she would not learn until later that afternoon what caused the hostility she'd just been subjected to. Christina's maid, Jenny, was only too happy to reveal the argument she'd overheard between Silver and his mistress earlier that day.

"He has insisted that you be in attendance this evening for the barbecue being given for everyone on the plantation. It is going to be a night of celebrating like nothing you have ever seen before," Jenny assured her. "You will have a wonderful time."

"And of course, Rhea does not wish for me to attend?"

Jenny nodded sadly. She liked this young woman so much more than the wild, untamed Rhea Francesco, but she feared Rhea. More than once, the Spanish woman had laid into her with a belt for not replacing the many gowns just so in the armoire that Silver had bought her. "She is afraid of losing him to you," Jenny confessed. "She believes him to be in love with you."

"Why, that's nonsense!" Christina replied.

Jenny only shrugged. "I am not so sure. He has never acted this way before, not even around Rhea."

"No wonder the woman despises me so."

"And she can be very dangerous, that one. Please be careful," Jenny warned Christina.

"Yes, I shall indeed," Christina agreed. But to herself

224

she thought of the possible advantage if what Jenny had told her was true. Could he be infatuated with her? Was this the reason he refused to allow her to leave or to contact anyone? And could she somehow use her womanly wiles to escape from this place? It was certainly worth the try. Tonight's barbecue would be the perfect place to start. With renewed vigor, she sorted through the gowns lying in a heap on the bed.

A short time later, Christina stood before the looking glass and surveyed her hastily chosen attire. She tugged upward at the snug material that covered her bosom in satin splendor.

She had chosen a simple skirt fashioned in the Spanish style, a swirling full skirt with deep ruffles that swept about her shapely legs. Christina surveyed the colorful material with a critical eye. She couldn't suppress the surge of excitement as she viewed herself dressed so uninhibitedly. She gasped. "Why is it I am always drawn to the style of life that I should not assume?" She frowned at the low cut neckline of the cream-colored peasant blouse, which gave her full breasts the appearance of spilling over the top. Her hair had been brushed until it shone like newly minted gold, secured into a sweeping cluster of waves over one side of her face, and fastened into place with a tortoise-shell comb. A crimson rose was tucked behind her exposed ear, and a drop of Jenny's perfume had been dabbed on a lace hanky and placed in her waistband. To complete the ensemble, she had accepted her maid's offering of long, golden earrings that practically reached her shoulders and glimmered sensuously each time she tossed her tawny head.

Satisfied, she fastened a pair of thin-strapped sandals upon her feet and swept from the room.

He was waiting in the hall below, dressed to look the part of the Spanish cavalier. The midnight-black jacket and tight-fitting velvet breeches contrasted perfectly with his gleaming silver hair. Upon his fingers were heavy silver rings, and ornamental spurs of the same complimented his shiny boots. Taking her cool hand, he touched her fingers lightly to his lips.

"You look as though you belong here," he stated, his topaz eyes burning intensely into hers from behind his black mask.

"Must you conceal your face from me even tonight?" she inquired with a sigh of disappointment. "I thought that being here among your own people you would not find the need to wear it."

"It must be so," he stated simply. "Let us join the others." He led her outside to a cool-shaded arbor that lay beneath a cluster of tall, breeze-ruffled trees. A servant came with a tray of goblets. Silver accepted two and handed one to Christina.

"This is very good," she said as she tasted the refreshing wine in her glass.

"I'm glad you like it. It is mixed with several fresh fruits and fermented for over a month just for our barbecues." He directed her attention to a narrow, long pit that had been dug in the ground, from which fragrant aromas and wafting spirals of smoke caused the eyes to burn and the mouth to water. "Let's go help ourselves to some of the roasted meat. I guarantee satisfaction, beyond any doubt." He guided her by the elbow toward the food tables that swayed under their heavy burden. He had eyes only for Christina and was oblivious to his mistress, who stood by a few feet from the couple.

The tranquil atmosphere was interrupted as Rhea's voice rose with simmering anger. "And you may count on my wolf's guarantee, *Señorita* Duprea. For he never boasts lightly. Do you, darling?" Rhea purred in forced sweetness. Her dark eyes flashed as she summed up the lovely, sensual creature by her man's side. This slip of a girl was going to present nothing but trouble. Rhea formed a mental picture of the couple in the faded daguerreotype that was safely hidden in her room. She wasn't certain . . . it couldn't be, damn it! The moisture stains and the elements of time had blurred the images considerably. But there were similarities . . . she could see them now as she looked over the fine bone structure of Christina Duprea.

"Rhea!" Silver's voice snapped.

"*Sí,*" she replied, bringing her thoughts back to him.

"I wish to spend some time with our guest—alone. Would you leave us please?" He gazed at her unfeelingly. "I believe you can find someone else to escort you this evening, can you not?"

The icy calmness of his tone filled her heart with bitter, seething rancor. Casting a dark, killing look Christina's way, she spun around on her heel and fled toward the house. The seed of hatred which had been planted in Rhea's mind and nurtured by Silver's cool indifference toward her sprang forth in full bloom, wrapping itself tightly about her heart and leaving only one objective in her soul: to rid herself of Christina Duprea any way she could. She observed them from the second-floor gallery off her bedroom until her eyes grew too misty with tears to see. She forced herself to remain when the dancing began, even after she recognized the slow, heartrending strains of the Spanish love song.

As Silver led Christina to the raised dance platform, he began to explain why he had chosen a Spanish theme for tonight's party.

"It is very romantic," she told him, as she smiled seductively. "You surprise me."

"The Spaniards that settled in this land in 1770 were just such people," Silver told her. "Many here tonight who support our cause are direct descendants of those Spaniards. I wished to show them my appreciation; however, I am happy that you too are pleased."

The throbbing tempo of the music became more intense, and Christina could not help herself as she became caught up in the aura that surrounded her. "It is so primitive, so uninhibited," she sighed breathlessly as she whirled about his tall form. He smiled to himself as he observed her tiny, slippered feet tapping in step with his upon the wooden floor. Colorful strands of lighted candles flickered overhead.

"It is a flamenco, *chérie*," he explained. "A dance for lovers." He heard her sharp intake of breath at his remark, barely audible over the clicking of the castanets and the strumming guitars. "Nothing else exists, Christina, but this moment, this place, and these people." His arms swayed above his head and hers, almost wrapping themselves about her as he swayed ever closer.

The candlelight illuminated their forms, casting silky, gliding shadows in the dusky night. Christina's body moved lithely of its own accord to the pulsating music. Her eyes were closed and a soft, dreamy expression had fallen across her face. In her mind was another's face, another's arms she longed to feel about her. *Where are you darling? When will you come for me?* she called silently.

Silver observed her from beneath half-closed eyes. She was so beautiful and illusive, unlike anyone he had ever seen before. He longed to be alone with her—had to be! Reaching out, he surprised Christina and himself by taking hold of her wrist and pulling her after him into the shadows of the gardens.

Rhea Francesco, watching all of this from the second-floor balcony, gripped the wrought-iron railing between her fingers and cursed the woman who had cast such a spell over her man. That's what it was—Rhea was certain of it now. She had bewitched him. Sobs rose up inside her and she fled to the solitude of her bedroom. At that moment she promised her soul to the devil if he would intercede on her behalf. She thought the devil must have responded and accepted, for at once the image of Simon Baker became vividly imprinted in her mind.

"Yes! Yes!" she sobbed wildly. "Of course he will help me. And he will be more than delighted. He is the one who has been stalking her, so let it be him that she casts her spell on. Let it be him that she takes to her bed." Flinging herself across her bed, she dug beneath the mattress and withdrew a weathered leather pouch. It was the kind used by enlisted officers during the war—a sabretache—to hold maps, papers, and personal items. This particular one was heavily stained and worn.

Rhea glanced over her shoulder before she opened it to ensure that she was alone. Then she slowly withdrew several items: a straight razor, keys, a looking glass, several maps, and at last the daguerreotype, faded by time

229

and the elements. She gazed upon the images in the picture, and then scowled as her eyes rested solely upon one figure.

"This is the damnedest thing, Jason," Big John McGurk fumed. "I've followed Baker all over the countryside and he hasn't made a wrong move yet." He paced back and forth in his office on board the *Lucky Lady*. "I'm beginning to believe he doesn't know where she is any more than we do."

Jason drew in sharply on his cheroot, his booted feet propped up on the heavy oak desk. His mood was black, his thoughts heavy.

"I'm going to follow that son of a bitch myself, Big John," he growled angrily. "And if necessary, I'll beat it out of him! I think he knows more than we do, and I intend to find out just what. I'm going crazy not knowing what happened to her." His voice almost broke, so deep was his anguish.

Big John crossed the room to answer a soft tap on the cabin door and Martinique entered. Her face too bore a troubled expression. "Thank you, John," she said, obliging him with a weak smile.

"Jase," she called, turning her attention to the dejected figure staring off into space.

"What is it, Marti?"

"I have something to tell you, and I don't quite know what to make of it."

His head shot up and his eyes sought hers. "What? Tell me, for God's sake!"

"A Spanish woman was just seen going into Simon Baker's mansion by one of our contacts. She is known to be the mistress of that rebel leader, the Silver Wolf." Hope sprang forward in her next words. "Perhaps this could mean something. Maybe our first lead has presented itself."

Jason's legs were cramped and his back ached from his two-hour vigil outside Simon's mansion. Secluded behind an outbuilding to one side of the main house, he would be certain to see this Rhea whenever she left.

"How long has she been in there now?" Big John McGurk whispered as he nudged his friend in the side.

"About fifteen minutes longer than the last time you asked me." Jason attempted to stretch his legs within the confines of the shrubbery that surrounded them.

"Are you seriously going to follow her when she leaves here?"

"Yes! Now, will you quit your flapjawin' before someone hears you? It would be a damn sight embarrassing for us to be found squatting in Baker's flower garden."

"Well, you just be careful, Jase," Big John warned. "Because I don't have the vaguest idea where to find you once you've been swallowed up in them bayous along the trace."

Jason nodded his answer and both men's attention riveted upon a small figure, wrapped in a dark, concealing cloak, that had just emerged from a back entrance of the mansion and was now making its way toward them.

"Wish me luck, Big John," Jason said as he slipped silently from his hiding place and shadowed every step the small figure took.

*　　*　　*

It was well after midnight when Jason's steps halted just outside the iron gates which marked the beginning of the illusive highwayman's sprawling acreage. He had to admit that this was a long shot. Christina may not be here at all; but something had been gnawing at his insides ever since she'd told him of the bandit's intervention with Baker on her behalf. Christina was a beautiful, desirable woman. She was also earning a good deal of money from her enterprises. Could there be a possibility that the Silver Wolf wanted payment for her safe return? Or was it her beauty alone that drew the legendary figure, Jason thought, his eyes darkening as he visualized her lovely body in the arms of another man. It was all he could do to keep from rushing forward, storming the house, and demanding that she be returned to him. She was his! No other man had a right to touch her! He would kill the bastard if he so much as laid a finger upon what belonged to him!

"I vow to reclaim what is mine," Jason whispered fiercely. "And I'll kill anyone who tries to stop me." His hand closed around the pearl-handled Bowie knife. He knew he must be patient, wait a bit until he'd gained some knowledge of the layout and the people that lived here. "I I am here, my darling," he whispered, willing her to feel his presence. "I've come for you."

Silver twisted and turned, flung his hands forward, then brought them back to cover his contorted face. He could hear screaming, awful, anguished cries. He heard his voice begging, pleading for help. And he knew without the slightest doubt where he was: it was the bottomless pit. It had claimed him again. All around him the walls were crumbling; it was impossible for him to climb out. Why was he here? From somewhere up above him came the sound of dripping water. To his horror he realized the water was slowly filling up his prison. It was rising rapidly now, reaching his knees. Terror gripped his insides as he tried calling for help. No one answered. As he looked up, straining his eyes to the edge of the pit, he caught sight of a lone form standing at the rim. Whatever it was, it just stood there watching. Not one sign of compassion could be observed on the shadowy face. Silver tried reaching up to it, begging it to save him from drowning. Just as the murky water lapped at his nostrils and began to trickle down his throat, the mysterious figure threw down a rope. It beckoned for him to grab hold. At last he was free! He would not drown. He could feel himself being pulled up to the top of the pit, smelled the fresh air as it hit his face. Opening his tightly closed eyes he gazed upon his savior. His breath caught in his throat. How could this be? It could not! The hideous vision that met him made him reel back in terror. It was totally encased in a flowing black robe. The only visible part was the face. A face that looked exactly like his. Except this one was suddenly engulfed in searing flames. The mouth opened in silent screams of anguish as the clawlike hands reached out to him. As it finally managed to touch his flesh, he heard himself begin to scream. "Let me be! Let me be!" he cried unashamedly as the flames danced their way onto his writhing body. He felt them eating away the flesh on his arms, working a path to his face. The only means of escape was the pit. To keep himself from being burned alive, he threw himself headlong down into the murky water. As always, just before he hit the bottom he awoke. His body was drenched in sweat and his fingers clawed at the scars upon his face. He heard his voice moaning.

"Oh, God the pain . . . the awful pain." He curled himself around the comforting body whose arms encircled him.

"It is all right, my darling. Rhea is here . . . will always be here for you." She stroked his trembling shoulders and held his shaking body in her arms until finally he realized he was safe. It had only been the dream.

He shook himself, as though to ward off any more demons in the night. Rising to a sitting position, he reached over to the bedside table for a cheroot. His hands still shook as he lit it. "I'm all right now, Rhea. Go back to sleep," he said as he swung his bare legs over the side of the bed and stood up. "I need some fresh air."

"Lie back down, *querido*. I will make you forget."

"My sleep is over for tonight, Rhea." He began pulling on his clothes. "I'm going to check on a few things, love. I'll be back later."

With that he was gone. And she knew exactly where he was headed. "She is not the answer," she could not help but cry out to him.

Christina did not know what it was that caused her to waken. Unconsciously, her eyelids slowly lifted and she found herself staring about the dark room. Someone was here in the room with her; she could feel them, sense their presence. Fear gripped her in its wake and she was afraid to move lest she make them aware that she was no longer sleeping. She gripped the edge of the sheet that covered her and held it beneath her chin. Straining her vision to search the corners of the room, she fairly reeled in terror when her eyes made out the form of a man sitting before the fireplace. He was facing her, staring at her, yet he never made any attempt to come closer. Summoning up her courage, she spoke.

"What is it you want of me?" The voice that answered took her by complete surprise.

"Only to be near you, *chérie*," replied her captor. "Nothing more."

A queer tightness constricted her breathing as she saw the silver-haired highwayman rise from the chair and advance toward her bed.

"Please, *monsieur*. You should not be here."

"And neither should you, he returned smoothly, but you are."

"That is hardly my doing!"

"No, . . . it is mine."

She felt the mattress sink under his weight, and flinched when he laid his hand upon her brow, caressing it gently.

"Do not be afraid, I will not harm you."

She shrank from beneath his touch. "Don't," she whimpered frightenedly.

"You have no say in the matter," he replied huskily as his hand moved to encircle her slender throat and close around it. "I could snap your neck in two, if I had a mind to," he stated, more as an afterthought than a threat.

Christina felt as though she were indeed the fox in the painting and had at last been caught by the hounds.

He felt her swallow constrictively and immediately loosened his grip. With a despondent sigh, he said. "I did not come here to molest you, *mademoiselle*. I find that I do not have a desire to love you physically." He paused. "Does that surprise you?"

"I must admit, yes, it does," she sighed with obvious relief.

"It is true."

"Then why?" she questioned, her voice but a whisper.

"To talk with you some more."

"But you already have," she reminded him. "We talked at great length in the gardens during the barbecue this evening."

"That was nothing more than polite talk."

"What is it you wish to know that I have not already told you?"

"Many things, *chérie*," he whispered. He stood and crossed the thick carpet to stand before an open window. "But most importantly, what it is about you that stirs within me feelings, strange feelings . . . as if we have known each other in another time . . ."

It reached her ears as almost a plea, and it drew her first feelings of compassion for this man, who seemed reluctant to ever let her go.

"Why do you think that I have the answers, *monsieur*. I don't really know you, and have never even set eyes upon you before. At least, I do not think I have. With that mask between us, how would I know?"

His voice was strained at his next admission. "I am not wearing it now."

Silence settled about the room, broken only by the sound of two frightened people breathing deeply, seeking to come to terms with feelings they did not understand.

"Turn around," she ordered softly, "and come over here to me."

She thought at first that he would ignore her, perhaps refuse to acknowledge he'd even heard her. But to her surprise, he turned toward her and moved across the room in the direction of the bed.

*   *   *

Rhea sat bolt upright in bed. "I can stand this no longer!" She hurled her pillow across the room. "Damn that *gringa!* He is still with her—I just know it!" She flung herself out of bed, pulled a wrapper over her nakedness, and hurried down the long hallway until she stood before Christina's door. Her hand raised of its own accord but paused in midair, did not meet the wooden surface before it. From inside came the sound of two people talking companionably together. Not able to stop herself, she placed her ear against the door and listened. And inwardly she seethed with fury as she pictured them together.

"I wish you would allow me to light a candle," Christina stated as her slim fingers skimmed feather-soft over his smooth, lean cheeks. The high, prominent cheekbones and the clean, chisled profile spoke of fine ancestry. Christina thought he must have been dashingly handsome before the accident, which had caused deep, jagged scars along one side of his face. "This is why you do not want your face revealed, isn't it?"

"Isn't it a good enough reason?" His fingers reached out to close gently around hers. He brought her hands away from his face. "I could not bear to see the pity and disgust my enemies would bestow upon me. This way I command respect, and I receive it."

They were sitting together upon the Brussels carpet that covered the floor. The only light came from the moon, which cast a pale yellow glow through the lacy curtains at the windows and upon the two people who sat cross-legged and inquisitive in its light.

"Did you receive this in the war?" she asked.

"It is possible."

"Why can you not give me a straight answer?" she inquired intensely.

"Perhaps it is because I do not have one for you," he replied hoarsely.

"I—I don't understand," she stammered, somewhat confused.

"There are many things that are best left alone, *Mademoiselle* Duprea."

Christina pulled her hands away from his. "Then why did you come here at all if you feel that way?"

The soft light filtering into the bedroom revealed the tense lines in his face. "I could no more have stayed away from you than will myself to stop breathing." He rose to his feet. "But I think it best if I leave you now."

She observed his shadowy, lean form stride toward the door. "Wait," she called out, rushing to him. "You told me earlier that you feel drawn to me," she bowed her head. "Well, . . . since we danced together and talked in the gardens, I have had similar feelings about you—almost as if I had known you before."

"I know these same emotions," he said, inhaling deeply.

"Wha—what are we going to do about them?" she posed shakily.

"I don't know, *chérie*," he whispered as his hand closed around the doorknob. "I wish I did."

"At least allow me to talk with you again," she pleaded as she watched him open the door. "Perhaps together we can dredge up old memories that will enable us to remember where we might have met."

He shook his silver mane. "It would be useless."

"Why? Why would it be useless?" she cried.

"Because," he admitted, "if the truth be told, I do not

238

have any memories of my past to recall."

Gasping, she stammered. "No—nothing?"

"Nothing," he replied.

"*Mon Dieu*," she gasped, laying her hand upon his arm.

He jerked away from her. "Do not show me pity! I could not stand to see sympathy in your eyes each time you looked at me!"

"I'm sorry," she hurriedly replied. "I could not help it."

His response reached her ears as bitter and hard. "So, now I am an object of your womanly concerns. It becomes your duty to help the poor freak discover himself, is that it?" he snapped.

"No, no," she defended. "It is for my benefit as much as yours."

His smile was jeering as he replied, "Very well. If you truly mean what you say, then we shall begin first thing in the morning. But I warn you, I am not easy to be around for very long. We will soon find out if your are indeed sincere." The door closed softly behind him before she could find her voice to reply.

Rhea tiptoed quickly back to Silver's bedroom just seconds ahead of him. Her heart seemed lodged in her throat from her near escape. Pressed flatly against the wall outside of Christina's bedroom when she had first heard his hand upon the doorknob, she'd held her breath waiting for him to step out into the hallway. But he'd lingered long enough for her to slip away unseen. And as she climbed back into the high bed, she knew that the pact she'd made with Simon Baker had been her only

239

recourse. She tried to tell herself she was not actually betraying Silver. She was helping him more than anything. Just as she'd always done, since the beginning when she had found him nearly dead floating in the Mississippi. He had needed her help unknowingly then, as now. He had to be protected from this woman who had bewitched him, this *maldita puta* who had been sent to destroy their love.

Chapter Twelve

Christina's bedroom-prison was on the second floor of the Silver Wolf's octagon-shaped mansion. It was of a most unusual design for a Southern home, and upon first viewing it in daylight, Christina had likened it to an Arabian palace complete with a small moat. There were six floors to the structure; the eight rooms on each floor all centered around a rotunda complete with windows. The sunlight filtered down through the windows and upon mirrors, which reflected bright cascading sunbeams through each level.

As she lay soaking leisurely in the copper bathtub, Christina allowed her head to rest on the tub's rim while she watched the sun beam downward and play upon the dark mahogany furniture. It was a large, comfortable bedroom, filled with soft colors that were pleasing to the eye. In addition to her canopied bed with its peach spread and the two Queen Anne chairs upholstered in muted shades of olive green, it contained a tan brocade sofa, several other wood pieces, and the round claw-footed table which now held Christina's breakfast tray. It would have been a delightful room under ordinary circumstances.

As it was, the only thing on her mind at the moment was escape. Her mixed feelings about this highwayman were beginning to confuse her.

"Time to be getting out of there, Miss Duprea. Silver himself told me to have you ready within the hour." Jenny handed Christina a towel. "He's planning on showing you about the place himself, so hurry up with you. Heaven knows, he is not a man of patience."

Christina allowed Jenny to help her with her toilet; she brushed Christina's hair a hundred strokes but left the thick mass of curls flowing freely about her face.

"Silver told me to style it this way, ma'am," she explained to Christina's questioning look. "Said to leave it like a gypsy's, that it would suit you perfectly."

Christina nodded somewhat apprehensively, but deep inside she thought it best that he had taken such an interest in her. It would make it easier for her to win his trust—and her means of escape.

Brilliant gold strands of hair blew in the breeze, whipping about her face and his as they journeyed over the many roads that wound through Willow Wind plantation. Christina reached with one hand to hold her hair in place.

"Don't, *chérie*," he urged her. "Leave it be. Let it blow freely; it suits you."

When he talked in that manner and gazed at her so intensely, she began to feel a bit guilty for plotting behind his back. But she realized that if she didn't, he might never let her go of his own accord. She wasn't certain

242

how stable his mind was. He was a strange and haunted man, and he could very well be planning to keep her here indefinitely. Her father and Jason must be frantic.

Silver halted the buggy on a slight knoll and then assisted her to the ground.

"Come with me," he told her, "I wish to show you something." Hand in hand, they walked until they stood looking out on endless rows of cotton.

"I'm truly impressed," Christina told him. "Is this all yours?"

He smiled down at her. "Mine and theirs." He pointed to groups of workers that were busy tending the fields.

"Much the same as we do it on our plantation," she responded softly, "tenant sharecroppers."

"A man works harder if it's to put food on his own table," he stated simply. But it was a phrase she'd heard many times before.

"Yes, my father believed this even before the war," she informed him.

"A smart man, your father."

"Yes," she replied, looking up at him strangely, "he is."

"I strongly feel that this is ingrained in me somehow," he revealed to her. "It is not an opinion with me, but a way of life."

He did not notice that Christina's face paled considerably, nor that her hands were trembling slightly as they returned to the buggy.

Christina was not surprised in the least to find Rhea waiting in her bedroom when she'd returned from her outing with Silver. But she was not prepared for the

243

scene that followed. She barely had time to close the door when the Spanish woman began screaming accusations at her.

"I have taken just about all I can stand of you, you *puta!* I know what you are doing, how you are making Silver believe that you enjoy being with him while you look for any opportunity to escape." Her red lips curled up at the corners when she saw the naked truth on Christina's face. "Ah, . . . I thought so," she sneered. "Silver believes you to be his friend, and all along you have been using him. He will not be happy to hear this."

Christina regarded the woman warily. "Do not make trouble where there is none, Rhea." She stood blocking the door.

Rhea laughed wildly. "Do you think a *gringa* like you can stop me from doing anything I have a mind to?" She advanced slowly toward Christina. "He will kill you for deceiving him."

Christina crossed her arms over her chest and stood her ground. "What is it you're really afraid of, Rhea? What is it about me that frightens you so?"

The Spanish woman halted her steps and gave Christina such a look of hate that it sent chills throughout her body. "You'd like to kill me you despise me so badly, wouldn't you?" Christina murmured, somewhat dazed by being face to face with someone who would take her life as casually as one would swat a fly.

"Yes!" Rhea hissed, "I would. He is mine. . . . He has been from the first day I set eyes on him. I do not intend to share him."

Christina saw the embers of madness in those dark, fathomless eyes and knew that she should prepare to defend herself. She watched helplessly as the woman withdrew a shiny, slim dagger from the inside of her boot and held it firmly in her grasp.

"Now, let's see how much my man will want you after I finish carving up your pretty face." She lunged suddenly, landing upon Christina and knocking both of them to the floor.

Instinctively, Christina threw her hands up to protect her face. The razor-sharp blade sliced across one arm, bringing forth a cry of pain and surprise from her and a satisfied grunt from Rhea. Christina could not believe this was truly happening. It was insane, absurd! But as the knife plunged downward toward her face, Christina realized that if she didn't concentrate on defending herself she would be cut to shreds. She reached out with both hands and grabbed hold of the woman's wrists, using strength that she did not know that she possessed.

"*Puta!*" Rhea cried as she desperately rolled along the floor in an attempt to free herself from Christina's viselike grip.

"I will kill you slowly. I will slit your throat!" She continued her attempt to slash at Christina's face.

Feeling her arms growing weary, Christina frantically tried to think of a way in which to gain the advantage. Shifting all of her weight to one side she rolled over, taking the spitting Rhea with her. Her long skirts wound around her legs, making it impossible for her to straddle Rhea. With both of her hands busy wrestling Rhea, and her legs bound up in her petticoats, Christina desperately sought another recourse. Swiftly, she brought her face to the startled Rhea's and doggedly clamped her teeth around the woman's delicately shaped ear.

"Ayee!" Rhea screamed in pain and outrage as she felt Christina's fangs sink into her fleshy ear lobe. "You are trying to bite off my ear!" she cried in disbelief. *"Dios! You are loco!"*

Christina held on for dear life and shook her head from side to side, looking every bit like a persistent, feisty terrier who had gotten the advantage of a vile mongrel.

The pain became so excruciating that Rhea released the knife and let it fall to the carpet. Immediately, she threaded her fingers into Christina's long hair and began pulling it by the roots. "Let me go, you cannibal!" she demanded in a voice heavy with tears and anguish. "You are going to rip it off if you don't stop! Please . . . please," Rhea began to sob.

"Christina!"

Even the sound of Silver's voice could not break through the red haze that lay before her eyes and made her continue to hold fast to the caterwauling Rhea. She was sick of everyone pushing and threatening her until she didn't know from one moment to the next whether she would be dead or alive. The taste of fresh blood was warm upon her lips and the need to destroy prevalent in her mind.

"Damn it, Christina! Let go!" Lean, hard fingers jerked upward on her golden tresses, pulling her away from the wildly sobbing Rhea and up onto her feet. Rhea immediately fled.

Christina's small fist began swinging as soon as Silver yanked her away. She feared that he would take up where his mistress had left off. Clawing, kicking, and shrieking at the top of her lungs, she gave even Silver pause.

"What the hell is going on here?" he growled in a

demanding voice, all the while throwing out defensive blocks to ward off her blows.

"I'm sick of you people, that's what!" Christina let loose with a bloodcurdling howl. "I want to be left alone! To myself! You get the hell out of my room!" She brought her tapered nails within inches of his face, then curled them into the soft fabric of his shirt. She ripped at it viciously, and before he could stop her she had torn it into so many strips.

He stared at the little savage, who now stood silent before him, in total disbelief. Her eyes lay riveted upon the flesh of his bared shoulder. She brought up her hand to cover her open mouth and swayed faintly upon her feet. Silver swept her up into his arms and carried her over to the bed.

"Are you hurt, Christina?" he asked anxiously. "Tell me, what is it? Did she manage to stab you with that damn dagger?" A quick sweep of her limp form revealed only a slight arm wound. "Why are you looking at me like that? What is it?" he fairly shouted.

Her wide green eyes looked back at him as though she had seen a ghost. Her mouth was opening and closing but no sound came forth. Her fingers found their way along his arm, upward to his shoulder, and then lay pressed against the crescent-shaped birthmark now revealed where his shirt had been torn away.

His hand closed over hers. "It is just a mark on my skin," he said as his eyes circled back from where her fingers touched him to rest upon her face. "It is nothing to get so upset about."

Wordlessly, she lowered one shoulder of her gown until her own creamy skin lay bare to his eyes. "Isn't it?"

she managed to choke out. "You bear the same birthmark as I . . . the Duprea birthmark."

There was complete, absolute silence in the room. Only the mahogany clock which chimed in the corner broke the eery, pregnant stillness.

The man sitting upon the bed had not moved, had not even blinked an eyelash. Her words kept repeating themselves over and over inside of his head.

Christina was still in shock but with certainty, a name had formed upon her lips. "Curt . . . Curt, . . . my darling brother, you are alive," she breathed incredulously. She reached shaking fingers toward the concealing mask. He pulled back from her.

"No, . . . no," he murmured, his voice heavy with suppressed emotion. "It cannot be, surely, you are mistaken."

"I'm not mistaken," Christina was quick to reply. "I should have known—in fact, deep down inside I had begun to suspect. But I did not believe anything so absurd could be possible. My brother, Curt Duprea, alive and the legendary Silver Wolf. How? Why? Please, I must know." She sat up, holding back tears and wrapped her arms about him and laid her cheek against his. "I've missed you so," she sobbed.

His hand found its way to the back of her tawny head and stroked hesitantly at first, and more assured as she continued to repeat the name "Curt" with each touch of his hand.

"Oh, God, I wish I could remember. What I would give to recall the memories I have lost. I cannot even tell you what you wish to hear."

Christina drew back from him and very slowly, so as not to break the bond of emotion that now flowed between them, reached and untied the mask from his face. "I have to know. Do not be afraid," she soothed as the knot on the black cloth was undone and the mask fell away.

He averted his eyes from hers and felt the coolness upon his entire face as he allowed this woman who claimed to be his sister to gaze upon his scarred image. He had never felt so afraid in his life. This mere slip of a girl had induced fear in him such as he'd never known before. He was a proud and fierce leader, respected by many and dreaded by his enemies. How was it that he could be reduced to this quivering mass of humanity if he did not somehow, in the deep innermost part of his brain, believe that what she told him was true. Her next words brought tears to his eyes.

"I never thought that I'd see you alive again, my brother, but you are. You sit before my eyes, in the flesh . . . Curt Duprea."

Rhea Francesco lay upon her bed with tears in her eyes. Anger, furious, overwhelming anger consumed her at the thought of the man whose life she had restored and the woman who was determined to take him from her.

"*Mi amor, mi amor.* She shall not have you." Silently she tread from the room and fled outside. She was haunted by the image of Christina standing next to the tall, handsome man in the daguerreotype that lay hidden in the Confederate sabretache. It seemed obvious to her that Christina was his old flame, left behind at the onslaught of the war.

"You shall not have him," she vowed as she tore across the lawn toward the path that led to the bluffs overlooking the river. "I would see you dead before that." She removed a mirror from her pocket.

Two men sat in a small boat, idly watching the saffron-colored water of the Mississippi go rushing swiftly by them. They had been told by their leader, Simon Baker, to come to this spot and wait for a flashing signal from the craggy bluffs along the hillside.

"As soon as you see it," Simon had informed the men, "you hightail your butts back here to me. The nightriders and I will be ready to move out." His gray eyes narrowed threateningly. "And don't blow it like you did the last time," he warned, "or I'll make you regret it. We are going to surprise that Spanish slut of Silver's. She thinks I'm going to wait along the road for her to lure Christina to me. Well, I may have agreed to that. But that's too damn bad. We're moving in on the area where the signal is seen, and I'm going to wipe them all out." He ran his forefinger across his throat. "Just like that. All except one, and by the time I get through with her, she'll be begging to join them in death."

Jason stood unseen in the waning shadows of the setting sun, observing the octagonal design of the mansion which held his love a prisoner. He had never seen anything like it. It appeared to only be half completed, as the top portion of the six-story structure contained no glass in the windows, no sign of being occupied. It looked every bit like a sheik's palace—or would, if it was ever finished. While not as opulent or elegant as others in Natchez, it still held one spellbound with thoughts of the imaginative genius that lay behind it.

Paying particular attention to the many windows on all sides, Jason formed his plan of rescue. It was now or never, he reasoned. He had been watching for his chance since his arrival, and had made a mental note of the plantation's activities. His only chance of getting Christina out of there alive was to act after nightfall. His stomach rumbled, reminding him that he hadn't eaten since arriving here yesterday. Reluctantly, he tore his eyes from the architectural wonder before him and slipped furtively back into the forest of moss-draped trees where he'd been hiding.

"Rhea will not be joining us for dinner, do not fear," Christina's new-found brother informed her as he entered the room where earlier they had rediscovered each other. He smiled warmly at the look of relief on Christina's face. "I feel somewhat consoled by having at least asked her, but inwardly I cannot say I am truly distressed by her refusal."

"I have tried to understand how she must feel," Christina said. "But I have to tell you, Curt, the woman had murder in her eyes when she attacked me."

The lean highwayman strode over to the table that had been set for two before the fireplace. "Jenny and the rest of the servants will not be used to this new name I suddenly find myself with. It would be best for a time if you refrained from calling me Curt as much as possible."

"If you wish it," she replied, disappointment heavy in

her voice. She walked over to accept the chair that he held back for her. "You do believe me, now . . . don't you?"

"How can I deny it? The picture of the two of us in your cameo locket proves what you say. It is me all right, beyond a doubt." After seating Christina, he took the chair on the opposite side of the table.

"I'm glad you decided not to wear the mask, at least tonight," she said, her eyes brimming with tears. "It is such a joy to look at you, alive, well."

He lit the two candles on the table and then proceeded to serve dinner from the covered dishes on a serving cart beside them.

"It is not easy for me. That is why I requested dinner in your room, away from prying eyes and inquisitive ears."

"We do have ourselves a problem, don't we?" Christina stated, concerned.

He looked at her glumly for a moment. *Truer words have never been spoken,* he thought. But to the beautiful woman watching him so anxiously he only replied, "Don't go worrying your pretty head about it tonight." He extended his arm across the table and laid his big hand over hers. "Tell me, sister," he urged. "Tell me of our life as you remember, of our father and mother, and how we lived before the war." And so she did for the next several hours.

All too soon their celebration dinner was over. The candles had melted down to mere tallow stubs, and Christina had told him everything there was of life as it once had been for them, and even of the tragedy of their mother's death. He took it well. But then, he did not actually have any memory of this woman she told him about.

As they sat staring into each other's eyes, wine glasses raised and touching rims, Christina and her brother were not aware of the man outside below the window, who was now climbing hand over hand up the thick vines along the side of the house.

"To my dear Christina," her brother proposed, sipping the vintage wine. "May we never be parted again."

"Yes," she agreed, her eyes shining. "Oh, yes."

Sighing, he unfolded his body from his chair and stood. "I best be going now so I can go look in on Rhea." He walked around the table and placed a kiss upon her cheek. "I only hope I can make her understand and believe that you are truly my dear sister. Pleasant dreams."

"You too," Christina called after him, blowing him a kiss.

After her brother left, Christina called to Jenny, who was in her own bedroom off of Christina's. "Don't worry about helping me undress tonight, Jenny," she informed her. "I plan to stay up awhile longer and perhaps sit out on the veranda."

Jenny replied. "Very well, miss. But do call if you should need me. I think I'll be turning in then, goodnight."

"Goodnight, Jenny." She peered around the doorjamb at the girl who was just climbing into bed. "I'll close this so I don't keep you up. Pleasant dreams."

As the moon rose higher into the sky and the peaceful sounds of the night settled in across the delta, Christina stood before the wrought-iron railing on the veranda and listened to the plaintive sounds of a guitar that came from the courtyard below. The melody was beautiful and the female voice that accompanied the passionate love song was husky and filled with emotion. She sang each note with a throaty quality that made Christina shiver with the longing and memories it evoked. A heavy, sweet ache travelled heatedly, throbbingly, to her loins. In her mind a vision took shape. It was a familiar one. A tall, broad-shouldered, lean-hipped man, whose eyes were hot with desire as they sent unspoken messages to hers. Unconsciously, Christina's hands caressed the contours of her body, visualizing his, and moaned softly her need of him.

The sensual music, the smell of jasmine in the air, and the thought of his fingers caressing her so assuredly, provoked a burning need inside of her to dance. She began swaying her lithe, young body to the feverish heat of passion revealed in the pulsating tempo. Her eyes closed, her slim arms moved gracefully above her head.

"Jesus Christ," Jason muttered in disbelief as he swung his long legs over the sill of Christina's open window and observed her alluring performance. She whirled and swayed, and moved her hips in a slow-heated motion, whose message he understood with a knowing smile. She did a pirouette into the bedroom and began to remove her clothing piece by piece.

The sight of such beauty and uninhibitedness caused all thoughts of everything but her to leave him. She swirled near, eyes dreamily closed, her face bearing a wanton look of desire that stirred him so that he almost gave way to tumbling her right then and there.

The moiré dress buttoned down the front, and with trembling fingers, Christina undid each one. The heat of her body demanded a release, an end to this heavy, breathless cloak of desire that had consumed it. Like a silken cloud, the gown floated down about her slim form

254

to lay quickly forgotten at her feet. Jason's breath caught in his throat as her palms cupped each full breast and a small gasp escaped her lips. Petticoats were kicked aside and pantalets soon followed. Unknowingly, she stood before him clad only in a thin chemise, ruffled drawers, and a pair of semisheer stockings held up at the thighs by frilly lace garters.

A blatant, heated expression met his as she heard him call softly and knew—without having to look—who would put out this fire inside her.

"Little gypsy cat," he whispered, his voice husky with desire. "You are magnificent.

"Jase, . . ." she breathed, "at last you are here." Her gold-streaked hair, tangled and flowing about her half-naked form, gave her the appearance of a wild, willing she-devil who had been put on this earth explicitly to prove how weak Jason really was.

"Yes, baby, I am here." He thought for a brief moment of the danger of being caught with her. But it was not strong enough to put a stop to this confrontation which was leading them to one final conclusion. Possession . . . complete, dominating possession of her body, her thoughts, her soul. He snaked one arm out and drew her up against his hard body. "I have come to claim what is mine . . . all of it."

Smoldering green eyes, flecked with electrifying gold, gazed unyieldingly into his. He saw the glistening sheen of sweat upon her skin, and tasted of its saltiness as he lowered his lips to her heaving breasts that swelled above the chemise.

Her fingers tangled in his dark hair. "Oh, Jase, . . ." she moaned, "I've missed you so."

"I know, sweet," he murmured, "as I have you."

"There is so much to tell you," she whispered.

"Shh. Not now, sweet." He silenced her protests with his burning kisses, his tongue filling her mouth with such warm, wet delight that she soon forgot everything but the ache to feel him even closer.

Boldly, she touched the tip of his tongue with hers as her hands wound about his neck to hold him close. Her small tongue thrusting against his drove Jason almost crazy to possess her. Imitating his suggestive motion, she caressed every inch of his mouth, intermingling two breaths, two desires, two hearts as one.

When her overpowering love and need of him became too much to bear, she drew back and whispered breathlessly. "I want to make love to you. I want to show you how much I've missed you." Her slim fingers traced a feather-light pattern of fire along his kiss-swollen lips.

"Sexy lady," he replied softly, "wild horses couldn't drag me from this spot. But do lock all the doors before you take me on love's delightful journey. I have no desire at this moment to tangle with anyone but you." His eyes followed her every movement.

"Is that so," she purred, and laughed throatily as she began to untie the ribbons on the chemise. "Well, heaven knows we mustn't make you suffer any longer." She slid the garment from her shoulders and down her arms, dropping it upon the carpet. Smiling teasingly, she advanced toward him, her firm bosom gleaming enticingly in the moonlight. When she stood before him, she gently pulled him down with her to lie upon the thick, soft rug. Lying over him, Christina offered one aroused, taut nipple as she leaned toward his mouth.

"Kiss it, darling," she urged him hoarsely.

Sucking gently, he nipped and swirled his tongue

around the stiffening peak until she moaned and writhed in his arms. Her eyes were closed, her lips parted in ecstasy as she moved one breast and then the other for him to worship. And worship them he did, until at last her body cried out for more. "Lie still, Jase," she said as she rose to stand directly over his prone body. Her fingers curled in the waistband of her frilly drawers; deliberately, and very slowly, she lowered them over her hips and down her long, stockinged legs until they lay upon the floor. Raising her arms over her head, she swayed them in an exaggerated gesture behind her. This thrust her breasts forward in all of their glorious splendor for him to adore. Her legs stradled him, the lacy garters about each silky stocking tempting his fingers to caress each band. Jason's long fingers ran up her slim calves and along the inside of her knees to rest on the curve of each thigh and gently push each limb wide, so as to allow him access to the golden triangle of curls that was to be his prize. She twisted as his fingers found her, moved inside her, and set her nerves on fire as they explored her satiny warmth.

Small, panting gasps tore from her lips as he delved into her willing flesh, withdrew, then repeated the action again. A shudder encompassed her as he increased the tempo of his action and moved to kiss the place his fingers had just explored.

Violent shudders started from deep within her as the first all-consuming throes of ecstasy began to rack her body. Sensing the burning ache now flowing through her limbs, Jason pulled her toward him.

"Undress me, sweet," he commanded huskily, "and I will love you fully."

Her eyes, glazed with desire, looked down upon him

and she fell without question to her knees. After she had divested him of his clothing, she seated herself upon his muscular thighs, and began to show him that she too could play this game of love. And when he was moaning and twisting his big body from side to side from her persuasive ministrations, she took pity upon him, and herself, and lowered her satin sheath around his rigid staff. Caught up in their love for one another and the release they so desperately sought, neither Jason nor Christina heard the footsteps down the hallway that began to draw increasingly near her door.

Jason rolled Christina onto her back and thrust his loins repeatedly against her slim hips. Heaven, for both of them, was but a heartbeat away, and they strained and drove each other's bodies in a frenzied, heated motion to obtain it.

Christina observed the intense expression on his face as he lay deeply embedded within her and realized she alone had brought him to such heights of pleasure.

Together they played each other's bodies toward that final exhilarating peak of pleasure that sent her senses reeling and his name escaping into the night upon her lips.

The very pinnacle of sublime ecstasy consumed them both, rocking their bodies in its intensity, and fusing them as lovers for all eternity. Even after their passion was sated, and they lay with legs entwined, heads resting together, they did not have any desire to separate. Though joined as man and woman, they were still somewhat in awe that anyone could love another as passionately as they both did.

"I love you, Jase," she expressed to him openly.

"I love you, little cat," he replied, surprising her by

his words.

Raising her head from his shoulder, she said. "For always, . . . right?"

"Until the end of time," he vowed, his lips once again capturing hers in a gentle, sweet declaration of his love.

It was the soft knock upon her bedroom door that at last drew them apart and sent them scurrying for their hastily discarded clothes.

"Who the hell is that?" Jason demanded in a hushed tone.

"It may be my—I mean, Silver." She halted her sentence, a vision of Jason and his mission taking shape within her thoughts. *If he is truly here as some sort of agent for the government and is attempting to stop this reign of violence and corruption, then my brother could be in jeopardy if I reveal his true identity to Jason.* She blanched at the realization. It was true! Jason had been Curt's friend before the war, but Jason was a Yankee through and through. He would not hesitate to have the notorious Silver Wolf brought to justice. It was his job. And he would see it to the finish no matter what. Her brother's only chance lay in Christina's protection.

"Quickly," she warned Jason. "You must leave here before he sees you!"

Jason stood and stared at her as if she'd lost her mind. "I'm not leaving here without you, Christina."

"You fool!" she hissed in desperation. "Don't you see I don't want to leave here yet? Now go! Go . . . before he kills you!"

Jason sprang forward and grabbed her by the wrist. "The hell you won't go!" He pulled her along behind him. "You and I are leaving here together and you can explain your feelings for this man to me later. I think,

259

madam, that you owe me that much!"

"No! No!" she protested heatedly. "Let me go, damn you!"

The sound of the door being kicked open took both of them unawares. Christina's brother Curt appeared before them, his scarred image contorted with rage by what he assumed had taken place between his sister and this man. "Let her go, you bastard! Let her go or I'll kill you!"

Jason withdrew the Bowie knife from its sheath and readied to send it flying. To his astonishment, his lady grabbed his arm and held on for dear life.

"No!" she screamed. "You can't kill him!"

"Christina!" Jason growled. "What is the meaning of all of this?"

The three stood with stunned expressions, observing each other warily. Jason eyed the highwayman keenly but then glanced away, no recognition apparent. His eyes blazed at Christina.

"I can't tell you," Christina mumbled, almost in tears. "I'm so sorry, Jase."

The silent highwayman viewed the scene before him and at last spoke. "You are my prisoner, *monsieur*. You shall remain here with us." The gun pointed at Jason would tolerate no denial, no argument.

With a face that looked as though it were set in granite, Jason stood and viewed the tawny-haired temptress before him. "I always knew never to trust a woman. I don't know why I ever thought you would be different, sweetheart." His heart was as hard as the expression on his face as he allowed himself to be led from the room and down the long hallway.

Christina collapsed upon the bed and sobbed her heart out. How would she ever straighten out all of their lives? Was it even possible?

Chapter Thirteen

Jason cursed Christina, the Silver Wolf, and the leg iron that was securely clamped around his right ankle as he lay, at last exhausted, with his head upon his arms.

Turning his attention toward Christina's bedroom, he saw her standing on the veranda, looking in his direction.

Christina's heart beat steadily; inside she felt as though she were dying. She relived the awful events of the evening over and over again in her mind. She heard once more Jason's mocking drawl as he'd been led from the room, and her brother's fury as she'd tried to explain that Jason was an old friend of them both.

"I have no friends that are Yankees," he'd snarled at her. "Do not try and tell me that I do just so that I will spare his life."

Two more stubborn, hard-headed men I have never met, she said to herself as she pondered her next move. *I just don't know what kind of man my brother is, and I don't think I can take that big of a chance with Jason's life.* It was with that thought in mind that she crept barefoot from her room and stole through the deserted rooms and foyers

261

until she reached the front door. With a sigh of relief, she turned the knob and felt it give freely. And stopped just as quickly when her brother's voice called to her.

"Christina? Just what do you think you are doing running around alone this time of night?" He stood watching her from the parlor.

With a frightened, wild look in her eyes and a cry of despair on her lips, she ran through the open door and across the yard toward the black-clad figure of the man she loved with all her heart.

Jason saw her running toward him, her nightgown blowing freely about her and her face as white as the material she wore.

"Jason! Jason, my love!" she pleaded as she drew near. "Please do not doubt my love for you, please believe in me as I did you."

His arms ached to hold her near as he watched her striving to reach him. It was then he saw the men move out of the shadows behind her, and his heart plummeted to his feet.

Simon and his nightriders had ridden into the Silver Wolf's domain as if they had every right to do so. Simon allowed his hard gray eyes to fall upon the lovely woman who had just emerged from the house and ran toward the dark shadows beyond the yard. She was calling out something, a name it seemed, as she desperately tore away from the silver-haired man running behind her.

"Leave it to my cousin to have all of the men in Natchez hot on her footsteps," Simon sneered to himself. "That son of a bitch has probably had her too, just like that damned blue-belly. Used goods is what I'm getting. But she shall pay for her alley-cat ways when she finds out what old Simon has in store for her. I'll teach her ways she never dreamed." He wiped the bloody tip of his sword on his pants leg, having used it to dispose of Willow Winds guards, and spurred his mount forward toward Christina.

Christina saw his horse bearing down upon her and willed her legs to move, to flee, for her life. But her concern for Jason made her hesitate, make certain that the hooded figure followed after her and not toward her beloved, who was helplessly shackled and defenseless. Simon did not even notice Jason in the darkness. He had eyes for only the half-naked girl fleeing across the yard. Laughter burst forth from inside him as he reached her side, grabbed her long, flowing hair and hauled her into the saddle before him.

Christina brought her hands up to pull off the mask and claw his face, but he anticipated her action this time and smashed his hand across her mouth, knocking her senseless in his arms.

The Silver Wolf gave heated chase, his gun firing from the hip at the hooded figures charging forward, swarming over his land. But there was nothing he could do to prevent Simon from taking Christina from him. He wanted to fire at the despicable bastard's bloated form, but it was too great a risk—he might hit his sister instead.

His men had been roused from their sleep by the sound of gunfire and were now running to their leader's aid. But the nightriders had accomplished what they'd set out to do. All around lay fallen comrades and burning buildings. Women were screaming as they discovered husbands and lovers lying mortally wounded in front of them.

Christina's moans mingled unheard with the sobs of

others. Already, Simon's hands were doing cruel, sadistic things to her flesh as he slipped into the swamp, taking with him the woman that at last would be his.

Jason was beside himself as he stood and watched Simon ride off with his darling Christina. His closed fists were raised and his face was furious with the look of death upon it.

"I'll come after you, Simon! I'll cut out your heart and leave you for the buzzards. I'll find you if I have to follow you to hell!" He looked up to see Silver Wolf running toward him, gun in hand. This is the end, he thought silently as the forty-four was levelled at his chest. "Go ahead!" he growled tersely. "Finish what you have wanted to do since you found her in my arms."

The face that looked back at him did so proudly. "I would not want to kill someone who had been my best friend," he said. "Even though I find his presence in my life a bit disturbing at this time." His amber-gold eyes looked directly into Jason's. It was a moment that Jason would not soon forget. Curt Duprea, literally back from the dead it seemed.

"Curt Duprea . . ." Jason uttered, stunned. He could not help but stare at the cold visage of the infamous Silver Wolf. The golden hair he remembered had been replaced by a silver mane but still, even with the scars, there was still something very memorable about him. As Jason watched his former companion closely, he felt the first stirrings of sorrow that their worlds were so far apart.

"How did it all come to this?" Jason asked as the highwayman hunkered down beside him and set him free of his shackles.

Standing, the haunted man replied grimly, "That's

easy. It was the war. Just like it destroyed our friendship, it destroyed my life and my memories."

Jason, thinking of his own misguided future since the war's end, could only nod silently.

"Come," the highwayman insisted. "I need every man I can get to go after Baker and save my sister."

"Say no more," Jason returned, already hurrying to a nearby horse. "We are united for now, Silver Wolf, to save the woman we both love. The future of the country can wait until she is once more safe. Our differences can be discussed at another time."

"I am bound to this cause until its conclusion," the highwayman stated.

Jason urged his mount onward. "There has got to be a way for all of us, Yankee and rebel. There has to be if any of us are to survive."

There was no further conversation between the two men as they urged their horses into the swamp and concentrated on picking up Simon Baker's trail.

"Drink it!" Simon forced the cup of bitter liquid to her lips and poured the foul-tasting brew down her throat. "There . . . that's a good girl, Christina." He patted her on the head like a small child who had just been rewarded for a good deed.

"What was in it?" Christina's voice could not hide the note of fear that caused it to tremble. She clutched at her throat, and then her head as everything before her began to swim hazily in circles. "Wha—what did . . . you put . . . in that?" she asked again, her voice reaching her ears as nothing more than an incoherent slur.

"It's not going to poison you, sweetums. Only make

you a bit more receptive to my plans for you." Simon chuckled, watching her stagger about drunkenly. He glanced over at one of his raiders. "You say this stuff will make her tame as a pussycat?"

Marcus Trudeau smiled and replied. "If you need something to handle your woman, Simon, I guarantee you that's it. It's a potion I picked up from one of them voodoo priestesses in the bayous. She said it was powerful good stuff for persuading a body to warm up to you." He leered at Christina's half-naked form. "If you can't handle her, how about giving me a go at it?" He laughed at his own lewd suggestion.

Simon viewed the group of nightriders now camped out in the hillside with him. "Don't any of you get any notions in your heads about taking what belongs to me. We're going to get on just fine, just the two of us. Aren't we, honey?" He pushed her ahead of him through the mouth of the cave. "Our day of misunderstandings are over."

Even in her semiconscious condition, Christina's eyes opened shockingly wide at the dark, damp cave in the hillside.

"I've had this all fixed up just for you, cuz. I hope you like it." He lit a lamp hanging from a bracket on the wall. "It's just the two of us tonight." His eyes gleamed with anticipation as he pushed her down onto a pallet on the floor. "I know it isn't quite as elegant as you are accustomed to, but for now it will have to do."

Her eyelids kept threatening to close on her, and she had to concentrate on keeping them open. She had no idea what he would do to her if she should pass out. She remembered the night when his raiders had burned her cotton and how he'd attempted to rape her in the creek

266

bed. Was that his intention now? If it was, she would fight him like before. She vowed he would not have his way. She would claw his eyes out first! "I despise you for the scum that you are," she hissed.

"You can hate me all that you want," he chortled. "Fight me, I love it when a woman struggles in my arms. Do anything your little heart desires, Christina dear. For this time . . . I shall claim my treasure. There is no one here that will come to your aid." He sat beside her and began to rub his hand up and down her leg. "To the victor belongs the spoils."

To Christina's mortification, she found that she could not move her limb from beneath his hand. Whatever he had given her to drink had sapped her strength entirely.

At first he laughed shrilly, pleased that she was going to tolerate his exploration of her enticing curves. "See how easy it is to love me, my wild, sweet rose." He reached forward and with one swift yank tore the flimsy gown from her body. His face flushed with heated desire as he crushed her down onto the pallet and fell on top of her. He wasted no further time on preliminaries. He had a burning need to possess the woman beneath him, whom he'd longed for all of his life it seemed.

Christina's instincts were to fight him. She wanted to scream, scratch, anything but just lie here and allow him to take what she swore he'd never have. But her arms and legs were like dead weights and her throat felt completely closed when she opened her mouth to scream. She knew the liquid he had forced her to drink was making her unable to move. Hot, salty tears ran down her face and fell upon the lumpy mattress. No one would ever find her shut away in here. She was doomed to be Simon's plaything; as his hands slid over her cold flesh and pushed apart her legs, she could do nothing to stop him. She allowed him to position them without complaint. It was then, when she felt certain that he would possess her, that he threw her roughly to one side and cursed unendingly. "I don't want a woman who just lies there like some paid whore waiting for it to get over with." He slapped her roughly several times. "Move, damn you! That potion was supposed to make you hot for it!" He continued to swear, rant, and curse to the heavens, but all to no avail. Simon Baker's member was as limp as a sail without any wind. "I'll have you one way or the other, and if not in body, then in spirit." Frantically, he pulled her to her feet. "We'll see how your Yankee lover feels about you when he hears that you are my wife." He gave a satisfied laugh as he wrapped her in her gown.

The cave to which Simon had taken Christina was connected by a long, dark passageway to an underground tunnel that ran beneath his mansion. At the end of this tunnel there were stairs leading up to the secret panel in Simon's study. It was through this secret door that Simon now carried Christina's inert form. His housekeeper, Lucinda, was polishing the furniture and gasped, startled by what she saw before her.

"Don't just stand there with your jaws hanging open, you stupid woman!" he snapped as he strode with his burden through the room and proceeded toward the stairs to the second floor. "Go fetch Trudeau for me, quickly. I have something for him to do. And after that, get yourself up to my room and bathe her. Make her presentable for a wedding."

"A what?" she cried out in total surprise.

"You heard right, woman! Now do as I tell you. I can't have a bride unless there's a ceremony." He cast a

268

threatening look toward the distraught housekeeper. "And Lucinda, remember to keep your mouth shut about what goes on here tonight. . . ."

"Yes, suh," she hurriedly replied, wringing her hands in distress.

"You won't get a second chance to wag that tongue, Lucinda," he further threatened for good measure. "Is my meaning clear?"

Her knees shaking with apprehension and fear, the housekeeper ran to fetch Marcus Trudeau.

Simon stretched Christina out upon the bed and stood staring down at her with malicious intent. "Tonight is the night that will change both of our lives, my lovely." He licked his full lips. "And one that will haunt you forever . . . I will make certain of it."

Lucinda returned within minutes to help Simon prepare his bride. Simon stood beside the housekeeper as she removed the tattered nightgown from the unsuspecting girl and tossed it aside. Suddenly, she remembered the note that had arrived earlier in the day. Withdrawing it from her pocket, she handed it to Simon. "This came for you. That man of yours at the Freedmen's Bureau left it."

"It's about time, Simon growled, ripping open the envelope. He fairly beamed with pleasure at the revelation inside. "I knew it. I just had a suspicion about those two, but it took a lot of digging to uncover anything."

"What two?" Lucinda inquired as she washed and perfumed the drowsy girl lying on the bed.

"It really is none of your business," Simon reprimanded her. "However, just so you'll remember how much power I wield, I'll let you in on the secret. That

Yankee my darling Christina has been sleeping with has been buying liquor from my operation and having it shipped up North to his investors. Except for one problem . . . there are no investors, Lucinda." He grinned triumphantly. "This message confirms that the liquor is going to the O'Roark warehouse in St. Louis for repossession by the Federal government. The bastard is trying to set me up so that they'll have enough on me to prosecute." He strolled confidently toward his bathing chamber to prepare for his wedding. "But after tonight he'll have so much to think about that I doubt he's going to find the time."

A wedding . . . Christina smiled as she viewed the somber people standing around her through blurry eyes. Whose wedding, though? At last, the realization seeped through the murky corners of her brain and she nodded to herself. Of course . . . her wedding day. A day of great joy. She felt his fingers, her groom's, curl about her right hand in a strong, unrelenting grip.

Oh, Jason, she giggled inwardly, *how anxious you are to claim my hand, to make me truly yours.*

She stared in confusion at the preacher. "I've . . . seen you . . . somewhere before." He was indeed a strange man of the cloth, as he wore a gun on his hip. She turned to the man at her side. "You don't look like my Jason," she mumbled in a slurred voice.

"Shh, sweetums, just be still now."

Hushed, hurried words were spoken and then a cold ring was pushed onto the third finger of her left hand. She stared down at it in wonder.

"Just get to it, will you? The man and wife part. I want

270

to make sure that she says it . . . and remembers saying it." He jerked her by the arm. "Repeat it again, Christina. Say the words like a good girl."

She burst forth in giggles at the serious expression on everyone's faces. "Oh, of course . . . I do take you for my husband."

"Is that it?" Simon questioned the clergyman.

"Suppose so," the man replied. "You may kiss your bride."

Her chin was captured in a cruel grasp and tilted upward to receive a slobbery kiss. *This is not my Jason!* she thought. Opening her eyes wide, she found Simon staring down at her. "No. No . . ." she began to protest, and struggled even more when a cold goblet was pressed to her lips and the now familiar bitter liquid poured down her throat.

"Not so much, goddamn it. I don't want her to stay like a rag doll all night," Simon complained.

"Well, better that way than a fighting hellcat," Marcus Trudeau warned. "She'll be easier for you to handle." He chuckled jeeringly.

Simon could not bring himself to admit that a fighting hellcat was just what he needed. He sighed inwardly, watching Christina go limp once again . . . just as he did.

Christina awoke to the bright sun pulsating upon her eyelids, and a feeling similar to a hangover. "I feel terrible," she moaned, looking about her strange surroundings and making note of the masculine decor. "Where in the world am I?" She sat up and tried to piece the events of last night together. "Jason . . . married me. No, it was not him. Oh, God, no!" she gasped. "Simon is

271

my husband!" She glanced down at her nakedness and the purplish marks shaped like so many fingerprints all over her breasts. "What happened last night? What did he do to me?" she whimpered, more afraid of the answer than the black, empty void that was her memory. "I can't remember. . . . I don't know what he did." Simon's voice interrupted her thoughts as he strolled into the bedroom dressed in a maroon satin robe and slippers.

"Good morning, my little turtledove. And how are you feeling today?" He winked suggestively at her as he handed her a goblet. "Here, drink this, my dear. It seems to make you feel so much better."

Christina tossed the bitter brew back in his face. "You bastard. You can kill me if you like, but I won't drink another drop of that vile stuff!" In the background she heard a disturbance on the floor below, but did not attribute it to anything out of the ordinary. In Simon's house there was much dissension among everyone, and arguing was not uncommon. But when she heard the deep voice outside the bedroom door, her heart began to hammer in her chest.

"Is this where he's keeping her?" the familiar voice demanded. "Unlock it, or I'll kick the damned thing in!" The terrified housekeeper hastily unlocked the door and then ran for her life.

Simon did not appear at all disturbed that his lovenest was being invaded by unwelcome guests. He deliberately snatched the sheet away from Christina when she tried to cover herself, wiped his face dry, and pasted a sick smile upon it. His moment had come.

The door swung open and Jason's big body filled the doorframe, his eyes doing a quick observant sweep of the room.

272

Christina noticed a wrapper at the foot of the bed and quickly put it on.

Christina would remember the look in his eyes for the rest of her life, as they slowly travelled the length of her to rest upon her face. They were filled with confusion, hurt, and lust for blood. The latter prompted him into motion, and leaping fluidly across the distance between them, he wrestled the smiling Simon Baker to the floor.

Simon screeched at the top of his lungs as he tried vainly to scramble from the angry man's reach. "She's mine! I made her so last night! I can have you arrested for breaking into my home and for attacking my wife and me without provocation."

Jason's fist, which had been poised over Simon's face, halted and the color drained completely from his face. "What . . . do you mean?"

Simon wrenched free of him and sat up on the floor. "You heard me," he sneered bravely. "She came to my home with some wild story of having escaped from that awful Silver Wolf person and begged me to give her protection in my home." Christina's wail of denial interrupted him and he glared at her. "Hush, sweetums, you know you're just overwrought from your ordeal." He turned back to Jason, who stood with a look of total disbelief on his face. "She wanted me to marry her—at once—and keep her safe. She felt I was the man who could do it."

"I don't believe you, Baker," Jason snarled.

"It's true," Simon grinned. "She said she was at the end of her rope and wanted to start things fresh between us." He shrugged. "We Southerners do stick together, suh, no matter how much we may squabble,"

Other footsteps could be heard rushing up the

stairway, and before Christina had time to recover from the shock of Simon's story, her brother burst upon the scene, the mask once again in place.

"What in the hell is going on here?" he demanded as he viewed their faces. "Will somebody please tell me, for God's sake."

Jason spoke first. "Simon claims Christina found her way to his door last night seeking refuge from her kidnapper, the Silver Wolf. And that she begged him to marry her and keep her in his protection."

"That's ridiculous," he glanced at his half-clad sister. "Isn't it?"

"I'm afraid there's more," Jason continued. "Simon claims they were married last night."

"What?"

"It's true," Simon interrupted, "and I have a paper to prove it."

"I'd like to see that paper," Christina's brother demanded.

Simon hesitated only for a moment. "It's right over here." He started toward the bureau, but Jason's anger at last exploded full force; his fist made its way forward and connected with Simon's jaw.

"I know you must have forced her. She would never have married you otherwise!" he spat.

Christina ran to Jason's side. "Oh, darling, I never did anything that he said. I never came to him. He's the leader of the nightriders who raided the Silver Wolf's land. He kept me here against my will and kept making me drink this awful-tasting liquid so that I would do everything that he told me." She buried her face into her hands.

"And did you?" Jason asked hoarsely.

"I don't know," she wailed. "There was a ceremony, but I can't remember very much about it, and nothing of what happened after. I blanked out."

Simon lay upon the floor where Jason's blow had sent him sprawling. He was rubbing his sore jaw, yet gloating inside at his victory, as evidenced by the defeated expressions of the three people before him. "I told you I would best you all!" he crowed.

"No, suh, you haven't," the housekeeper, Lucinda drawled sarcastically as she strolled into the room. "I just can't stand by and let you destroy any more lives when I know what I know."

"Shut up, Lucinda!" Simon snarled.

"No, suh, I am not going to anymore. I may have stood back last night and allowed all of them things to happen to this poor girl, but I won't any longer."

"Go on," Jason urged the woman as he cradled Christina in his arms. She was still crying brokenly, as if she could not summon up enough strength to stop.

"There is a lot to tell. But first I want to show you this." She pulled a hooded mask from within the bodice of her gown. "It's his," she pointed at Simon, who had picked himself up from the floor and was watching Lucinda through narrowed eyes. "And he was the one who attacked you last night. He's done a lot of horrible things in these parts to poor folks, too."

"I suspected as much," Jason replied.

"Yes, I know many people did, but they've just been too afraid of his influence to defy him. He has a powerful lot of friends in government positions."

"Well, we're not afraid of him!" Silver said menacingly.

"Downstairs," Lucinda continued somberly, "he has

275

invoices regarding his liquor transactions. He hasn't paid a dime of tax on any of those shipments."

"I'll make certain I have those invoices before we leave," Jason remarked. But at that moment Marcus Trudeau was removing the incriminating evidence from Simon's study; without it they would have a difficult time proving anything.

Simon Baker was beginning to sweat profusely. The veins in his neck stood out like rope he was so furious with Lucinda for exposing him. Desperately, he turned toward Jason and pointed an accusing finger his way. "You all think that I'm the clever, cunning one, don't you? Well, ask him . . . ask Agent Woods why he's really in Natchez." He quickly produced the message that he had received earlier. "He's even managed to take you in," he sneered at Silver. "Take a good look at this." He handed him the note.

All eyes turned to Jason.

"Are you here to bring us in?" the Silver Wolf calmly asked.

"I'm here to do my job, to help the government," Jason replied, meeting his burning gaze.

"The Federal government!" Simon shouted. "The Yankee government!"

"I knew it . . . I knew it," Christina moaned, her face white.

"Are you here to get us to knuckle under to your government's beliefs, Jason?" Silver persisted.

"I don't wish anyone to knuckle under. I only want what is best for everyone."

"And just what is that?" Silver inquired coldly.

"To clean up corruption in the government in Natchez and to get rid of parasites like Baker. I am here to quiet unrest in any way that I think necessary."

"I suppose that this includes putting a halt to everything that I've been striving to obtain," the highwayman snarled.

"If I find you to be a threat to our government, . . . yes."

Both men, once the best of friends, now faced each other for their moment of truth.

"And do you?"

"As the Silver Wolf, yes, . . . I do."

"That's all I wanted to know, *mon ami*." He moved to take his sister from Jason's arms.

"I won't allow you to take her from me again," Jason warned him.

"And I won't be separated from her again."

The two friends stared at each other in a silent stand-off, as Simon snuck furtively behind his housekeeper, clamped one meaty hand about her neck and then twisted it. Her anguished screams filled the room.

"Don't come near me," he warned them. "If you try and keep me here, I'll snap her neck in two." He edged toward the door, using Lucinda as his shield. "You fools!" he smirked. "You're too soft, both of you. The girl you're fighting over isn't worth it," he grinned once again cocky and self-assured. "I should know, after last night."

Helpless, lest Simon make good on his threat, the threesome could only stand and watch the leader of the nightriders slip away.

Chapter Fourteen

"Mr. Baker?" The voice startled Simon, who squinted his sun-blinded vision to distinguish his addressor. Simon had just emerged from the secret passageway, and the darkness of the cave had temporarily rendered him unable to see. With his round, little body, and his beady, peering eyes, he had the appearance of a mole emerging from his burrow.

"Yes, who is it?"

"It's Larry, sir," the nightrider answered. "You left word for me to get things assembled for you on the riverboat."

Simon pulled Lucinda along after him as he strode over to join his men. "Did you get my message?"

"Yeah, and it's all ready to go."

Simon glanced around him. "Where's Marcus?"

"He went on ahead, suh. Says not to worry, that he will meet you in New Orleans and there is nothing left in the house to connect you with anything."

"To connect Marcus is what he meant," Simon sneered. "He's protecting his own hide, not mine."

Another of Simon's men came rushing over to him, his face twisted with anxiety. "Mr. Baker, we've got trouble."

"What kind of trouble?"

"A posse's been here since early this morning. They have the place under surveillance, sir."

Simon snickered. "Oh, that. If that drunken sheriff and his deputy are trying to put on some kind of show for the town, then let's give them one. Send a few of the boys out to meet them."

The nightrider shook his head back and forth. "It's not just the sheriff . . . there's some of those government men with them. They've got us surrounded."

Simon's shrewd gaze darted about the heavily shrubbed area before coming to rest upon Lucinda. "Don't worry about a thing, I've got it all under control. You boys take the rest of the men and head out of here along the secret pass. I'll stall them off with our beauty here and meet you in New Orleans." He watched them hurry away and then he turned to the terrified Lucinda. "Okay, my dear, it's time for your performance. And if it isn't good, you're a dead woman."

John McGurk had been flabbergasted to learn that his partner had been observed riding up to Simon Baker's mansion, bold as brass, in the company of none other than the Silver Wolf. He had hurriedly gathered what men he could and set up a stake-out all around the house. He wasn't quite certain what to make of Jason's association with the notorious highwayman, but he trusted his friend enough to know it could not have been by choice. The Yankee agent and the Southern rebel were united for a definite purpose. John felt absolutely certain he knew what the common objective was—Christina Duprea.

"That young woman has been more trouble than any ten," he commented wryly.

"What did you say, John?" Martinique Summerfield questioned, her violet eyes still resting on the scenery around her. She was dressed the part of her profession. Gone were the silks and jewels, replaced with a dark linen shirt, matching pants, black knee boots, and a pistol strapped about her shapely hip.

"Oh, . . . just my thoughts voicing themselves out-loud, that's all," Big John replied, smiling reassuringly at her.

Martinique removed the gun from her holster and flicked open the chamber. Spinning it, she made a note of each bullet. "I hope I don't have to use this thing," she mused verbally. "But if I do, I want to be ready."

"That's why I brought you along, Marti. I know I can count on you to be on my side when the shooting starts. I don't share the same sentiments about the rest of these people."

Martinique glanced around her at the frightened, apprehensive faces of the sheriff and his men. "Baker sure knew who to get elected for sheriff in this town, didn't he?" She watched with disgust as the sheriff removed a flask from his pocket and drank deeply; he then passed it around to his cowering posse. This had gone on for over five hours, and John and Martinique knew help from these men would spell more trouble than purpose.

Several hundred yards away, a woman suddenly appeared from the dense growth of bushes and trees and walked forward some distance before stopping. She remained far enough away that no one could get to her without running through open ground. In a shaky voice she called out.

"I'm Mr. Baker's housekeeper," she explained. "The Silver Wolf is still inside with hostages. He sent me out here to tell you that he will kill everyone if you don't pull back and give him some space." She began to cry softly. "He . . . means it. Please, . . . he will kill all of us if you don't go."

Big John regarded her suspiciously. "Where is Baker?"

"He managed to escape last night," she called back without hesitation.

Martinique looked over at John. "Very convenient for him."

"Yes, but at this point I don't know what in the hell is going on."

"Do you believe her?"

"Have I a choice, and can I take the chance with all of their lives?"

"Then we have to fall back. Or at least make it seem as though we have." Big John signalled to the sheriff and his drunken men to disperse. One by one the posse fell back, as did John and Martinique.

Jason looked down from the gallery at the scene below. "They're moving out. All of them. It appears as though the housekeeper told them something that convinced them to do so."

The Silver Wolf sat on the edge of the bed, cradling his disheartened sister in his arms. "At least the poor woman is still alive. Simon must be using her to save his own skin. He's probably trapped, just like we are."

"Yeah, but how he's going to save that skin of his is what's bothering me," Jason said, his brow arching quizzically.

"You said you recognized two of your colleagues among the posse. I suppose that means you'll be turning me in as well?" the highwayman predicted.

"It's my duty," Jason answered in a tight voice. "I don't wish to get your sister killed—or us—if they should rush this place. It will be far better if we go out quietly."

"Even though you know there's a price on my head, dead or alive," Silver pointed out. "They'll shoot first and ask questions after. They're all too frightened of me to do otherwise."

Jason swung around to face his former friend. "I promise to help you. I'll speak to the government on your behalf. If you walk out of here right now you can save a lot of bloodshed." Jason stared at the weeping girl in Silver's arms. "I think we had best get her to a doctor."

"You're right," Silver replied, "about Christina, that is."

Christina's head snapped up and she grabbed her brother's arm. "No! Baker has a five-thousand-dollar reward for your capture. It is posted all over the area. How long do you think you can keep him alive, Jase, after he walks out before those men out there? They'll see dollar signs immediately. Why, some of them are trying to support starving families!"

"Jason and I can handle them," her brother spoke up. "And you do need medical attention." He stroked her bowed head. "I want you to get out of this without anyone realizing that you are involved with me. I want that to remain our secret."

"Don't do this," she begged him with tears in her eyes.

"I have to. If you were injured I'd never forgive myself."

Christina threw her arms around his neck. "Please don't go out there, either of you. I just know something is going on that isn't right. They'll be hiding . . . waiting."

The Silver Wolf removed her arms from around his neck. "Get dressed. I've made up my mind."

She turned her pent up fears upon Jason. "I'll never forgive you if you take him out there!" She flung herself at him and hit his face with her tiny fists. He bore it silently, grimly. "I despise you! You just want to take him from me as some sort of punishment for finding me in Simon's bed and for being his . . . wife," she choked.

Jason stared dispassionately down at her tear-stained face. He gently held her hands in his. "I admit I'm angry. I'm damned angry, as a matter of fact. But at who, I don't really know—perhaps myself more than anyone else. I've put duty before anyone and anything, and now I'm going to have to do it another time. And it's going to cost me much, let me tell you." He released her and walked toward his friend. "Are you ready?"

The highwayman nodded silently. He kissed his sister on the forehead. "Wait until the coast is clear before you come out. Jason will take care of you." He patted her cheek. "Don't worry, *chérie*. We'll be together again, I promise it."

"Oh, Curt," she sobbed brokenly. "Don't leave me! Don't leave me!" She was still calling his name as the two men's footsteps descended the stairway below. Hurriedly she dressed, ran quickly down the hall, and raced down the staircase. Fear was like a living, breathing thing inside of her as she tore open the door and ran behind her two men.

John McGurk saw them coming and rode slowly from the trees, where he'd fallen back, to assist Jason. Martinique watched, her heart in her throat. It didn't appear as if Jason was being held at gunpoint. What was going on here? Without warning, a shot tore through the dense brush and whizzed by John McGurk's head. He ducked over his horse's neck and urged the animal toward cover.

The drunken posse was too far away to notice from which direction the shot had been fired. They assumed it to be the work of the highwayman, and so they opened fire.

Jason and the Silver Wolf hit the ground, tumbling, rolling, dodging the wild volley of bullets that followed Simon Baker's carefully planned shot.

Simon Baker replaced his gun in his holster, a satisfied smile playing across his mouth. He now had the diversion necessary to escape unnoticed. Mounting his horse, and pulling Lucinda up behind him, he spurred the animal deep into the bayous, toward his riverboat and freedom.

John McGurk had no choice but to return to the posse. He cursed everything he could think of as he guided his mount into the brush and began shouting orders to the crazy, drunken men around him.

Christina crawled along the ground until she reached her brother's side.

"Goddamn, Christina!" he yelled, "I thought I told you to stay put!"

"You should know by now that she never does what

you tell her," Jason growled.

"We've got to get out of here!" Christina screamed to her brother over the deafening noise. She threw Jason a calculating glance.

"He's still in my custody," Jason warned her, interpreting her thoughts.

She pulled a small pistol that she had taken from the bureau in Simon's room. "Now he is in mine." She pointed the gun at Jason.

He stared down the barrel into her glittering cat eyes. "I'll come after you, Christina—both of you." But they were already running, fleeing for their lives and taking part of Jason's with them. He swung his gun hand around until he had brother and sister within his sights. But he knew he could not bring himself to pull the trigger. He'd sooner turn it on himself.

The foolhardy posse issued forth a volley of shots. Jason called angrily to the men in the brush to cease firing as he carefully made his way toward them.

Big John had just convinced the men to stop shooting at every moving object when Jason ran snarling into their midst. But it was too late. Forced to flee in order to save his life, the Silver Wolf had disappeared, and Jason had lost everything that meant anything to him. His thoughts were grim as he was united with his partners. The three agents realized that this was not the end of their ordeal. They would report today's fiasco to their superiors and then be off after their target again. But this time there were three. Simon Baker, the Silver Wolf, and Christina Duprea Baker.

*   *   *

Rhea Francesco had been waiting anxiously for her man's return. She knew that she was responsible for the death and destruction that surrounded her. She felt awful inside. Even if he cut out her tongue after she'd made her confession, she still was determined to do so.

"I never meant for it to come to this," she wailed, looking about at the fresh graves, the burned out buildings and homes. She dropped her head in her lap and cried brokenly.

"What is it, *muchacha?*" he said comfortingly when he found her there, amidst the rubble of the garden house crying out her soul. He laid a palm upon the back of her head and stroked it tenderly.

"I only wish I had been killed with our people," she choked out. "I deserve to die! I am so wicked, my love." She turned her tear-stained face upon the man she loved more than life itself. "I did all of this to you, . . . to them. My awful jealousy for the golden one made me betray you and everything that I believed in."

"What are you saying, *mi mujer?* This was not any of your doing."

"You don't know—it was." His gasp caused her to blurt out her tale. "I went to him, that horrible Simon Baker. I told him she was here," she sobbed. "But I did not know he was going to use me just to find out where our home was so he could do this!" She spread out her hands and then clamped them over her head. "Kill me! I deserve it for betraying you!"

He regarded her with hard, cynical eyes as he took hold of her hand and pulled her to her feet. "I don't know how you could have done this to me. You have surely killed everything I ever felt for you, Rhea. I came back to get you, to tell you and our people that I must go away for awhile. I risked my life to do so." He spat at her feet. "And what do I hear when I get back? That my woman is responsible for this knife that has been stuck in my back."

"I will make it up to you, darling. I promise you," she burst out.

"There is no way you can make up for this, Rhea."

"Y—yes," she stammered desperately. "Just like I helped you rebuild your life after the accident, so will I do now. Remember how I tended your burns and wounds and rode by your side? I am the one who saved you from the river's grasp. I can save you from these men. I know just where we can go."

"Where?" he questioned, giving her a harassed glance.

"We will go down river, to New Orleans. From there we can obtain passage out of the country. It will be easy, *querido*. Anything can be bought for a price in that city."

"Very well," he agreed. "I do owe you something. But once we're out of the country, Rhea, . . . we're through." He left to inform his sister of their destination.

Christina stood some distance away observing the catastrophe that had befallen her brother's home, Willow Wind. Even the first floor of the mansion had been burned out. The smell of smoke and charred human flesh invaded her nostrils and caused her empty stomach to heave threateningly. She fell upon her hands and knees, and cursed her stepcousin—her husband—until she had no breath left to do so. Her heart was bleeding for her lost love. She looked over at Curt, who sat with Rhea, talking earnestly. What the woman was telling him, Christina did not know. But she prayed he'd hurry. They all had to leave here at once. For she knew that Jason would not be far behind.

Christina glanced over her shoulder a dozen times the rest of that day. They rode for hours—her brother, Rhea, and herself—frantically trying to reach their destination in the swampy bayou bordering Louisiana. Rhea knew a Cajun family there, and was certain the man would take them by boat the rest of the way. Christina could only pray that they would make it to the border. Again, she turned and searched the passing trees and moss-draped oaks. *This is stupid, he'll not find us here*, she chastised herself. But deep inside, she knew that Jason was an excellent tracker, a survivor like no one she'd ever seen before. He had said, "I'll come after you, Christina—both of you," and she knew he'd meant every word. It was possible that he was behind them, beside them, or maybe waiting up ahead in ambush.

It wasn't until the second day that he finally caught up with them. The three fugitives had made it to the border of Louisiana, to the Cajun's shack in the bayous. Christina had been alone loading one of the piraguas. He had slipped like a shadow out of the dark green jungle, and before she had time to even scream a warning, he'd captured her in his arms.

"So we meet again, sweetheart," he drawled mockingly, that deceptively lazy tone of voice that she knew could be so deceiving. She choked as his big hand clamped firmly over her mouth. Frustrated tears welled up in her big green eyes.

Frantically, Christina's eyes searched the area, praying that her brother would not come and be forced to defend her. She didn't want either man killed, but she had the feeling that this was what it was coming down to.

Jason stared down at her, feelings welling up inside him that he was trying desperately not to think about. No matter how much they fought he still loved her, wanted her. "If I let you go, Christina, you've got to promise not to cry out."

She nodded her head.

"Good, I'd hate to have any more bloodshed, but I won't hesitate if you push me." He turned her loose and grinned lazily when she hissed like a little wildcat.

"Ooh! I should have shot you when I had the chance!"

"I've told you before, don't make threats unless you're prepared to back them up."

Narrowed, emerald eyes stared hard into piercing blue. "I am," she said, emphasizing each word.

He tossed his gun at her. "Then, go ahead, damn you! Shoot, if you have the guts!" You're always telling me what you'd like to do to me, but I've yet to see you make good on any of your threats. I don't think you will this time either." His voice had turned soft and silkily dangerous.

"Don't do this," she whispered, her frightened eyes watching him slowly advance toward her. She looked away from him down to the gun on the ground.

"I want to take him back alive," he stated, still coming toward her.

She bent down and wrapped her fingers around the cold handle of the gun. Picking it up, she held it in shaky hands. "I can't let you . . . now stop where you're at. . . . Please, you're frightening me."

"And what I've watched you become is frightening me," he retaliated.

Terrified of the emotions he was evoking within her, Christina pleaded. "Just go, Jase. Go back and tell them you could not find us. I don't want to hurt you."

"I can't," he replied softly. "We both know that."

"Are John and Marti with you?" she queried, her eyes searching over his shoulder.

"I lost them a ways back, when I saw that I was close to catching up with you."

"Purposely?"

"Yes."

"It's just us, then, isn't it?"

"God, how I wish that were true," he whispered huskily as he continued to talk to her to distract her from his movement.

He had just about managed to reach her when he caught sight of Rhea Francesco emerging from the cabin, her arms loaded with supplies. She began walking toward the water and stopped short when she spotted Jason.

"Damn," he swore softly.

"Silver! Silver!" Rhea screamed, her eyes, wide with fear.

"What in the hell's the matter?" the highwayman ran through the open doorway, gun in hand. He froze when he saw his sister holding the gun on the Yankee agent.

Christina did not turn around to acknowledge them. She did not move a muscle, but called over her shoulder instead. "Go, Curt! Take Rhea and get out of here. The other two agents cannot be very far behind."

"I can't leave you," Curt said.

"Yes!" she snapped at her brother. "You can, and you must! He's not going to harm me. I know him well enough to realize that." But the eyes that held Jason's penetrating stare revealed her uncertainty.

Rhea grabbed Curt's arm and urged him toward the piragua. "Do as she says, we must get away from here. What good will it do any of us if you are in jail—or worse, dead?"

Hating himself for having involved Christina in the first place, the highwayman made his painful decision. "Okay," he told his sister, "but I'll not forget you for this. I'll be back when things die down." He ran for the piragua with Rhea. "I'll be back! I love you, Christina!" He continued to call out to her until the piragua disappeared around a bend.

It was the tears blurring her vision that allowed her guard to slip for just a fraction of a second. Somehow, and before she knew what had happened, Jason had grabbed her gun and attempted to wrestle the pistol away from her. She didn't even know it had discharged until she heard the explosion, a grunt of pain, and saw his fist shoot forward with surprising speed to clip her solidly on the jaw.

She was floating . . . blackness consumed her consciousness as she fell helplessly into his waiting arms.

Chapter Fifteen

As she ascended back to consciousness, Christina's eyes flew open in startled confusion. She could see the ebbing sun, its rays less intense as it filtered through the expanse of green tree tops.

Licking her dry lips, she silently reminded herself to remain calm. The enormity of it all threatened her sanity, and she had a sudden urge to jump up and run as far from this place as her shaky legs would take her. Her ears strained to catch any sound that would tell her what she so desperately wanted to know but was too afraid to see with her eyes. Had she killed him? She could not hear any sign that he was there. Praying silently, she slowly turned her head to search the area where they had last stood, hoping above all else that he had not been killed.

Suppressing a groan, she lifted her stiff neck from the ground; her jaw felt as though she left it where she'd fallen as she forced herself to a sitting position.

"Christina?"

He wasn't dead! Her eyes focused on his tall form, the Cajun convincing him not to move by waving a shotgun in his face. Her thoughts immediately flew to her brother. Did he escape?

"Are you all right?" Jason said, his voice breaking.

"Did—did my brother get away?"

"Yes," he replied through clenched teeth, "he did." As he stood helpless, he watched her rise uncertainly to her feet. She turned her gaze upon the Cajun.

"It's all right, you can take the gun off of him and leave us. He won't harm me." She watched the man nod and then silently walk away. She shook her head to clear it, and stumbled as the earth rose up threateningly. Gingerly, she rubbed her jaw.

Jason was beside her at once, reaching out for her. "Damn you for making me do that! I've never hit a woman in my life." His voice sounded strained as his fingers reached tentatively to caress the bruise slowly forming on her jawline.

She turned scathing eyes upon him. "You can't wait to hang my brother and you're worried about hitting me! You Yankee hypocrite!"

Jason's hand fell away from her face as both physical and mental pain wracked his body.

Christina observed him skeptically. It was then she noticed the red stain upon his shirt, on his right arm. "Jase, you're hurt. Why—I've shot you!"

His eyes, those chilling shards of blue ice that caused her to shiver as they locked with hers, glittered determinedly. "I'm not going to die if that's what you're hoping."

She reached out to him. "You fool, you should have let us go.

"Don't blame this one on me," he snorted.

"Oh, hush!" she ordered. "We've got to get that

bleeding stopped before you pass out on me." She led him toward the Cajun's shack.

"You're a lousy shot, Christina," he said, allowing her to lead him to a cot in the corner of the one-room shanty.

Christina turned to the other occupants. "Do either of you know anything about doctoring?" she asked the man and his frightened wife.

"Never had cause to treat any gunshot wounds before," the Cajun replied. "But my wife here can gather some herbs and roots for you so leastways he won't get blood poisoning." The woman hurried from the shack with a basket over one arm.

"Great," Jason quipped wryly. "Now you're going to experiment on me." His eyes grew wary as she withdrew his Bowie knife from its sheath.

"That bullet has got to come out, Jase." She ran her finger along the sharp edge of the blade.

He flinched with discomfort as she began to examine the wound.

The Cajun handed her a bottle of liquor. "This will hold him still."

"Drink this, you're going to need it," she stated baldly, handing the bottle to Jason.

The liquor flowed down his throat with practiced ease. Within a short time, he was grinning lopsidedly at her.

Gently, she cut the black shirt away from his upper torso, and did her best to avoid looking at the corded muscles along his broad chest and the lean flat belly that had never failed to quicken her breath in the past. She felt his piercing gaze upon her as she leaned over him and his warm breath, scented with brandy.

"I must say, . . . I like that . . . style of clothing," he slurred comically, referring to her man's shirt and tight

295

trousers. The top button had been torn off revealing rather more than she wished of her heaving breasts.

"Lie still and be quiet. You always were too hot-blooded for your own good."

"And yours," he grinned.

"Jase," she chastised, exasperated that he hadn't passed out yet. "You've a good chance of bleeding to death if I don't get this out and cauterize the wound."

His eyes at last began to glaze over. As he closed them, she heard him whisper, "But if I am to die . . ." His words trailed off as his head rolled to the side and his eyelids closed.

Anguished sobs rose up within her as she absorbed the enormity of the situation she now found herself in. One slip, and he was dead. An artery accidently severed would ensure his death. Hand trembling, she eased the knife inside the wound.

"So, you're awake."

Jason opened his eyes to peer into Christina's. "Am I in heaven or hell?" he quipped, smiling rakishly.

"Neither." She bit back her laughter. "And I can see you haven't lost your glib tongue." She sat in a chair beside the bed.

"I'm surprised, considering the many times you threatened to remove it for me."

"Yes, well, it was indeed tempting, but I controlled the urge." She began spooning a foul-tasting liquid into his mouth.

He grimaced in disgust. "I hope like hell that this isn't a sample of your cooking!"

She sighed patiently. "If you must know, it's made

from the bark of the willow. Keeps the fever down."

"Learning a little voodoo now, are we?" he teased.

"You'd be surprised what I've learned in this bayou the past week."

Jason attempted to sit up. "Week?"

"That's how long you've been under."

"I suppose you sort of helped me along, didn't you?" he growled.

"It was for your own good," she replied shortly.

"And Curt's."

She shrugged.

"Where's the Cajun and his wife?" he said noticing that they were alone.

"They had some pelts to take down river. They said they'd be gone for a few weeks or more."

She raised a hand to brush the tousled hair from his face. Then she began to tidy up around him, careful not to allow her fingers to touch any part of his bare skin.

Like a magnet his eyes were drawn to the wide gold band that encircled her third finger.

She glanced down at her left hand, remembering that in the confusion she had not found time to even remove Simon's ring from her finger. She did so now, slipping it off and dropping it onto the earthen floor at her feet. She ground her heel over it, smiling victoriously as she felt the gold band sink into the hard dirt. She only wished it could have been Baker himself. Oh, God, how she wished.

"That doesn't really solve anything, you know. You are still his wife." Jason almost choked on the word.

"So he tells us. But the entire night was so fuzzy to me I find it impossible to think of myself as Simon Baker's wife. And I most certainly will not be known as such," she added firmly. "I am Christina Duprea."

"He claims there is a marriage certificate."

"Did any of us see it?" she quickly countered.

"You do have a point," Jason agreed. "And it is something to look into first chance that we get."

"There should be a record of it in Natchez."

"Exactly."

"And until that time?" she questioned.

He sighed heavily, running his fingers through his hair. "I wish I could readily answer that."

"Damn it, Jase!" she retorted hotly. "Do you think for one minute just because that evil man tried to come between us that we should go on letting him. We can't just turn off these feelings inside us because Simon is now claiming I am his! I will never be Simon Baker's— never!"

There was an indiscernible change in his eyes as he looked at her. His voice was thick with suppressed emotion when he spoke. "Nothing has ever been easy for us . . . since the first day I laid eyes on you when you were nothing more than a runny-nosed, feisty brat."

She thought she was imagining the slight mistiness within the fierce, longing gaze he now cast toward her. Could this hard-driven, ruthless Federal agent, long for her as much as she longed for him?

"Jase," she whispered, trying to read the answer on his anguished face. Her eyes went beyond the fierce look, the dark, concealing beard, back to when they were children, and to a love that had been written on the winds of time, never to be denied. She put her arms on either side of him.

"Christina . . ." he groaned, as her mouth descended over his.

He was just as helpless as she to deny what their virile, young bodies thirsted for. Their love, and their passion demanded to be acknowledged, to be sated. Jason clung to her as she did him.

"Hold me, darling, . . . hold me tight," Christina whispered against his soft, burning mouth. And he did, until she ceased to tremble in his arms and responded as he knew she could.

He pulled her onto the mattress next to him and she snuggled her face down into his familiar warm neck, entwining her fingers into his thick, black curls. "My heart and my love are only yours."

"I want to bury myself within you, and never let you go," he moaned. "I need you so, . . . love you so."

Their lips sought each others in a desperate, all-consuming kiss as they tried to bind themselves so closely together that even thoughts of Simon Baker could not break through.

Sighs of pleasure escaped from her throat as his strong hands tore away her shirt to cup her firm breasts, his thumb lightly flicking each nipple to an erect little peak. A low, throaty growl rumbled from his chest to die softly upon her straining breasts as he buried his face in her heavenly scent. He removed her garments, needing help to pull off her trousers, as his wound hindered the movement of one arm. When they both lay naked, he ran his hands lightly over her compliant form, kneading gently the soft flesh of her inner thighs. Then he replaced his hands with his lips, nipping incessantly there, his tongue scorching a path to her womanhood as he lapped at golden curls.

For a moment she wondered why their lives had been turned about so, and if things would ever be right for them again. But as she felt his fingers on that pulsating bud where his tongue had just lingered, she gave up such thoughts to enjoy this moment of unity, knowing it might very well be their last. She felt him spread her unresisting legs, his fingers biting into her hips, lifting them high to receive his first thrusts. Beads of sweat covered them both as they fought to hold back their passion, to enjoy their time together to the fullest.

Jason looked down into her face as he moved his hips in a slow circular motion against hers. His eyes were heavy with passion, his lips murmuring her name.

"You are mine . . . only mine, Christina," he gasped, driving into her, consuming her, conquering her. "Never could he love you the way that I do, know your body as I do." Again and again he thrust forward fiercely, then agonizingly slow, making her come to him, withdrawing, stroking, forcing her to succumb completely to her need of him. "Tell me it is true, . . . tell me."

The exquisite sensation became too much and at last she half-sobbed, "No one can ever love me as you—no one." She clung to him tightly as the flames enveloped her body and consumed her soul. He molded himself to feel every part of her pressed against him.

Burying his face against her throat, he gave himself to her fully, spiralling down into her very being and leaving his mark deep within her. Their passion spent, they lay still joined, and slept.

Later, when they woke, she removed herself from the circle of his arms and padded naked to the washstand. She dipped a clean cloth into a basin of cool water; returning to him, she sponged his body. The firm soothing motion with the wet cloth and refreshing water prompted him to stretch his lean form beneath her ministrations.

"That feels absolutely wonderful," he murmured, eyes once again closed.

Her gentle fingers worked around the bulky bandage on his shoulder, trying so hard not to cause him any more pain. She never wanted to cause him anguish again. Touching the beard on his chin, she voiced her sudden notion.

"Why don't we get rid of this now? There doesn't really seem to be any need for it. You're not exactly working undercover any longer."

He opened one eye to stare up at her. "Would you like for me to shave it off?"

"Yes," she replied eagerly. "I'm anxious to see if you still look the same as I remember."

He chuckled. "The beard doesn't hide that much." He swatted her bare rump as she knelt on the bed next to him. "All right, get the razor."

When she'd returned with the necessary toiletries, she proceeded to lather his face with soap. Very carefully she began to remove the dark stubble from his face.

Jason laughed at the serious expression she wore as she concentrated upon her task. "Does it look that bad underneath?"

"On the contrary, it appears to be rather handsome, I think." She sat back on her haunches, soap suds clinging to her chin and the tip of her pert nose, and surveyed her handiwork. "There . . . I've left you a mustache." She handed him a mirror. "Looks nice, doesn't it?"

Jason peered at the image in the mirror. It had been so long now since he'd seen his chin without hair on it that he was stunned by the contrast. "Rather naked, I would say."

"Goes with the rest of you," she teased, her eyes roaming his torso.

"Well, yours doesn't," he grinned, wiping the suds from her chin and nose with his fingertips.

She stared into his face intently. "You are a handsome devil, Jason O'Roark. Too handsome for your own good, and mine."

"Jason O'Roark, is it?"

"It goes better with your new image. Sharp, smooth, and fast."

"Fast?" he queried playfully.

"You managed to catch up with me, didn't you?" she taunted with a teasing smile.

"That I did. But I'd say you were the fast one, madam. I'm the one who caught the bullet, remember?"

Her face sobered at the remembrance. "Don't remind me of that, it was awful."

"Yes, well, it's all over now, sweetheart. And accidents do happen. That's all it was."

"One I shall never forget," she replied soberly.

Seeking to draw her thoughts elsewhere, Jason said. "You say I've been here for a week?"

"Yes, why?"

"I was wondering about Big John and Marti. I didn't think John was so rusty that I could lose him so easily."

"Don't pat yourself on the back too hard, Jase," Christina responded.

Jason carefully measured the smirk upon her pretty face, and frowned. "What aren't you telling me, minx?"

"They were here. Just left yesterday when they were

sure you were out of danger."

"Why didn't you tell me sooner?"

"You didn't exactly give me a chance."

His eyes met hers, and they both began to laugh.

He sat up on the edge of the bed, testing his strength. Christina protested immediately. "Just what do you think you're doing?"

"Where did John and Marti head to Christina?" He reached for the trousers that were neatly folded beside the bed.

"To get the *Lucky Lady*. We're to meet them in a slough just this side of Baton Rouge. He said you'd know where he meant."

Jason's vivid sapphire eyes stared back at her in the dim light. "It's the cutoff we used to shorten the trip and stay hidden when we were carrying liquor back from New Orleans."

"John also told me some other news—unpleasant news."

"What's that?"

"Simon's housekeeper, Lucinda. He killed her," she choked. "He shot her and dumped the poor woman in the brush along the river road. She—managed to crawl out onto the road and one of your people found her." She swallowed, closing her eyes for a moment before she continued. "Before she died she told him Simon had headed for New Orleans."

"The man is worse than an animal," Jason snarled.

"The courier managed to trail Big John and Marti into the bayou and caught up with them. He told them their orders were to proceed directly to that city. Big John told the man he was going to find you first because if you found out about it you'd try and get to New Orleans on your own." She smiled weakly. "He said I should tell you he couldn't let anybody else look after your worthless hide but him. He said he's the only one big enough to handle the job." She began rummaging about the room gathering up supplies. "I've already begun loading the piragua. I know there's no sense in trying to persuade you not to go."

A wry smile worked its way to Jason's lips. "And it just so happens that New Orleans is where your brother and Rhea have gone, isn't it?"

"Yes," she whispered, "and I need your help in finding him." She tucked some extra food into a knapsack. "I suppose I best tell you. I made no mention of my brother's destination to your friends, and I don't intend to."

"That doesn't surprise me in the least."

Christina's lips suddenly trembled as she looked directly into his eyes. "Don't kill him, Jase. Please?"

Jason began to pull on his trousers. "I hope I can locate him before someone else does or before he slips away from us both and leaves the country."

"Perhaps that is the only answer," she said with a solemn face. "At least there he will be free."

"Running again? And for how long?" He shook his head. "No, I don't think that your brother would be happy in Mexico. The past he is seeking is here."

"I'll not let you lock him up," she stated, her tone of voice firm. "You'll have to go through me to get him."

They stared at each other, their expressions grim.

"I don't want to see your brother spending the rest of his days behind bars, either. I know he didn't have any idea who he was when this all began, and I'm willing to make some concessions—if he is. A lot depends on Curt. We'll just have to see.

"And on Rhea." Christina shuddered just mentioning the woman's name. "She is like no one I've ever encountered before. She reminds me of a witch, the way she has my brother completely under her spell. The woman treats him like he is her creation, her possession. And I feel the only way we can break this hold she has on him is to give him back his identity, and bury the Silver Wolf forever."

A dawning awareness stole over Jason's crisp, clean features. "I think you may have just come up with the solution to our problem, and your brother's."

"How's that?"

"I can't let you go to him without me along to protect you. So together we will find him, and bury the Silver Wolf once and for all. I am bound by my honor to put an end to his activities." He grinned devilishly. "You told me once that we were a heck of a team. So together we will bring back your brother, Curt Duprea. He is the one who will emerge from the funeral of the Silver Wolf."

Christina felt hope surge up within her for the first time since their flight began. "You'll do this for us?"

"And for myself," he replied huskily. "When we leave New Orleans—if all goes as it should—it will be Curt Duprea that you take home with you." He held her gaze with his. "Agreed?"

"Yes," she said in breathless anticipation. She hugged him to her. "Thank you, darling, thank you so much."

Nothing in Christina's life had ever prepared her for the backbreaking task that she faced now. Sitting in the rear of the piragua, it was up to her to guide them safely through the treacherous currents and around hidden sand bars.

Jason, hindered by his wound, could only paddle for short periods. As he watched her guide the boat into the mouth of the cutoff where they were to meet the *Lady*, Jason turned and gave her a mock salute.

"Couldn't have done better myself," he grinned crookedly.

The piragua sailed smoothly into the calm, dense jungle growth that surrounded them on every side, and Christina took the opportunity to stretch her cramped, aching back. *"Mon Dieu*, if Mammy could only see me now." She ran slim fingers through her tossled hair. "I must be as brown as an Indian," she sighed disgustedly.

Jason chuckled at the disgruntled expression on her peachy-gold face. "I like you looking all sun-browned and healthy. Never did like a woman with skin like milktoast and a soft, flabby body to go along with it."

"Yes, well, you won't have to worry about that with this lady. I'm developing muscles to rival the best of them," she remarked dryly. Leaning back in the vessel, she propped her elbows on the sides and observed her surroundings.

The area teemed with heavenly scented flowers and rich green foliage. She inhaled the mixed fragrance and sighed at the heady sensation. Wiping her moist brow with her neckerchief, she pocketed it and reached out to run her fingers through the silvery-green Spanish moss that trailed from the tall trees down into the black water. Cabbage palmettos, their leafy fronds spread out like enormous fans, harbored squawking flocks of pink flamingos that took to flight when their haven was invaded.

Lovely pink and red flowers graced the shoreline, looking out of character snuggled around the verdurous bull alligtor who lay among them.

Jason lit a cheroot and inhaled deeply. "It shouldn't be too much farther to the cove where we're supposed to meet the *Lady*."

"I just don't know how you ever managed to get that big boat through here at all," Christina said skeptically, making note of the shallow depths in some areas.

"Our pilot, J.W., is a veteran. He could take her through here blindfolded and still miss every snag and sand bar."

Up ahead in the distance and around a sharp bend in the narrow channel, a short blast of a riverboat whistle could be heard.

Jason sat up quickly. "I'd recognize the *Lady*'s whistle anywhere."

Christina heard the long blast, followed by several shorter, higher notes. She picked up the paddle and began to direct the piragua toward the sound. Jason made a game effort to assist her.

As they rounded the turn in the twisting glade, the *Lady*'s tall, ornamental stacks could be seen through the trees. Belching forth black smoke, the sternwheeler glided cautiously through the water toward them.

"It's them all right!" Christina shouted, happy to see friendly faces.

"I see J.W. in the pilothouse," Jason remarked, his face wreathed in smiles. "Damn, if he isn't a sight for these eyes."

The calliope began playing a merry welcome "Oh, Susannah" as the piragua drew alongside the *Lady*. The big riverboat had docked in a cove which would allow her to back out into the channel upon departure. She was like a regal, gilded queen in a setting of green velvet.

"Jason! Christina!" Big John McGurk shouted from his position on the prow. He waved and hurried to greet them. Martinique stood on the promenade, a smile spread over her lovely features. She called to a steward to set two extra places for the evening meal, and to serve something extra grand, befitting a celebration.

Chapter Sixteen

New Orleans! The name itself conjured up stories and images in Christina's mind of bright, sinful gambling dens, narrow cobblestone streets and secluded courtyards.

Eagerly, she leaned forward over the guardrail, straining for her first glimpse of the busy river city. Jason explained to John and Marti that he was taking Christina to stay at Diamond Sal's on Royale Street.

"I've been acquainted with them for many years. I feel she'll be safer someplace other than a hotel."

"I think you're right," Big John agreed. "Marti and I will be over at the St. Charles. We'll get in touch with you in the morning after we've all had a chance to settle in."

"Does that meet with your approval, little cat?" Jason inquired of her.

"Whatever you say, darling," she responded demurely.

Jason could not get over the transformation in her. It had only been two weeks ago that she'd led him on a merry chase through the Louisiana bayou and then shot him with his own gun. Was this indeed that same creature? He said nothing of this, but talked of Diamond Sal's instead. "You'll like Sal and Black Jack O'Leary, her husband. He taught me every trick of the trade. He's the best when it comes to cards."

"Are all of your friends Irishmen, Jase?" she teased.

"The ones I trust," he grinned, and then laughed with his friends.

It was mid-September, a sultry warm afternoon with only a faint breeze blowing off of the river, as the *Lady* nestled her way up to the empty slot at the levee. Jason smiled down at Christina who stood by his side looking stunning in a watered silk of lemon-gold complemented by a black velvet sash about her tiny waist.

"You look excited, madam," he teased lightly, wrapping one arm around her bare shoulders.

"For two reasons," she replied, returning his bold appraisal.

"And may I venture to guess what they might be?"

"I'm certain you are already aware of one."

"Tell me, tell me anyway," he said with a serious glimmer in his eyes.

"To be completely alone with the man I love more than life itself in one of the most romantic places in the world," she whispered, kissing the tip of his smooth chin. she touched the cleft, now visible. "I forgot you even had that. It gives you such a rakish air."

Jason laughed. "And what's the other reason?"

"Because I know my brother is here somewhere. And that you are going to find him for me, and help him."

He put a finger up to her lips. "Do not talk too loudly,

310

Christina. Remember, John and Marti think we are here only to search for Simon. They have no idea that the Silver Wolf headed this way too."

"Yes, . . . Simon," she sighed, her light mood dampened, "and . . . that night."

"That night," Jason growled. "What I wouldn't give to forget it ever happened. I see you in his arms at least a hundred times a day. I wish I would have killed him when I had the chance."

Christina held him close.

"That's my girl," he praised. "Simon will be nothing but a passing memory very soon . . . I promise you." He spoke as though their task would be easy, but deep inside him, where the vision of Simon with Christina still danced across his mind, there remained considerable doubt.

They pulled apart as the riverboat came to a standstill next to the rows of other vessels nestled along the levee. Huge, ocean-going ships lay out in the harbor: sternwheelers, sidewheelers, flatboats and brigs, all floating side by side forming an endless chain of deck that a man could walk upon without his feet ever once touching water.

Jason conferred with Big John as they made their way down the gangplank toward a waiting carriage. When the foursome was seated comfortably within and the carriage rumbled over the cobblestone street, Christina grabbed Jason's arm.

"I've never seen anything quite like it, it's marvelous!" Her tawny head swivelled from side to side at the passing sights. "Look, Marti! That black man over there is dancing in the street and people are throwing coins at him."

Martinique smiled. "He's a common sight here, dear." She motioned for the young woman to look in the direction of a magnificent, towering cathedral. "Over there is the St. Louis Cathedral, and the square facing us, The Place d'Armes, with its beautiful gardens."

Christina's eyes shown brightly at each new sight she encountered. "And that narrow street there. Is that not where Jean Lafitté, the famous privateer and buccaneer, was said to have operated his clearinghouse for contraband?"

"That's the place all right," Jason answered her, bemused. "I think my lady has a hidden penchant for rogues and pirates."

"I'm here with you, aren't I?" she smiled sweetly.

"I have a feeling," he drawled, "I will be fighting duels in St. Anthony's Garden when these romantic citizens get but just one view of your loveliness."

She gasped, remembering stories of the famous duelling ground which once rang with the clashing swords of hot-blooded Creoles.

"No, dear," Martinique was quick to intervene. "He's just jesting with you. It's a bit more civilized than it was."

"That's comforting to know." Jason heard her reply, and noted with amusement the slight disappointment evident in her voice.

As the carriage rumbled to a stop in front of the impressive St. Charles Hotel, Jason and Christina bid their friends farewell for the day; they continued through the busy French Quarter to their destination at Royale and Bourbon Streets. The excitement here was contagious as people rushed to and fro, while others reclined at sidewalk cafes enjoying mint juleps and steaming cups of café au lait. And behind high-bricked walls still others enjoyed sitting under the fragrant shade of an orange tree next to a cool, splashing fountain while they drank their repast.

They pulled up before an enormous brick building with two massive front doors of rich, polished oak. "This is Diamond Sal's gambling emporium," Jason said, helping her from the carriage onto the banquette.

"You certainly didn't exaggerate." Christina's eyes made note of the gleaming brass lanterns hanging on either side of the entrance. Enormous brass pots, boasting green, leafy palms sat under each lamp. Somewhat hesitantly she followed him inside.

"Anybody in here awake yet?" he yelled.

A tall, willowy woman made her way down the grand staircase in the center of the room. Christina stared up at her in awe. She was gowned in a black satin sheathlike creation; one leg was revealed by a slash in the gown, which was hidden by tiny ruffles until the wearer stepped forward and exposed it. She was by far a woman of quiet sophistication and allure. Pale gold curls spilled about her delicate diamond-studded ears, and diamonds winked from her throat and fingers as she stepped forward to greet them.

"Yes, may I help you, *monsieur?*" she presented her hand to Jason.

"I think you may at that, madam," Jason replied with a twinkle in his sapphire eyes as he bent forward to place his lips upon her hand.

"How may I be of service, *monsieur?*"

Jason stood straight and smiled back at her. "Sal . . . don't tell me it's been so many years that you don't remember your most ardent admirer in all of Louisiana." He feigned a crushed look.

The woman, who Christina realized was Diamond Sal herself, stared in amazement.

"Jason O'Roark, is that truly you, you scoundrel?"

"None other," he replied, gathering her into his arms, "It's been too long, my pretty lady, so I thought I'd stop in and pay you and Black Jack a visit." He set her aside and gazed about him. "Where is the best damned card player I've ever run up against, anyway?"

Sal nodded her head in the direction of the staircase. "He's up in his office going over the books. You know Black Jack; everything has to be in order and running properly before he sets himself down to deal tonight." She turned her inquisitive gaze upon Christina. "Jason," she admonished, "are you going to keep this enchanting creature's identity a secret, or are you going to tell me her name?"

Before Jason could respond, Christina replied eagerly. "Christina Duprea, *Madame*. I am most happy to make your acquaintance."

"And I yours," Sal smiled. "I take it by the luggage your driver left over there that you are planning to stay with us a spell?"

Jason nodded. "For as long as you'll have us."

"Good!" she beamed. "I'll have one of the girls show you to your rooms and then we can surprise that wily husband of mine."

Jason and Christina followed Sal as she led them up the oak stairway to the second floor.

Christina's neck craned upward. She gasped in appreciative wonder. It looked the size of a Roman coliseum with three stories boasting balconies encircling the circumference of each floor.

"I especially designed it myself," Sal explained

314

proudly. "This way my customers can roam about on each level and sit along the railings observing the activity in the main saloon below." She nodded at several brawny men standing about. "These are my guards. I post them about each floor at various strategic points to watch the goings on. From up here they can spot the first sign of trouble and stop it."

When they reached the third tier, Christina glanced down to the main level at the stage draped in red velvet hangings. "Do you also have entertainment?" she inquired.

"Yes, we do," Sal replied thoughtfully.

"Oh, won't that be nice!" Christina turned to Jason.

Jason's eyes held an unreadable expression. He took Christina's hand. "Let's go freshen up a bit and then we can have a bite to eat. I guarantee you Sal's cuisine is outstanding."

"Here comes one of the girls to show you to your rooms," Sal said. "I hope they will meet with your approval."

"I'm sure they will be just fine." Christina followed behind the maid, and then turned back when she discovered Jason was not in step with her. His head was bent next to Sal's and they appeared to be talking in earnest. Looking up, he caught Christina's eyes upon them and waved with a smile.

"I'll be there in a moment."

Soon after, he caught up with her and escorted her to her suite of rooms. Swinging open the door, he kissed her on the tip of her nose. "You have a rest, sweetheart. I'll be by in a little while to take you to dinner." With that, he left her to enter his own suite which was next to hers.

Closing her door, Christina leaned against it and

315

sighed. She was disappointed that they wouldn't be sharing a room. Was it just to protect her reputation? Or was there an ulterior motive behind their separate sleeping arrangements This was his town, these were his friends, and it was here that many memories for him remained. Christina could only hope that it remained just that . . . memories.

"I've never met anyone like you before, my love. You are all fire and passion, and breathless uncertainty, but still you are mine. . . . And I do not intend to lose you, ever again."

John and Martinique had been thoughtful enough to lend trunks of clothing to both Jason and Christina. Jason was forever grateful as he dressed for the evening and his meeting with Black Jack O'Leary. He had chosen a dark blue jacket, matching trousers, and a snow white linen shirt. He tucked a pistol in the pocket of his jacket.

As he stepped out the door into the hall, he heard a clear, sweet voice singing a song that was familiar— painfully familiar.

"Teressa St. Clair," he whispered, stunned. Rushing down the hall to the railing, he clutched the wood as his eyes rested upon her exotic-looking face three stories below.

She was as lovely as ever. Lost in song, head thrown back, eyes closed, arms stretching wide as if to draw energy from some unknown source, she was rehearsing for this evening's performance, a performance that she had promised to Diamond Sal many years ago before she was famous. She had come back to the place where it had all started for her. That was like Teressa—she never forgot anyone who had helped her along the way. Sal's would be overflowing this evening, even though Teressa's performance was by invitation only. Sal would turn a huge profit from the elite group who eagerly paid for the privilege of attending the famous singer's return performance in New Orleans, three years after taking the world by storm.

Jason's eyes were glued to her. He was lost in memories of another time when Teressa St. Clair had been everything to him.

"She was always an exciting woman," he breathed.

"Yes, she still is," said a soft voice behind him. He spun around.

"Christina," he started. "I didn't hear you come up behind me."

"Obviously, your thoughts were elsewhere."

Their gazes locked. Jason tried to hold his eyes to hers, to assure her that his love for her was all that mattered to him. But Christina looked away, still stung by the words she had heard him whisper about another. "Is it she? The one Marti told me about—Teressa St. Clair?"

Jason reached out to her but she pulled away. "Yes, it is, . . . if that matters anymore. You are all the woman that I want now, Christina, the only one I've ever truly loved." His deep gaze bore into her. "You are all that matters to me, not Teressa." He reached out once more and placed his hands upon her shoulders. "She is simply an old memory and always will be. I was just surprised that she was here, that's all."

Christina allowed him to pull her close then. With her face pressed against his hard chest and his arms locked securely around her, she felt at that moment that she could take on the world.

"We don't have to stay here." He turned her face up to meet his. "We can stay on board the *Lady*."

Christina shook her head. "No, we're here now and I'm not about to turn tail and run. Running from old memories doesn't work, particularly those kind."

His hand trailed lightly across her perfect features. "How about the two of us going on downstairs and meeting some old memories head on?"

She tucked her hand within his and together they strolled toward the stairs.

Black Jack O'Leary, a jolly good-natured fellow who looked upon Jason as the son he'd never had, jumped up from his seat at the card table upon spotting the young man entering the room. He rushed forward to grab Jason in a crushing bear hug, the mug of beer he held in his hand threatening to slosh over the sides. Christina observed the reunion with a smile.

"Jason, me boy, what did this old Irishman ever do to you to keep you from visiting me and my Sal?" He stood back and observed the young man from beneath bushy brows. "Tell me the truth now, lad, was it because I skunked ye so bad in cards that last night you were here?" He paused thoughtfully. "'Tis, isn't it, lad?"

"Whoa, . . . whoa, Black Jack," Jason laughed. "First things first." He drew Christina to his side. "There is someone here I'd like you to meet before we get into flapjawin' about the old days." He smiled at the appreciative glint in the older man's eye when he looked upon Christina. "Miss Duprea, may I introduce you to Black Jack O'Leary."

"No need to be answering me earlier question, laddie. I

can see with me own eyes why 'tis you've been away for three years. She is the prettiest colleen I have ever seen, except for me Sal, of course."

"I couldn't agree with you more," Teressa St. Clair spoke up as she made her way into their midst.

Christina had watched her approach. She walked with an assured, sensual grace that made most women despise her immediately. But Christina was determined to not let jealousy cloud her feelings for the woman. She smiled warmly at her.

"Why, thank you, how nice of you."

Jason stood between the two women, his new love and his old, and attempted to perform introductions calmly. "Teressa St. Clair, may I introduce Christina Duprea."

The two women surveyed each other critically from head to toe.

Dark, almond-shaped eyes gazed at jade-green, admiring the tawny-streaked curls entwined with black velvet ribbon, and the slim figure gowned in a green and black striped silk. For her part, Christina descreetly observed that Teressa's long brown hair brushed her hips, and her white satin gown clung revealingly to ripe curves.

"It is a pleasure to meet you, Miss Duprea," Teressa replied sincerely. But Christina could not help but notice how her eyes kept straying to the tall man by Christina's side. "And you, Jason, it is good to see you once again."

"We heard part of your rehearsal. You sounded wonderful, Teressa," Jason said with a polite smile.

"Yes, . . . well, it is my life, you know. It is everything to me." Her meaning was directed to Christina, and the young girl did not miss the hidden message in her words.

Black Jack coughed. "Why don't you young folks come join me for a drink?" he interceded smooth as silk.

"Sort of for old time's sake."

Teressa shook her head negatively. "None for me, thank you. I have a performance shortly and alcohol is bad for the voice. And Cornelius is waiting for me to dine with him. I really must leave you all now."

"Old Cornelius is still hanging in there, is he?" said Jason.

Teressa smiled enigmatically. Christina breathed a sigh of relief when the singer at last left.

"Cornelius is her beau?"

"You might call him an admirer," Jason chuckled.

Their first meal at Diamond Sal's was just as Jason had promised, absolutely excellent. She and Jason sat at a small, intimate table in a curtained alcove off to one side of the vast stage.

Jason's eyes kept straying to the delicate curve of Christina's shoulders as he toyed absentmindedly with his dessert. Desire for her welled up inside him as he admired the swell of her full breasts revealed by the cut of her gown, and the soft, loving light in her eyes each time his gaze caught hers. This woman meant everything to him. He loved her more than life itself and all she had to do is lift her sweet lips in a smile to arouse him. So why did he specifically tell Sal that they wished separate rooms? What made him suddenly feel the need to be alone with his thoughts? The answer was difficult for him to admit, but he knew it was the haunting memory of Christina in Baker's bed. He closed his eyes trying to blot out the awful picture imprinted in his brain. *Damn you Baker*, he thought.

"Jase, you're as white as a sheet," Christina's anxious voice reached him through the cloud of his emotional anguish.

320

He hesitated briefly. "It's nothing for you to concern yourself about. . . . I'm fine."

"It's Teressa, isn't it?" Christina's voice quivered.

"Teressa was yesterday," Jason said slowly.

"Yesterdays have a strange way of leading to tomorrows," she replied bitterly.

"It is not *my* yesterdays that plague me, Christina," he retorted before he could stop himself.

She threw him a crushed look. "It is mine . . . isn't it?"

A muscle jerked in Jason's jaw.

"Isn't it?" she persisted, angry now.

He did not answer, nor look at her, but trained his eyes upon the rising curtain instead. The deafening applause when Teressa St. Clair was introduced halted any further conversation between them. But while Jason's eyes were trained on the alluring beauty on the platform, he could feel Christina observing him and regretted his nasty words.

Teressa, the Golden Girl of New Orleans, performed like the true professional she had become, and the eager audience responded with wild enthusiasm at the end of every song. They applauded her last song as soon as she introduced it. It was one they all knew, the song that had made her a star. She had written it several years ago. The words fell upon Christina's ears and she died a little inside. There could be no doubt now for whom it had been written. Each note, each word about a love that had been lost and mourned, and yearned for again, was for the man sitting next to Christina.

Christina's soft words were only whispered, but Jason heard and turned to gaze into her eyes. "She has never forgotten you, Jase."

He allowed his eyes to look upon the woman at his side, and then upon the woman onstage. The glow of the gaslamps at the foot of the velvet-draped stage bathed Teressa's gold satin dress in gilded hues of shining splendor. Her long dark hair swayed across her hips as she moved feelingly to the haunting melody. And when her eyes closed in feigned ecstasy at her lover's return, Christina could bear no more. She left.

"Christina!" Jason called in a hushed voice. Before he could follow her, Teressa's performance had ended. As she did at the close of each performance, she tossed a single red rose into the audience. Whichever gentleman caught it was invited backstage to her dressing room to meet her. The rose landed directly in Jason's lap and there was nothing he could do but accept it graciously.

Sands Of Time

Chapter Seventeen

"Did you enjoy the show?" Teressa sat at her dressing table in the dusky, smoky glare of the gaslight, and smiled invitingly at the man who had just entered her dressing room.

"Yes, I did, very much," Jason replied, leaning against the doorframe as he studied her from head to toe.

Teressa's eyes did the same to him, not missing anything about the tall, broad-shouldered man for whom she still carried a soft spot in her heart. "Where is your friend?" she asked with raised brows.

"She's a bit tired from all of our travels. She went to her room.

"*Her* room?" she questioned.

"Don't pry, Teressa, sweetheart, it is not your style."

She looked down and stroked the fluffy white cat that sat in her lap. "Ooh, . . . did you hear that, Cornelius?" she mocked. "The gentleman does not wish to discuss his relationship with the lady." The animal purred at the touch of her hand and wrapped his bushy tail possessively about her arm.

Jason pretended to examine the rose in his hand, inspecting each petal. "Why did you do this?"

"I wanted to be alone with you."

"And did you think I would feel likewise?"

"You are here, aren't you?"

"Yes," he answered quietly.

Teressa had seen so many dandies in the years of her fame that the sight of him before her looking so tanned and healthy and strong, made her heart beat queerly against her rib cage. "I have to ask you something," she said, studying the rugged face closely. "And you must give me an honest answer."

He looked at her suspiciously and then nodded.

"Do you love her, Jase?"

The room became deadly silent. "Since you have asked me so directly," he replied crisply, "I will answer you in kind. Yes, very much. . . . I think I always have." He tossed the rose back into her lap.

"I think so too," she murmured, her face wistful. "I am happy for you," she amazed him by saying. "I am relieved, as a matter of fact."

"Relieved?" he said, puzzled.

"*Chérie,* we would make a bad pair, you and I. I can admit that freely now." She smiled with a touch of sadness. "Although I do regret it. I wish I had more to give a man such as you."

The tension between them began to vanish as their place in each other's lives began to take shape and clarify itself.

"Please, have a seat," she said, indicating a couch against one wall. When he'd sat down and relaxed, she called to a maid to bring them some wine. The girl returned immediately with a bottle and two long-stemmed glasses.

Teressa dismissed the woman and poured two drinks. "Here. I think we both can use a little of the grape to unwind a bit." She handed him a glass.

"Thanks," he said, "I couldn't agree more."

She resumed her seat across from him and appeared to examine the liquid in her glass closely. "I can't lie to you, Jase, and say that I have forgotten you and the love we once shared. We were too close for that. But it is in the past. I chose my career, the only path I could follow and be truly happy. And in doing so I lost something special, and I've mourned that, oh, so very much."

Jason shuffled his glass from hand to hand in brooding silence. He looked up at her. "You don't have to tell me any of this, Teressa."

She nodded. "Yes, . . . yes I do."

"I know how you are feeling at this moment," he said softly. "I will never truly forget what we shared either. I don't blame you anymore . . . we were both too young, too starry-eyed. It wouldn't have worked out for us. We're too much alike when it comes to wanting every last drop out of life that we can grab."

"I think that is the reason for my inviting you to join me tonight." She extended her glass to his. "Let's bury the past . . . right now, this minute," she offered with a smile. "We can go on from here as two friends and that way we can stop avoiding each other." She stared at him pleadingly. "The slate will be wiped clean and I can be happy knowing that you are happy."

Jason returned her smile. "Sounds good to me." They drank a toast to it. He set his glass back on the table and rose to his feet. "I really must be leaving now. I have a bit of explaining to do, I'm afraid."

"Good luck with your life, Jase, and your lucky lady." Her words halted his steps at the door. "If you ever need me . . . you know I'll always be here for you."

He appeared thoughtful as he looked at her. "Do you mean that?"

"Just name it," she replied quickly.

"You meet many people in your career, do you not?"

"Yes, I do at that. Why?"

"Would you try and find out something for me? See if anyone in the city has seen a young man with silver hair, with either a black mask on his face or a terrible scar. And another man—he's short, hefty, and has eyes as cold as a snake. His name is Simon Baker."

"Are you tracking them for your government? You are still doing this?" she inquired somewhat astounded.

"I know I can trust you to keep this quiet," he answered. "I am involved in one last assignment. And it is imperative to many people that I find them both. One's life I must save, and the other's I may end, if necessary."

"I will do my best for you," she promised without hesitation.

With a quick wave of his hand Jason disappeared into the dark corridor. Teressa's eyes were wide and dry as the man who had been her first and only love walked out of her arms forever, and into another's.

Christina was in her private bathroom, relaxing with a glass of sherry and soaking in a tub full of hot, scented water. Whenever she had a serious problem to resolve, it helped to just shut herself away from everything and lie in the warm soothing water and think. She examined this strange square wooden tub with the copper lining. Above her, there was a spout with little holes in it which could shower water down if a person desired to bathe standing up, instead of in the conventional way. When the maid had showed her the room earlier, Christina had wondered how one could carry water up so many flights of stairs. But the maid had quickly explained.

"It's a built-in system, ma'am. The water is boiled in a copper boiler downstairs, and the steam from the heat allows the water to rise through the pipes and come out here." She pointed to the fixture with the tiny holes in its surface. "Mr. O'Leary himself designed it especially for his wife. All of our suites boast this luxury. New Orleans has everything . . . don't you know?" she chuckled as she departed the bathing chamber.

Christina sighed and slowly closed her eyes; she was so weary. And she felt so empty inside . . . so alone. Jason invaded her thoughts as she lay there. A soft, sad cry escaped her lips at the remembrance of his face when he'd gazed so longingly at the beautiful singer who had been so much a part of his life at one time. Was she again? Could he be with her at this very minute, holding her in his arms, making sweet love to her as he'd done so many times with Christina? Hot, scalding tears began to flow down her cheeks and she rubbed at her eyes absentmindedly, forgetting the soap on them. The sharp stinging of her eyes made her cry even more.

"You are so stupid, Christina!" she ranted. Standing, she groped about with tightly squeezed eyelids for the towel she knew to be near. Without her knowing, long fingers reached out to hand it to her. She wiped at her soap-filled eyes, and nearly jumped out of the tub when she opened them to find Jason standing in front of her, a mocking, appraising smile upon his lips.

329

"Tsk, tsk, little cat. Such a fuss over a bit of soap." His voice was husky and deep as he smiled lazily. The towel fell unnoticed into the water.

"It is my life, Yankee, and if I wish to bawl my eyes out over a bit of soap, then I will!"

"Can I help you?" he drawled.

"Yes! You can leave me alone. Get out of my bathroom! You do have your own, you know. Or is that being occupied at present?" She found to her mortification the words popping from her mouth.

"For your information, it is not. My room is very dull and lonely. And you're going to catch your death if you keep standing there like that, all wet and glistening with bath oil."

She gulped at the throaty quality in his voice. "I—I need another towel. . . . I seemed to have dropped mine into the water."

Her eyes observed his darken and smolder with embers of desire.

"So I see," he replied.

"Hand me another—would you please, Jase," she stammered, feeling so helpless and vulnerable under his scrutinizing appraisal.

Her sigh of relief turned to a gasp as he offered a replacement and grinned devilishly as it slipped from his fingers to the floor.

"Come get it."

"You think I won't, don't you?" she shot back, jade cat-eyes flashing and rising to the bait of his challenge.

"I think you want to scratch my eyes out. I think you're imagining I have just come from another's arms to yours."

"And have you?" She cast him a withering look as she

stepped slowly from the tub. Without saying another word, she stood before him and leaned over to retrieve the towel. She smiled at his sharp intake of breath, and knew without a doubt that his eyes were feasted upon her tempting derrière and long legs. Deliberately, she held her form, drying each slim little toe of excess moisture.

With a soft groan, he caressed the smooth curve of her back, her hips and the delectable curves revealed to him. She responded to his gentle touch by arching her back against him, pushing her buttocks upward to receive his caress. Her head began to spin dizzily as his lips soon followed. His warm body pulsed hotly against hers. She could feel every inch of him, smell his clean, masculine scent in her nostrils.

Practically lifting her from the floor, Jason pulled her soft form upward until she was standing, still presenting him her delectable backside.

She moaned in pleasure when lean fingers found their way around to the front of her body and stroked gently the satin flesh before slipping downward to entwine themselves in tawny curls. Small panting gasps escaped her.

"My little she-cat," he whispered against the nape of her neck as his lips nipped along the graceful column, "you are so beautiful and I love you so."

"And I don't intend to let you forget those words, my blue-eyed rogue," she replied. "You belong to me, not her. Only me."

"I could no more forget about you than tell myself to stop breathing," he stated hoarsely as he urged her down onto the hardwood floor and explored her exquisite body with his hands and lips. Lovingly, he caressed her pink-flushed breasts with gentle, arousing fingers until the

331

nipples rose willingly to his touch and she moaned her pleasure beneath him.

"I love you, Jase, and I want you, so terribly much it scares me."

Her words were like a devouring flame upon his blazing passion, and without hesitation he freed himself of his confining clothes and took her there upon the floor, amidst the water and the soapy bubbles that had started it all. His hands teased the smooth satin flesh along her spine, kneading, stroking, until she purred in ecstasy and rotated her hips to receive the full length of him deep within her.

"You're wonderful, Christina, . . . and you feel so warm, so good." Kneeling over her, his eyes watched every movement of her gently rounded hips. Wordlessly, he stared down at the joining of their bodies; so perfect, as though they were made only for each other and this moment. The visual sensation was lustily provocative, and feeling his release come upon him in a rush, he slid one hand beneath her, stroking her, encouraging her to seek her own fulfillment.

Christina writhed beneath him, crying out helplessly as his hot, piercing manhood thrust between their bodies. Unbearable pleasure raced through her, claimed her, and made his possession of her complete. Their love was all consuming, and as they rushed to meet the overwhelming wave of ecstasy that claimed them, they knew deep in their hearts that it would never change. They would be together always and forever.

Breathless, she lay beneath him, their bodies entwined, quiet now and totally satisfied. It had been as wonderful and exciting as always, and she knew that he was just as content and happy as she. She turned over onto her back, wrapping her arms about him and pulling him close. She could feel the pounding of his heart grow slower and smiled in dreamy wonder. What more could she possibly desire?

Silence had settled in the room, and so had understanding and peace. Unfortunately, it wasn't to last very long. A persistent tapping on the door sent her from his arms toward the bedroom to grab her robe. Slipping it on, she hurried toward the sound as Jason grumbled unhappily in the background.

"Big John!" she gasped, opening the portal wide. "What is it? You look absolutely awful!" She moved aside so that he could enter the room.

His face was ashen and his hands were trembling.

"I don't know where to begin," John whispered brokenly.

Jason, alerted by the note of alarm in her voice, straightened his attire and joined them.

"What happened?" Jason suddenly felt very cold. He glanced around the room. "Where . . . is Marti?"

The big man's shoulders shook as sobs wracked his body. Christina urged him to sit on the couch. Jason rushed to pour him a glass of brandy and handed it to him. John gratefully gulped it down before answering.

"It's Marti . . . Someone deliberately ran her down when she was crossing the street a little while ago." He ran his fingers through his thick hair. "It's bad—real bad," he choked, tears welling up in his eyes.

Jason swore under his breath. Christina sagged against him, grabbing him for support.

"Who would do such a thing, and why?" As soon as Jason uttered those words, a vision of Simon surfaced in her thoughts. She looked up at Jason, and immediately

333

knew that he was thinking the same as she.

"I didn't want her to go out by herself." Big John bowed his head and pounded one big fist against his knee in helpless frustration. "She wanted to walk over to the market and get us some fresh fruit. And I was too tired to get up and go with her."

Christina clutched at his coat sleeve. "Where is she?"

"At the hospital. I left after they told me there was nothing more that could be done for her. We'll just have to wait and see if she is able to hold on through the night." He blinked his eyes, fighting his runaway emotions. "She's several broken ribs, a concussion, and possible internal injuries."

"We'd best go over there, Christina," Jason said tersely. "Would you hurry and get dressed please."

"Of course, right away." Christina disappeared into the bathroom.

Big John turned an anguished face to meet his friend's. "I want the person responsible for this, Jase. There were witnesses who told the authorities that the buggy appeared to come out of nowhere. The driver was a portly man, middle-aged, and saw her—damn his rotten soul! He did this on purpose!"

Jason took a seat next to his devastated friend. "She'll make it. Marti is a fighter. I know she will, partner." He patted Big John upon his broad back. "And I promise you this, my friend, we'll get the person who did this thing. We will hunt him down and make him pay dearly."

Christina appeared in the doorway and the threesome left for their vigil at the hospital. In each of their minds was the same thought. Just don't die, Marti . . . don't die.

* * *

334

Martinique Summerfield battled valiantly for her life for over a week before she finally surfaced from the coma she'd been in and smiled weakly at John McGurk.

The doctors shook their heads in awe that this mere slip of a woman could overcome such mortal injuries. Still, they warned, it was not certain that she'd ever walk again. Nerves in her legs appeared to be seriously damaged. But then, they couldn't be certain.

Thinking of her vitality and zest for life, Big John broke down and wept unashamedly. Jason and Christina clung to each other, horrified that something like this could have happened to their vivacious friend.

As they were leaving the hospital sometime later, John confided: "I'm going to buy Marti a lovely house we saw the other day. It is in the Garden District and can be purchased for a reasonable sum. She's been wanting a place because she wants to establish roots. I expect we'll be staying in New Orleans longer than I had intended." His voice dipped low to a snarl. "I wish I had my hands on the bastard responsible for this right now. God help him when I find him!"

"You just concentrate on Marti," Jason replied. "I swear to you I will locate him, and when I do you can have the first swing."

"Marti told me that she remembers very little about the man's appearance. Everything happened so fast."

"So she couldn't recognize her attacker?"

"I doubt very much if she'll be much help." John appeared to suddenly remember something. "You know, she did say he was a heavyset man, and appeared to have hard, blunt features."

"That fits the man I have in mind," Jason replied.

"Tell me his name if you know," Big John snarled, his

expression fierce. "I'll fix him so he never does anything like this again."

Jason contemplated his friend's dark face, and then he answered. "I believe it's the work of Simon Baker."

"So, he strikes again."

"It isn't surprising."

"He must have recognized Marti in the posse, and decided that if she was out of the way he'd have one less government agent on his tail."

"One by one he intends to eliminate us, I'm afraid."

"Then it is more important than ever that I keep her secluded."

Jason nodded. "Yes, it is."

Big John's hazel eyes met Jason's. "We'll get that son of a bitch yet! We'll put him six feet under and smile the entire time we're doing it."

Although Christina still did not trust Teressa St. Clair, she was wise enough to keep her thoughts and opinions to herself. The woman seemed to go out of her way to be kind to her. Even though she and Jason had appeared to mend their differences, she still found it difficult to understand his relationship with Teressa. Just friends, he'd told her. *Ha!* she thought hotly as she watched the scene before her unfold.

Jason strolled down the center stairway, nodded in acknowledgement at Christina and Diamond Sal, who were sitting chatting over tea in the dining room, and left the gambling house without so much as a word. Shortly thereafter, Teressa, looking absolutely stunning in a gown of cream satin and twirling a matching parasol over her lustrous curls, did the same.

"What do you suppose that was all about?" Christina said as she turned to Sal, her teacup poised in midair, her heart plummeting.

"Darling, their affair ended years ago. This is something else altogether . . . I'm certain of it."

Christina's lips formed into a tight, white line. "Is that why he spends so much time with her of late? He hasn't even kissed me in over a week." The thoughts inside her head made her miserable.

Sal's fingers, glittering with diamonds, tapped upon the surface of the table. "There is more here than meets the eye, more than either of us can see. I've known Jason a good many years, and while he may be a bit of a hellion and a stubborn-headed cuss, he's not one to trifle with a lady's affections. One thing he is, and that's in love with you."

"We are in love as differently as two people can be, Sal," Christina said emotionally.

Sal glanced down at the lace napkin in her lap, and thought a moment on Christina's words. "You're not telling me everything, are you?"

"It's all so complicated," Christina sighed. "We are in a tangled web of deceit, and the only thing that keeps drawing us together is this shameful lust we seem to have for each other." She blushed at the admission. "At every turn, there appears another unexpected person to drive a wedge deeper and deeper between us. And soon there will be . . . another." She closed her eyes against the hot tears that threatened to spill forth.

"Darling?" Sal put her hand over Christina's, which were clenched in her lap. "Tell me, who is . . . this other?"

Christina's answer was barely audible but Sal heard,

and her heart went out to the beautiful young girl. "Our child."

"Oh, honey, you must be feeling frightened out of your wits. Does Jase know he's going to be a father?"

Christina shook her head mournfully. "No . . . he knows nothing. I only just figured it out myself. You see I missed my . . . my woman's time . . ."

"With all that you've been through, it could very well just be your nerves," Sal offered hopefully.

Christina's face brightened somewhat as she looked up. "Yes, . . . it could, and with my life turned upside down at present, I wouldn't doubt it one bit." But somehow, Christina knew in her heart that the seed of life was growing within her. She only wished she could be certain as to the child's father. She would like to believe that Simon had failed to consummate their wedding vows. But had he? Did he? Flashes of his angry, sweating face and his frustrated efforts lurked in the corners of her mind. *I am almost certain he did not make love to me.* But she knew that almost was just not enough. The thought chilled her.

Jason's carriage stopped before the wharf and he stepped out of the carriage to gaze upon the one story barge that lay next to an old paddle-wheeler which had seen better days. A sign above the barge's entrance read *Showboat*.

Jason's eyes searched the levee for any sign of Teressa. Within minutes another carriage drew up alongside Jason's, and her pretty face appeared in the open window.

"Is the coast clear?" she giggled.

Jason grinned, delighted by her playfulness. She could

still charm any man right out of his boots if she chose to. "Step down, Teressa, our secret is safe."

"This is rather fun," she said breathlessly as Jason helped her from the vehicle.

"I'm glad you think so."

"You're worried about Christina finding out we're meeting each other, aren't you?" She led the way toward the showboat. "Do you think she suspects anything?"

"She certainly would have to be blind not to after today." He followed her flurry of skirts inside the showboat.

"After you see why I brought you here, I think you will feel better." She smiled in understanding. "You asked for my help, remember?"

"Yes, I remember." But he also remembered the sight of Christina's stricken face as he'd casually left today. He hoped that this hunch of Teressa's panned out. All the others had been nothing more than a wild goose chase.

"Let's sit here," Teressa said, indicating a seat on a plank bench.

Jason smiled politely at a plump matron who begrudgingly moved over so that they could sit down. He looked down at Teressa with a droll expression. "You know, we have to stop meeting like this in these romantic places."

"Shame on you, Jase." She wagged her finger at him. "You never did appreciate the arts as you should."

The curtain began to rise and the audience eagerly applauded the tall man who stepped out onto the stage.

"There, look—he's coming out now," she said smugly as the lead actor began to deliver his lines. He was a distinguished looking gentleman, and his erect bearing drawing Jason's gaze to him immediately. His hair was

339

covered by a dark wig and his features disguised by the clever application of stage make-up. It seemed to Jason that the actor stared directly at him, their eyes holding for a brief moment before the man turned and walked to the opposite end of the stage.

Teressa's voice was close to his ear, and Jason nodded at her words. "He is a new actor, so my manager tells me. Quite good, isn't he? There's a rumor circulating about this gentleman that intrigues me. They say he wears theater make-up at all times. Perhaps to cover some sort of scars . . . h'm?" She watched Jason intently as he studied the performer's face with great care. "Is this the man, Jase?"

"It is quite possible, my dear," he replied softly.

"What are you going to do now?" she inquired, her face alive with excitement.

"Sit back and enjoy the show."

"What?"

He grinned at her. "And then afterward, you and I shall go backstage so we can congratulate him on his performance."

Her brown eyes gleamed. "Is there going to be any gun play? Perhaps even a duel . . . with swords?"

Jason only shook his head, his lips continuing to smile wryly. "I'll leave all of that to you, my dear. I'm sure you could hold your own with the devil."

She sighed in exasperation. "Oh, Jase, you really are no fun at all anymore."

"With age comes wisdom, and thank God for that."

The man, sitting in the cramped dressing room amidst the clutter of discarded costumes and stage props, was thoughtful. Gaslight flickered overhead and in the dim light he began to remove the heavy, greasy make-up. The dark wig lay discarded on the table and his own silver-streaked mane was revealed. A woman entered without knocking.

"Silver." She crossed the room to stand behind him, her worried face reflected in the mirror in front of him.

"Yes, Rhea, I know," he answered. "I saw him too."

She placed her hands upon the back of his shoulders. "We must get away from here! He will come looking for you—he'll find us!"

"I can't run any longer. I'm tired. Besides, I've found something here that has finally given me peace in my life," he smiled weakly at her. "I'm sorry."

"It's that woman again, isn't it?" she spat the words, furious. "You tell me she is your sister but she has taken you away from me as surely as any brazen woman."

"Yes, if you must have an answer. It is Christina. I must find out what became of her." The removal of his make-up complete, he viewed the image revealed in the mirror. "She is all that I have of my past."

"I am the only past that you need, *querido*," Rhea Francesco murmured enticingly, her eyes seeking to hold his in the mirror.

"No, . . . I need more now."

A knock upon the dressing room door caused Rhea to jump. She was panting for breath her heart beat so furiously.

The highwayman turned actor rose and faced the door. "Come in," he said firmly.

The door swung wide, and Jason stepped through its entrance; Rhea slunk into the far corner of the room, into the shadows.

341

Teressa stood behind Jason peeking around his wide-shouldered stance.

"So, *mon ami,* we meet again," Curt Duprea greeted him, a sardonic smile turning up the corners of his mouth.

"Yes, it seems as though we are forever destined to cross each other's paths, doesn't it?" Jason returned.

Each man stood silently viewing the other.

"How is she, Jason?" Curt Duprea blurted out. "And where is she?"

"She is well," Jason said. "But I cannot reveal to you where she is."

"Surely you can tell me more than that!" Curt snapped in agitation. "I've been half out of my mind worrying about her. I heard a shot fired from where I'd left her. It nearly drove me mad thinking she was hurt and I was running out on her."

Jason sent Curt a warning look and then turned to address Teressa, who was staring with avid interest at the actor. "I'd like to speak to Curt alone for a few minutes. Why don't I meet you at home later."

Disappointment crossed her pretty face. Glancing reluctantly at Curt Duprea, she quietly left the room.

Jason turned back to Curt. "Your sister understood why you had to leave her. She's waiting for you, my friend. I want to take you to her, but first I must have a promise from you. And I think you know what it is."

Curt sneered. "Why should I trust you?"

"I'll help you every step of the way."

"Does that include tightening the noose when it's placed about my neck?"

"On the contrary. I have a plan, and if you'll come with me, I will explain it all to you. I believe we can both obtain what we're seeking," Jason urged, his voice intense but steady.

It took every ounce of will power that Rhea Francesco possessed to stay out of sight, hidden behind a dressing room screen. Her man had changed. Ever since he'd laid eyes on that woman he claimed was his sister, he'd thought of nothing else. There was something about this *gringa* that made men want to kill for her. It was the same with that other one, the fat, heavy-jowled nightrider who had approached Rhea yesterday as she left the sanctuary of the St. Louis Cathedral. He was certain Rhea knew the girl's whereabouts, and got violent when she told him she had no idea where Christina was. It was then that he'd threatened her.

"I have no qualms about turning him over to the authorities. I will find him through you." He'd grabbed her arm hurtfully. "I'll follow you one day when you least expect it and you'll lead me straight to him." He'd demanded she locate Christina for him.

She'd stood facing him with contempt in her eyes. "I don't know where she is, I tell you. And while we are making threats, Baker, what is to stop me from telling the authorities where you are?"

His hand had reached out to squeeze her throat between meaty fingers. "This is why," he laughed as she gagged for air. "I will kill you if you tell anyone about seeing me. Do I make myself perfectly clear?"

Tears had sprung to her eyes but she knew she really didn't have any choice in the matter. Now that she knew Christina was in New Orleans, she would have to tell Simon Baker. For if she did not, she would be signing her own death warrant, and that of her lover.

Chapter Eighteen

Even if Simon Baker had not made his presence known to Rhea Francesco, she would have realized that he was in New Orleans by the wave of violence in the papers each day. Chaos and murder erupted in epidemic proportions as the hooded and masked devils terrorized the countryside with their nightly visits. White robes had been exchanged for red, a suggestion of Baker's to make his followers less recognizable as nightriders. But their tactics and methods did not change. With torches blazing and sitting astride their red-robed horses they presented the people in and around New Orleans with a sample of their supreme power as they made their nightly visits.

Rhea picked up a copy of the New Orleans *Picayune* and read the account of Simon's latest house call.

"Several Negro farmers and their families, their bodies mutilated beyond recognition, were found yesterday on the outskirts of the city." Rhea read out loud and then swallowed the bile rising in her throat. The weak and the poor, these were Simon's prey. "He thrives on the horrible atrocities he commits." She threw the paper across the room, her heart pulsing irregularly. "You are a pig, Simon!" she hissed under her breath. "And damn my soul to hell for what I'm about to do. . . . But I must, I must." Her mind was racing furiously as she ran from the small cabin toward the city. She needed to secure a horse and then she would go in search of the devil. She didn't think it too difficult to find him. After all, the devil could only hide in one place.

The horse was anxious to run and fought the bit.

"All right, my beauty," Rhea urged, loosening her grip on the reins, "fly like the wind. Take us into the devil's den." The animal surged forward, tossing his great head and viewing his surroundings with wild-eyed suspicion as he galloped with thundering hooves down the river road and into the vines and growth that cloistered the swamps within.

She halted the horse beneath a thick cluster of massive ash and willow trees beside a pool of black still water. A shrill cry, like that of a bobcat, split the quiet atmosphere sending winged herons and egrets screeching into the air. The horse tossed his head and pranced skittishly in circles. Rhea, always superstitious, blanched as the dark atmosphere was broken by an eery green light wavering across the water.

"*Dios!* It is the merry fire, an evil omen." She hastened to turn her mount around and leave. The Cajuns knew that this was a sign not be taken lightly. An evil omen to be sure.

"Move one step farther, lady, and it will be your last."

She glanced over her shoulder to see a red-robed figure

346

on a huge horse peering through a slitted mask at her. "Do not shoot—please," she managed to stammer. "Your grand leader is expecting me. He told me to come."

"Get down slowly and walk over here to me."

Rhea obeyed without hesitation. "Sí, sí, just don't shoot me."

The ghoul handed her a handerkchief to tie around her eyes. "Make certain you can't see anything or you might find yourself with a lot of problems."

Rhea flinched when a bobcat scream rent the still atmosphere once again. "It is you, a signal of some sort?"

The voice answered her with a chuckle. "Yeah, it was me. The call suits our purpose just fine, don't you think?"

Her answer died in her throat as the cry was returned. Rhea shivered in the dampness as the bloodchilling sound drew closer. The horse stopped in front of her and she did likewise making certain she clung tightly to the man's flowing robe. She would not want to wander about in here on her own. It wasn't long before a voice spoke to her. It was a strange voice, one that she'd not heard before.

"*Señorita Francesco,*" Marcus Trudeau greeted her. "How nice of you to join us here. Simon will be pleased that you decided to go along with his suggestion."

"You make certain that your leader knows I am doing this only for one reason," Rhea told an amused Marcus. "Because he threatened to kill me and turn the man I love in to the authorities."

"You've made a very wise decision," Marcus said.

"I doubt that it is wise, *señor,* but it is necessary."

347

"Do not get too cocky with me, you Spanish *puta,* or I shall have you killed this instant and fed to the alligators. Be very careful with your answers."

Rhea did not cower away from him as he expected, but stood her ground, haughtily proud. It irked him unbearably that he was not able to induce her to cower in fear. He snapped the whip he was holding forward and it hissed like a snake as it wound about her ankles. When it produced a startled cry of fear from her he laughed, pleased at last.

"That's better, *señorita.* You now know who you are talking to."

"Just get on with it," she whispered breathlessly. "How do you wish to get her away from Silver and that Yankee agent?"

"It is not Simon or myself who will do this, it is you."

"Me!" Rhea cried.

"It will be far easier for you to get to the girl. Do not let us down, my dear woman," he warned in a threatening tone.

"How am I to do that?" she blurted.

"That is for you to figure out," he chuckled sarcastically. "Why don't you try using your head, both of us may just be surprised at the outcome." His voice grew distant as though he were walking away. "Simon will be waiting . . . don't disappoint him."

Quiet settled in around her and she realized that they had left; she was alone. With a sob of relief she tore the blindfold from her eyes and fled on furiously pumping legs back in the direction of her horse. "I must do this . . . I must!" she repeated over and over again. But deep within she hated herself for her consorting with the vile Simon Baker and his band of filthy murderers. None of them were to be taken lightly and she shivered thinking just how close to death she had been.

Curt Duprea's reunion with his sister was a touching moment for them, as well as the blue-eyed man whose gaze rested upon them before he closed the door to Christina's suite and walked away.

Black Jack O'Leary was about to descend the stairway to the game room when his green eyes noted Jason walking down the hall in his direction.

"Jase, me lad, where have you been keeping yourself? I've asked me Sal a dozen times about you and she said to ask Teressa."

Jason fell in step behind Black Jack as they made their way to the gaming tables. "I swear to heaven, why is it everyone around this place thinks Teressa and I are having some kind of torrid love affair?"

Black Jack signalled the bartender to bring his usual mug of beer before answering. "'Tis because you don't seem to deny it." Accepting the foaming brew he drank deeply and then smacked his lips. "And your Christina, the poor wee lass is heartsick over your treatment of her. I'm ashamed for you meself." He glanced scornfully at Jason who scowled back in return.

"You don't know the half of it, Black Jack."

"Then perhaps you'd like to tell me." He settled into a chair.

"I wouldn't even know where to begin," Jason replied taking a seat across from the Irishman.

A fresh deck of cards was called for, and Black Jack proceeded to artfully spread them out before him and with a practiced flourish flipped them skillfully from side to side. "How about a wee game, lad, just for old time's sake." He smiled blandly.

"You old gold digger. You never do anything just for old time's sake, and I've already lost a month's winnings to you since I came here. What do you want, my last damned gold piece?"

"Now, now, Jase, you know I would never be doing such a thing as that," he grinned. "I just happen to think that you have more than that one gold piece left." His eyes twinkled with delight.

Jason gave him a quick glance. "Deal," he said resignedly.

As the day wore on and the afternoon sun withdrew its brightness from the room, the two men were still engaged in the game.

Black Jack saw to it that a fresh bourbon was set before his young friend as soon as Jason's glass emptied. It took some doing, but at last Jason began to talk. As the liquor continued to flow, so did his need to bare his soul. Black Jack, always a good friend and listener, sat quietly without passing judgment and studied each deal set before him.

"The woman is driving me crazy," Jason snapped, throwing in yet another gold piece.

"How's that, lad?" Black Jack tossed in another to up the bet.

"Right now she is upstairs with her brother Curt, whom she was afraid she'd never see again. Teressa and I had found him at the showboat this evening, and then brought him straight here. And do I so much as even get a thank you from her? No, . . . not even a hello. She just rushes into her brother's arms, casts me a narrowed, suspicious look, and ignores me thereafter." He gripped the glass of whiskey in his hand. "It's all this business with Teressa."

"Did you explain to her how Teressa was involved in all this?" Black Jack queried.

"Explain? Explain!" Jason exploded. "She doesn't listen to a word I say. Besides, can't she see that my every move, my every breath, is just for her?"

Black Jack again produced cards equalling the sum of twenty-one. "Just the luck of the Irish, lad," he beamed.

"I'm glad someone reaps the benefits of their heritage," Jason grumbled.

"Now, Jase, what you should be doing is having your lady listen to some of the things you've been telling me. Talk to her. Me Sal and I talk to each other about everything that's on our minds, good or bad. I suggest you do the same." He inclined his head toward the upper floor. "Don't let it stay like this too long. It does neither of you any good."

Jason stood and turned his trouser pockets inside out in a show of complete devastation. "I'm busted, Black Jack. I leave you to another poor sucker."

His voice bright-edged, Black Jack called to Jason's fast-retreating figure. "Better luck with your lady, Jase! And remember, a good Irishman never lets a woman get the best of him!"

"That's easy for you to say," Jason grumbled under his breath. "I've never seen you lose at anything in your life."

"So you see, my darling sister," Curt Duprea said, "if not for your Jason and this entertainer friend of his we might never have found each other. We should be

351

forever in their debt. He's risked much for us both."

"Oh, Curt," Christina sighed, her hands dropping into her lap. "Why is it I am such a jealous shrew where Jason is concerned? And I've been awful to Teressa as well."

"It is love, *chérie*. I am afraid we are all guilty of doing things we hate ourselves for."

Christina muffled a sniff as she looked over at her brother. "You and Rhea, what is to become of the two of you?"

"I find myself in much the same predicament as you." He moved his shoulders in a helpless gesture. "I cannot just turn off this love I feel for her. But what she did to you and my people through her conniving with Baker has made it impossible for us to go on together. I will be going home to Oak Meadow alone."

"I can hardly believe that you are willing to bury the Silver Wolf once and for all," Christina said, barely able to comprehand the fact that he was indeed going home at last. "And Jason has agreed to let you wipe the slate clean and begin your life again as Curt Duprea?"

"That was our agreement . . . as long as I help persuade the Southern people to accept his government's policies."

Christina bristled. "Damn that Yankee and his compliance to the Union!"

Curt unfolded his long legs from his chair and strode over to comfort his sister. He held her close for a moment. "It will be all right. The worst is over." He kissed her cheek. "Now, I think I'd best leave you to get some rest." He placed his hand upon her shoulder. "You're looking pale and tired."

Christina tried to smile reassuringly. "Don't worry about me, you just take care of yourself." Her fingers rested upon the curve of his jaw. She studied the area where the deep scars were cleverly concealed by theater make-up. "You know, Curt. If you were to grow a beard it would do much to cover the scars. And I think it would look quite dashing also."

Her brother appeared skeptical. "It may not be possible because of the damage to the tissue. But if you think it would look pleasing, perhaps it couldn't hurt to try."

"Good," she replied.

"I will even try to do without the eye patch. I've been attempting to go for longer periods with my weaker eye uncovered," he explained. "I believe I'm regaining some of the strength in it."

"The new look will befit the man—Curt Duprea, the actor."

After Curt left she sat for some time and dreamed of their return to Oak Meadow. But soon she found herself nodding off in her chair. She could not remember ever feeling so tired and washed out before in her life. Stumbling over to the bed, Christina stretched out fully clothed and fell into a dreamless slumber.

It was quite late when Curt Duprea slipped into the cabin that he shared with Rhea within the confines of the showboat. The sparse room was equipped with two bunks. Rhea was lying upon one, staring up at the ceiling, her eyes focused on nothing in particular. She expected him to take the other bunk as he did every night and go to sleep with only a whispered "sleep well" in her direction. She expected nothing from him in the way of an explanation of his reunion with his sister, nor any indication as to what he was going to do from here. Therefore, when she saw him cross the room in the moonlight to stand beside her bunk, she could not stop herself from reaching out to him.

"*Querido*," she whispered. "You have returned to Rhea."

Curt could not find it within himself, even after all of the heartache that she'd caused, to scorn her, to turn away. He intended to hold her in his arms for only a moment before telling her he would be leaving her behind when he returned to Oak Meadow.

Rhea clung to him desperately, as if some how she knew that this would be the last time she was to feel his arms around her and his virile body pressed next to hers. "Kiss me, darling," she whispered as her lips thirsted for the taste of his. Her fingers threaded their way into his thick mane of silver hair and urged his lips toward hers. The sheet that had been covering her, fell away as she rose up to embrace him, and his breath caught in his throat as her lush form lay naked to his gaze. In the dimness of the moonlit room, the memories of the love they'd once shared overwhelmed him and brought forth a soft cry of need from his lips as they surrendered to hers. Hungrily, he explored the warm, searching mouth beneath his, tasting, forcing her lips apart so that their tongues met and embraced. Having denied himself the pleasure of her body for so long, he was now like a man cauterized by the fires of his own desire.

Gently, so as not to break the spell of the moment, Rhea moved over, suggesting by her movement that he should lie next to her. Curt stretched his lean body fully against her familiar form, pulling her roughly against him as his fingers cupped one small breast. The mouth beneath his moaned softly as he gently teased the taut nipple between his fingers while his free hand stroked downward to her smooth abdomen and around to cup the contour of her buttocks. She draped one of her legs over his side as she moved her hips against him, urging him to touch her there, between her legs where a slow heat had turned to a burning ache.

Pulling his mouth from hers, he whispered in a voice ragged with desire. "Let me undress, it will only take a second."

Her fingers reached out to help him with the buttons and soon his clothes lay in a heap beside the bunk and he had rejoined her as they were. With lips that burned each place that they touched, Curt explored every curve of body with infinite sweetness.

Rhea was aflame from within as his need of her lay pressed between her thighs at the gate to her femininity. She wanted him so inside her, to fill her completely as only he could. Her head turned wildly from side to side as he awakened raging desires within them both. And at last, with his name a cry upon her lips, he slid smoothly into the warm, moist place so eagerly awaiting him. His big hands spanned her tiny waist as their hips thrust heatedly and furiously in the throes of passion.

Curt's amber eyes lay closed, but he could feel her dark eyes upon him, seeking some sign that he forgave her, that this was the reason for this rapturous moment of love that he so willingly shared. As his hips increased their motion, so did hers, until at last they felt their senses engulfed with their emotions and they soared together to heights so exhilarating that each clung to the other, wanting never to let go. All too soon, with passions spent, their world was righted and Curt felt an enormous wave of guilt wash over him. Abruptly, he withdrew from her and sat up, his legs planted over the side of the bunk.

"What is it, *querido?*" Rhea questioned sleepily, her hand touched the broad back that she loved so well.

"Damn it, Rhea," he swore softly. "I never meant for this to happen."

The gentle stroking fingers upon his back rose in their motion. "Wha—what are you saying, Silver?" the small voice whispered.

He kept his back to her, could not bear to see the anguish upon her face that he sensed even now was there. "I am leaving you, Rhea. I am going home to my family." A great weight seemed to lift off of his shoulders at the admission. "The Silver Wolf is dead, he died back at Willow Wind in the blazing inferno that destroyed everything that he had built and dreamed. You betrayed me with Baker, Rhea, and I told you then that I would leave you. You're safe here. It's time for me to move on."

"No!" she cried out as a searing pain tore at her heart.

"Yes," he whispered, "it is the only way."

"You don't mean what you are saying. She has confused your feelings, your thoughts with her sentimental rubbish!"

The silver head shook gently. "I have thought carefully and clearly upon this. I can do more good for myself and our people if I speak out freely against the perfidy of our enemies. Not everyone in government is dishonest. There are several influential people that are in Natchez at this moment to try and help us in this fight."

"You fool," she spat at him. "They will betray you. She will betray you in the end! You think that by going back there that you can recapture the life that you don't remember." When her accusation was met with silence she laughed bitterly. "I thought so. You will never remember this Curt Duprea that you were. You are the Silver Wolf . . . I created him for you. Together we shaped your life and our future. And I do not intend to just let you walk away from me because some fancy woman comes along dangling tidbits of your former life before you."

He stood and walked across the room to peer out of the open shutters. The misty river met his probing gaze. "It is not my sister. The answer lies out there somewhere, lost in the grasp of that river. I lost it there the night the riverboat exploded and I was tossed into his realm. He is a greedy one, the Mississippi." A cooling October breeze blew in to caress his perspiring face. "It is not Christina who continually torments me with my past . . . it is that infernal river. But one day he will have to relinquish to me what was stolen, for I will never give up my struggle to regain it."

"But you will give me up?" Rhea interjected, flinging back her thick black hair in an aggravated motion.

He began retrieving his clothing from the floor. "You have come to think of me as your possession, Rhea." He dressed as he spoke, his eyes resting upon her stormy features. "Your love has changed, it is not the same as I remember it. Or perhaps I was too blinded by my need of you to see how things actually were."

"I think, my wild wolf, that it is now you are blinded, not then," she said through stiff lips.

Slowly he shook his head. He picked up a silk scarf that he had seen her wear often and whispered. "For old time's sake." And then he was gone.

*   *   *

In the weeks that were to follow, Curt Duprea's engagement on board the showboat drew to a close. Tonight had been his final performance, and a successful one it had been. Curt Duprea was making a name for himself within the circle of theater people that he now surrounded himself with.

As was the custom, a late night champagne supper was held in his honor at a very elegant restaurant. His sister, Jason, and their friends, John McGurk and Martinique Summerfield, were all personally invited to join him.

He was a bit nervous about his first confrontation with the two agents, who he feared might remember him as the notorious highwayman, the Silver Wolf. He stood to lose everything if either of them recognized him.

"Don't worry, Curt," Jason had tried to reassure him. "With your hair styled so much shorter, and that very distinguished silver beard, you look more like a philosopher than a highwayman. Who would ever guess that you were the most sought-after revolutionary in all of the South?"

"My brother, a philosopher?" Christina teased. "I don't think so."

They sat in Antoine's, New Orleans' most famous and exclusive dining establishment, awaiting John and Martinique's arrival. The menu was entirely in French, and Curt did the honors of ordering several appetizers.

"I'll eat whatever it is you ordered," Jason grinned. "I'm starved."

"You are always starved. I never saw a man that can consume so much food and manages not to gain an ounce," Christina said. "It's not fair."

"Is that why you haven't been eating with your usual gusto of late? Watching your figure?" he remarked, biting back a smile.

Christina sent him a look of mock displeasure. "Gentlemen should never mention a lady's eating habits."

They enjoyed an assortment of delectable tidbits, all washed down with a bottle of white wine. The conversation began on a light note, but as the wine began to mellow their moods it turned to the one subject that was on all of their minds but had not been mentioned.

"So, now that your performance is ending, you and Christina will be returning to Oak Meadow, correct?" Jason said calmly.

"I have nothing more to keep me here," Curt replied. "It is time for me to move on."

"And you, Christina?" Jason questioned, his eyes searching hers.

"It's best this way, Jase," she whispered. "We both have much to sort out in our lives. This mission of yours . . . I don't think when it's over you will be content to settle down."

"I hoped once we were free of Baker and all the unpleasant memories he's left you with that I would settle down with you." He reached out his hand to touch hers.

"Oh, Jase, . . . you don't know what you're saying. Sometimes I think I know you better than you know yourself."

Curt Duprea sighed. "So much of this is my fault." His eyes were deeply sad.

"I don't think anyone is to blame except Baker himself," she said.

"I swear I will get to the bottom of this for you," Jason vowed.

"I'm afraid it may already be too late." She was thinking of the child she carried inside her and the scandal she would face upon her return to Natchez. Everyone would assume she was carrying Simon Baker's child. Could she stand up to it all? And though she wanted passionately to believe it was Jason's child, what if Simon heard, and came to claim what he would think was rightfully his? What if? Unknowingly, she shuddered.

Jason sat back in his chair with a sense of great loss. Christina was leaving him. It was something he wasn't ready to accept. He clamped down hard on the cigar between his teeth. Just then the sound of John and Martinique's joyful arrival broke the tension. Jason performed the introductions.

John positioned Martinique's wheelchair next to Christina.

"I never thought John had it in him to live in a real house on solid ground," Martinique exclaimed smiling up at him. "But he assures me he is happy in this new role he's found himself in."

"Never happier," John replied with confidence. "I found out nothing in the world means a damn to me unless Marti is there to share it with me. And I can live anywhere, overcome any obstacle, and live the rest of my life as a very happy man as long as my lady is with me."

Jason observed their radiant faces and the love that was in their eyes, then turned his gaze on Christina.

"And listen to this all of you," Martinique said, her eyes bright. "John and I are going to be married soon, and we want all of you to attend the wedding." She held up her hand. "It's official—see?" A lovely diamond and sapphire ring winked back at them.

"Oh, Marti! John!" Christina blurted. "That's the best news I've heard in ages."

Jason stood to kiss Martinique and shake his friend's hand. "Congratulations, you two! It's about time!"

"Better late than never," John chortled.

"This calls for a bottle of the best champagne Antoine's can produce," Curt Duprea proposed, extending his hand toward Big John. "Congratulations." The waiter appeared and Curt ordered champagne for everyone.

They drank glass after glass of the delicious bubbly. Dinner was a festive affair and they all ate the scrumptious fare with zest. Everyone but Christina, whose meal remained untouched.

Jason studied her closely, noted the pallor of her complexion and lifted a brow in thoughtful silence. This was not at all like his Christina. Whether she liked to admit it or not, she had an appetite that could put a roustabout to shame. It worried him when she just sat and picked at her food; it worried him a great deal. He was growing alarmed at the thought of her possibly ill . . . seriously ill perhaps? He quickly averted his eyes when she turned and caught him staring moodily at her.

What are you thinking, Jase? she wondered, studying the strong features, the firm lips, the well-chiseled jawline. *Now that Teressa is gone from our lives, do you find that you miss having me in your bed? Was there only friendship in your relationship? Did you not even once yearn to hold her in your arms, as you did so many times in the past before me? And what would you think if you knew that I am going to have a child? I feel in my heart that it is your child . . . but would you believe me? And what right do I have to want you when the baby may be claimed by Simon? I love you so, and I can't bear for you to hate me when you learn of the child.*

Jason suddenly grasped her hand within his and rose from his chair, drawing her with him.

"I apologize to everyone for cutting this evening so short," he explained to their companions. "But I think I will see Christina back to Sal's She appears exhausted, although I know she'll deny it." He took her gently by the arm and escorted her from the table.

"I'll be along later," Curt called after them. "I think I will talk to our friends about the plans for this upcoming wedding of theirs." He watched happily as Jason and Christina left the restaurant arm in arm. It was the first sign of a reconciliation between them, and as his eyes met those of Martinique and John he knew that their thoughts were the same as his own.

Chapter Nineteen

The air was balmy for early November as Jason and Christina left Antoine's, and stepped out into the velvet night. Cabs were lined along the roadway awaiting the rich and elite that would soon be exiting the opera house and surrounding dining establishments. Jason obtained a cab with little difficulty, looking every bit a part of his surroundings, and seated Christina comfortably inside. He gave the driver their destination and swung in to sit across from her. As the cab lurched forward, so did her stomach, and she couldn't help the small protest that she emitted. Immediately, she felt his eyes, warm and concerned upon her.

"What is it, Christina, what's wrong?"

"I'm afraid the champagne didn't agree with me tonight," she managed to answer, although his face was beginning to swim before her.

He viewed her skeptically, reaching over to lay his palm across her damp brow. "And neither did your dinner. I noticed you never even took a bite." He withdrew his hand. "You don't feel warm."

"I'll be fine," she snapped testily. "As long as you stop fussing over me like a mother hen!"

His expression was impossible to discern in the shadows, but his voice held a note of impatience as he replied. "I hope your mood improves also. I've never known you to be this cantankerous, although I must say you always were a trying little package."

In the flicker of the coach lamps, he saw her sweet mouth purse itself in indignation. "I did not ask you to whisk me away from the restaurant, *monsieur*. You are responsible for that, so don't complain about having to share my mood."

He thrust his long legs out before him, accidentally brushing hers as he did so. She withdrew them as though she'd been burned. "I see your reflexes are as sharp as ever," he drawled.

"Jason, . . . please. I'm not up to fencing words with you this evening." She was mortified to sound so weak and fragile, but at any moment she felt as though she would literally drift away. Her head lolled back against the cushions.

Now he was truly concerned. This was more than just an ordinary case of the vapors. He was beside her immediately, laying her head upon his shoulder and talking soothingly. The cab rolled to a stop and the door was opened for their departure.

"I'm going to carry you, Christina," Jason informed her as he scooped her tiny frame into his arms. She did not protest in the least. Her face appeared as pale as death, Jason thought as he took the back entrance to Diamond Sal's and hurried toward Christina's rooms. Nudging the door open with one booted foot, he strode across the floor to deposit her ever so gently upon the satin coverlet of the bed. He yelled impatiently for her maid.

"Miss Christina is ill. Get your mistress at once!" he commanded the young girl. She hurried off to do his bidding.

Jason called softly to the pale figure on the bed. "Christina, sweetheart, I'm going to loosen your gown and stays. I think this should help you." The gown was a luxurious wine velvet, and Jason could not help thinking how much the feel of the fabric reminded him of her soft skin and how his lips felt when pressed against her silky flesh. Agilely, he undid the back of the gown and attacked the whalebone stays of her corset.

"It's no wonder women give way to the vapors confined in these damned things," he ranted, at last completing the task. Noticing a pitcher of water on a washstand next to the bed, he went to it and dipped a cloth in the water and returned to wipe Christina's brow. Her eyes opened and gazed up into his.

"Jase, . . . what happened?" she attempted to sit up but was promptly halted by a firm hand upon her shoulder.

"I was hoping that you would tell me," he replied.

Diamond Sal stood in the doorway contemplating the scene before her. "I was hoping she would, too," Sal blurted out.

Christina moistened her lips that were suddenly feeling quiet parched. She could feel what little color that had returned to her face drain completely away once more. "Sal, please, this is not something I wish to discuss now."

Sal's eyes met Christina's, and she almost was persuaded by their look of sheer terror to keep still. But

Jason's acute look of worry convinced her to persist. "I believe this is something you need to share."

"What the deuce is going on here?" Jason growled. "Christina, if this concerns your health . . . tell me." His hard blue gaze raked the young girl's slim form, and then shifted to her face in dawning awareness. His eyes settled upon the lush, full breasts that suddenly seemed so much riper than before, then travelled downward to her stomach. His hand reached out to lay gently upon it, the folds of the billowing gown cushioning his fingers, but still he could feel the gentle swell beneath it. "My God, Christina! Why did you keep this from me?"

Sal quietly left the room, closing the door behind her.

"I wasn't certain that you would relish the news," she admitted in a miserable voice.

"What do I look like, some sort of monster who would abandon you in your time of need?" He smiled narrowly. "Don't answer that."

She managed a weak smile that tore his heart.

He brushed the damp strands of hair from her brow. His lips followed, kissing her gently at each temple.

"This child is ours. Do you think I'd let you go through something like this without me?"

"*Non, . . . non,* but . . ."

"Are you saying that I overestimate myself?" He drew back from her, somewhat piqued by her hesitant answer.

Her words, haltingly spoken, were forced to her lips even as her heart protested vehemently. "Jase, . . . you must know. . . ."

"Know what?" he prodded.

"The baby . . . I am married to Simon as far as we know. H—he has rightful claim," she stammered at last.

366

Jason's face leaned over hers, searching the depths of her soul with his piercing hard stare.

Her gaze was soft and luminous as she held his. "There is no doubt in my mind who the father is. Is there—will there ever be—?"

The handsome face above hers darkened with suppressed fury at the images which flitted across his thoughts. He frantically swept them aside so that they were not mirrored in his eyes that still rested upon the face he adored. "My heart has been so empty without your love to fill it. I can't let you walk away from me. . . . I can't let you leave me," he said hoarsely. "I have people on Baker's tail even at this minute. They'll have him cornered soon and then I'll go after him. When we have him in custody it should be relatively easy for you to obtain a divorce. Hopefully, a quiet one. I will not have my child born with that man's name," he finished with a snarl, "so I promise you, if that bastard causes any problems I will make you a widow and solve this fiasco a much easier way."

Christina gasped at the cold, killing look on his face. She had no doubt that he meant each and every word that he said. Her hand reached out to grasp his arm. "Don't say that—ever! Simon has so many enemies he could turn up dead at any given time. And who do you think they will come for if you go around issuing threats upon the man's life?" She shivered, suddenly very frightened.

Jason gathered her close into his arms against his beating heart. "I will love this baby you carry with my entire being."

A tear coursed down Christina's cheek. "How glad I'll be if he arrives, his face alight with a lopsided grin and his eyes the color of the sky."

"I pray it is so, my darling . . . for both of us, and our child."

He unbound her arms from around his neck and rose from the bed. "Try to get some rest now. I'll just be over on the settee if you should need me."

She reached a hand out to stay his leaving. "There is plenty of room in this bed for two."

"I know," he replied quietly. "But you need your rest and if I lay that close to you I doubt whether either of us will get any."

"Is that the only reason?" she questioned at the look in his eyes. It was uncertainty that she saw there.

He did not reply, but turned on his heel and blowing out the lamps, retired across the room upon the settee.

When she awoke in the morning, Jason was gone. Had she only imagined last night, and his tender understanding and show of support? And then it came to her; her doubts, her hidden fears. He's left! She was certain he had! Throwing back the covers she padded across the room to the settee where she had last seen him moments before she'd fallen asleep last night. A smile lit up her classic features as her eyes fell upon the gold case upon the side table. Picking it up, she flipped open the lid and was immediately assailed by the aroma of the imported cigars he loved so well. The thin black cylinder of tobacco was like an aphrodisiac to her senses and at first, when she heard his voice, she did not realize that he was indeed in the room with her.

"Did you sleep well, sweetheart?"

She nodded almost shyly as their eyes met and held.

Trying not to be conspicuous, she set the gold case back down on the table and scurried to cover her thin nightgown with a robe. She felt so shy before him with the slight roundness of her stomach plainly visible through the sheer material. His gaze rested there, still in wonder over what she'd revealed to him last night. A child . . . his child?

"You look in the peak of health this morning," he said thickly, the sight of her sending his composure reeling.

"I have never had anything happen like that before." She cast her eyes downward. "But then, carrying a child is all so new to me."

"And me," Jason replied softly. He took her hand in his. "I have just the thing to bring the color back in your face. So, why don't you hurry and get dressed and I will take you there."

"I should love it!" she exclaimed. "But what of breakfast?"

"I've taken care of that." He started back toward the door. "I'll send the maid up to help you. Wear something casual and take a cloak—you may need it. It's a bit cool this morning."

"I'll be ready," she called, hurrying to do his bidding.

The early morning mist was just rising from the waters of Lake Ponchartrain as the carriage pulled up and the occupants stepped out.

"I never asked you whether you liked sailing boats or not." Jason grinned at her. "I hope it will agree with you."

A refreshing breeze blew in from the lake and tugged at the hood of the fur-lined cape that framed Christina's

369

face. She smiled happily.

He grabbed her hand in his and enfolded it close to his body. She felt so secure and protected whenever he was with her. Like nothing in the world ugly could touch her. Jason wouldn't allow it.

The sun shining through the mountainous peaks of cumulus clouds overhead turned the blue-gray water into an ocean of wavering, glistening ripples as the vessel skimmed lightly over the surface.

Christina stood with Jason's arms embracing her, her body reclining against his, and gazed out upon the endless spectacle before her. "When you talked of sailing, Jase, I had no idea you were speaking of doing so aboard a beautiful clipper ship such as this." She turned her head to peer up at him. "Who does it belong to?"

"Need you even ask?" he replied with a slow and tantalizing smile.

"Somehow, I rather suspected," she grinned back at him. "Although why I'll never know." They both laughed in unison, a sound that delighted them.

His lips brushed her temple as the sleek ship with its long slender lines and tall raking masts carried them over the water toward his destination. The shoreline of the city slowly receded into the distance until even squinting her eyes, Christina could see nothing around them but water. Was he taking her out to sea? The thought sent thrills racing through her. It was almost as though he was playing the part of a pirate, and she his willing captive. With his dark locks blowing in the wind and his smooth profile complimented by the curved moustache, he gave the appearance of just that. His alluring mouth was but inches from hers, and as she stared up at him she noticed the grooves on either side of it, deepen as he returned the

370

appraising look.

"Something wrong?" he teased, eyes dancing merrily.

"*Non*, everything is just right I would say."

He smiled remembering himself saying something very similar to her upon their first meeting. Had it only been months ago? With everything that had taken place since then it seemed more like years. "Are you glad you came, little cat?" he whispered, lips brushing across hers tenderly.

"Oh yes, my love, . . . so glad," she replied dreamily.

"You are all mine for the day, and perhaps I shall decide never to go back at all." He spun her around to face him. "Would you go away with me now, if I asked it?" he surprised her by saying fiercely. "Without asking any questions—just sail away with me to an island where it would be only us, no one else?"

"Is this the surprise?" she inquired a bit apprehensive, nervous.

"I may say yes," he replied in an intense voice, "and then what would you do?"

"I could jump overboard," she exclaimed.

"I'd come after you."

She saw the intense, possessive gleam in the blue depths of his eyes. "Yes, . . . I believe that you would." The thought pleased her.

"Make no mistake about it. I told you, you are mine, will always be mine . . . forever." The breeze whipped the full-sleeved linen shirt that he wore about his hard, muscular form. He held her tightly against him. "I came after you once, and it was not for the sake of capturing your brother. I could have let someone else handle that."

"I know," she whispered, rising on tiptoe to place her soft mouth against his. He crushed her against him and

371

tasted the sweetness of her kiss.

A discreet cough broke them apart. Jason looked over his shoulder from his place overlooking the prow of the boat. "Yes, what is it?" he questioned the young crew member standing there.

"Captain says to tell you we're almost at your destination, sir. Says you might want to view it first through this here spyglass." The crewman handed Jason the glass.

"Tell the captain, 'thank you'," he replied, and then turned back to Christina. "Here, look over the starboard bow." His finger directed her.

Christina adjusted the cylinder until she spotted, off in the distance, a dot of land, a curving shoreline coming into view.

"Is that our destination?" she questioned curiously.

"That is it," Jason replied. "We should be there within the hour. Why don't we go below first and get a bite of breakfast. I can assure you this will be no ordinary pirate's fare."

And indeed it was not. They sat below in the warm galley and feasted on fresh pineapple, oysters, cracked crab, and piping hot muffins, all washed down with coffee, thick with clotted cream.

"That was absolutely superb," Christina praised the beaming cook. "And I must have your recipe for those divine muffins to give to Mammy when I get back home."

At mention of her leaving, Jason's face immediately darkened. "So, you are still planning on leaving at the end of the week?"

She looked down at her plate. "I must," she replied gently.

"I don't like the idea of your being away from me and

my protection," Jason drew a ragged breath.

"I won't exactly be alone. Curt will be with me."

"I realize that."

"You're not having second thoughts about Curt?" She looked anxious. "You don't foresee any problems in telling your commander that the Silver Wolf is dead so that my brother can begin his life anew?"

Jason shook his head. "No, no, I've already wired him that the Silver Wolf no longer exists. I am satisfied with my decision."

"Good," she said, relaxing once more. She stood up and followed behind him as he led her down the narrow passageway and toward the stairway. "If you are worried about having to go without a companion to John and Martinique's engagement party, well, cease worrying. I intend to have you as an escort, have no doubts about that."

"I only wish that were my primary concern."

"Well, thank you, *monsieur*. I must say you certainly know how to make a girl feel important," she mocked as though offended.

He halted, turning around so suddenly that she bumped into him. "It is your importance to me that drives me to distraction with trying to protect you, Christina. I would kill any man who tries to harm you."

Looking into his hard, intense visage, Christina had no doubt that he meant every word that he spoke, "You scare me when you talk this way, Jase," she whispered.

"It is not you who needs to beware, my love . . . not you."

The day passed before them in glorious abandonment

as together they explored every nook and cranny of the small inlet that Jason had spirited her to. The clipper ship sat anchored in the tranquil setting of their private bay, the crew enjoying a day to just relax on board and bask above deck in the warm sun. It was indeed a splendid day, the air perfumed with late blooming flowers, and the sand on the beach soothing as Christina sifted the toasty granules between her toes. Her stockings and slippers lay discarded atop the deep blue cloak. Jason dropped down beside her, tossing a handful of wiggly crabs in a basket beside him.

"I bet you've never been to a clam bake before, have you?" he asked as he stretched out his long body and propped his head upon his hand to view her through narrowed eyes.

"I can't say that I have," she turned her head to observe him, and caught her breath at the glint of desire she read in their depths.

"We'll have one, then. Tonight."

"You *do* intend to keep me here forever, don't you?" she whispered, resting her arms back over her head, and smiling to herself as the tops of her breasts spilled further from the décolletage of the simple wheat-colored muslin she had chosen to wear.

His brown fingers reached forward to trace along the velvety satin of their alabaster splendor. "If you would be willing . . . or perhaps even if you're not," he said softly. He could feel her breathing quicken beneath his caressing fingers. "But somehow, I think that you are . . . willing."

He lowered the gown down one slim shoulder until slowly a firm amber-tipped breast peeked forth. His tongue moistened his lips suggestively, purposefully.

"And you?" she countered boldly.

His answer was to lower his head to place his lips about the already hardened peak tempting him.

She gasped at the shock waves coursing through her as he suckled gently.

"Jase," she breathed against his mouth as it covered hers. She surrendered herself completely into his keeping.

His lips were everywhere, upon her temples, her closed eyelids, and moving downward to the wildly beating pulse at her throat. One sinewy arm held her still beneath him as he lowered the gown completely to her waist.

"Jase," she protested weakly. "What of the men? Can they not see us?"

"No," he assured her, "the rowboat shields us. They can see nothing. And besides, we are just going to renew our acquaintance a bit, whet our appetites, so to speak." His eyes took on a promising light. "The best we save for last."

His hands closed about her waist, lifting her bodily. His fingers slid the gown further downward, until it lay in soft folds across her hips. She closed her eyes, a bit afraid as to his reaction when he had unclothed her completely. Only this morning a look into her full length mirror had told her that she was not going to be one of these fortunate women whose pregnancies lay hidden until the last months. Her abdomen continued to grow rounder by the day, it seemed. She felt the cooling breeze upon her bare skin and burrowed deeper into the warmth of the sun-warmed sand as his body encompassed her to protect hers from further chill. The heat from his stroking fingers served to bank the fires of her desire as he explored, with infinite slowness, each curve, each pulse point, each soft warm place that he intended to claim. He tugged once, and stripped away her remaining confinements, and she lay naked beneath him, and so very shy.

Feeling her tremble, he said, "Cold? Do you wish for me to stop?"

"No," she breathed, barely more than a whisper. "But . . ."

"But what, love?" he coaxed gently.

She turned her head to one side. "I do not look quite the same as the last time we made love."

His fingers caressed the small mound lovingly, reassuringly. "And I love you more than the last time, little cat. So much it tends to frighten me." He kissed her stomach lightly.

The sun was an orange-red sphere of burning fire as it bathed the two naked lovers in its heated glow and baked the white sand beneath them into a hot bed of desire. They ravished each other's mouths with glorious abandonment, their tongues tasting the honey of that warm place and making them shudder with suppressed longing to be joined by yet another action.

Jason could feel her silken hips moving against him, and the moistness of her as she pressed against his thigh, urging him to her, to fill her, to bring her rapture as only he could.

"Not yet. I wish to savor every inch of you first. It's been too long since I've held you like this, tasted of you in that way that I desire."

Christina twisted almost frantically beneath him, her fingers clutching his thick black locks as she tried desperately to seek her relief. His lips were relentless as they broke free of hers and nibbled along the lobe of each ear, his tongue so warm as he traced such delight over her skin. Her full breasts, the nipples aroused and longing for his touch, were not forgotten. First one, and then the other was warmed by his swirling tongue. And when she felt certain that she would surely explode from the pleasurable sensation, he moved on, downward, to explore with gossamer lightness the curve of her abdomen.

Watching him through heavy-lidded eyes, Christina realized at that moment that her life would mean nothing without him to share it with. As his hands gently spread her thighs and his mouth found the core of her femininity, she gave herself up to the sensations that overtook her. And Jason, to his delight in giving it to her.

When the earth had ceased spinning beneath her, and had righted itself once again, she opened her eyes to see him staring at her, his desire as yet unslaked. She held her arms out invitingly. He chuckled.

"The best is for last . . . remember?" Reaching for her velvet cloak he wrapped it snugly about her and then proceeded to move about as he built a cheery fire. Having placed driftwood in a pile earlier, a match was all that was needed to reap the benefits of its warmth. "I thought it best to start the fire before the sun goes down which is just about now." Opening the wicker hamper that they had brought along with them, Jason took out a bottle of peach brandy and two glasses. He poured two, and handed one to Christina, "Sip on that until I get back. It should warm you up nicely." He winked at her suggestively.

She watched as he gathered some seaweed and returned. By that time the fire was roaring and she noticed he had placed large rocks about the blaze. Scooping the clams from the basket where he'd tossed them earlier, he placed them upon the heated rocks and covered them with seaweed. Then he sat back on his haunches and sipped his brandy.

"So, this is what you were trying to explain to me. A clambake, right?" she laughed.

"Exactly as it sounds," he replied, laughing along with her. He reached inside the hamper again and withdrew a loaf of crusty bread and yellow cheese. Tearing off a small hunk of bread and then cheese, he moved next to her and placed it before her lips. She nibbled daintily from his fingers, her white teeth taking small bites as he continued to hold it for her. A few crumbs of cheese clung to the edge of her lip and he brushed it away with the tip of his finger. She caught it playfully between her teeth and ran her tongue suggestively across the tip as she sucked gently upon it. She was aware immediately of the effect it had upon him as there was nothing to hinder her seeing. A gust of wind blew into their private cove and whether he shivered from desire, or a chill, she did not know, but opening her cloak, she invited him to share in the warmth within.

They huddled closely together by the fire and as the clams lay wrapped snugly and smouldering within, so did they.

At last, Jason declared the shelled delicacy ready to eat. With a cloth he removed them from their bed of seaweed and placed them in a napkin before her.

She cast him a smiling inquiry. "What should I do with them?"

Picking one up, he removed the Bowie knife from its sheath that lay within reach and began to pry open the shell. Steam escaped as the shell was forced open and the succulent meat was revealed. He loosened the flesh of the

378

clam with the Bowie and then held it to her lips.

"Use your tongue," he urged with a mocking smile.

"This hardly seems decent." She grinned as she tested the texture of the offering with the tip of her tongue. Deciding she had eaten worse, she sucked it neatly from the shell into her mouth.

"Very good," he praised. "Very good, indeed."

Swallowing, she cast him a derisive look. "What is? My methods, or the fact that you actually talked me into eating these things?"

"A little bit of both," he drawled, popping a bit of clam meat into his mouth. "You look like you've been doing this sort of thing for years."

Christina's eyes became transfixed upon a droplet of clam juice that had lodged in the cleft of Jason's chin. He caught the direction of her gaze and watched amused, as her eyes followed the droplets meandering trail as it trickled through the thick furring of his chest, over the flat belly, to disappear tauntingly below his navel. His amusement quickly evaporated as her finger reached out to trace the very same path of that droplet. From the small indent in his chin, along the broad chest, teasing lightly the lean muscles of his abdomen, and meeting his look of longing head on when her fingers dropped below his navel and wrapped unhesitantly around him. A glimpse of her soul was revealed in the jade cat eyes that stared heatedly into his. There was a primitive abandoness about her now that quickened his blood and fired his passion. The sun had long since set and it was the moon that strove for its rightful place in the deep purple sky. The night had brought with it a fine mist that wrapped a second cloak about them and insured them privacy. The velvet cloak fell away unheeded as they allowed the warm

379

sand to embrace their bare skin. Christina thought how scintillating the coarse sand was as Jason pressed her hips into it with his own. It was a moment of glorious unity when he joined at last with her pliant body and felt the hunger that had been denied for weeks take fire in his blood. He was drugged on her passionate kisses and drowning in this whirlpool known as love. His entire being was filled by his love and need of her. She was his everything.

Christina felt his mouth searing her own and his heart cry out his pledge of love for all eternity. It was a wondrous, all-consuming moment and as she held him deep within her she returned to him these very same emotions that he had given freely to her. And for a brief period in time they were unhindered by the demands of their world, and their peers, as they soared together above it all to a plateau where nothing existed but them . . . and love.

Chapter Twenty

Curt Duprea found the memory of Rhea Francesco constantly on his mind. He had banished her from his life, but he was unable to keep the vision of her from his thoughts. Memories assailed him whether he was awake or asleep. He had rented a suite of rooms for her, deposited large sums of money in her name at the bank, and denied her nothing material. Emotionally, she received no indication that he still cared.

Rhea stood in her comfortable parlor and studied the last statement from the bank that listed each deposit that Curt had made. The paper crinkled tightly in her hand. "You are trying so hard to bury the memories of me without feeling guilt for doing so, aren't you?" she mused. "The last thing you want to feel is love . . . but I'm certain there is still some feeling left for me. We went through too much together." She closed her eyes as a familiar, painful knot seemed to swell in her chest. "I still love you, want you . . . and I am sorry for everything I've done that has brought us to this. If only you would give me the chance to make it up to you." She considered her words, and found them to be true. But how would he ever know if she couldn't get him to even talk to her? She had refused to pay a great many of her accounts in hopes that he would hear of it and seek her out for an explanation. The lovely apartment that he had secured for her was the only concession that she made. After all, if she was going to win back his affections she would need a place to set her plan of action into motion. This was the only thing that kept her going and fostered in her the strength necessary to keep up the struggle. Love him she did; to the point of sacrificing everything possible, even her life. Several times she had seen him around town with his sister or some of his theater friends. There was never a time when she could manage to see him privately, and she desperately needed to talk with him. She had made an important decision. She was going to tell him of Simon Baker's forcing her to agree to help him in kidnapping Christina. She had to regain his trust and his love, even though it was decidedly dangerous to double-cross Simon Baker.

Her thoughts growing increasingly darker, she grabbed her cloak on impulse and fled from the lonely apartment and out onto the busy street. She wandered aimlessly through the marketplace, pausing at this stand or that vendor to examine their wares and then move onward. She was cautious as she strolled along, glancing over her shoulder at any unexpected noise, and keeping her distance from dark alleys. She knew she was taking a chance walking unescorted and unprotected. Simon Baker could be watching every move that she made, and probably was.

Suddenly out of the corner of her eye she caught a glimpse of a seedy looking man who seemed to be following her. Terror overwhelmed her.

Rhea glanced around frantically for a place of refuge. She could not resist looking his way another time, and panicked when he smiled at her as though she were his prey and he was a hungry mountain cat. She fought the urge to scream for someone to help her. Like a frightened doe she ran through the crowds in an effort to lose him, but the man doggedly kept up with her. She darted into the first shop that she came to.

The proprietor glanced up from her work and seeing who it was that stood in the doorway went forward to greet her with a fixed smile.

"Miss Francesco, what an unexpected surprise. I hope this means you are here to pay off your account." Her words were discreetly spoken and her manner most polite, but the look in her eyes, brooked no argument.

Rhea cast a furtive glance out the window. The man was still there . . . waiting. "Is there an empty dressing room where we might discuss this in private, madam?" Rhea said, trying to keep her voice steady.

The woman nodded crisply and ushered Rhea to the back of the shop and into an empty dressing room.

Rhea breathed a sigh of relief when the door was shut behind them. She was safe for a little while and would use the back exit when she felt it safe to return to the street. She turned to address the woman standing before. "*Señora*, I have every intention of meeting my next installment. I just need more time before I pay off the entire amount."

The woman's lips formed a tight angry line before she snapped. "I cannot allow you to order another thing from my store until the balance of your account is paid in full." She favored Rhea with a stern, no nonsense look.

"And I do hope that will be soon."

Rhea's face twisted in outrage as she lashed back. "I do not like having my intentions questioned by you or anyone? After all, it is a small sum, surely not big enough to make such a fuss over."

Rhea and proprietor continued with their heated discussion as the Spanish beauty sought to gain a few precious minutes before she had to return to the streets. She would argue all day with this woman if it meant she remained free of Simon Baker's clutches.

The sharpness of Rhea's voice carried through the thin walls and captured the attention of the couple who had just entered. Curt Duprea had agreed to escort his sister to the dress shop for the final fitting of the gown she'd ordered to wear to John and Martinique's engagement party. Upon hearing Rhea's voice, he instantly regretted that decision.

Christina's eyes flew to her brother's face. "Curt, let's just go. I can come back later today."

"Absolutely not," he replied in a flat tone. "If she insists on staying in the same city as me then I suppose I will have to become accustomed to running into her from time to time." He escorted her to a chair as the heated tirade from the dressing room continued.

"Excuse me, will you Christina?" Curt didn't wait for her reply but had already started forward, toward the sound of the voice now arguing hotly in Spanish. Christina's face flushed crimson when she recognized a few of the choicer words. She cast her eyes downward and pressed her lips together.

Rhea tensed in fear as soon as she heard the tap on the dressing room door. She stared unbelievingly at the man who opened the door and stepped inside.

Curt was the first to speak. "Hello, Rhea." He smiled apologetically. "I'm sorry for intruding upon you but I couldn't help overhearing your conversation. I thought perhaps you did not receive my message informing you of funds deposited for you at the bank."

"I received it," Rhea replied solemnly. "I choose not to touch it."

The shopkeeper hurried to smooth over the awkward moment. "Sir, please accept my apology for this most unfortunate incident. This is nothing for you to concern yourself with, I assure you."

Curt smiled politely. "I understand that perfectly, madam. But if you will just leave us alone, I am quite certain I can arrange for things to be worked out to everyone's satisfaction."

The shopkeeper threw him a doubtful glance. She exited with a swish of her skirts and Rhea was left facing her former lover alone.

"Why have you not used any of the money?" Curt said.

"The apartment is enough; quite generous, actually." She appraised his new appearance and mulled over the conventional image he now presented. What had she expected, she thought? He had even discarded wearing the eye patch, although upon her questioning him about it, he did explain that he wore it about in his own quarters.

"My new appearance confuses you, doesn't it?"

"Somewhat . . . but it is becoming." She did not reveal that inwardly she was disappointed that he could remain so fit and devastatingly attractive without her presence in his life. "Actually, I like the look very much; the beard, the clothes, even the shorter haircut."

"In all fairness, it was Christina's idea."

"Of course," Rhea said bitterly.

"Do you still despise her that much, Rhea?" Curt could not help but ask.

Rhea countered without hesitation. "I might ask the same of you." She hoped she had not misread the light in his eyes when he'd first entered the dressing room and saw her.

"No," he replied softly. "We shared too much for me to ever hate you, even though I have tried."

"Have you forgiven me, just a little?" She favored him with a sultry, pouty look, her full red lips parting in a guileless smile.

"You look like a little girl who was caught with her hand in the cookie jar, rather than a woman who connived with her lover's worst enemies."

"Am I never to be forgiven for that one mistake? Are you going to punish me for the rest of my life because of it?" she insisted, her large dark eyes brimming with unshed tears.

"I do not wish to punish you, Rhea," Curt explained patiently. "I just want to get back to my life as I knew it before all of this."

"And before me?"

Curt desperately sought to sway the conversation back to safer ground. "I think I have shown that I am not unaware of the great debt I owe you."

"Oh, you are generous enough." She stared deliberately into his eyes. "But it is not your money that I am after, my Silver Wolf."

A sigh escaped him. "Silver Wolf no longer exists."

Without hesitation, she advanced toward him, and watched his eyes fire as they followed the sway of her hips. "This is just a reminder, *querido,* that he does." She stood on tiptoe and wrapped her slender arms about his neck as she pressed her warm lips to his. Her mouth parted and her tongue probed the softness of his lips, but went no farther. She intended to prove to him that his words were easily spoken; his emotions, on the other hand, were an entirely separate matter. The man she knew and loved was still there; would always be there. She smiled inwardly when she felt the tip of his tongue search out hers and delve heatedly into her mouth. She pulled back from him and whispered only inches from his lips.

"You see, *querido,* for Rhea, he appears."

Passion lurked in the depths of his golden gaze as he murmured. "Yes, he hungers for you, you Spanish witch. Night and day since he left you, he yearns to feel your lovely little body thrashing beneath him." He framed her face in the palms of his hands. "Why . . . why didn't you leave me be, Rhea?" he groaned in defeat as he crushed her to him.

"Why didn't you send me away if that is what you really wished?"

He grabbed a handful of her lustrous hair and buried his face in its rose petal scent. "I couldn't . . . I can't, even now," he whispered, "God help me, I wanted to. I can't live with you, Rhea, and yet I find that I can't live without you."

Hope surged within her. "We belong to each other, you and I. No matter what you say, it was meant to be this way."

His fevered kisses roamed over her slightly flushed face. "I can make no promises."

"Just hold me, my Silver Wolf, hold me tight."

He crushed her to him, molded their bodies in a familiar embrace. "I've wanted so to forget you," he stated, his voice raspy with desire, "but it is no use . . . I can't."

"Will you come to my apartment later this evening?" she ventured to ask. "I must talk with you."

Rhea longed to tell him all of the things that were in her heart; all of the fears in her soul, but his lips silenced anything she might have said. His kiss was possessive and hungry, and Rhea responded freely in return. Heaven was in this man's arms . . . her world was nothing without him.

Christina kept looking toward the closed dressing room door. He had been in there with Rhea longer than she had expected. When she saw him at last coming her way, she held up her new gown.

"How do you like it?" She saw the myriad of emotions that her brother could not readily conceal as he glanced over at her.

"Very nice," he replied absentmindedly, and then turned to the shopkeeper. "The young lady in the back dressing room. I wish to settle her account with you. And anything else that she should desire—see that she has it, without fail. I will be personally responsible for payment."

The proprietor beamed with satisfaction. "Very good, Monsieur Duprea. It shall be as you request."

A puzzled frown marred Christina's features. She clutched the bombazine gown to her bosom and stared up at him.

But at the moment Curt Duprea was feeling a desperate

need of some fresh air. He tossed some bills at the matronly dressmaker. "This should take care of my sister's bill. Madam, would you please wrap her gown for her?"

The ride back to Diamond Sal's was uncomfortably silent for both Curt and Christina. As soon as the carriage came to a halt, Curt sprang forward to help his sister from the vehicle. They walked briskly through the doors of the salon and were greeted immediately by none other than Black Jack O'Leary, who kissed Christina soundly upon her cheek.

"If you have any sense about, lass, you'll turn yourself around and head right back out that door." He rolled his green eyes skyward.

"Problems, Black Jack?" Curt inquired.

"Singular, son. Problem. Sal."

Christina could not contain her smile of amusement as a lilting voice yelled forth from the kitchen.

"Black Jack, you old rascal, where have you run off to now?" Diamond Sal, rolling pin in hand, came forth in search of her husband. Dustings of flour clung to her fingertips and chin as she descended upon the trio. "You are supposed to be helping set up the dining tables in the main salon, and look at you." She eyed the mug of foaming beer in his hand with a scathing, disapproving look. "Just let me turn my back on you for one minute and you're loafing." She thrust the rolling pin in his direction for emphasis.

"Now, darlin' Sal," Black Jack cooed in a soothing voice. "I wasn't deserting you, honey; just taking me a well deserving rest, that's all." He grinned innocently in her direction.

She pursed her lips in indignation. "You are so full of Irish malarky a body doesn't know when to take you serious and when not," she reprimanded. She pointed toward the large salon that had been closed off in preparation for the big event to take place the following night. "Go—now!"

Curt laughed heartily and grabbed Black Jack's arm. "Come on, my friend, you look like you can use some help."

Christina's eyes uneasily followed her brother's departure.

For a heart-stopping moment Curt Duprea paused in the doorway of Rhea Francesco's suite.

Rhea stood on the other side of the threshold, her eyes locked with his. There was something very different about her now, and as he followed her to the sofa it struck him what it was. Honesty and truthfulness, two qualities that had been lacking in their relationship for a long time.

"It's very nice," he said, glancing about the cozy apartment.

Rhea had forgotten anything else existed besides Curt; shaking herself free of her dreamlike state she invited him to sit down.

"Thank you. I'm glad that you like it, Curt."

"Curt?" he repeated in surprise. It was the first time he'd heard his given name upon her lips, and the sound warmed his heart.

"I am ready to relinquish the past and go forward into the future . . . together . . . if you are," she said softly. She sat beside him, her body brushing his in a seemingly accidental motion. It triggered a response in him that brought a reminiscent smile to his lips and his long fingers to brush across her cheek.

"Oh my fiery Rhea, you can't know the hell I've been through until this moment." The house was quiet except for the crackling fire and the sound of their quickened breathing.

"I need you," she whispered, "very much."

"I tried to tell myself that you were the lowliest woman I ever had the misfortune to meet. I promised myself I would forget you, drive my feelings for you from my soul and purge your memory from my mind."

Her eyes filled with tears at his words. "I would surely wither and die if you should do this," she whispered.

"It is an impossibility," he murmured, his mouth moving closer to hers. "I found that you were with me everywhere. In the wind I heard your sigh, in the black satiny night, envisioned your raven hair cascading like velvet about your shoulders; but most of all I missed the feel of you," he eased her into his arms, "against me . . . like this."

She murmured his name as her parted lips accepted his with wild abandonment. "I love you, darling," she said quietly when at last they parted.

Curt stretched his lean form out on the sofa and urged her beside him, tucked within the curve of his arm and pressed full length against him. He inhaled the sweet scent of her as his head dipped to the beckoning valley between her breasts.

Rhea closed her eyes to enjoy this moment to the fullest. She held no doubts in her heart about what she was doing. Even if Simon Baker found out that she had betrayed him and killed her, it would be worth just this one night in Curt's arms. Gently, but urgently, they removed each other's clothing and went on with their heady exploration of love's secret delights until at last they came together in a fierce explosion of all-consuming passion.

"Make this night last forever, *querido*," she breathed huskily, and sighed with contentment when his arms closed around her. She had no fears at that moment, not even of dying by Simon's hand. Curt was here in her arms making love to her as she had dreamed for so long, and for now, that was enough.

On the day of the engagement party Christina rose bright and early and began to dress for breakfast with Martinique at the prospective bride's home. She hadn't slept very well. She was worried about Curt. Was he never going to be free of Rhea?

Christina drew herself from her brooding thoughts. She looked up to see Jason's wandering gaze upon her.

"It's a bit early, sweetheart."

She smiled at the picture he made sitting there looking so dark and handsome against the ivory satin sheets. His black hair was sleep-tousled about his face, the dark curls upon his forehead making him appear so innocent and vulnerable. "I just wanted to get an early start on the day. I promised to have breakfast with Marti this morning, remember?"

Jason grinned teasingly. "I'm sure you ladies have much to talk about and fuss over before the gala event. However, it means I am forced to seek out another breakfast companion."

Christina's brow arched. "One I approve of, I hope."

Jason's grin broadened. "Do I detect a possible note of jealousy?"

Christina attended to the rest of her toilette as his eyes followed her every move. "I don't deny that," she admitted, glancing back at him through the cheval mirror. "But I think it is a two-way street, my darling rogue; so remember that!"

She started for the door, turning one last time before she left to face him. "Marti and I have a surprise for you later. We've been saving it just for tonight so be certain that you are downstairs on time." She waved happily and went on her way.

Curt Duprea roused himself from Rhea's arms and stared down at her sleeping form. What she had revealed to him late last night, after they were both exhausted and content from their session of love, had whirled around in his head the entire night. Could he believe her? Could he trust her after she had deceived him before? This new revelation nagged at him sharply and he had a sudden desire to grab her roughly by her shoulders and shake her, demand that she swear her loyalty or risk her own death this time. His voice was but a whisper as he spoke to the sleeping woman.

"I will kill you myself if you deceive me and endanger my sister's life another time, I promise you that." Then he rolled away from her and off the sofa to gather his clothes and dress hurriedly.

Curt Duprea strode through the early morning crowds toward an outdoor cafe that he frequented. After he had seated himself and ordered breakfast, he mentally sorted through the facts Rhea had presented to him concerning her contact with Simon Baker. Her words kept ringing in his ears.

"He wants your sister, the woman he claims is his wife and rightfully his. And if I do not help him to obtain her, he has threatened to turn you in to the New Orleans police and, most certainly, end my life."

Her voice had trembled so when she'd told him as she'd lain so open and vulnerable in his arms that Curt felt certain that this time he could rely on her to help him save Christina from Simon's grasp. He now had two women's lives to protect; two that he loved very much.

The future had never seemed so precious as it did at that instant to Curt. Always he had been so concerned over the past. Now he found it wasn't so important to him any longer and prayed that God would help him find a way to ensure all of the tomorrows for his sister, and for the woman that he loved.

Martinique Summerfield laughed gaily as she observed the delighted expression on her dear friend's face. "Don't move, Christina. I'll come to you." Very carefully she moved from where she had been standing in the garden of her lovely home and walked quite well toward Christina.

"I'm so happy for you!" Christina said excitedly. "You've done it!"

Martinique indicated for Christina to follow her and they entered a side door to a large, airy bedroom that was papered in soothing lavender cream flowers. "I told you I had every intention of walking down that aisle at the church and I meant it!" she stated with finality in each word. She picked up a silk gown from the bed for Christina's inspection. "Do you like it?"

"It's beautiful," Christina replied.

"I'm wearing it tonight." She held up the deep blue gown with its smooth flowing lines in front of her. "John is going to be so surprised when I show him what you and I have managed to do. I can never thank you enough for your faithful support."

"You are an inspiration for all of us, Marti," Christina praised. "Never let someone give you tough odds, do you?"

Martinique's eyes gleamed. "I'm not one to crumble when the going gets tough, if that's what you mean. And as for odds, well, I've learned a bit from my gambler friend Jason. When they are not in your favor you just sway the odds a bit to your side. And if you work hard enough you just may find that they've been equalized."

Christina's expression revealed her thoughts. "I suppose I could take a lesson from that."

Martinique read her thoughts.

"At least you've told him at last. I was beginning to worry you would have the child away from him somewhere."

"I'm still going home with Curt as soon as your wedding is over, if that's what you mean."

"To Oak Meadow? Without Jason?"

"Jason has never said one way or the other if he would care to join me there," Christina revealed.

"Why don't you ask him and find out?" Martinique sat down at last upon the bed.

Christina flopped down in a forlorn heap beside her. "Until the truth is learned of my marriage to Simon, I am not free to ask anything of Jason. It's just an awful mess and to make matters even worse, I've got to go home and try to explain this situation to my family."

Martinique wrapped a comforting arm around Christina's over-burdened shoulders. She had sworn to Big John that she would not tell Christina they had located Simon Baker's secluded hideaway, and it took all of her will power not to do so now. The agents had agreed that if Christina were told she might insist upon coming with them or take some impulsive action that would endanger her life.

The secret was safe, for only the three agents knew its location. It had been discovered by a fluke while Big John had been gator hunting with a group of Cajuns. Their boat had happened upon a seemingly abandoned riverboat in one of New Orleans' obscure bayous. It had aroused Big John's natural curiousity. Keeping carefully hidden, John had managed to identify some people who had appeared on deck. One of them had unmistakably been Simon Baker himself. Big John had not wanted to risk a surprise attack without being properly equipped with firearms, so he had to leave that day. But he had promptly relayed all of the facts to Martinique and Jason, and the three agents had immediately made plans. Martinique could still recall the intensity in Jason's voice as he had briefed them on their plan of attack for the last time.

"Baker is mine. He is going to tell me everything I want to know by the time I'm through with him and I don't want interference from anyone. Is that clear?" She and John had nodded silently.

"What's left of him you can have, Big John. I know I promised you that."

"Just leave me something to take into custody, Jase. I want the pleasure of watching him hang."

"I'll try like hell not to get too carried away," Jason had replied.

"I think you both need me along just to keep you from killing the man," Martinique said, casting them both a simmering glance. "We are agents of the federal government, you know. Our personal feelings are not supposed to become involved here."

"I admire that quality about you most, Marti." Jason had the first signs of a smile. "You remain cool no matter what you're up against."

"Yes," she replied emphatically, "as I expect both of you to do. I'm the one who should be wanting to put a bullet in him. After all, we know who it was that ran me down that day. And now I have to stay behind and remain in control of our home base while you two rob me of all the glory." She heaved an exasperated sigh.

"Now, honey," Big John interceded, "if you could walk you know Jase and I wouldn't hesitate to take you the whole way with us. But as it is, there is just no way. I'm sorry . . . I really am."

"Big John's right," Jason responded firmly. "It's too dangerous to expose you to Baker a second time. This is not going to be easy, not at all."

Martinique had agreed, but deep within her a plan, and an even stronger resolve, began to take hold. If she could walk, John had said. If she could walk . . .

Her thoughts returned to the present and to the young woman beside her. Martinique remarked with conviction. "Yes, both Jase and my handsome captain are going to be astounded." She smiled at Christina. "I can hardly wait to see the look on their faces!"

Chapter Twenty-One

The engagement party for Big John McGurk and Martinique Summerfield promised to be an affair that New Orleans would remember.

On the eve of the event, Diamond Sal, in whose casino the reception was being held, stood in the main salon issuing last minute instructions to her efficient staff. She looked stunning in a pale blue taffeta and silk gown with her blonde hair swept up sleekly into a fashionable roll. Her jewelry, consisting of aquamarine stones and diamonds, sparkled beneath the glow of the crystal chandeliers. Everything seemed to radiate the glimmer of excitement in Sal's blue eyes.

Dinner was a sit down affair for over one hundred people. Sal watched with a critical eye as the waiters brought forth hearts carved of pink ice and placed them in silver punch bowls filled with champagne delight. Floral arrangements of pink and white roses were artfully placed about the room and upon each individual dinner table.

Black Jack O'Leary, looking a bit uncomfortable in his

dark jacket, walked toward his wife all the while tugging at his starched cravat.

Sal thought him exceedingly handsome this evening and placed a well-deserved kiss upon his lips.

"What's that for, me sweet flower?" Black Jack blustered.

"For being so dashing," Diamond Sal replied with a coy smile.

Black Jack beamed. "For you, me darlin', 'tis an easy task."

Sal went to compliment her hardworking staff. As she did so she could be heard mumbling about the blarney of all Irishmen. But still, a very discernible smile could be seen curving the corners of her lips.

True to her earlier prediction, Martinique did indeed astonish her betrothed when he came to her bedroom that evening to escort her to the party. Big John tapped upon her door and when she bade him enter he was more than astounded to find her standing before the fireplace, looking every bit like a vision from heaven—so beautiful and radiant, his glad heart cried. Rushing forward he took her hands gently in his as though she might crumble if he wasn't cautious.

"Oh, Marti," he sighed, his eyes bright from suppressed emotion, "I can't tell you how good it does my soul to see you standing there on those gorgeous legs of yours once again. But how—how did you manage to do it? Although, knowing your spirit woman, I don't know why I even need to ask." His glowing face revealed his admiration.

"I did have help. Christina," she answered his

questioning look. "She came every other day to massage my legs and keep the muscles from deteriorating beyond repair. I owe her so much, John, and I'm hoping now that I can walk again," she paused to show him just how well as she demonstrated a few steps, "that I can repay some of the debt."

John swallowed over the lump in his throat, finding it difficult to speak so deep were his feelings at the moment. He felt like his life had just been given back to him seeing the shining light in Martinique's eyes once again. "I'll second that," he agreed simply.

"Oh, John, I'm so glad that you agree with me, and I know just the way." She quickly seized her opportunity. "The mission to go after Baker . . . I want to go the entire distance," she pleaded. "Just like we used to, the three of us . . . as a team."

Big John started to protest. Her finger came up to his lips to silence him.

"One of the last things you told me that day you and Jase were going over the plan, was that I could be there for the arrest on board Baker's boat if I could walk. Well?" She knew she had made her point.

Big John shook his head in defeat.

"All right, Marti," he conceded with a grin. "But you stay clear of the rough stuff. And I mean that!"

"Of course, darling," she responded obediently as they started from the room. "Whatever you say . . ."

John smiled broadly at the smug look upon her face. "I should know better than to ever underestimate you Marti. You have proven the best of them wrong time and again, and this time, I'm so very glad you did."

*   *   *

Christina thought she never saw anyone look more radiant than her friend, Martinique, as she entered the crowded casino on John McGurk's arm. They created quite a stir with their dramatic entrance and no one was happier than Jason to be witness to it. With Christina by his side, they went forward to extend their well wishes.

"Thank you, both of you," Martinique beamed.

"I don't know what we would do without your friendship," Big John added, "and I hope that one day soon we'll be attending your engagement ball.

They all turned at the sound of champagne corks popping softly throughout the room. Waiters in full black livery began threading their way about the tables filling glasses with champagne; for with the arrival of the guests of honor the celebrating officially began. The musicians began playing a waltz that invited everyone to step out onto the dance floor.

Jason took Christina's hand in his. "May I have this dance, beautiful lady?" he requested, looking so handsome in formal black attire.

"By all means, *monsieur*," she replied with a smile.

Jason led Christina to the dance floor while Big John and Martinique circled throughout the room conversing with their guests. However there was one guest that the couple didn't greet, for he kept hidden, watching with avid interest the festivities below him.

Simon Baker stood on the second floor balcony of the casino, his hungry eyes devouring the golden vision swaying gracefully in her lover's arms. She had no idea how just the sight of her heated his blood and fed his desire. It had been so long since he'd feasted his eyes on her beauty that he'd risked the chance in coming here tonight just to do so. He withdrew the marriage certificate from his pocket and glanced down at the names that were upon it—his and Christina's. A hot flame of lust ignited in his loins at the thought of the night when he would truly possess her completely. He had to have that luscious body of hers in his embrace soon, he groaned to himself. And this time he would show her he could be just as much of a stud as that son of a bitch who held her in his arms now. And she would fight him, oh, how she would . . . and he would perform like a stallion until he was tired of her and had made her his slave.

The evening wore on with much laughter, good food, plenty of bubbly, and feet that never grew tired of dancing. Christina noticed that Jason seemed more relaxed with her than usual. He wasn't moody or preoccupied as he had been of late and Simon's name had not been mentioned even once.

During the musicians' intermission, when Jason had departed to smoke a cigar with Big John, Christina cornered Martinique.

"It is as though Simon's whereabouts do not concern him, that he doesn't even care any longer about the man. The animosity is gone, his earlier tension nonexistent, and in my mind there is only one thing that could bring about such a change." She paused, waiting for a reply from Martinique. She was disappointed when it came.

"I don't have any idea what you're talking about, Christina," Martinique lied, even though she hated doing so.

"Don't give me that, my friend," Christina returned stubbornly. "I know you three have cooked up something. You've been spending a lot of time together of late, and without me. You've located Simon, haven't you?"

Christina noticed Martinique tense slightly at her words. "Tell me. I have a right to know."

Martinique was saved from giving an answer by the arrival of Curt Duprea. But Christina remained determined to find out what it was that they knew. Even if it meant she had to do a bit of investigating on her own. She turned her attention toward her brother, and when the music resumed she happily accepted his invitation to dance.

Martinique took a deep breath and exhaled slowly. As discreetly as possible, she went in search of her fiancé and Jason. Heaven knows they couldn't have anything go wrong in their plans at this late date. The mission was set to go tomorrow night. They would have to divert Christina only for a short time, and then all of the answers the desperate girl sought would be there for her. As long as nothing happened to mess up their plan of action, it should all go down quite smoothly. But as she explained her concerns to Jason and Big John in the privacy of the casino garden sometime later, and viewed their serious expressions, she had an undeniable sense of foreboding.

"Christina must not know," Jason said. "I don't want her doing anything foolish. Baker must not have a chance for one second to get near her. Once was enough," he finished grimly. "I don't want him getting an opportunity to take any hostages."

"We understand, Jase," Big John replied. "Just hang in there until tomorrow evening and soon your lady will be free."

"I was beginning to wonder if you intended to show up

at all this evening." Christina favored her brother with an inquisitive look. "Where have you been keeping yourself of late . . . or need I even ask?"

The sound of the music floated about them as Curt led her expertly around the floor. "I have something I wish to tell you," he ventured with bated breath. "And I'm not certain you are going to be pleased when you hear."

"Oh?"

"My whereabouts of late . . ."

"Go on," Christina urged.

"I've been working out some differences with Rhea, at her apartment."

"Curt!" Her expression was one of great distress. "How could you?"

Their eyes met and held; his burning with intensity, hers, disappointment.

"She's changed, Christina. She really has."

"Do you expect me to believe that?"

"I was hoping that you would trust my judgment."

Christina squeezed her eyes tightly to still her rising anger. "I do trust you, Curt. It's that woman who has torn all of our lives to shreds that I do not trust. She and Baker are the ones that belong together, two vipers."

They exchanged heated words; Curt in Rhea's defense, Christina in bitter accusation. At last, Curt told her: "Rhea is outside waiting for me. I want you to come outdoors and talk with Rhea and me."

Christina reluctantly allowed him to escort her through the room and out into the cool night air. With her arm tucked in her brother's, she followed him to a nearby carriage.

Curt held open the vehicle door and aided Christina in stepping inside. She sat across from the dark-haired Rhea and glared as she saw Rhea's hand reach out to snuggle into Curt's.

"This is a cozy scene I never thought I'd have to play witness to again," Christina said icily.

"We love each other very much," Rhea replied calmly, "and we intend to be together—always."

"So, you've won, *Señorita* Francesco . . ."

Curt interrupted, seeing that the conversation was not going as he'd hoped. "Ladies, come on now, let's try and discuss this like reasonable adults."

"I am willing," Rhea offered, "but I don't think your sister is."

Christina flounced back against the cushions. "Can either of you blame me? I mean, here I sit, my life torn asunder by your little liaison with Simon Baker that very nearly cost me my life, and did many of your own people!"

"I am trying to tell you," Rhea hurriedly pleaded, "that I know how I've wronged you and I would like to help undo some of it, if possible." She did not back down from the wrath she saw in Christina's eyes. "Please, . . . allow me."

"I don't see how you could undo so much wrong," Christina said coldly.

"Oh, but I think there is a way," Rhea rushed on without thinking what she was revealing, "and it concerns Simon Baker."

"Rhea!" Curt snapped. "That's enough!"

Christina sat up straight, her eyes riveted on Rhea. "What do you mean, Rhea?"

Rhea lowered her eyes to her colorful skirt. "I am sorry Curt, but she will never believe of my sincerity if we don't tell her."

"Damn it!" Christina fumed. "All evening I'm being protected by everyone and I am sick of it! Now, will you please go on Rhea? Finish whatever it is you want to tell me."

"I am too ashamed to reveal to you how all of this came to be," Rhea began unhesitantly, "But Curt and I are going to capture Simon Baker."

Christina's frantic gaze flew to her brother's impassive face. "You cannot do this, Curt! He is a vicious killer and you both could be killed." She clutched at her brother's arms. "Let the authorities take care of Simon."

"No one does what he did to us and gets off without punishment," he whispered harshly.

Christina's vision began to blur and a sick feeling came over her. She gasped and touched her forehead with a trembling hand.

"Christina?" Curt questioned with a frown. "Are you ill?"

"I'll be fine in a moment." She moved closer to the open window, hoping that the cool air might soothe her somewhat. It was then that she saw the figure hurrying across the street. "Simon!" she gasped, just before she slumped over into her brother's arms.

Rhea craned her head around Christina's crumpled form and she too saw the figure of Simon Baker hurrying through the shadows to a waiting carriage.

"Driver!" Rhea called out to the cabby as she took charge of the situation. "Follow that carriage just ahead of us. The one with the bays pulling it!"

Curt's head snapped up to glare at Rhea. "You can't go after him now, for God's sake! She's fainted and needs a doctor."

"Women swoon at everything, *querido*," Rhea declared. "It is more important that we go after Baker and see just where his headquarters are. Even though we are poorly equipped for such a venture we need the element of surprise on our side, and tonight is as good a night for that as any other." She felt Christina's forehead. "She will come around soon."

Curt cradled his sister close. "I will send her back in the carriage as soon as we arrive at our destination. I don't want to take a chance of Baker knowing that she is nearby."

"I agree," Rhea said. "It will be as you say."

Rhea looked up at Curt and read in his eyes everything that she had prayed she would see there once again. It buoyed her spirit for the task ahead, and filled her heart to overflowing with love for him. Even if she did not make it out of this alive tonight it was worth the price just to see the glow of love in his eyes.

Chapter Twenty-Two

Christina's eyelids fluttered open, but she remained motionless as she blinked and looked up to see her brother's concerned face watching her carefully. She attempted to smile reassuringly.

"Are you all right?" he asked in a worried voice.

"Yes, seeing that man just took me by complete surprise." Christina sat up and peered out of the carriage window. "Where in heaven's name are we?" She found her gaze mesmerized by the flickering yellow flames in the distance. Lantern lights, that's what they were! She twisted around to face Curt. "You followed him, didn't you? To that riverboat moored in the distance?"

"Yes, we felt it might be the best chance we'd have of finding him. I don't want him slipping away from me again."

"Oh Curt," Christina breathed softly. "If you are dead set on this vendetta then I suppose there is little we can do but help you every way possible. I don't want anything happening to you."

"You, my dear sister, are going back just as soon as

Rhea and I depart."

Christina bristled, "That's not fair. I can be of assistance."

"We need all of the help that we can get, *querido*," Rhea pointed out. "Look closely, there are men and guns everywhere on that boat."

"You need some sort of diversion if you intend to sneak on board without being noticed," Christina said.

"And I suppose you plan on being that diversion, sister?"

"I don't see you coming up with a clever plan. Rhea and I together should provide a better diversion than even an armed escort," she quipped.

"You're leaving here—now," he snapped.

"I seem to constantly have to remind you and Jason that I am not a child to be bullied about any longer." Her chin came up defiantly. "And I hope you also realize that I am not letting you do something as foolish as killing Baker. I'm going along with you and your foolish scheme just to keep you from putting your neck in a noose."

Curt's brow lifted in a sardonic gesture. "My sister, the bodyguard?"

A tender smile touched her lips. "Someone needs to be. Now, will you listen to my suggestions?"

"How did she manage to talk me into this?" Curt Duprea asked himself as he huddled in the damp, chilly mist that surrounded him and stared intently at the scene by the riverboat. He was more than a bit angry at himself for giving his sister the chance to change his mind about sending her back to town. But he had to admit grudgingly, as he watched Christina and Rhea flirting outrageously with the guards stationed at the entrance, that they just might be able to pull this off neatly and efficiently. Christina had promised faithfully that once Curt had managed to steal on board that she and Rhea would then sneak away from the guards and back to the safety of the carriage that was hidden down the road.

Curt stood watching as Rhea, laughing gaily, her red skirts swirling temptingly about her ankles, teased and flirted with the guards with Christina following her lead.

"You poor devils. You don't stand a chance," Curt mused under his breath as he began to move cautiously forward. "And I should know." His lean frame kept to the dark shadows as he crept unseen on board the boat.

Jason was frantic. He had looked everywhere inside and outside of the casino and Christina was nowhere to be found. Neither was her brother Curt, and one of the servants had added to his fears by telling him that he thought he saw them leaving together over an hour ago. "Where? Where in the hell did they go off to?" he murmured, his eyes doing one last sweep of the room. He caught sight of Black Jack hurrying toward him, a frown deeply etched upon his brow.

"Jason, me lad," he said breathlessly, having reached his side. "Me men reported some disturbing facts to me."

"What's that?" Jason waited expectantly.

"'Tis Simon Baker. He was in the balcony watching Christina all evening, I'm certain of it."

"How do you know this?"

"Me men attempted to detain him because he was acting so strangely. They tried their best to restrain him but he managed to get away."

"Did they give you a description?"

"Yes," Black Jack replied. "They said he was of medium height, overweight, with wild gray eyes. And Jase, he kept raving about his right to be near the lass—said if anyone had a right to her, he did."

"It was him," Jason confirmed, his concern increasing for Christina. "Will you keep this under your hat, Black Jack. I don't want to cause any undue anxiety, but I have a strong hunch that Christina and her brother have followed Baker from here."

Black Jack scowled. "Can you blame her, lad? When I heard the story meself I could not believe it. If Sal hadn't assured me she'd heard it straight from Christina, I would have scoffed in disbelief. It is incredible that such a man exists!"

"No, I don't blame her for anything. I blame Simon. And before this night is over, I intend to find out the truth of that night in question, or kill Simon in the trying."

Simon Baker was more than surprised to look up from his paper work and find his old enemy viewing him from the doorway. He was astonished, but his eyes revealed nothing as they stared into Curt Duprea's.

"So, we are to have our last stand after all," Simon sneered.

"Without fail, this time, Baker," Curt remarked casually. Even his stance, with thumbs hooked nonchalantly in his belt, gave credence to the air of unconcern that surrounded him. It made Simon furious realizing the corner he now found himself in. He glanced furtively over Curt's shoulder, searching, Curt knew, for his men.

412

"They are . . . indisposed," Curt said.

Simon's breath became thick in his throat as he wiped at the moisture suddenly pouring from his brow. "They'll come, and they'll kill you. You were a fool to come here."

"You were a fool to show up at the party tonight. You led me straight here." Curt grinned coldly. "You're slipping."

"You have a very lovely sister. She completely captivates a man so that you find yourself doing things you would not normally do." Simon kept speaking as his hand slipped inside the desk drawer he had managed to partially open without drawing attention to it. He felt around for the derringer he knew was there.

"Like forcing women to marry you?" Curt pointed out.

Simon's voice was steely-soft as he replied. "I believe I have just about stood enough of you, suh." He grasped the handle of the gun, feeling more in control with the cold steel against his palm. "I don't know what you thought you were going to accomplish by coming here alone and unarmed." He laughed shrilly. "This is a joke!"

It was then that Simon noticed Curt's hand was inside of his coat pocket. "What do you have there?" He looked wary, and suddenly terrified.

"What I call my powerful persuader," Curt drawled.

Simon sat frozen in undecisive motion. He began to blubber nervously. "If you use that gun my men will be here within seconds after you pull the trigger." His hand was itching to withdraw the gun he held, but the fear of being shot kept him immobile. He began to talk rapidly in an effort to buy himself more time. "I know what you came here for tonight . . . yes, I do. It is because of your sister. You wish to learn the truth about what took place between us, don't you?"

"You've almost destroyed her by what you did to her that night," Curt stated fiercely. "She didn't deserve that . . . but what I have in store for you you deserve." He moved menacingly toward Simon.

Simon looked pathetically frightened as he watched the tall man descend upon him. Too much a coward to challenge Curt outright, he waited until Curt stood directly before him, impossible to miss when he shot him. "Your sister was warming that blue-belly's bed long before I got hold of her," Simon growled. "I didn't do anything to her that hadn't been done already. She was used goods."

"Damn you, you heartless bastard! I'll thrash you within an inch of your life for saying that!" Curt roared as he made a lunge toward Simon, his hand withdrawing from his pocket.

"You never had any gun at all!" Simon crowed as he quickly withdrew the derringer and aimed it at Curt. "Stop or I'll blow your face away!"

"Go ahead, you rotten son of a bitch!" Curt growled as his foot swung forward, catching Simon by surprise. The derringer went off with a soft popping noise. The two women and the guards rushed toward the sound.

"Curt! Curt!" Christina screamed as she ran toward the sound of the struggle from within a far cabin.

The next few minutes were like a terrible nightmare that Christina felt certain she would awaken from at any moment. She was the last to reach the cabin and the sight that met her eyes when she rushed into the room stopped her dead in her tracks.

414

Curt was bleeding from a wound on the side of his head but still he was furiously pounding the screaming Simon with his fists. Three guards were attempting to pull him off of their fallen leader, but to no avail. Rhea Francesco had a dagger clutched in her hand and was slashing out at anyone who tried to subdue the silver-haired aggressor.

Christina's screams mingled with Simon's as one of the burly guards raised the butt of the rifle over Curt's head and brought it down forcefully with a vicious chopping motion. Curt slumped immediately on top of Simon. Rhea attempted to go to his aid, but was back-handed across the mouth and crumpled unconscious to the floor.

It was all over before Christina could even think to move, and by the time that she did, Simon had pulled himself from beneath Curt's inert form and was leaning heavily upon the desk. A wide gash ran across his nose, which looked smashed and pulpy and was bleeding profusely.

"He broke it," he sobbed in disbelief. "My nose . . . he broke it."

The guards raised their rifles now that Simon was out of the line of fire and prepared to shoot the two attackers. Christina threw her body in the line of fire and Simon called out sharply.

"Don't shoot them in here, you fools! You'll make a mess! Haul them outside and tie them up. We can come up with a better way to end their lives than to simply put a bullet in them."

"Please, Simon, I beg of you. Don't do this," Christina's voice pleaded softly as she faced him. She was crying great, gulping sobs as she knelt down beside the two bodies, so broken, so still. "I'll do anything you ask if you'll just spare their lives." She looked up at the man whom she feared and hated more than anyone, and cringed at the insane, gleaming light she saw in his lifeless eyes.

"Anything, my darling?" he purred, reaching down and pulling her up to him by her long hair. He smiled when he saw her wince in pain.

"Yes, . . . anything," she repeated.

Her breath nearly whooshed from her lungs as Simon's mouth twisted over hers, sucking the very life from within her as he kissed her.

Christina let him have his way with her as his men stood laughing lewdly in the background. Simon's hands were cruel and hurtful as they roamed and caressed her body. His slobber dribbled down her chin and his hips moved in a suggestive motion against hers. She bore it all without complaint. Curt and Rhea lay upon the floor. If they weren't dead already, they eventually would be, unless she could bargain for their lives. As she felt Simon's fingers at the back of her gown, and the coolness upon her shoulders as the night air caressed her spine, she knew what it was that she would bargain with.

So did Simon Baker, and he could not help but smile inwardly at the thought.

Christina lay upon the bed in Simon's quarters clutching the cover about her nakedness. She could hear Simon coming from the dressing room and approach the side of the bed. Her eyes looked up into his and saw not one shred of compassion. He smiled when he noticed how dilated and fearful hers were. His hand reached out to grasp the edge of the sheet.

"It's all up to you, you know—whether they live or they die." He fastened his eyes on her heaving breasts, as he slowly pulled the cover downward to reveal their naked splendor to his licentious gaze. "Your brother and that traitorous bitch, Rhea, are tied snugly about their wrists and are standing upon crates next to the rail." He yanked upon the coverlet another time so that it slipped downward an inch. "Do I have myself a willing woman here, or are there going to be tears and resistance?"

There could be only one answer . . . she nodded her head, and squeezed her eyes closed as the cover was yanked completely off of her. They flew open upon the cry of absolute disgust that erupted from Simon's lips. He was staring at her abdomen, and the distinct swelling that could only indicate one thing.

"You're carrying a child—that blue-belly's, aren't you?" he screamed in outrage and disgust.

"Yes," she whispered, pride revealed in her voice, "I am."

"Damn you to hell for that," he cursed her. "My sordid tramp of a wife!"

"You never completed the act that night we were together, did you Simon? You were just as impotent then as you are now!" she taunted.

"Don't laugh at me, you whore. It's not me—it's you! That's the reason I can't perform. I'll fix you for doing this to me a second time!"

The laughter died in her throat as she realized the full impact of his words.

"It isn't so funny anymore, is it?" he sneered. Get dressed, bitch! You and I have an appointment with the executioner up on deck."

"But I did keep my end of it!" she lashed back. "It is

417

you who cannot consummate it, not I!"

He growled viciously as he backhanded her across the mouth. She fell across the bed in a defeated slump. "Get dressed, I said. For the last time, or I'll be throwing you over the side with them if you don't."

"You rotten scum, Simon Baker. May you rot in hell for all of the atrocities you've committed."

Simon laughed jeeringly as he recovered his composure and went to the dressing room to retrieve his clothes.

Curt Duprea kept his eyes trained forward as he tried to concentrate on something other than the rushing sound of the river directly below him. Something kept drawing his attention down river to a flutter of movement behind a grove of trees along the curved shoreline. Was it only wild hope that made him think he saw figures moving furtively behind those trees? Or could someone else have discovered Baker's hideaway; someone who was even now hurrying to help them.

One only had to look upon the bound figures standing precariously upon the crates next to the guardrail to know what fate Simon had decreed for them.

"Even after all that you've done, I never actually thought you'd go through with something so awful," Christina said shakily as she stood on the deck next to Simon and stared at her brother.

"I'm surprised that you, of all people, would underestimate me," he chided with glee.

She was truly desperate now, and the fear in her voice

was apparent to him. "If you tell your men to get both of them down I swear to you that I will stay with you, I'll never leave you."

"Oh, my sweet, . . . we both know that's a bunch of bullshit," he said.

"Simon, what can I say or do that will change your mind?" she begged, knowing that she'd fall to her knees and kiss his feet if he told her to.

"It's too late. I warned you and you failed to keep your end of it."

"I tried. It was—"

"Shut up, bitch!" he hissed, glancing around him to see if any of his men were listening.

Pushed beyond her endurance, Christina ran across the deck to throw her arms around her brother's legs. "I won't let you do it—I won't! You'll have to throw both of us in the river!"

"Christina, get away from here," Curt moaned.

She gazed up into his face, wincing when she saw how battered it was. "No, I won't," she replied stubbornly.

"You're making it harder for him!" Rhea told her sharply. "Do as he says!"

"I can't . . . I can't," Christina wailed.

Dressed completely in black, and moving as steathily as he could, the man moved sleek and deadly through the mist. He had only one thought flowing through his head, one burning objective that kept him thinking clearly: to rescue the woman he loved. His two companions followed in his footsteps.

The leap from the dock to the deck of the riverboat was accomplished with effortless ease by the two men and the woman. Somewhere on this boat was their prey; and as they moved silently through the shadows toward the boat's prow they heard the distinct sound of Simon Baker's voice and knew that their search was over.

Christina clung to Curt, her arms wrapped about him, her head bowed in total defeat—at least, that was how it appeared. In truth, she was working furiously at the rope that bound her brother's wrists.

"It's time," Simon stated, gesturing to one of the guards to move Christina away from her brother.

She fought, scratched, and bit the hands that grabbed for her until Curt, fearing for her safety, yelled at her to do as she was told.

Hatred like nothing she'd ever experienced before assailed Christina as she was dragged beside Simon, who stood soberly viewing her display of temper with obvious amusement.

"The Spanish woman is to go first," he said to the guards who shoved the barrels of the rifles they held into Curt's and Rhea's backs.

"Rhea, . . . remember I love you," Curt said quietly, standing tall and brave, his manner now calm.

Rhea was sobbing softly, but she heard and nodded. She felt the rifle prodding her, urging her to take that last step. A sound from behind gave them all pause; it was a man's voice telling Simon to halt immediately or he was a dead man.

"Jase! Oh, Jase, you found us!" Christina cried, spinning around to meet his hard, piercing stare.

"Yes, I found you, little cat," Jason said huskily. "Come over here by me, sweetheart." He kept his pistol levelled at Baker's chest. "Unless you have any objections Baker?" he finished with a tight smile. "And while we're at it, have your men over there drop their guns."

Simon looked frantically around him, now noticing the bodies of his men lying still about the deck in the distance. He saw another agent come forward, rifle in hand, to join Jason. It was obvious he was in a precarious position, Simon thought. He would have to try and keep his wits about him if he intended to get out of this without being apprehended. "No objections, O'Roark, take her. She's a pain in the ass and not worth two cents in bed, anyway."

Jason cocked the trigger of the Colt. "Be very careful, Baker, of how you move and speak while this gun is pointed at you. It has a hair trigger." He inclined his head toward Curt and Rhea. "Tell your boys to help them down. We wouldn't want anything happening that shouldn't, now would we?"

Something in Simon's eyes warned Jason that he was not going to give up without a fight.

"Christina! Move quick!" Jason yelled. She moved forward to obey his command, but Simon caught her and shoved the derringer that had been hidden in his coat sleeve into her back. She gasped as she felt its bluntness against her spine.

"Jase, he has a gun!" she cried out.

"Throw your guns on the deck!" Simon shouted, his face set in determination.

"Do as he says," Jason murmured to his partner; John McGurk was gritting his teeth in frustration. Their only visible means of protection clattered to the deck at their feet.

"Very good, gentlemen. Now walk over there by the guardrail next to your friends," Simon commanded. His guards, seeing their chance to escape with their lives, ran like frightened jack rabbits.

Simon called after them, demanding that they stay and help him. His men paid no attention and fled the boat in haste.

"Go on, you cowards! I'll take care of myself!" he screamed.

Martinique Summerfield swung her long legs, encased in tight-fitting trousers, over the guardrail of the open gallery and balanced precariously on the ledge. She willed herself to remain strong.

Simon Baker stood directly beneath her with Christina in front of him. Martinique knew she would have to move fast. She reholstered her pistol, realizing she couldn't take the chance of shooting and possibly hitting Christina. There was only one thing left that she could do. Leaping feet first from the balcony, she lunged toward Simon and rammed a booted foot in his fleshy ribs. The force of the impact sent him reeling across the deck and into Rhea Francesco, catching her off balance.

Christina heard a shot ring out as she was knocked to the hard deck. Splinters gouged into her hands and knees, but she was so numb from terror that she didn't even feel them. An anguished wail of terror met her ears and she rolled onto her side to see Jason dive across the deck.

Simon and Rhea grappled with one another, fumbling, cursing, each of their faces a mask of complete and stark terror.

Curt Duprea had freed himself from his bonds and lunged forward to grab Rhea. She teetered on the edge of the railing, with Simon's enormous bulk continuing to force her toward the black, yawning space she was fighting so hard to avoid.

Curt struggled to reach Rhea, kicking out at Simon at the same time. He was finally successful in securing Rhea.

Simon fell against them both just as Jason reached for a hold on the man. Simon's bloodcurdling scream pierced the air as the weakened guardrail gave way beneath the force of their impact, sending Curt, Rhea, and Simon Baker hurtling over the side to disappear from view.

Christina raced to Jason's side and together they leaned over the guardrail to desperately search the fog-covered water for signs of survivors.

"Oh, Jase, they've drowned! I know it," she sobbed.

"Don't give up on Curt yet," Jason said hoarsely. He dove over the railing into the blackness; the only proof of a river below by the splash of his body as it hit the water.

Shadow In The Moonlight

Chapter Twenty-Three

"Try to kick your feet, Rhea!" Curt demanded. "Don't just give up!"

"My hands—they are still tied. I keep going under," she choked, struggling to keep her head above the water.

"I'll help you," Curt replied, summoning up the stamina to keep both of them afloat. He wrapped one arm about Rhea's slim shoulders and fought with all of his strength against the current that kept swirling them farther out into the main channel. He knew he had to keep them away from it or they were both doomed. All around them logs and other debris floated within arm's reach. If he could just grab onto one they would stay afloat. His numb fingers clawed at a small tree that drifted near; he held on as the river tried to wretch it from his grasp.

"I've almost got it," he shouted.

"I can't make it. . . .We're both going to drown. . . . Save yourself, let me be," Rhea gasped weakly before her head disappeared under the water.

"Rhea! Rhea!" he called hoarsely, groping in the water in an effort to find her. "I won't give you up—I refuse, goddamn it!" Reaching downward, he yanked with all of his remaining strength and felt a surge of joy when

Rhea's head once again bobbed to the surface. She was coughing and gagging on the water in her throat, but still she was alive—and he intended to keep her that way.

Curt kicked with everything he could muster but her added weight and the sucking grasp of the undercurrents made him realize they might not be able to make it—they were slowly drowning.

Rhea also knew that they were not going to survive. The thought of his dying brought back the memories of their first encounter. They had come full circle, she and her Silver Wolf. She would win his life for him, just as she'd done before, three years past when the explosion from the troop boat sent him hurling into the Mississippi, and into her arms.

"You will not have him—he is mine," she swore to the challenger. "I took him from your embrace once, and I can do it again."

With that, she twisted out of his weakening arms and kicked away from him before he could grab her.

"Rhea! What are you doing?" he screamed in panic. "Come back!"

"No, my darling, . . . it is the only way. *Adios, querido.* I give you back to your other life." She slipped away into the fog and disappeared.

The full impact of her loss began to sink in. She was truly gone; had given her life so that he might save his. And then the nightmare that so haunted him seeped into his consciousness.

"Oh, God, not now!" he begged.

But the images would not stop and flashed across his mind's eye in rapid succession. The fire was all around him, burning his face and body. His only thought was to escape the flames; he could feel them eating away at his flesh. And then the final explosion rocked the troop boat. His body was thrown like a feather through the air; he had the sensation of floating, drifting aimlessly. He hit the water; the river would suck him under until he would feel his lungs burst from the lack of air. And then there was nothing.

The chilling waters of the Mississippi brought him back to the present. As he floated in the river, he realized that bits and pieces of his long-locked memory had begun to surface. He could think beyond his years as the highwayman, the Silver Wolf, back to the night it had all happened.

It was a cold night in winter, just like tonight. He and his fellow enlisted men of the Confederacy were being shipped down river to another point of battle. They had been sitting companionably, desperately trying to bolster each other's spirits as they always did prior to a confrontation with the Yankees. The first low rumble began. Before any of them became aware of impending danger, the overburdened boilers burst open in a spew of fiery death, sending pieces of steamboat and human cargo into their watery graves.

It all came back to him now in a rush. He understood the reasons behind his recurrent nightmare; it had been of that night.

"I can remember . . . I remember it all . . . all of it," he whispered as he once again fought the river for his survival. "Please don't let me die now, not when I've just rediscovered my life."

Resolutely, he struggled to keep himself awake as the cold river swirled him around and around, lulling him into a false sense of reality. Rhea then appeared as a vision, calling out words of encouragement to him as she'd done in the past.

"Rhea! Help me, darling," he called out weakly to the wavering shape before him in the water. "Oh, Rhea! I thought I'd lost you for certain." He thrashed blindly about. "I'm not going to make it, *mi vida,* my only love." He later swore that a gentle hand had grasped his and guided him the rest of the way until he felt solid ground beneath him. He had looked up and seen her beautiful face hovering anxiously near, whispering words of inspiration, commanding him to hold on, to fight.

"I will hold on for you, my Rhea," he murmured, "only for you . . ." His head dropped onto the wet sand as his consciousness slipped away from him.

Curt Duprea's life had been spared. The Silver Wolf was truly dead now, and the man who was found in the cold light of dawn on a partially submerged sandbar was virtually reborn. Curt was the only person to be rescued. Rhea had sacrificed her life for his; Jason found her still body not far from Curt's. Simon's was not found.

Christina stood on the deck of the *Lucky Lady* and viewed the covered body of the woman who somehow, even in death, had managed to save Curt Duprea. She firmly believed that Rhea had guided Curt to the sandbar where they had found him several hours after the tragic accident. Christina bowed her head and closed her eyes.

"Thank you, Rhea, for giving him back to me."

Jason walked to her side, his face registering his fatigue. His eyes were all that Christina saw as she glanced up at him. "You tried your best to save them both, Jase. You almost drowned yourself."

He placed a hand gently upon her slumped shoulders. "Come below with me, sweetheart," he urged. "You need to get some rest."

When they had reached a warm, dry cabin, Jason began at once to remove her damp clothing. He knelt down on one knee to remove her sodden slippers and stockings. Nothing was said between them for a few moments. The realization of how very close they had come to losing one another had left them both melancholy and so very aware of the depth of their love.

"Jase, get out of your wet clothes. Stop worrying so about me."

"I will after I get you dry and settled," he said, glad for something to concentrate on. The piece of paper that Big John had handed him only moments ago seemed to burn through his clothes and sear his skin. It was a marriage certificate, and it had been found in Simon's desk when John had searched it. They had promised not to say anything to Christina about it until Jason felt it was the right time. At present, it wasn't the right time, and Jason didn't know if and when it ever would be. What was the point? Simon was dead, drowned, and gone forever. The scandal of being Baker's widow would be too much for Christina to bear. And what of the child she carried? Did he want everyone thinking that Christina was carrying another man's child, when in truth, it was his own. And if she gave the child Baker's last name, he would die! No, there was another way, a way to avoid all of the gossip and scandal that would forever haunt her. Jason was going to marry her; now, before they went back to Natchez.

Christina's hand reached out to still his as they continued to chafe her half-frozen feet between his palms. "Is he—is Simon . . . dead?"

He did not look up to meet her gaze but simply answered yes.

"But you did not find his body, did you?"

431

"No one in Simon's condition could have managed to just swim away, Christina."

"I'm so frightened," she sobbed.

He reached up to gently cup her chin in his hand. "I promise you he will never bother you again. He's gone out of your life—forever."

"I know it is wrong, but I am so glad." She smiled weakly.

"And before you have a chance to get away from me I want you to marry me, Christina."

"You do?" she gasped.

"Yes. At once, sweetheart," Jason replied, enfolding her in his protective embrace. "If you'll still have me."

"I have never wanted anything or anyone more in my life," she answered before placing a kiss to seal their love upon his lips.

"There will never be any doubt over anything, again," Jason stated determinedly. "You are truly mine and you're free of him at last."

The trip back into New Orleans was spent by Jason and Christina in each other's arms. They lay upon the narrow bunk in the cabin of the *Lucky Lady* and renewed their vow of love with a new awareness and intensity that neither had ever felt before.

"There is nothing that can ever separate us again," she whispered into the curve of his neck. "Nothing. . . ."

The next few days passed in a blur as plans for their wedding preceded everything else. Christina tried to involve her brother in their plans as much as possible following the solemn burial of Rhea Francesco. He was a changed man and Christina was worried about him. At least once a day he would disappear for hours on end and everyone knew it was to the small church cemetery that he went. Christina was secretly glad that Rhea was buried here in New Orleans and that they were going home in just a few days. Perhaps then, everything would begin to turn around for them all.

Captain John McGurk and Martinique Summerfield were married at the St. Louis Cathedral in New Orleans the day before they departed for Natchez, Mississippi. It had been a beautiful and moving ceremony, but it had not been theirs alone. Jason and Christina joined them in a double ceremony. The two women had insisted that there was no better way in which to begin their new lives than to share in each other's happiness this way. It was a moment none of them would ever forget, least of all Jason. He had vowed to love her and cherish her for the rest of their lives; he did not take promises lightly, especially this one.

Christina would go home to Natchez as Mrs. Jason O'Roark to await the birth of their child. Her new husband would make his home with her at Oak Meadow and life would go on from there as though Simon Baker had never really existed in their lives at all. At least this is the way that Christina hoped it would be as she stood at the rail of the *Lucky Lady* and waved goodbye to Black Jack and Diamond Sal, who had come to the wharf to see them off.

"Don't be forgetting, lass," Black Jack called forth. "We expect to be notified of the wee one's birth, and we'll be coming north to see all of you when he's christened!"

"We'll look forward to seeing you in the spring!" Christina returned, wiping at her brimming eyes.

Christina and Jason stood at the rail until the boat backed out into the channel and the levee was left behind in the distance.

Then Christina gazed up at him lovingly and whispered, "And so it begins . . . our new lives, together."

"Yes," he replied, kissing her upon the mouth. "Today is the start of the rest of our lives. Yours and mine, together, with our child."

Martinique and John McGurk were convinced to spend a few leisurely weeks in quiet splendor honeymooning at Gardenia Place. Christina and Jason had insisted, and as Martinique awoke to the tantalizing smell of frying bacon she could not help but agree that the decision had been a wise one. She had never felt more rested or healthier in her entire life. Pushing aside the soft blanket, she stretched her limbs gracefully.

It was a sight that warmed John's eyes and his big body as he stepped into the bedroom, a tray of food in his hands. He set it down beside the bed, forgetting his stomach. The hunger had shifted in intensity and need. It was of a different sort altogether, this all-consuming ache that gnawed at his insides. And he knew of only one way to appease it. Reaching out to the woman who was his life, he felt himself near to bursting in his need of her.

"Make me your woman . . . like last night," she whispered. "Make this moment in our lives last for eternity." Her hands grasped his and their fingers laced together.

John slowly lowered his mouth over hers, gently pressed their entwined fingers back over her head so that he could feel her full lush breasts beneath the sheer nightgown pressed against his chest. He eased himself over her. The thinness of her gown enticed his senses as to what lay beneath.

His muscular legs tangled about her slim ones as the need to join his hard body to hers became the sole, consuming thought for them both. She moaned as his hard, throbbing flesh probed demandingly atop her, pressing into her soft thighs as the gown worked its way up over her hips and exposed her womanly charms to him. He claimed them with a fierceness that brought with it extreme pleasure. Martinique writhed wildly beneath him, matching his passionate movements with her own. He buried his face between her breasts and murmured love words and sex words, one mixed up between the other. Her uninhibited response sent him beyond anything he had ever experienced with her before. It was a time for complete surrender, a time to pledge undying devotion. But most of all, it was a time he would remember for the rest of his life. And he knew it was the same with this beautiful woman that shared his love completely in every sense of the word.

Afterward, they splashed and frolicked like water nymphs in the large wooden tub that was big enough for two in the private bathroom. They made love again amongst the bubbles and then raced for the big bed. There they wrapped themselves in each other's arms and quiet conversation.

The day passed quickly for them; before they realized it, they had laughed and loved the entire day away. Twilight was settling in at Oak Meadow. Martinique roused her husband from his nap to dress for the dinner Christina and Jason were giving tonight at the main house to officially announce their marriage.

*　　　*　　　*

Jason removed the last of the whisker stubble on his chin with a flick of his pliant wrist and the sharp razor he held in his hand.

Christina, for the first time since he'd known her, was finished dressing before him. He glanced at her image in the shaving mirror above the washstand. She was standing looking down at the slight protuberance of her velvet gown. She patted the roundness lovingly and looked up, meeting his gaze through the looking glass and smiling shyly.

"It was a good idea, marrying before we came back to Natchez," she commented.

"For once, we agree upon something," he replied in a teasing voice. He continued on with the removal of his whiskers.

"Well, we've been getting along splendidly since we were married," she beamed, her radiant glow contagious to anyone who came near her of late.

"How many of your neighbors responded to your invitation to meet your Yankee husband?" he inquired with a grin.

"Surprisingly, almost everyone. There should be at least ten couples at dinner. They are doing their best to try and mend the differences between the North and South, Jase. But it will not be done overnight."

"I'm willing to meet them halfway, darling, and it appears by their acceptance of your dinner invitation, that they are willing also."

The dinner party was a huge success; as Christina glanced in the direction of her new husband, she felt certain that Jason had been the primary reason. He seemed to go out of his way to make everyone feel at ease

436

in his company. Even now he stood with his arms crossed over his chest, engaged in conversation with her brother Curt and some of their neighbors. Politics no doubt, but she felt assured that Jason could handle himself well. If she had known they were discussing the increasing concern of the plantation owners over the attacks upon their fields and workers, she might have been uneasy. But Jason urged the men into the study for brandy and cigars, and their conversation continued away from inquisitive ears.

"You say that president-elect Grant has promised to outlaw the existence of the nightriders by sending a bill through Congress in the near future?" Curt asked Jason after they were all seated comfortably and the butler had served their brandy.

"He intends to wipe them out completely," Jason replied.

"Well, I for one can go along with any president, Democrat or Republican, if he can make good on that promise," one man spoke up.

It wasn't long before everyone in the room agreed.

"This is a beginning, gentlemen," Jason said, raising his glass. "Together we shall work to destroy those who oppose peace and equality and hide behind masks to do so. You shall have an honest government in Natchez and be given the right to farm your lands and vote as you see fit. I promise you that I will do everything in my power to help you. We are united as one people in this cause."

Sometime later, the men all ambled back to the parlor and took seats next to their wives so that Martinique could entertain them by playing the piano. Christina caught the determined, set look upon Jason's face. She suddenly sensed that life as a plantation farmer was not exactly what Jason had on his mind at present.

I knew it . . . I knew it, . . . she mused to herself. *He is never going to be satisfied until honest government reigns supreme in Natchez. Would he then be itching to take on some other city, in some other state?* She lowered her eyes to her hands folded in her lap, and tried to resign herself to the fact that he would never truly be all hers . . . never.

The holidays were fast approaching. There was a nip in the air and frost upon the fields each morning when Christina went for her morning ride. The McGurks had departed, promising to return soon.

On this particular sunny morning, Christina came down to breakfast with Jason to find the household buzzing away in preparation for the Christmas celebration next week.

The mantel in the parlor was strung with bright green garland and a holly wreath hung over it. The smell of sweet confections drifted out from the kitchen door as Mammy came forward with steaming cups of hot chocolate.

"Ah wuz jist comin' up wid your chocolate," she said with a look of surprise. Every morning since Jason had effectively charmed her into accepting him into the family, Mammy had made it a tradition to wake them with her offering.

Christina smiled at her. "We can have it by the fire in the front parlor. It's warmer there."

"Dat fine wid me. Dat fine wid y'all?" she inquired of Jason.

"Whatever my wife says or does is fine with me, Mammy," Jason replied. He followed Christina into the parlor. "She's the boss, you know." At Mammy's raised eyebrows, he quickly amended, "After you, of

438

course, Mammy."

"Dat man learns quick who it is dat rules de roost, don't he, sugar?"

"Yes, he's a charmer," Christina replied, taking a seat by the fire. "How else do you think he got me to marry him?"

"Ah won't git into dat, no, suh," Mammy chuckled, setting down the tray of chocolate and taking her leave.

Christina looked over at Jason who was watching her quietly. "I haven't seen very much of my brother of late. It concerns me. I know he misses Rhea terribly and I had hoped our returning to Oak Meadow might ease some of his pain."

"He'll be just fine," Jason replied, but Christina could not help but notice the slight frown that creased his brow.

"What is really going on around her, Jase?" she demanded. "Why is Curt always on some errand, and when he returns you two lock yourselves up in the study and stay there for hours?"

"He's just getting to know the land once again, darling, and his neighbors. It's been difficult for everyone, you know. They can use all of the help that we can offer them."

"Yes, I agree whole-heartedly. But why must our workers leave at midnight to go help with their farming?"

"Stop allowing that mind of yours to work up all sorts of unrealistic things," he said, grinning broadly. "You have more important things to concentrate on than the running of our field hands."

"I concern myself with everything that goes on around here," she stressed to him. "Everything . . ." She unfolded her legs from beneath her and stood. "Now, if you'll excuse me, I promised George Washington I would help him go over the list of seed choices for the spring planting." By her frosty departure he knew she was upset.

Jason stood for a time after she'd left, staring into the blazing hearth. How in the world was he going to tell her that he was going to Washington right after the holidays to attend the president-elect's inauguration? And to report on their efforts to oust the crooked politicians that were still in office in Natchez. It had been his decision — and Curt had agreed—that Christina be kept in the dark due to her condition. She had been through enough already and neither of them wanted to cause her any more worry. But, God, it was getting increasingly difficult to keep up the charade. And if Christina knew that her brother was involved . . . Jason could only hope that it would all be over soon. With Simon now out of the picture, how many more could be left? Surely, the end was near. . . .

Matthew Duprea entered the parlor. The huge wooden rocking horse in his arms brought Jason's attention around to him.

"Made it myself," he informed his new son-in-law, whom he had welcomed into the family upon learning that Jason was the son of his old shipping colleague. With Curt and Christina's safe return, a new Matthew had emerged. Each new day brought him closer to his old self.

"It's a fine piece of craftsmanship, sir," Jason praised.

"It is my Christmas gift for my grandchild-to-be."

"I thought it might be," Jason nodded.

"Won't be too much longer," Matthew reminded him cheerfully.

"I know," Jason replied softly. "It's the exact same thing that I've been standing here thinking about myself."

Chapter Twenty-Four

Christmas Eve at Oak Meadow was beautiful. The air was crisp, clear with a touch of frost. The small family within the main house gathered around the piano singing Christmas carols. They had just finished dining on a succulent ham studded with cloves and red cherries, candied yams, and thick slices of fragrant fruitcake.

Christina had volunteered to lead them in song, and they eagerly joined her in a rousing version of "Deck the Halls." It was a holiday that would be remembered by each as one of particular significance. It was the first time in years that Matthew, Christina, and Curt had celebrated Christmas together, and with Jason's presence the occasion was truly special.

When their voices grew weary of singing, they moved to the corner of the parlor and to the splendidly decorated pine tree. There, beneath its twinkling majesty, Matthew proceeded to distribute the gifts.

Christina sat before the fireplace, her lap covered with brightly wrapped boxes. She looked especially radiant, Jason thought, her cheeks flushed pink with happiness and her figure so beautifully draped in a red gown trimmed in white ermine. He watched her every move, his heart feeling as though it would overflow with his love for her. He had saved his gift for her until last. It was special, and he wanted to wait until they were alone to give it to her.

"Jason, look at the rocking horse Papa made for the baby—just like the one that I used to have."

"An' rode until it broke from her bouncin' on it," Mammy chuckled.

"I'm glad you like it, daughter," Matthew replied, pleased.

"And what a lovely quilt you made," Christina smiled at Mammy, holding up the expertly made coverlet.

"Open mine next," Curt urged, pointing to a large carefully wrapped package.

With eager fingers she tore at the wrappings. Tears misted her eyes as she found the cradle that had been hers as a baby. Curt had restored the wood to a rich deep color and padded the inside with soft bunting. "You've all been so wonderful and your gifts are just perfect. Thank you very much."

The rest of the evening was spent exchanging gifts for the rest of the family. Before they knew it it was time to retire for the night. Christmas Day would mean open house, and all of the workers at Oak Meadow were invited to the main house for the day.

When the bedroom door finally closed behind them, Jason gathered Christina in his arms and kissed her lovingly. "Merry Christmas, my darling wife," he said, raising his lips inches from hers.

"And to you, my love," she whispered.

He led her over to the big bed. "Sit down. I have

something I've been saving as my special gift to you." He opened one of his bureau drawers and withdrew a package. Walking back to her, he laid it in her lap. "Open it, please." He sat beside her.

Removing the wrapping, Christina found a beautifully bound picture album. When she opened the cover and read the inscription he'd written inside, she wept with happiness, so much had his thoughtfulness touched her. It read: "To be filled with loving photos of times shared together with our child. May the memories it will call forth in the years ahead all be happy ones, filled with love."

She reached out to caress his smooth cheek and lay her head upon his comforting chest. "I can't tell you how much I love you, Jase. At this moment, words seem so inadequate."

"Then show me, sweetheart," he whispered in her ear, his long fingers already at the buttons of her gown.

"Mmmm, what a nice suggestion," she purred, lying back on the bed as he slowly disrobed her.

When he had removed his own clothing he stretched out beside her and cradled her against his dark, matted chest. "I love it when you do that," he groaned, delighting in the feel of her full breasts and aroused nipples rubbing against him so erotically.

She raised up on her knees and bent over him. "And do you like this?" She cooed as she arched her back and moved against his warm lips. She sighed as his tongue curled about her nipple and awakened the pulsing bud to exquisite sensations. She found herself aching to feel him inside her.

"Turn over on your side, love," he said softly.

"My side," she questioned in surprise.

"It will be more comfortable for you this way." He nuzzled the back of her neck with his lips and pulled her snug against his body. His fingers explored the warmth of her womanly place and made way for his entry. Snuggling her round bottom into his muscular form, Christina felt an unbelievable surge of heat in her loins as he eased himself inside her. Jason rotated his hips against her firm derrière until he felt her straining back against him as little gasps of ecstasy escaped from her lips.

"I told you you would like it, didn't I?" he whispered, as he nibbled the back of her neck and then along her spine.

"It's positively wicked," she returned, "and, oh, so wonderful."

Jason grinned as he lost himself within her charms, and took them again along love's blissful path where they totally surrendered themselves to each other. His exploring hands slipped beneath her to gently squeeze her nipples. His adoring body coupled with hers, they soared into a world where only their emotions and feelings mattered. They both revelled in the oneness that they'd found and whirled together into the heated fires of desire.

"Jase," she breathed, as indescribable waves of ecstasy swept her into an ocean of consuming passion that left her clinging weakly to him when it subsided. His release was deep within her; and they both fell immediately asleep wrapped in each other's arms and feeling absolutely and thoroughly loved.

The new year, 1869, arrived at Oak Meadow with a minimum of fanfare. The holidays were now officially over and had been spent pleasantly with a few close friends sharing a lovely reunion with Curt and his family.

It was now time for Jason to leave to attend the newly-elected president's inauguration in Washington, D.C. He broke the news to Christina on their morning walk over the plantation grounds. The only sound that could be heard after his statement was the sound of the crunching shells beneath their feet as they strolled along the walkway.

"I have to go," he finally said, breaking the tense silence.

"Duty calls," she replied crisply.

"It's more than that. President Grant and I go back a long way together. I am going for personal reasons."

She stopped in her tracks and stared at him. "Can you honestly look me in the eyes and tell me that you are not going to discuss anything political?"

Jason didn't reply, but he stopped walking and pulled Christina into his arms. His chin rested upon the top of her golden head. "I'm not working undercover any longer, if that's what you're worried about. Everything will be above board."

"So you admit you've still got a hand in things?"

"Maybe, just a couple of fingers . . ."

"And Curt?"

"This is something that he must finish, darling, If you try and prevent him from doing so he will not listen and it may just cause hard feelings between the two of you." Jason ran his hands along her stiff back. "We both love you very much, Christina, but there is still much that needs doing. This fight between government and the scum that has infiltrated it has been almost as bloody as the Civil War itself."

Christina sniffed back her tears. "I know that, and I understand why you and Curt feel the need to clear them out of this area. You're both fighters, and believe in freedom, and honesty."

"We cannot allow the existence of an organization such as the scum that hide behind masks and go about as the nightriders. Nor the individuals who support them, and pretend to be real neighbors!"

"Just be careful, Jase. I don't know what I would do if anything should happen to you." Her voice was trembling with emotion.

"I promise nothing is going to happen, to any of us." He kissed her to banish her fears.

Curt Duprea, George Washington, and Jason O'Roark sat upon their horses overlooking the valley below. It was a cold, blustery night and the trail they had picked up just before nightfall was obliterated by the sudden darkness.

"How many raided Thompson's place?" Jason asked George.

"Not many," George replied with a snort, "but hell, one of dem devils is too many. Grant's election has really set dem back on dere ear. Dey's fit to be tied and we's goin' to feel it, ah knows it."

"Were there any survivors?" Jason inquired further, waiting in tense silence for the reply.

"No," Curt growled. "They strung them all up. The whole family."

"Jesus!" Jason sighed.

"Jase?" Curt said softly. "The New Orleans authorities contacted me."

Jason's voice became gruff. "They found his body?"

"What was left of it anyway. The remains had to be buried immediately but his personal items were sent to me," Curt explained. "I recognized a ring with his initials. It had to be Simon's body, I'm certain of it."

"So, I suppose this proves even more that he's truly dead."

"Yes, it looks that way," Curt replied.

"Christina will be relieved. This may just be the proof she needs to put her mind to rest." But as Jason strained his vision to the tracks imprinted in the soft ground he found himself wondering. "You know, Curt. I think before I leave for Washington, D.C. I'm going to pay a visit to the recorder's office in Natchez. Just to check and see if there's any record of Simon's marriage to Christina."

Curt's eyes focused back on Jason. "Something gnawing at you, *mon ami?*"

"As long as we're tying up all the loose ends I thought I might gather up one last strand, just to make certain . . ."

Curt stared over at Jason, a concerned frown furrowing his brow.

"He's dead," he said emphatically.

Jason's eyes burned into Curt's. "I never said one word to the contrary, did I?"

Christina missed Jason terribly and he'd only been away for twenty-four hours. He was to be gone for two weeks—two long weeks, she thought as she walked along a path at the river's edge. The sun dipping behind the trees produced a brilliant pink sunset, transforming the river into an eye-catching panorama of color. She halted her steps amidst the quiet sounds of evening and heard

447

the first call echoing through the trees. She tilted her head toward the shouting and brightened when she recognized the call.

"Showboat! Showboat is a comin'!" one of the workers on the plantation was crying excitedly.

She hurried toward their private landing and looked up and down the river in search of the vessel. The plantation crier came racing toward her. She turned at the sound of his voice.

"Melvin, run along to the house and tell Mammy we will be having entertainment for the evening. Have everyone come to the landing."

"Yes, missus," the man beamed. "Ah surely do dat right now." He dashed off in the direction of the main house, leaving Christina to watch the old paddlewheeler push the long, one-story barge containing the playhouse to the landing. They would remain there for several days provided they were made welcome. This would give the families in the area an opportunity to attend the show and, hopefully, draw the menfolk to the games of chance on board the paddlewheeler. The calliope was sending forth a melodious repetition of song that was certain to have every neighbor within miles scurrying to Oak Meadow.

Christina felt gay as a young child again as she stood and watched the occupants emerge and gather on the deck.

The entire evening was spent being entertained by a troupe of performers who were both charming and talented. When the last fall of the curtain signified the end of the show, Christina rose to her feet with everyone

448

else and eagerly applauded their performance. She glanced at her brother standing next to her and could not fail to notice the enraptured expression on his face.

"You miss all of this very much, don't you?" she queried, feeling her heart sink just a bit.

"I would not be telling you the truth if I told you otherwise," he replied quietly. "But no one is forcing me to stay here, Christina. This is my life for now."

"But you had plans to travel about the country. Why is it they've changed?"

"They haven't. Postponed a while, that's all," he answered.

"Until you've wiped out every last nightrider and therefore avenged Rhea's death? That's what it's come down to—think about it."

"You, sister dear, have got to stop worrying about me." He attempted to sound lighthearted. "You have a husband to concern yourself with now."

"Who is just as stubborn as you are," she grumbled.

"Runs in the family," he grinned charmingly.

A female voice interrupted their conversation, to Curt's relief.

"Curt! Curt Duprea!" The attractive young woman approached him with a pleased smile upon her face. "What in the world are you doing in this part of the country?"

"Lila Monroe," Curt acknowledged the female performer. "I might ask you the same."

Her brown upsweep of curls bounced delightfully as she laughed good naturedly. "Fair enough, but you first."

"Believe it or not, Lila. I live on this plantation." He turned to present his sister to the woman. "And this is my sister, Christina.

"Pleasure, ma'am," Lila nodded.

"Likewise, Miss Monroe," Christina replied.

Lila's brown eyes swept up to Curt. "Do you mean to tell me that you come from a place as grand as all of this and you were working on a showboat in New Orleans? Why, for pity's sake?"

Curt laughed heartily. "For pure fun, dear lady. What else?"

"Sure as hell wasn't for the money," she grinned, "although this guy here pays us all pretty well."

"I was wondering what could entice you away from New Orleans," Curt teased.

"Monsieur Marc pays us well."

"Perhaps you might introduce us to this Monsieur Marc. I would like to talk with the man, possibly for future employment," Curt stated.

"Why don't the two of you go on ahead without me." Christina stifled a yawn. "I'm afraid it's been a long day and I'm going to retire."

When Christina had left, Lila took Curt toward the private offices located in the lower confines of the riverboat. She knocked once before she entered the owner's office, but as they crossed the threshold it became obvious that the room was empty. A stack of paper work was piled on the desk and a smoldering pipe still lay in a receptacle, its fragrant tobacco lingering heavily in the room.

"I guess he must have stepped out for a spell," Lila assumed.

"That's okay, honey, maybe some other time," Curt told her.

"Yeah." The disappointment left her face. "Hey! Why

don't you come backstage with me and talk with some of the troupe? I bet you'll remember quite a few of them."

Curt smiled indulgently. "Okay, but just for a little while.

Christina walked along the deck proceeding toward the gangplank when she happened to notice a strange man talking with Tyrone beside the carriage. At first he gave her quite a start, what with his stout figure and prominent features outlined against the backdrop of the full moon. But upon closer observation she found she could breathe a sigh of relief.

"When will I ever feel completely free from him? Simon is dead," she reminded herself. She approached the carriage with a sure step, glancing only briefly in the stranger's direction. Tyrone opened the door, but before he could help her inside the vehicle, the stranger rushed over to do so.

"My dear young woman, I know I am being most forward, but please, allow me to assist you." Before she could open her mouth to say otherwise he had her by the elbow and was staring down at her in open admiration.

"Sir?" she questioned. "Is there anything the matter?"

He appeared to shake himself from his contemplative study of her features. "You are so like her," he whispered almost weakly. Releasing his grip on her arm, he appeared to sway on his feet.

"Are you all right, *monsieur?*" Christina asked in growing alarm.

Steadying himself he nodded. "Yes, yes. I am sorry. It's just that you remind me so of my poor daughter that it unnerved me quiet a bit when I saw you."

"Your daughter?"

"She's dead now," he whispered brokenly, "a hunting accident."

"Oh, my, how awful," Christina sympathized.

He swallowed with difficulty. Then remembering himself he straightened his shoulders. "I must beg your forgiveness. I behaved most inappropriately."

"There's nothing to forgive, *monsieur* . . ."

"Marc," he replied in reference to his last name.

"Are you a new resident in this area?" she inquired.

He laughed, erasing the harsh lines in his face. "I own the showboat you were just on."

"Oh, yes, one of your performers was just mentioning you to us. My brother Curt would enjoy talking with you. He is a former actor. I am Christina O'Roark. I live on this plantation with my husband and family." She favored him with a welcoming smile.

Christina didn't know why this man should have such an overpowering affect on her, but he did. Before she thought twice about what she was doing, she had invited him for breakfast the following morning. He accepted eagerly, and as she seated herself inside the carriage and observed his departure, she noticed that one of his arms hung lifeless at his side. She was even more pleased that she'd extended her home and hospitality to a man who was obviously a casualty of the war and had suffered so much personal tragedy.

Marcus Trudeau smiled to himself as he strolled away. Everything was going along exactly to plan.

If Christina had any misgivings about inviting the

showboat's proprietor, they were soon forgotten by the time everyone had finished breakfast. The man was a charming storyteller and had them all enthralled with tales of his worldwide travels. Everyone took to him at once, and he had promised Curt a job when he decided to get back to acting.

"Thank you, *monsieur*," Curt replied. "But I have many things to take care of here before I can consider returning to acting."

"Surely a plantation that is as efficiently run as this one could spare you for a few months? I need a strong male figure for the lead. I can't think of anyone who would be better than you."

"Think about it, Curt," Christina found herself encouraging. "When Jason returns he can assume the responsibilities here. And we all know how very much you've missed acting."

"You say your husband will be returning soon?" Monsieur Marc asked Christina with innocent concern, although he knew that Jason was gone. He had checked purposely before he had arrived.

"Yes, he's been to the presidential inauguration," she told him with pride. "I expect him back next week."

"As much as I would hate for you to leave us, son," Matthew added, "we all know that this is not the life for you. You've been travelling the country the past few years, and to tie such a young man down to a life that can be quite sedentary is a bit too much to ask."

"See, Curt?" Monsieur Marc intervened. "Your family agrees with me."

"We'll see, *monsieur*, how everything works out after my brother-in-law returns."

"Very well. I suppose I will have to respect your

wishes, Curt." Monsieur Marc turned to Christina. "Would you be so kind, lovely lady, to indulge an old man in a fanciful whim?" He gazed at her with an adoring, wistful look that caught her heartstrings.

"What is that?" she asked.

"Would you go for a drive with me about your plantation? I would love to see the entire place."

"It is a small request, *monsieur*. One that I am happy to comply with." An odd feeling crept over her as she observed the look of gratitude the man bestowed upon her. *What is the matter with me?* she wondered. *This unfortunate man requests a few hours of my time and I react with a ridiculous foreboding.*

Monsieur Marc's face beamed with pleasure as he walked beside her toward their waiting carriage. When they were seated within the vehicle, he said, "Your husband is a very lucky man. I would not leave one as lovely as you for any reason, especially knowing of your . . ." Remembering his place, he quickly sought to apologize. "Oh, my dear, please forgive me for my outspokenness." He placed his hand over hers. "It is just that you remind me so of my Elise, and the grandchildren I shall never have." His gaze seemed to consume her, almost overpower her.

Christina shifted uncomfortably, desperately trying to calm her racing pulse. "It is all right, *monsieur*, no offense was taken. I do understand." She gently removed her hand from beneath his and placed both of her hands in her lap. "We really should begin. It will take some time to show you just part of the plantation."

The gray-green eyes blinked, and he replied gently. "Of course, my dear, we shall begin our exploration at once. There really isn't much time, is there? And we have so very much to discover, . . . so very much indeed."

During the tour through the grounds, the man sitting next to Christina kept having to remind herself to periodically comment on the plantation. He really had no interest in anything at Oak Meadow. It was all just a ruse to be alone with this beautiful woman, the wife of his old nemesis and gambling partner, Jason O'Roark. Marcus Trudeau had played out his hand to perfection on this occasion; she didn't suspect a thing. No one did. And by the time he was finished winning them all over, it would be too late. Simon may have bungled it, but Marcus knew that he wouldn't. He would take his time and when the moment was right, he would have the pleasure of informing them that their idealistic life was over. Jason O'Roark owed him plenty. Now that he had managed to wheedle his way into Christina's good graces, getting it all back was going to be easy. He only had to wait patiently for the birth of the child.

Chapter Twenty-Five

In the days that followed, Christina and the showboat owner became good friends. As they became better acquainted she dismissed the things that had first disturbed her about him.

It was obvious to everyone at Oak Meadow that Monsieur Marc doted on the mistress of the plantation, and appeared very reluctant to be on his way. However, he didn't wish to overstay his welcome.

"I will have to be leaving you soon, I'm afraid," he explained one afternoon as Christina was showing him about the newly decorated nursery. He had been holding Christina's precious picture album.

"You haven't been here all that long," she responded, a note of disappointment evident in her voice.

"Too long already, I fear. My performers are urging me onward, back down river to New Orleans." He smiled at her and touched a soft spot in her heart, as he always did. "I only wish I could take you along with me this trip."

His statement took Christina by surprise and she did her best to cover her confusion by laughing lightly. "I'm afraid my husband would have something to say about it if he returned and found that his wife had departed for New Orleans on a showboat."

"I cannot say that I would blame him."

"I wish you could stay longer so that you could meet him."

"I'm afraid I cannot, but perhaps I can stop by on our return trip."

"When will that be?" Christina questioned, a thought already forming.

"In the spring, after Mardi Gras."

"If you make it late May, the baby will be here by then and you can stay over for the christening," she encouraged him.

He seemed genuinely pleased that she would consider inviting him. "It's a confirmed date, then. I will be here for certain, of that you can be sure."

That evening her admirer escorted her into the city for a shopping trip and supper at one of Natchez's finest restaurants. Her brother and Lila Monroe had promised to meet them at the dining establishment following the evening performance, Curt was filling in for an actor who had fallen ill, and had been enjoying himself thoroughly.

As Monsieur Marc and Christina mulled over the dinner choices and talked about the events of the day, their waiter presented them with news of an approaching storm.

"It is sweeping toward the city in an icy gale," he warned them. "I would suggest that you not linger long if you are travelling very far this evening."

Christina had wanted to depart at once for the plantation, but Monsieur Marc insisted she at least have supper first. He would not take no for an answer, and appeared unconcerned about the storm.

"More Madeira, please waiter," he'd ordered. "That should help to put my friend's mind at ease." He smiled kindly in her direction. "Do not deny me my last evening with you my dear," he coaxed. "I have been looking forward to it for so long."

Christina took another sip from her glass and as the soothing wine spread warmly throughout her system she shrugged. "If you insist. How can I refuse you?"

"Good," he beamed with pleasure. "Two adventurers we are. I knew you were a woman of spirit." He refilled her glass another time.

The evening was spent in lively conversation with Christina doing most of the talking, and her admirer listening enraptured to everything she said. He cared little to talk about himself, preferring instead to listen to Christina. She found herself going on especially long tonight. It was the wine she thought. It was beginning to have an effect.

"I believe I have bored you long enough for one evening," she said apologetically, her eyes overbright and her face slightly flushed. "Perhaps we should be getting home now, don't you think? It looks as though Curt and Lila could not get through the storm." She turned a worried gaze his way. "I hope nothing has happened."

"I'm sure they decided not to venture out," he answered. "I can see by that look on your face that you're not going to enjoy another minute of this evening worrying over your brother." He stood, signalled the waiter, and then took her arm. "Come, my dear. We'll see about leaving at once."

They hurried from the establishment and out into the blustery, cold night, only to find that the waiter's warning had been most accurate. A mixture of rain and sleet pelted the two figures as they ran toward a waiting carriage. The driver was quickly informed of their destination and they set off as fast as the weather would allow.

The air was very cold for Natchez, and it was unusual to see a storm of this severity—so much so that it unnerved Christina. She sat huddled in a corner, cold, frightened, and absolutely terrified.

Her companion's voice was soothing as he spoke to her in gentle tones. Again, he probed her about her life, her husband, and their plans for the future. It irritated her to find herself continually going over the events of her life when she wished instead to know a bit more about him. But still, he was so kind, and forever considerate of her every need. She immediately felt guilty and therefore indulged him once again. Their companionable exchange took her mind completely off of the inclement weather until the carriage gave a peculiar lurch that sent her tumbling into his lap. His good arm tightened around her, holding her fast, for what seemed to Christina an uncomfortably long period. She quashed the feeling when he righted her onto the seat and apologized for his ungentlemanly grip on her person.

"I was afraid you might hurt yourself or the child," he said with a sheepish look on his face. "Are you all right?"

"Yes, but what happened?" She could tell they had come to a standstill.

"I'm not sure. I suppose I'd best step out and see if our driver is still with us." He grinned. "He just may have abandoned ship after that mishap." He disappeared out the door and Christina was left shivering and suddenly

460

feeling very frightened.

He wasn't gone very long; when he'd hoisted himself back in the carriage Christina could tell by the expression on his face that her fears were justified. "I'm terribly sorry, Christina, but it seems our vehicle has broken an axle. The streets are quite slick and we've slid into a fallen tree limb that was lying on the road. I think it best if we seek some sort of shelter until our driver returns with help."

"He's gone for help?" she questioned.

"Yes, and I expect it will take him some time to make it back."

What was the matter with her? Christina was suddenly uncomfortable in his presence. It was the storm and their situation, that was all. He was still the same kindly gentleman who had only her best interests at heart.

He saw the uncertainty in her eyes and hurried to lay her fears to rest. "Don't worry, dear. Our driver tells me there is a house on top of the bluff where we can seek shelter. Someone should have a nice warm fire and a hot toddy right at this minute." He began to help her out of the carriage. "Come, I'll not allow anything to happen to you."

Christina's thoughts were a mass of confusion as she allowed him to direct her toward the large house that loomed in the distance. It wasn't until they were almost on the veranda that Christina noticed where she was.

"Falcon Hurst!" she gasped in shock.

"You know the house, and the family then?" her companion questioned.

"Yes, . . . and all too well." She balked at going any further. "Take me back to the carriage at once. I'd sooner freeze to death than take shelter here." She could feel his penetrating eyes upon her and suddenly wished she was safe at Oak Meadow, and that her husband was by her side and not the man who was with her.

Sensing her fear, Marcus ushered her back to the carriage as she requested. He could see that she was trembling as they sat across from each other. "That house has disturbed you terribly, hasn't it?" he pried carefully. "Why?"

"It's any ugly story. And one I don't like remembering."

"Sometimes to remember and recount an unpleasant event helps it to go away."

She shook her head vehemently. "Not this one. I've buried it all along with that night, and I never wish to think about it again."

Marcus sat back with a satisfied feeling inside him. She didn't appear to recall his part in the wedding ceremony the night she and Simon were married. That pleased him enormously.

Christina did not see Monsieur Marc again after that night. Their ordeal had ended with the return of their driver with another carriage returning her to Oak Meadow no worse for wear and very grateful to have her concerned family around her. The showboat had left Oak Meadow at daybreak.

When the clock struck seven the following morning, Christina was awakened to feel a persistent pair of lips upon hers, kissing her until she sighed with bliss.

"Jase, . . . you're home, at last," she murmured against his mouth.

"I've missed you so, Christina," he whispered,

462

stroking the softness of her satin skin.

"What took you so long?" She stared into his handsome face. "I thought perhaps you had changed your mind about having a rebel for a wife and went back to St. Louis," she teased him.

"I'm so sorry, sweetheart," he apologized, "but Martinique and Big John just happened to be in Washington for the inauguration too, and we had a lot of ground to cover with the president on the nightriders." He tilted her chin and kissed her lovingly. "And there isn't a woman alive who could hold a candle to you, darling." He patted her rounded tummy. "Even if you are getting a bit fat and sassy."

She scrambled from his arms and hit him playfully with her pillow. "Fat and sassy, am I?" she mocked. "And who, pray tell, do I have to thank for that?" She gave him a mighty blow from her pillow, which sent them tussling playfully among the covers. When he saw that she was tiring, he eased her back upon the bed and kissed her into peaceful surrender.

"I'm so glad you're back," she sighed. "Now everything, at last, is right with my world." Her arms wrapped about him, as his did her. They stayed in their room for the rest of the day, renewing their vow of love and talking of things that had occurred at Oak Meadow while he had been gone.

Sometime later, as she lay with her head snuggled against his shoulder, she related her acquaintance with Monsieur Marc. And she found herself leaving out some of her misgivings about the man.

"It sounds like he became quite taken with you."

"Nonsense. He simply thought I reminded him of his deceased daughter. That was the only reason he doted on me."

"Just the same," Jason said softly. "I'm glad I shall be here when this Monsieur Marc returns for the christening."

The remainder of the winter sped by in a wondrous daze for the newlyweds. Spring was showing signs of bursting forth in glorious bloom and for Christina, it couldn't happen soon enough. The baby was due any day now, and then their lives would truly be complete. The future did indeed look bright. The plantation was prospering, and so were their other ventures.

Jason was searching for suitable offices in Natchez where he could work undisturbed. He had contacted his family in St. Louis to tell them of his marriage to Christina and his decision to remain in Natchez. He was working very hard with his friend Curt to establish unity in the area. Many of the people who had been leary of this Yankee who had married one of their own now encouraged him to consider political office. Through his efforts, the reign of terror that had once gripped the city was now almost nonexistent. There remained only isolated instances for them to deal with. Jason knew that much of this was due to the death of Simon Baker and the efforts of President Grant. The president's campaign speech delivered one message to the people that he was determined to enforce: "Let us have peace." It was a concept that North and South both were ready to accept.

As Curt Duprea and his sister sat in the parlor one warm day playing chess and sipping lemonade, she could not help but remark at his improved state of mind.

"Some of the pain has eased from losing Rhea, hasn't it?"

He was caught off guard for a moment by her statement. He hadn't realized that he was finding it easier to laugh again, and that at last he was beginning to make some plans for his future. "Yes, I believe it has." He sighed. "Although part of my life died with her, I will never forget any of it—or her."

"I suppose we all have things in our lives that we must put behind us."

He knew she was referring to Simon Baker. "You have nothing to worry about, honey. Jason and I checked the authorities' story of finding Simon's body. Although they were not able to make a positive identification, the rings and personal effects proved beyond any doubt that it was him. You saw them yourself when they were sent here . . . they were his."

"I know," she murmured. "And I have put it behind me." She looked over at him with a question. "Now, tell me, what is this about Teressa St. Clair contacting you regarding a part in a play she is producing?"

"Who told you?" he said in mock disappointment. "I wanted to surprise you."

"A little bird," she laughed.

"Let me guess . . . Jason?"

She nodded. "We're both so happy for you. And I'm pleased that she's coming here when the baby's christened. I suppose you'll be leaving here after that."

"Yes, I've already wired her of my decision, and Monsieur Marc. I felt it was the decent thing to do after his generous offer." He looked at her wistfully. "Teressa and I will be going north to Chicago, where the play is scheduled to open in early summer. I'm going to miss all of you very much but it's time for me to get on with my life and bury this bitterness. This will be something constructive."

"And fun!" Christina added. "Don't forget that."

"I intend to start having lots of that," he brightened.

"Oh, . . . dear," Christina unexpectedly moaned. She sat up straighter as a nagging pain stabbed persistently in her side. "I believe I've had enough bending over this chess board for one afternoon."

Curt reached out his hand to steady her as she stretched and placed her hand on the small of her back.

Mammy entered the room with a plate of sandwiches and upon seeing the look of discomfort on Christina's face immediately said, "Ah don't think dat chess game has a thing to do wid dis, darlin'."

Christina was inclined to agree as another pain followed the first one. She caught the meaningful gleam in Mammy's eyes and smiled. "The baby . . . it's time."

Curt anxiously grasped her hand in his.

"Curt," Christina said. "Send word to Jason that his child is about to enter the world. And have someone fetch Dr. Grady."

Curt jumped to his feet. "Just as soon as I get you up to your room." Sweeping her into his arms he carried her toward the stairway.

Chapter Twenty-Six

"I'm not leaving her side," Jason stated emphatically. He wiped Christina's damp brow with a cool cloth and stubbornly ignored the doctor's order to wait downstairs with the rest of the family.

"No use tryin' to git dat man to do anythin' he don't want to," Mammy informed the harassed practitioner. "Her and him is a good match." She inclined her head in Christina's direction. "He not goin' to leave her, I kin tell by de look in his eyes."

"This is unheard of!" the doctor said, shocked.

Jason grasped Christina's hand as she shuddered from another intense pain.

"Don't leave me, Jase," she whispered, very frightened.

"I won't, sweetheart. I promise."

As the hours dragged by and Jason continued to remain cool and efficient, Dr. Grady reversed his earlier opinion. This husband was making his task a whole lot easier.

Tirelessly, Jason would massage Christina's aching

back, doing everything he could to make her more comfortable. He soothed her with soft-spoken words and continued to hold her hand as he coached her during early labor. When she went into the last stages and they were certain the baby was in the birth canal, it was Jason who sat beside her and told her when to push and when to try to relax.

Mammy was clucking over her like a mother hen, and now and then bestowed Jason an admiring glance or two.

The pain was so intense that Christina thought she would surely die. Fear suddenly gripped her as she cried out from the severity of the spasms. Jason's hand holding fast to hers was her mainstay, as she fought to give birth to their child.

"When is this baby going to be born?" Jason asked the doctor, his face pale and drawn from witnessing his wife's exhausting trial.

Both Dr. Grady and Mammy were preparing Christina for the eminent birth and Jason could see the same emotions on their faces that he was certain must be on his own. The moment had come at last.

"Here it come, Papa," Mammy beamed. "Your baby is bein' born."

There was a moment of tense silence, broken only by Christina's labored breathing. Then Mammy straightened up with a tiny, struggling form in her hands. "It's a boy!" she cried.

The doctor tended to Christina while Mammy gently whacked the wiggling little body lightly upon his naked bottom. Nothing had ever made Jason feel as humble as the moment when he first heard his son's lusty cries.

"He's beautiful, isn't he, Jase?" Christina questioned drowsily.

Jason bent forward to kiss her lovingly. "He's just

perfect, darling. And I'm so proud of you." He stroked her damp face tenderly. "You were magnificent."

Mammy cleaned the baby and wrapped him in a fluffy blanket, all the while cooing and fussing over him. Taking him in her arms, she walked over to the proud parents. Tenderly, she laid him into his mother's outstretched arms. "Here is your new son, all perfect and strong."

Christina thought her happiness complete as she studied the baby closely, counting fingers and toes. "He is like a miracle, isn't he, darling?" she said.

Jason nodded silently, unable to speak over the lump in his throat. His hand found hers and together they examined each tiny part, from their child's downy black curls to his perfect little toes. They pronounced him perfect.

Mammy came back all too soon to collect her new charge. "Ah take him to de nursery now to meet his wet nurse and git some nourishment." She reached down as Jason deposited him in Mammy's arms. It was at that moment that the small baby opened his eyes. They were the exact shade of blue as his father's. Jason bent forward to place a kiss on his tiny cheek. "No one can ever say that you are not mine," he declared with pride.

"You go right ahead and strut around here like a peacock all's you want," she informed him grinning. "But ah wants it understood right now dat I ain't sewing on any of dem buttons dat you's in danger of poppin' off your chest."

Jason followed Mammy toward the door, peering over her shoulder. "I must say, Mammy, you did one heck of a job tonight. I hereby appoint you official mid-wife for all of the children that Christina and I will have."

Mammy shuffled away to deliver the baby to his wet

nurse, but not before Jason heard her reply. "Some Yankees ain't all dat bad. . . . Der is one or two dat a body could learn to respect."

Jason saw the anxious faces of Matthew and Curt peering around the doorframe as Mammy opened it. There were congratulations all around as they came into the room.

"A fine boy," Curt praised. He shook hands vigorously with Jason and kissed his sister.

"And what will you be naming my new grandson?" Matthew piped up.

"How does Shawn Matthew set with you?" Jason asked.

"For Jason's father and you, Papa," Christina explained.

Matthew couldn't have been happier. After stating his approval, he rushed from the room to spread the good news throughout the plantation.

Jason and Curt kissed Christina goodnight and quietly left the room.

"See you in the morning, darling," Jason called softly. "I love you."

"I love you more," she whispered back sleepily.

He knew they could spend all night debating that statement. "I don't know how that could be possible," he said thickly. But Christina had already drifted off to sleep and did not hear.

Life for the new family fell into a wonderfully uneventful routine. While Jason conducted his business from his recently acquired offices in Natchez, Christina busied herself with running the household, shopping, and taking care of little Shawn.

Twice a week she accompanied Jason into Natchez to go over the books on the *Rebelle Christina* and oversee the operation. Although she no longer travelled the river on board the luxury paddlewheeler, she insisted on remaining active in the business end.

Jason would drop her off at the riverboat and continue to his suite of offices that occupied the entire second floor of a magnificent brick building. The view overlooked his vast fleet of riverboats, harbored next to the *Christina*. It was here in these offices that he transacted business daily with their branch office in St. Louis. Jason's uncle still handled matters there with great efficiency, but made it known that he was happy to have his nephew back in charge of their vastly growing empire.

Jason had not seen his family in a long time; however, that was soon to be altered. He received a telegram from his mother informing him that she and Uncle Henry would arrive at the end of the week. They were looking forward to seeing everyone again.

"Well, I do believe I have remembered to invite everyone to the christening." Christina looked up from her task and smiled at the sight of her husband and son curled up together in a chair. She folded her guest list and forgot it completely as she observed with shining eyes the two most important people in her life. Her husband was animatedly discussing his latest coup d'état in Natchez with Shawn.

"We managed to conduct an election without one shred of violence or reprisal on the people in this area. They all voted for the candidate of their choice." His voice was alight with satisfaction. "Honest government is returning, son, and by the time you run for president all of this hatred and prejudice, I pray, will have passed." He kissed the tiny baby upon his curly head. "We shall never give up in our fight to end that, will we?"

"Between you and Papa, Shawn Matthew will be spouting facts, figures and political matters as his first words," she teased.

"S'pect dat boy to give us po women folk de vote when he becomes de next president," Mammy said as she came forward to collect her young charge. Jason reluctantly relinquished the baby for the evening. Watching them leave the room, he turned his attention back to his wife.

"John and Martinique will be bringing the O'Learys on board the *Lady*," Christina was saying. "Teressa is arriving by coach and Curt is to meet her. And you are to pick up Uncle Henry and your mother . . ." She paused to consider the grim look that now crossed her husband's face. "You are not pleased," she sighed. "Have I invited too many people?"

"Perhaps just one too many."

"One?" she echoed, somewhat bewildered.

"That Monsieur March fellow," he explained, "I checked into his background." He appeared thoughtful. "Puzzling . . . he doesn't appear to have one. I haven't been able to find out a damned thing about your friend."

"Most likely because there is nothing to find out," she replied. "Not everyone has a shady past, you know."

"But they at least *have* a past. This man appears to have none."

Christina sighed. "Oh, come now, Jase. While I admit he is a bit eccentric in some ways, he is just an ordinary man who runs a troupe on board a showboat. Perhaps he has led a very dull life."

Jason looked doubtful but said no more regarding the

man. Instead, he strolled across the room to join his wife upon the settee, and gathered her into his arms. "I'm getting a little tired, how about you?" he coaxed, his lips caressing the side of her slender neck. "Don't you think it's about time for us to call it a day?"

"H'm, did you have a trying one, my financial wizard?" she teased as she snuggled closer to him.

His hand slowly reached forward to tantalize the softness of her arm and then downward to lace her fingers in his. "I was busy making you a financially secure woman."

"I thought I already was financially secure."

"For three lifetimes . . . after today!"

"Tell me!" she probed excitedly.

"Remember that railroad stock that was in trust until you reached twenty-one?"

"Yes."

"Well, on May ninth, the Central Pacific and Union Pacific joined at Promontory, Utah." He lifted her fingertips to his lips. "And . . . that makes you, my dear wife, even richer than I. I am just a humble shipping magnate married to a railroad tycoon." He nibbled enticingly at her fingers.

A tiny flickering of heat began inside her, burning even hotter as he rubbed her fingertips against his moustache. "That pleases me very much," she murmured dreamily. His gentle, persuasive seduction of her senses overwhelmed any other thoughts she might have. It had been so long since they'd made love—since long before Shawn Matthew's birth—that she was weak from wanting him. "I think I should like to reward you for such devoted service," she whispered, sending him reeling as she smiled seductively.

"An excellent idea, madam," he replied.

Her hands moved toward his cravat as her eyes gazed heatedly and meaningfully into his.

A rueful smile touched his lips. "I put myself in your competent hands." His breath fairly left him as her fingers pulled open his shirt and curled into the dark fur on his chest.

Her fingers began to gently knead his firm muscles and lightly tease his flat nipples to arousal.

He swept her up into his arms and walked toward the staircase. "Tonight, you are all mine, in every sense of the word." His mouth closed over hers as he took the stairs two at a time and strode down the dark hallway to their room. The door was open, the chamber glowing softly with candlelight, the covers turned back to reveal amber colored satin sheets. The scent of lavender prevailed. As Jason and his lady gazed deeply into each other's eyes, he knew who had set the scene.

"I love you, my beautiful lady, I love you so much," he said fiercely, burying his face in the cloud of golden hair that had fallen free around her shoulders.

The door was gently closed, the distance to their love nest covered swiftly. Carefully, as though she might break, he laid her before him on the bed. The mattress gave beneath his weight as he sat beside her. His eyes darkened with passion and gleamed with intent; his heated gaze fired her blood to a fever pitch. With deliberate slowness, Jason removed each article of her clothing, allowing his fingers to brush her flushed skin as he prepared her for what was yet to come. When she lay clad only in her chemise he whispered, "And now it's your turn."

She shyly finished what she had begun in the parlor. She pushed the loosened shirt from his shoulders and down his muscular arms until it lay discarded upon the bed, and then lowered to unfasten his trousers. Lips as soft as rose petals covered every spot she revealed with moist, light kisses until the recipient stretched out upon the bed completely lost to her magic touch. Dreamily, he closed his eyes and formed a mental picture of perfection as his fingertips explored her satiny body. He smiled to himself, knowing full well that what he had retained in his memory had been exact. There had been no exaggeration; Christina was unequalled in her beauty or form.

Her hands left him momentarily to lift the chemise over her head. Her sultry cat eyes looked like two glowing emeralds as they met his and held.

His hands reached out to meet hers in midair, fingers entwining above their heads as she lowered her hips across his.

She lowered her mouth to cover his. The room spun crazily as they lost themselves in their private world where only love reigned.

Throughout the night, soft cries of ecstasy drifted from within the flimsy silk covering that surrounded the lovers within its folds.

Hands and lips took equal time, demanding, yearning to touch and explore what had been denied them since before their son's birth. Sleep, exhaustion, and the cares of the world were forgotten as Jason and Christina renewed their vow of love untiringly, again and again. Slowly, achingly, Jason claimed the satiny prison that lay so warm and inviting beneath him. Locked tightly within her, the quivering muscles of her flesh drove him to the brink of madness as she writhed provocatively beneath him. Her softness was so inviting, so willing; he felt he could lie within her forever, never caring to face a moment other than this one he shared with her.

Repeatedly, and with infinite skill, he renewed her hunger for him. Sometimes tenderly, sometimes demandingly, but always with words of love.

Once, after she had drifted into slumber, she found herself awakened by his lips caressing hers, his fingers touching lightly the nipples of each breast until she moaned with pleasure and willingly opened her legs to allow him to slip once again between her thighs. He did not enter as she had expected, but moved in a rhythmic motion with his rigid flesh pressed intimately against hers. The pleasure spot he rubbed so erotically swelled and throbbed until she was moist against him. The ache inside her began to grow and she urged him inside her by arching her hips.

"This time it's my turn to lead," he purred. His mouth locked over hers and she sucked hungrily at his tongue until he thrust it forward into her mouth as she demanded. Her hands caressed his buttocks and the softness between, tempting, probing him to exquisite bliss. And when both their bodies began to shudder for release, he thrust urgently inside her and brought them the rest of the way. Christina had never experienced anything like the trembling that swept her and the explosive heat that centered in her womanhood. Soft cries swiftly built in volume with each wave of ecstasy that claimed her. Her response sent Jason's senses soaring with hers, and together they again claimed the highest plateau to be sought, a blissful unity that they would share together for all time. Throughout the night, as soft evening breezes caressed them through the open French doors, they professed their love eternal until dawn crept upon the scene and claimed the night away from them.

Chapter Twenty-Seven

Together, Jason and Christina had created a bond so close that neither of them felt anything could ever intrude upon their newfound happiness again. Theirs was a private world, this lovely place, Oak Meadow, and they did their best to guard it and nurture it carefully. But sometimes, no matter how hard one tries, ugliness can creep into beautiful places.

On the morning the guests were to arrive for the christening, Christina was up at the crack of dawn picking flowers from her abundant gardens. A gentle spring breeze drifted across her face as she chose each bloom with discriminate care. A woven basket cradled over her arm, she went about her task unaware that someone was secretly intruding on her quiet moment.

Marcus Trudeau kept himself carefully concealed in the thick bushes surrounding the house as he watched her closely. He had made the trip to Natchez on board the showboat but had departed at Natchez Under the Hill on the pretense of taking care of some unfinished business. He also informed his touring company that they would be expected at Oak Meadow plantation before two P.M. to give a performance for some very noteworthy guests. They were to tell Mrs. O'Roark that Monsieur Marc was detained in the city due to some last minute business, and that he would attend the festivities as soon as he could. Marcus planned to hide here in the shrubbery until everyone had left for the christening. He could not allow anyone, especially Jason, to see him. He had to be careful that he wasn't discovered before he was able to enact his plan. When the house was deserted except for the servants, Marcus would slip unseen to the nursery and wait.

He knew the schedule of everyone in the household, and thanks to the warm hospitality of the family, he knew the layout of the mansion. His eyes travelled to the nursery window. That was where the child would be returned at two o'clock sharp for his feeding. It would be just the baby, his wet nurse . . . and Marcus. The rest of them would be attending the performance given on the showboat at exactly the same hour.

He sat back to review his plan once again. *Once I have the child in my possession I shall take him to the hidden room beneath Falcon Hurst.* He grinned at his brilliance. *I will send a ransom note to Oak Meadow and demand payment for his safe return.* He pursed his lips. *And I think I shall sign it with Simon's name. The stupid woman will believe it. I am certain that, in the back of her mind, she has misgivings about Simon being dead.* He smiled benignly and continued to observe Christina from afar until she went back inside the house.

The child was christened Shawn Matthew O'Roark in

478

the tiny chapel where the family worshipped each Sunday. He was surrounded by loving faces as the guests packed the church to overflowing.

Christina's brother Curt, and her dear friend, Martinique were the baby's godparents. It was a moving ceremony for everyone and Christina stood next to Jason, her hand in his, and cried tears of pride and happiness. She felt at peace, and so very lucky.

Afterward, they gathered on the lawns of Oak Meadow for a day of festive celebration. It was a beautiful afternoon; the sun shone brightly, seemingly giving its blessing to the assembly and adding an aura of serenity to the atmosphere.

Christina left Diamond Sal chatting with a group of admirers, who were listening attentively to life in her famous gambling emporium, and walked over to join her mother-in-law, Anne Marie.

Anne Marie had fallen in love with her little grandson. Everyone else was hard put to get near him, she doted on him so.

Lucy Washington was leaning over the back of Anne Marie's chair, a cookie in one hand while the other tickled Shawn Matthew beneath his dimpled chin. He was cooing and laughing, and charmed anyone that happened to come near.

"Just like his father," Christina remarked with a wide smile as she approached her mother-in-law. "He holds center court wherever he happens to be."

Anne Marie returned Christina's smile. "I can't tell you how glad it makes my heart to see my son so content with his life. He is not the same man who returned from the war." She cast a disapproving look in Teressa St. Clair's direction. "But for the life of me, I don't know why you invited her. She never helped Jason—ever. All she did was compound his problems." Christina's reply left her silently shocked.

"Oh, no, that's not true," Christina defended Teressa. "Without her help in New Orleans I might never have seen my brother again. I will be forever grateful for her assistance." Christina noticed the way in which Teressa and Curt chatted together throughout the entire day. They seemed totally enraptured with each other, and Christina had to admit she was secretly glad, for several reasons.

"Christina!" Jason called as he strolled across the lawn with his Uncle Henry. "Everyone is getting ready to go down to the landing. I understand that your friend, Monsieur Marc, is detained in Natchez for a while, but he sent the troupe on ahead to entertain our guests. They say they're ready for us."

"Wonderful, darling," she replied, "You get everyone together while I see that Shawn Matthew is taken to the nursery for his feeding." She leaned over to pick up the sleepy-eyed baby and tenderly cradled him in her arms. "You go on with Jase, Mother O'Roark. I'll be along directly." She took the child into the house as everyone else headed toward the carriages that would take them to the showboat.

Marcus Trudeau hid on the upstairs veranda, concealed behind some potted plants. Just ahead of him were the open doors that led to the nursery . . . and to his quarry. He could see Christina come across the lawn, up the walk and disappear inside the house. His pulse began to race rapidly as he picked up the sound of light footsteps on the center stairway inside. Her voice could be heard giving instructions to the child's wet nurse, and then she was gone—it was only Marcus, the nurse, and the baby. His palms were already beginning to itch; he could feel the money in his grasp. *Slow down, you fool,* he commanded himself. *Let the wet nurse feed the brat first and get him to sleep, then snatch both of them.* Marcus had thought it over; since he had no way to feed the child he would take the nurse as well. Once he had the money and was safely out of Natchez they could return to Oak Meadow. He didn't want to harm them, just make certain his revenge on O'Roark was complete. His eyes once again followed Christina as she departed in a carriage for the showboat.

It took only a half an hour for the child to have his fill of milk and fall contentedly to sleep in his nurse's arms. She rose from the rocker and gently placed him in his cradle. Marcus could not see her movements but he could hear her, and visualized each step that she took in his head. When he was certain that she had laid down on her bed across the room from her charge and he could hear her snoring softly, he put his plan in motion.

Withdrawing from his pocket the ransom note which he intended to leave in the crib, he crept forward until he stood beside the cradle. He glanced at the nurse, and then quickly snatchd up the mound of blankets that contained the sleeping baby. But when he felt around with frantic fingers for the little body, his fumbling meeting nothing but cloth!

"Cloth!" he yelped in outrage and shock. "Goddamn if it isn't!" He threw it angrily across the room and his furious stare met that of the tall man lounging casually unconcerned in the doorway.

"Hello, Trudeau. Looking for something in particular?" Jason's tone appeared coolly unaffected, but his blue eyes were narrowed and held a dangerous glitter within them. He made a motion toward the startled wet nurse that sent her scurrying from the room and away from the two men. He trained a pistol with careless ease on Marcus.

"How the hell did you know I was here, O'Roark?" Marcus growled. He looked like a trapped, frightened animal—one that might kill to get out of the corner he now found himself in.

"I did a bit of investigating on Monsieur Marc and found that he appeared to have no past, no ties," Jason smiled mirthlessly. "Nothing at all. In all fairness, Trudeau, I wasn't absolutely certain it was you until I walked in here and saw you. But I had a powerful hunch, you might say." Marcus began to slowly back toward the open door to the outside veranda. "There was a silent partner that operated with Simon Baker, a man that we never could quite get anything on. He cleverly kept to the shadows, and even managed to destroy any incriminating evidence that Baker had in his house. He was a difficult man to track down, and it took some doing, but I believe he stands before me now. I'd be willing to stake my reputation on it. And now that we have him, I suspect there will be no more nightly raids to contend with.

"You have no proof of any of this!" Marcus attempted to bluff his way out of the predicament he found himself in. "There isn't one person who will testify to anything you're accusing me of."

"Oh, I believe I have one witness," Jason replied.

At that particular moment Christina walked in and took her place beside her husband. "You should never have come back, Monsieur Marc," she said mockingly. "Or is it Preacher Trudeau?" At the unbelieving look in the man's eyes she continued. "Yes, I did at last place you. Your face was there in my subconscious. With Jason's persistence I was able to piece together the events of that night in Simon's house. You were the man behind Simon Baker and the nightriders."

"I began digging into the marriage records from Natchez around the time that Simon claimed to have wed Christina," Jason continued. "There was no record of their marriage." He smiled thinly. "Because a funny thing happened at the ceremony. Simon could not find anyone who would marry an unwilling bride, so he neglected to have a real preacher perform the service. He used you instead." Jason reached a hand toward the defeated man. "Make a clean breast of it, Marcus. Give me the ransom note you've been trying to conceal in your closed fist."

"Damn you, O'Roark!" Trudeau complained. "At every turn you have been a constant thorn in my side. I wasn't going to hurt the baby, I swear it." He appeared to wither in size as he hunched his shoulders and hung his head in fear. "I just wanted enough money to take me out of the country and then I would never have bothered you, or anyone else, again. Simon was the vicious killer in all of this, not me," he continued in a pathetic voice. "You left me destitute. . . . I had no choice but to try and recoup some of my fortune any way that I could."

"And as always, you sought to do it dishonestly," Jason said in a disgusted tone of voice.

Trudeau, seeing that his perfect plan had been foiled, attempted to make a mad dash for the veranda. Just as he had one leg over the balustrade, a shot fired over his head that halted him dead in his tracks.

"Don't give me an excuse to put an end to your miserable life," Jason threatened. The Colt was pointed at Marcus's chest.

Trudeau slumped to the floor in defeat as Big John and Curt came running into the room. Between the two of them they quickly had the man securely bound.

"We've done it!" Curt exclaimed with joy. "This is the last of those bastards."

"In Natchez, at least," Big John replied.

"At present, that is all that matters to me," Jason stated as he gazed deeply into his wife's eyes. "Get him out of here and to the sheriff."

"Sure thing, Jase," Curt agreed.

"With pleasure," Big John echoed as they pulled Marcus along toward the door.

"You haven't heard the last of me yet, O'Roark!" Marcus yelled in a desperate attempt at some sort of satisfaction. "I'm going to tell everyone about the night your wife spent in Baker's bed, and the fact that she turned up pregnant shortly thereafter! I'll fix you before you take me out of here!"

Jason shook his head unbelievably. "The man just never gives up, does he?" He walked up to the fuming Marcus; withdrawing a handkerchief from the man's own pocket, Jason tied it tightly about his mouth. "Marcus, you have played out your last hand. Now get the hell out of my life."

A quiet, tranquil twilight had settled in at Oak Meadow. Jason and Christina had seen to the needs of their guests for the remainder of that afternoon. But one had to only glance their way to tell that they were anxious to be alone. Most of the guests knew what had taken place here today. Those who were staying over at the plantation retired early. They would be leaving in the morning so a good night's rest was desired by all.

The wishing star shone brightly in the night sky, a full and glorious yellow moon accompanying it. It was a moon meant for love.

Two people snuck from the main house and ran toward the stable, hand in hand. They were laughing gaily, young lovers totally unconcerned with the world around them. Their devotion to each other was a beautiful, stirring thing to witness.

Curt Duprea stood on the second-floor veranda smoking a cheroot before retiring for the night. He had noticed his sister and her husband come forth from the house and disappear along the path to the stable. A smile crept across his lips and gladness welled up inside him.

"She will be just fine from now on," he murmured assuredly. "Her life with Jason will be a good one. And now I must go on with my own." His thoughts drifted to his own plans to become an accomplished actor. Having the beautiful Teressa St. Clair in one's corner was an added bonus. Curt felt a warm rush flow through him at just the vision of her in his mind. Something was beginning between them. He felt it, and he was certain that she did also. His life was going to take a definite turn for the better from now on. And as for Teressa becoming the new lady in his life? Only time would tell. "I shall always love Rhea, but one cannot live for memories alone." He retired to his bedroom with renewed hope for the future.

Jason tilted Christina's chin upward and repeated the words she had dreamed of hearing. "I'm through with it all, sweetheart. I told Big John earlier of my decision and I'm wiring the commander in the morning. I accomplished what I set out to do in Natchez. And I understand the president has several bills already in Congress that will see the end of these villains once and for all."

"Can you mean this?" Christina whispered, turning her eyes from their private pool to stare into his own. They had sought relief from a house full of people by escaping to their private place; an oasis still, as it would continue to be in the years ahead. "Will you not grow bored of this life before long and go seeking something else?"

Jason favored her with a lopsided grin, his blue eyes alight with dancing fire. "Married to you?" he snorted. "When will I find the time?"

Christina wrinkled her nose in a playful gesture. "I am not all that bad," she drawled.

"Life with you, my fair-haired colleen, has been nothing but one mad adventure after another." He laughed with wicked delight. "Why should it change at this late date? It hasn't been any different since the first time I laid eyes on you, tearing across this very same land on that feisty pony of yours like the world was yours for the asking. And since that time, if I may be so crude as to remind you, you've led me on a merry old chase. I've worked for you, gambled for you, battled nightriders for you, challenged the Silver Wolf for the right to love you, and bear a permanent reminder on my shoulder of just how protective you can be of those you love. But most of all," he whispered softly. "I've loved you, have always loved you, and intend to continue loving you for the rest of my life."

Her jade cat eyes filled with happy tears as she kissed him ardently upon the lips. "That should keep you busy enough," she whispered between kisses. "But in a most delightful way . . . I guarantee it."

Their mouths joined once more, the kiss deepening as he pressed her down upon the soft bed of moss and made love to her as sweetly and passionately as he had that very first time, so long ago, when she'd stolen his heart along with his soul and sealed their destinies together for all time.

Early the following morning, Christina and Jason said goodbye to their departing guests.

Diamond Sal and Black Jack were to travel back to New Orleans with John and Martinique on board the *Lucky Lady*. The O'Learys would be returning to their profitable gambling emporium, and the life they both loved.

The McGurks had agreed to continue operating the *Lady* for Jason and would keep their home in New Orleans for the times when Martinique felt a need to have solid ground beneath her feet. The arrangement suited their needs while also providing a way to visit their close friends whenever they had a layover in Natchez.

There were a few tears from the ladies when they made their farewells, but they all knew it would not be long before they would be together again; for theirs was a deep and lasting friendship that would endure over the years and events yet to come.

Teressa, the Golden Girl, and Curt Duprea were the last of the well-wishers to leave. Their departure had been detained due to a request from Christina.

The foursome had just finished with their lunch and were still lounging over coffee in the dining room when a knock at the front door brought a secretive smile to Christina's lips.

What is she up to now? Jason wondered, and hurried from the room to confront whatever was waiting for him firsthand. He came to an abrupt halt in the entrance hall when he found himself face to face with a photographer. At the perplexed expression on Jason's face, the man rapidly explained.

"Your wife, sir, she commissioned me to come here today." He pushed his wire spectacles back to their proper place on his nose. "I'm to remain with your family the entire afternoon and take pictures."

Christina came forward with the photograph album that Jason had given her for Christmas. She showed it to him. "It's for this," and then looking over at her son, who was bouncing on his grandfather's knee, "and for him. I want it filled with moments for him to recall in later years. I've dreamed of this since the day he was born."

"I had no idea," Jason said softly. "You never cease to surprise me. At every turn I find there is yet another side of you that has eluded me."

"That's as it should be," she said with a mischievous smile.

* * *

Shawn Matthew was dressed in his finest clothes and his very proud Mammy set him upon his father's lap; father and son looking like a duplicate picture of the other.

Christina, wearing the rose satin gown that Jason had admired and purchased for her from Madame Tulane, took her place by her husband's side, her hand resting in his.

The photographer thought he had never seen a more radiantly beautiful woman than Christina O'Roark as she smiled so enchantingly before his camera that day. He snapped, capturing the moment in time forever for them and future family members to recall.

And there were more to be taken, as Mrs. O'Roark had insisted. So the photographer stayed for the better part of the day to snap photographs of Uncle Curt with his nephew, and Grandpapa Duprea; and Mammy, standing with one arm around Christina and the other cradling Shawn to her breast.

Christina had photographs taken of Teressa and Curt. "You might just as well get some practice smiling before the camera, brother. Something tells me that things are just beginning for you—good things." Christina felt confident that he had at last found what he'd been seeking.

At the end of the day Christina was satisfied that she had enough pictures to fill a number of albums. The photographer was thanked and sent on his way and Teressa and Curt prepared to depart.

"I hope you will come home often so that we can do this again," Christina urged her brother. "I want our ancestors to look upon our family photographs in the years to come and realize the legacy of love that we leave them."

"Having such a loving family to return to will bring me home often," Curt replied. He kissed Christina on the cheek and whispered. "Home . . . at last I can say that with peace in my soul. Thank you."

As Christina watched them hurry to the waiting carriage, a sense of serenity settled within her. She shut the front door and stood for a brief time in the silent hall, listening and thinking back to the day when she had first entered this house after being away all those years. It had been such a haunting experience then. But now, she could hear Shawn Matthew laughing happily in the background, the delightful sound echoing through the passageway.

"No longer will these halls reflect the anguished cries of the past; from this day forward they shall be filled with children's voices and laughter." She walked toward her husband and son, who were waiting for her to climb the winding stairway with them and retire for the night.

After Shawn Matthew was tucked into his bed and kissed goodnight, his mother and father went to their own room. As the door swung closed behind them sealing them away from the rest of the world, Jason took her into his arms and kissed her with all of the love that had been inside of him for so long and that he was now free to express. There was nothing in his life to prevent him from doing so any longer.

Christina's response was immediate. All of the doubts and turmoil that had plagued their relationship from the beginning had finally been laid to rest. Her arms circled his neck and her fingers entwined in raven black curls as she moved her warm lips against his. Without saying a word, she let him know that night just how much she loved him, would always love him.

The night stars that shone brightly in the southern sky were no match for the glow of love that filled the room and blazed within them. And throughout the rest of the night, he sought to show her in every way possible just how very much she meant to him. Tenderly, deeply, passionately, and completely, until their bodies lay sated side by side.

His lips once again sought hers in hungry exploration and Christina knew her happiness to be complete. There would be no more shadows in the moonlight to further haunt her dreams.

At long last her blue-eyed talisman was with her. He had been her destiny from the beginning, as he would be until the end. . . .

Author's Note

History reveals to us that President Ulysses S. Grant was successful in his efforts to halt the violent, secret orders which wielded such political and terroristic power in the years that followed the Civil War.

Congress passed a series of bills in 1870 that finally ended their bloody reign and outlawed the existence of these organizations.

Eventually, they would fade into the twilight shadows and remain there for over half a century. There are some which exist even today. But none in this country would ever wield the power and influence of the group who had seen to its birth. The group described in this novel are fictional, as are the incidents.

Mary E. Martin

Dear Reader,

My tale of romance and adventure was written with you in mind. I hope you enjoyed reading REBEL PLEASURE. I would like to write what you enjoy most; so drop me a line—I'd be delighted to hear from you.

Mary E. Martin
c/o Finn Literary Agency
P.O. Box 28227A
St. Louis, Missouri 63132

PASSIONATE ROMANCE BY PHOEBE CONN

CAPTIVE HEART (1569, $3.95)
The lovely slavegirl Celiese, secretly sent in her mistress's place to wed the much-feared Mylan, found not the cruel savage she expected but a magnificently handsome warrior. With the fire of his touch and his slow, wanton kisses he would take her to ecstasy's searing heights—and would forever possess her CAPTIVE HEART.

ECSTASY'S PARADISE (1460, $3.75)
Meeting the woman he was to escort to her future husband, sea captain Phillip Bradford was astounded. The Swedish beauty was the woman of his dreams, his fantasy come true. But how could he deliver her to another man's bed when he wanted her to warm his own?

SAVAGE FIRE (1397, $3.75)
Innocent, blonde Elizabeth, knowing it was wrong to meet the powerful Seneca warrior Rising Eagle, went to him anyway when the sky darkened. When he drew her into his arms and held her delicate mouth captive beneath his own, she knew they'd never separate—even though their two worlds would try to tear them apart!

LOVE'S ELUSIVE FLAME (1267, $3.75)
Enraptured by his ardent kisses and tantalizing caresses, golden-haired Flame had found the man of her dreams in the handsome rogue Joaquin. But if he wanted her completely she would have to be his only woman—and he had always taken women whenever he wanted, and not one had ever refused him or pretended to try!